Red Archer

Red Archer

Book Two of the Red August Series

H.L. BROOKS

WEATHERHILL

www.hlbrooks.com

Acknowledgements

As with *Red August*, this book would not have been possible if not for the love, support and hard work of William Hardy. He is a great editor, grammar-lover, idea-flesher, blurb-writer, chocolate-supplier, kiss-giver and life partner. He makes me want be a better person. I also want to thank Brandi Brooks, Mary DeMarco-Logue, Sarah Riggle, and Natasha Lane for being amazing beta readers. This book is better than its first edited draft because of their efforts. Thanks to my daughters Amber and Jade for being such wonderful, loving and supportive spirits, even if neither of them came to my launch party (insert their eye rolls, head shakes, and huffs here). I can hear them now, "Mooooom." They really are wonderful girls though. I swear.

Thanks to Natalie Gibbs for modeling for the cover, and Leslie Gibbs for being my on-call rock and support when I needed some goddessy friend time. Also, many thanks to my friends and relatives who have helped me celebrate each little success, wished me well, or given me some encouragement when I needed it. Special thanks to Barry and Scarborough Fair B&B for hosting readings of my first book, and for having a B&B with a literary theme! Thanks to New Deal Café and all of my Greenbelt friends, supporters, and friendly faces who pitched in to make my book launch a success, and to my Southern Maryland friends who drove up to be supportive. I am lucky to belong to such a wonderful community. Thanks to Erica Winter and Raven Heights Radio for the podcast interviews and the sheer power of her enthusiasm. Additionally, thanks to people who have given me odd jobs to do when times were lean and hard, when my spirit was low, and the road seemed too long. You helped me, probably more than you know. And finally, thank you to all of the romantic loves I've had; I learned more about myself and the shape of love through my time with you. You know who you are, and you know if you treated me well, did your best, or … not.

For Love,

in all of its colors, heights, depths, and seasons

Chapters

Red Archer

Prologue
Conall Keep, Perthshire, Scotland
April 4, 1982

Somewhere deep in the wilds of Perthshire, a dark clutch of forest shrouded a small and ancient keep from prying eyes and chance visitors. Ciardha Conall paced the dusty stone floor of his tiny castle, his boots clopping hard, echoing throughout the main hall. His lycan blood coursed in his veins, and his agitation had caused his ears to begin their transformation from man to wolf all on their own. His chin too, and the back of his neck, were reacting to the surging adrenaline in his system and he rubbed them, stopping every few paces to glare at his wife as she cowered, looking tiny in her throne. After a tense, exhausting hour of pacing, trying to think of what to say to this impossible woman, he charged up on the throne. He pressed in close, grabbing her arms, his half-changed snout an inch from her nose.

"I give ye everything y' ask for! Everything! Don't I?" he ranted. His breath blew hot on her face and saliva dripped onto the lap of her faded, moth-eaten wedding gown. He would insist she wear it on days like this, though because she stepped into the gown of her own volition, and laced it herself, she wondered if it was fair to blame him. Yet she did, every time she donned the disintegrating thing.

He walked over to a honey-colored table of heavy, knotted wood, caked in layers of red candle wax, where a few baleful flames still flickered, melting their spires onto the mound of hardened lava. He picked up the crown of wild roses resting there, and brought it to her.

"Look, I twisted this for ye!" For all of his ferocity he sounded like a hopeful child seeking his mother's approval. "I made it just as I did that blessed day we were married. You loved it then, didn't ye?" His eyes were wide and a smile waited to spring forth behind the tight, uncertain mouth. "Clipped off all the thorns. Aye?"

She nodded and pasted on a smile for him, knowing what was to come next. "Aye," she said with as much tenderness as she could muster. Her faint smile faltered and he saw the glint of fear and worse, pity behind her eyes.

He placed it on her head. "I gie ye everything! All o' the things you love, all y' ever ask for. Don't I?"

She nodded—sullen, cautious. A small droplet of blood beaded on her forehead where a thorn dug in.

"I keep m' promises, don't I? I am a man of honor!" He studied her and waited.

She nodded, "Aye, ye are." It was a lie. They both knew damned well he didn't keep his promises.

"I'm the same man ye fell in love with. The same. Our hearts, they're the same that joined together, as then, as now. Always."

She inhaled and parted her lips to speak, but he interrupted. "And it's no different! No different now than it was then, lass." He took her hand and put it on his heart. "This heart is the same ye fell in love with. The same one ye left your family for. Is it not? You are the love of my life. And for you, I … I am …" He waited for her words, like a man who had crawled across the desert would wait for water.

She looked into his pale blue eye, then the gold. This was one lie she could not gift him, even for her own safety, because it dishonored her truest love. He would never be the love of her life again. She tried to reach up to his mane of dark hair and stroke the silver streak that parted the ebony from itself, and he growled. She did not flinch, and instead cooed his name, "Ciardha, Ciardha" in a lyrical hum—*Keer-ya, Keer-ya.* "Lover, I cannot make myself—"

He snarled at her. He did not want to hear the words that would come next, that had come hundreds of times before. He grabbed her by the wrist and yanked hard, lifting her out of her seat, sending the flower crown to the floor in a spray of petals. He pulled her along the cold rough stones, the sound of his anger echoing in every corner of the cavernous keep. She began to sob as the layers of her ornate gown entangled her feet, tripping her and sagging off of her boney shoulders. Twisted tendrils of dull hair, once a glorious golden-orange crown, hung lifeless and dull down her back, swaying with each jerk as he tugged at her. She endured it, as she had always endured his abuse, with tight lips and muffled criticisms.

He dragged her into her bed chamber and around the room, pointing at all of the fine things he'd given her. "Look a' this room! Look a' this bed, the finest silks and down! And this! Look at this painting I had made of ye, t' honor your beauty." His Scottish brogue was thick and urgent, spit flying from his teeth with each hard consonant. "Because I love ye! You said ye loved it! You said ye loved me!" He grabbed her head between his hands and searched her face for gratitude, but only found tears and regret. He flung her into a tufted threadbare chair; her teeth rattled as she crashed into it.

She was sobbing harder now and he softened. He drew his energy inward and took a deep breath. He squatted by her, petted her hair, his deep voice almost a purr, desperate. "Darlin', please … Please …" He stood and picked up a miniature cake, one among a tiered stack of rich, pastel-hued treats on the table next to her. "Look, love, I had these made for ye." He choked on his tears, or perhaps on his guilt. He held the confection out to her. "It's yer favorite, lemon and raspberry."

His wife remained still, her hands folded in her lap and a waterfall of tears streaming down her face as she swallowed her sobs.

He knelt in front of her again, put a crooked finger under her chin and said, "Please take it. Enjoy it. I will do anything you ask, if ye could only say … say that I am … I am …" he waited for her words again. The words he longed for and he was sure would bridge every chasm in him. Heal up every wound. If she would only say he was her love, the love of her life, he could be whole again, and then they could be happy.

"Ciardha, please …"

He looked desperate and put the delicate cake to her lips and nudged. "Eat it. Eat it!"

She tightened her lips and shook her head.

He pushed away from her and threw the cake across the room, where it splatted in the corner of her large gilded mirror. He swept his arm across the table sending small cakes and tiny sugar roses flying towards the low wall beneath a window. Standing there, in the center of the room, he let out a blood-curdling howl. Outside the trees shook as birds took flight, and the floor of the forest rustled and crackled with the fleeing of wildlife.

Ciardha then squatted down in the middle of the room and bowed his head, lacing his fingers behind his neck and sobbing until his legs were numb. He fell over on his side into a ball and lay there, shaking.

His wife got up from her chair and went to her knees next to him, petting his hair and the tops of his ears that were once again totally human. This was her fault. She knew it was her fault. She deserved every bit of rage and she would bear it as she earned it.

"I do love you, husband."

He shifted so that his head was in her lap, he grabbed fistfuls of the pale blue velvet gown and let the pain rush through him until he could breathe again, calm and deep. He let her pet and soothe his brokenness, though he knew the comfort wouldn't last. The questions would rise like bile again, too soon, and make him crazy with hurt and jealousy. But for now, he would inhale her smells and welcome her touch, and if he could burrow into her deep enough he could forget for a little while and just be lovers. They could travel back to a time where their love burned deep until it was written on their souls, all-consuming, and pure—that lost heaven where passion and curiosity were born, and thrilled, and made everything else blur and quiet.

She caressed his hair and traced his tanned forehead with a pale finger. She blamed herself for his misery, he knew this. She'd said it many times, her face full of anguish. She looked so much older now than she did just five years ago, worn down by the brokenness of hearts and her mistakes weighing heavy on her.

She gently tugged him upwards and took his face in her hands and they kissed. She pushed her mouth against him hard, their mouths open, tongues meeting and thrusting. Soon they were swept up in passion so powerful that in that moment they were new lovers again and nothing else mattered. Ciardha lifted his wife in one easy motion and took her to the bed where he tried to prove he was a good lover and she tried to convince herself that she still loved him at all. Moving inside her, feeling his urges reaching their peak, his body began to transform into his full lycan aspect, filling her as no human could. He howled into the night, and she answered him back with her own cries and moans of pleasure unlike any she had known with another—and in that he was the best, and he knew it. It was this carnal release that brought them here, time and again, bonding this way. The wash of chemicals and the pleasures of flesh let them both escape their misery until they collapsed, spent and reeling. It was the only thing left they did well together, the only way they could give anything to each other. They fell asleep, each nestled in their own lie as the sun dipped below the trees. A crescent moon rose to the peak of the tall gothic window that stared down at the ravaged bed where the two tormented lovers allowed the night to envelope them in peace. For these few hours of sleep, they could be as they once had been.

Ciardha awoke with the sun and the pain returned to his chest. He had dreamed, and his dreams told him what would come next— what would set the balance right again. He jumped out of the bed and put on his clothes and packed a bag. She stirred with the commotion, her heart beating hard at what appeared to be another episode of impending argument and abuse.

"Where are you going, Keer?" She kept her voice even, as though nothing were wrong, but pulled the covers up around herself tighter.

"It's those fecking Archers. We could be happy if it wasn't fer that lot."

He charged back to the bed, but pulled himself inward, made himself the lover he imagined she would want him to be. "There's no one matters at all in yer life but me. You said so yerself once, ye just can't see it now. But once you know there's nothing else, it'll all be clear again. You'll see. When they're all gone, you'll see." He pushed away again, grabbed his half-full bag, and strode about the room, a man with purpose.

She wanted to say something. Something brilliant and wise and loving and brave. Something to keep him from this cursed mission. He would never be happy. She turned away from him and stared out of the window at the sky, trying to imagine what other marriages were like, where you never feared the hand of your husband. Where you could work through your problems together, and the way to prizing your love again was by growing something finer in yourself, not burning down the rest of the world. Only a fool or a god would imagine that stripping away the people and things that somebody loves would make them better love what remained. Ciardha was the most powerful creature she had ever known, but he was no god.

Hunterlover

December 19, 1983

It was a year and a half since Ciardha had left his wife's side to chase his demons, real and imagined, hoping to silence the thrumming hate that pulsed and beat inside of him—an episode of peace in Conall Keep that had come to an end with his return. He told her how he had found Fletcher Evan Archer, and the hunter became the hunted. How he reveled in the sensations of flesh ripping and muscles snapping as he dragged his claws through Archer's body. It had touched something primal and ancient in him to tear apart an enemy, and since then he had been haunted by the longing the old ones called the *seann amannan*, the nostalgia for days long past, when lycans could hunt the *cumanta*—the common humans—without concern. But it did not end there, oh victory of victories! He slaughtered that bitch Sylvia Archer, too! She thought she had escaped him but he spilled her foul mixed blood in her own house, marked her five times over and sent her into the earth with her rotting mate. And to top it all he nearly finished off the matriarch, Sorcha, the start of all of this misery in his family. He left her shredded in her own bed, her guts bleeding into the blankets. "Never mind my hunterlover brother takin' her to hospital—she was na long for this earth after I was through with her." He smiled briefly, then let out a satisfied grunt.

This litany of bloody glories he recounted to his wife at least three times a day in the week since his return. Part of her hoped that this really would be the thing that would remake him into the man she remembered, while the rest of her wondered if he had ever really been as great as she once thought him. She felt sick at his stories, so full of hate and destruction, but she feigned her approval for the sake of peace. She imagined herself covering over the glowing coal of anger in her heart with the tattered ash that remained of her soul, trying to snuff it out. The first few days home, Ciardha had seemed happy, triumphant, but his tone of resentment soon crept back in. He began to pace and look at her with that pleading look—*Tell me you love me more than anything, more than anyone*—and each time she saw it spread over his face she would look away, and then try to start a conversation about something, anything, other than love.

A week later she saw him hunched and brooding, and his brow furrowed as he began to talk about the daughter that got away unscathed, the one called August. The one Faolan loves. She was amazed to realize how conflicted Ciardha was over the idea of killing his baby brother's lover. He was not so cold and pitiless—or at least he only was with his vengeance, she reasoned. He just wanted the Archers to pay for what they'd done to Ban, his father. Banning Conall had been Faolan's father too, Ciardha had raged, and they should be sharing their grief and the glory of vengeance. That was what brothers did.

Ciardha wondered aloud how Faolan could even love that mixed-breed. That mutt. How could he put her over his own family? But then there was that other hunter bitch he had a century ago. What was her name? Iseabail? In the end, though, it didn't matter. Whatever he thought of Faolan staining their honor, he was still his brother. Ciardha would let him have his Archer; she wasn't even born when the blood feud erupted anyway. He reckoned that it was the only thing he could give to Faolan—that and the hope that he would one day see the error of his ways and join him with the Veritas and make it strong again.

Ciardha looked up at his silent wife. "I got something for ye," he said, suppressing a conspiratorial grin.

"Oh? What is it?" She perked up; to do otherwise would have started a cycle of whining and irritation, with accusations that she didn't appreciate the things he did for her.

Between the murders of Fletcher and Sylvia, he had bought her a present in New York. She couldn't help but feel a little special when he presented her with the package, wrapped in a fancy box with layers of pink and lavender tissue paper. It was an elegant modern gown from some fancy boutique—no doubt some eager salesgirl had helped him choose it for her. Some part of her had always enjoyed imagining other women wanting Ciardha, though he was hers for life. Maybe he wasn't so bad, she would tell herself, knowing in her heart it wasn't true but clinging to it anyway. It was a pattern that had carried on for a decade now, which felt like both an eternity and also the blink of an eye.

"Go, lass. Put it on."

She went to her room, took off every stitch, and slipped on the dress, a silk organza in peridot green with a fitted bodice that bared her

9

milk-pale shoulders. In her mirror she appraised how her flesh had grown rounder and softer, her cheeks pinker again during Ciardha's absence—time she had spent on slow walks, reading, painting, and eating piles of roasted meats and dense breads with soft cheeses, rather than huddled and tense, with knots in her stomach whenever Ciardha's boots hit the floor. Now she filled out the gown as it was meant to be filled. She was rested and strong and beautiful. She pinned her shining hair up with rhinestone clips and rushed back to show him.

"Oh lass, you look good enough ta eat!" he rumbled with desire.

She smiled cautiously, though it did begin to feel sincere to her now.

"It's lovely, Keer!"

"Aren't ye goin' t' thank me?"

Forced smile, folded hands. "Thank you, husband."

Remaining guarded made her feel like she had some measure of control. It was a possibility, however remote, that she could find a way to love him the way she used to. But first there would need to be some trust, and if she couldn't find a way to trust him authentically, she would manufacture it from the shreds of her useless dignity. Just to prove she could be a loyal wife and love him the way he wanted to be loved. After all, she'd promised to do exactly that: to love him, forever. And promises only mean something when they are hard to keep.

"Would you make me another rose crown love? I'd like that. It'd be so bonny wi' my new dress, dinna ye think?" She allowed the flesh around her eyes to go soft, her words to take a gentler tone. He was mesmerized as she twirled around the room between sunbeams and shadows, the sparkling green fabric floating and trailing around and behind her. The scent of her, tracing spirals through the room, invited him in, and he went to her, placed his hands on her hips and looked into her pale blue eyes. He brushed away a rose-scented tendril of strawberry hair and inhaled to speak, but she spoke first.

"I love you, Ciardha."

It seemed more sincere to her, if she did it her way. And maybe if she said it enough times, it would be true. But also, if she said it first, she was in charge. It would be nice to be in charge again. Even if only in small ways.

He froze, enraptured, anticipating the words he longed to hear. He swore to himself that if she ever said them again he would focus on his duties as a husband. He would finally make a family with her. He could be all hers now because Archer and his mutt mate were gone. He was home and with the love of his life. If she said what he hoped she would say, he would have no need to do anything else but build their life together. Maybe he could even leave the Veritas behind him. It was dying anyway. He was convinced that once the rift between them was healed, they could finally have the babes they always wanted.

He pushed the other realities to the corner of his mind. His hypocrisies and crimes were quiet in their corners. He saw no conflict. He wanted her to say it. He willed her to say it. He watched her eyes shine, her sweet lips part.

"I love you, Ciardha, more than anybody. More than him." She almost choked on the betrayal she had just dealt to her true love. And her family. But she made herself believe it. "I love you, more than anything."

She'd said it. She said it! The thing he'd waited years to hear, and now here it was. He wasn't sure he was awake. He studied her, but smelled no deception. It was true, finally. She was all his again. He let out a howl and scooped her up and spun her around the room.

She laughed. It felt good to tell him something that made him so happy, like freeing a poor caged beast. It was her fault that he had been so miserable. It was her fault for falling in love with somebody else and breaking his heart. She ignored the warning at the center of her conscience. She buried it under more ash.

"You do, lass? Oh, are ya sure?" He beamed.

She nodded, "Aye, I'm sure, my lover."

"Och! Blair, ye've made me the happiest!"

He gave her another spin around the room and took her to her bed where they kissed and touched and he lifted up the dress he had so proudly brought her, and they wound around each other until they were exhausted. Ciardha crashed hard and slept deeply, like a soul unburdened. Sleep did not come so easily for Blair, but eventually it found her. She dreamed of her true love, and a son she hadn't seen in years. She dreamed of her dead brother, aglow with golden light, and said, "I'm sorry Fletcher Evan." And he hugged her and forgave her.

Red Eighteen
Mahigan Falls, Maryland
August 19, 1984

"Hurry up! Hurry!" August did an excited jog around the room while Faolan pulled on his shoes and hunted for his keys. Snow, though now a fully grown wolfdog after almost a year, barked and danced like a puppy after her, occasionally rearing up on her hind legs and pawing the air toward her mistress.

"You're something else, Red. Look at you, runnin' around the room like an elf-child." Faolan grinned and let out a small laugh. "Come on, I'm ready. You look lovely, by the way."

August felt her face flush. "I do?" She did a curtsy in her gauzy, dangerously short birthday dress and then spun around fast, momentarily flashing the laced edges of her panties. "I wore it for you." Wink.

"Well, thank you." Wink.

Once outside they paused in the sunshine and gazed at each other for a moment, each clearly enjoying the sight, before Faolan bent lower and offered her his back. She laughed and climbed on him, wrapping her legs around his torso, pressing herself tight against his back and resting her chin in the crook of his neck as he clasped his hands under her bottom. "Giddy-up!" she crowed, and he took off in a gallop down the hill toward her grandmother's house, dashing between trees and hopping across the creek at narrow points.

Bouncing and pressing against Faolan's body, with his hands so close under her, August was suddenly aware of how much she was tingling and swelling, and she knew if it went on much longer she wouldn't be in a presentable state for meeting anybody at her party. Faolan seemed to be having a similar thought when he stopped to lower her to the ground. "I think we'd better walk the rest of the way," he said a bit sheepishly, adjusting his kilt and looking almost apologetic. August was glad she was not the only one aroused, and the token of validation made her smile.

They continued down along the creek more slowly, with Snow ranging in a wide circle around them. Faolan would occasionally scoop a rock and throw it into the water, while August plucked a few flowers along the way.

"Is that a summer kilt, Fe? It looks hot."

"Aye, it's for summer. It's lighter than most. And most of the kilts y' see these days are not quite like those of my youth. They're easier to belt on, for one, and a good bit more comfortable."

"I don't see too many kilts at all, now that you mention it," she smiled up at him and gave one of his pleats a tug.

"Aye, that's true enough. It would attract a bit more attention than I'd want, most days, but this is an occasion."

"Too bad," she pouted. "As good as you look in your Levis, I get all kinds of ideas about a man in a kilt."

"Ahem. Right. I could say the same about girls in sundresses. Or one particular young woman, anyway."

She giggled, and they stood there a moment, again looking at each other, both smitten. She touched a finger to the crinkle at the corner of his eye and gently stroked the lines. He brushed a stray black curl from her pale forehead and gave it a kiss in the center. She knew that if he kissed her for real right now, they'd never make it there.

"So, onward to cake, then?" he said finally, and she sighed and took his arm.

"You always know how to tempt me, Mr. Wolf."

The Blue Rook soon came back into view. The towering Queen Anne house had been August's home for two years now, ever since her father died and she and her mother had moved to his little hometown in Maryland. Her father had grown up in the Blue Rook, and had slept in the same turreted bedroom that August called hers. Though, if she were being honest, she'd have to admit that she hadn't spent much time in her own bed since she and Faolan had fallen in love.

When they reached the huge front porch, they paused once more to straighten themselves a bit, while letting Snow slip inside ahead of them. August leaned over toward Faolan's ear.

"I'm going to want a nice long piggyback ride back up that hill," she whispered, and wiggled her brows.

"I hear ye, lass." He replied with his own wiggle. "You ready?"

She smoothed her skirt down. "Yeah."

He swung the front door the rest of the way open, but something seemed off to August. It was too dark and much too quiet. Smoke hadn't come to the door, or even barked. August took a couple of steps and peered into the living room. Nothing but quiet furniture and a crowd of family photos staring back at her from the wall.

"Is it the right time? Three, right?"

"Aye, three."

"Well, where is everybody?" A note of concern edged into her voice. Snow paced back to August and whined quietly.

"Sit girl."

August leaned into the library across from the living room. A ray of sun spotlighted the shelf of folklore. Her eye was caught by the ancient leather edition of Charles Perrault's *Le Petite Chaperon Rouge and Other Tales* displayed at the center, and a jolt of adrenaline flashed through her, as if it were an omen.

"Now I'm worried. Shit, what if ..." She sniffed the air for a clue, but the scent of cut flowers and sweaty dog was overwhelming everything else.

"Don't fret, dear girl. They probably left a note on the fridge." His voice was relaxed, unconcerned. "Maybe they want us to meet them somewhere else. Down by the barn, probably."

"Yeah, maybe ..." August padded cautiously down the hall, leaving Snow anxious to rush after her, checked only by Faolan's hand-signal to stay. August rounded the corner into the big room, as they called it, her hunter senses acute and reaching into every corner. Someone was here, she realized, and trying hard not to be noticed. Then a rush of movement and sound hit her like a wall.

"Surprise!"

Voices shouted at her from several directions and she wheeled back a little into a defensive pose, her ears transforming almost imperceptibly into furry points—then just as quickly receding as she recognized the beaming faces of her family. Her mother Sylvia and her grandmother Sorcha, dear old Brigid and gentle Abel, all were coming toward her with arms open and a babble of birthday congratulations. Snow bolted into their midst, barking, though she instantly switched to wagging her enormously brushy tail and licking any available hands, before getting into a friendly tussle with Smoke, who was already half her size.

"You nearly gave me a heart attack!" August protested with a relieved smile.

"Well, that's a fine thank-you!" Brigid said, her silver-bangled

14

hand on her hip. "When ye get to be my age, girlie, ye can talk about heart attacks." Her mock consternation melted as she put her strong arms around August's shoulders. "And just eleventy-one years t' go, love, afore ye get there!"

Sylvia and Sorcha both laughed heartily. "Oh, haud yer bragging, Brigid!" her grandmother quipped. "And get out o' m' way, let me hug my own granddaughter, would you? Happy birthday sweetheart!"

"I love you Gran!" August gushed. She felt arms and hands all about her as she was squeezed between the three powerful women in her life, with pats from Abel too, and the room filled up with laughter and chatter. Now turned around, she could see the decorations that had been invisible from the hallway: a neatly painted banner that read "!!Happy 18th Birthday!!" (no doubt Abel's fine signwork) spread high across the wall. There was a pastel rainbow of streamers twisted across the room, festooned from the ceiling with a spray of ribbons dangling at the ends, and clusters of pastel colored balloons on either side of a pale purple cake, with confetti all over the counter around it.

Sylvia was laughing as she slipped in a coral-pink lipstick kiss on August's cheek with a loud "mmm-wah!" Behind her was Sheriff Two Feathers in his usual stoic stance, though his eyes were smiling as he nodded his greeting, and beside him was the woman August recognized as the owner of Wynda's Bakery, a friend of both Sorcha and Abel, and probably responsible for the magnificent flower-covered confection on the counter. What really floored August, however, was the figure she saw standing off to the other side, behind Faolan.

"Hey," said the girl, and gave a little wave.

"Lainy! Oh my god!" August threw herself at her friend and they hugged each other tightly. "It's so good to see you!" she squeaked in her ear, feeling her throat tighten up. When she let go, her eyes were shining. "What are you doing here?" she managed to get out.

"I'm home from Berkeley for the summer, silly."

"I can't believe you came!" Now the tears really started flowing. She took a step back from Lainy and looked to Faolan, who was beaming down at her—though with a slightly crooked smile.

"You knew about this!"

"Aye," he nodded, and then came closer to her ear. "And we're going to have to work on those impulses of yours, lass. You nearly gave us quite a show."

August felt for the tips of her ears and looked a bit mortified. "Well I haven't been at this wolf thing quite as long as you have, Mr. Conall," she whispered back. She had a good bit more to say, but she had no idea how much talk of transforming Lainy might pick up on. "Well, I'm starving," she said, turning back to her friend. "Let's eat something!"

Abel and Sorcha had laid out half a dozen of their best snack platters, and August grabbed one of everything, while Faolan popped the cap from an apricot-flavored ale and handed it to her. Lainy piled her own plate high and they sat at the end of the table and talked and laughed as though no time had passed since they spent their lunch periods together at Mahigan Falls High School almost two years ago.

A boisterously off-key rendition of "Happy Birthday to You" began filling the room and August turned in her chair to see Sylvia carrying the cake to the table, the candles flickering as she came. Brigid was right behind her with a cake server and a stack of plates. August looked at all the smiling faces, and a wave of gratitude washed over her. So much had happened in the last year, and it all could have gone much worse if not for Faolan. And for Two Feathers. And Lainy. All of them, really.

"Oh, for heaven's sake, child!" Sorcha clucked at August's teary expression. "Let's just cut the damn thing, and see if Linda left anything out!" she cackled, elbowing her friend.

The wish August made was a simple one—that all of these faces she loved would be with her for a long time—but she blew out the candles knowing how big a wish it really was. She cut deep into the delicately fragrant cake, to the rousing cheers of her family, and strangely enough it seemed no one else wanted the piece with the biggest pink icing rose on top, so that one was left for August.

"This cake is amazing, Linda—what is the flavor? I can't quite figure it out."

"Lavender, hon," Linda said with a twinkle of pride. "From Mr. Jefferson's garden, in fact."

"Wow. You can eat flowers?"

"Sure, love," piped Brigid. "Eat 'em, paint yourself with 'em, relieve all kinds of ailments. Dinna y' ever read the labels in my shop, then?"

"It might be my new favorite flavor. After strawberry, of

16

course," August was quick to add. "I miss your old apothecary, Brigid."

"Aye, well—each in its season," she replied philosophically. "New frontiers, an' all that."

"To new frontiers!" Sorcha cheered, raising her whisky-laced coffee and giving Abel a squeeze.

"New frontiers!" everyone happily echoed her toast.

Someone had turned up the stereo, and Hall and Oats were playing in the background while August began tearing into her presents—fancy pens and markers for her journal from Mom, a silver clasp with knotwork and the face of a wolf from Brigid ("For your cloak, love," she noted), and nineteen one-pound notes from Gran (one for each year of her life and one to grow on—a Scottish tradition, as the card explained). From Lainy came a small stack of mix tapes with Queen, Heart and Led Zeppelin, and August delighted in the decorative labels and inserts she'd made, which featured rainbows and little creatures that looked like fluff balls with eyes and tennis shoes. Lainy also gave her a David Bowie poster—he was one of the artists that she had gotten her hooked on—and August wondered at how he seemed to be so elfin and mysterious, never aging, just changing. *Maybe he's part lycan*, August thought.

Abel reached over the table and handed her a cord with an arrow point dangling from the end. "One of your dad's old swallowtail broadheads," he explained. "For good luck."

"Thank you, Abel!" August gushed, and got up to come around the table and hug him. "You know I always love anything from my dad!" He hugged back with his good right arm while the artificial one hung at his side. August held the arrowhead out to Lainy, who came over and clasped it around August's neck. The cool metal warmed to her skin and she rubbed it with her fingertip, feeling a little choked up.

"One more from me and your gran," Sylvia said as she leaned across the counter to hand her daughter a small box.

August wiggled the gold-foiled lid off and found a shiny set of house keys inside, etched with her name. She looked up, somewhat perplexed. She already had a set of keys.

Sorcha chimed in, "Another tradition. It means you're grown darlin'. It means you can not only come and go as you please, you're always welcome: 'Where'er you may roam, 'tis always your home.'"

August welled up a bit as she smiled. "Thanks, Mom. Thanks

17

Gran. Now I'm getting all mushy again."

"Och, yer as sentimental as Goose ever was!" proclaimed Sorcha. "God love ye, child—ye are yer father's girl!"

August sniffed and looked to Faolan, smiling. Expecting, actually. She couldn't help but notice that he hadn't given her anything, and it didn't seem as though he was about to, either. Then she felt terribly selfish and ungrateful because she knew he must have worked hard to plan the party. But before she could even finish chiding herself for being a spoiled brat, he produced a bouquet of flowers that had mysteriously come from behind his back.

"I'm terrible, Faolan! I was already wondering why there was nothing here from you."

"Well, ye should have known better, a fine man like yours. Shame!" Brigid jibed from across the counter, then cackled and took a large swig of ale.

"Brigid, stop," Sylvia sniggered and swatted the woman on the shoulder. Abel just smiled and shook his head, while Lainy stared, a little wide-eyed. Teasing like this didn't go on in her family, and it took a bit of getting used to.

"Well, she's right, Mom. I should have known better." August was feeling a bit sheepish now.

"No worries," Faolan soothed. "Just open the envelope, love."

Her heart always sped up a beat or two when he called her that. August hugged the bouquet and buried her nose in the middle of it, then immediately sneezed and giggled.

"They're all Scottish wildflowers," Faolan explained. "I wanted you to have some blossoms from your homeland. Wild roses and bluebells, ling heather, and sweet woodbine. And of course your favorite, forget-me-nots." The smell of them immediately brought August back to their time spent by the stream, reading, talking, lolling among the flowers. The effect was stirring, almost magical. She had the urge to grab Faolan and squeeze him hard, and bite his nose and eat the flowers. But she didn't—she just smiled big and awkward and tried to look not completely crazy.

"Don't forget the envelope!" Brigid called out, then hiccuped.

"Oh, right." August finally looked at the envelope. Her initials, A.A. were on the front in elegant script, surrounded by loops and curlicues, probably drawn with one of the beautiful writing instruments on Faolan's desk. She herself hadn't quite gotten the hang of old-fashioned pens with fancy nibs and such, but she supposed Faolan had been using them for a hundred years.

"Ooh, it's pretty. What is it?"

"Well, you'll find out when you open it, won't ye?" he teased gently, and flipped it over in her hands so the back side was showing. There was a blot of dried red wax with a wolf's head in the center. In a flash August was taken back to her sixteenth birthday and the final gift she received from her father, the red cloak that she now wore everywhere in the cooler months. That gift had also been sealed with red wax, and it had been her first inkling of things like family crests and literal last names like Archer. And that cloaks are red because the lycan are colorblind and can't see that color when they're transformed for fighting, while the hunters can still easily see each other.

She felt a well of emotion rising again in her chest and hurried to open the envelope, hoping that if she cried right now, it wouldn't seem too weird to everybody. They were all looking at her and she wanted to crouch into a ball on the floor, but she also wanted to bask in their attention. *All these conflicting emotions*, she thought. *It's exhausting.*

She slid her finger in and ripped the long seam open and pulled out a cardboard folder. It had a big blue Pan Am logo on the front and two tickets inside for a flight from Baltimore to Prestwick on the last weekend of October—their anniversary of meeting.

"Scotland?" She said it almost too quietly. Why was everybody staring at her?

"Well, yes, we're going to arrive in Prestwick, then stay near Glasgow and from there drive to Edinburgh and Perthshire. And beyond." He gave a half grin.

Sylvia walked over to her daughter and put her hands on her shoulders, her eyes wet. "Sweetie, I want you to take your dad's ashes to spread over the Tay. He would have wanted that," she sniffed. Then she hugged her daughter and took a place next to Two Feathers, who handed her a tissue.

August looked at Faolan, speechless, her mouth agape. She could feel everyone looking expectantly at her.

"I don't really know what to say."

"Well then have some whisky, dear girl, and let's finish up this food," interjected Brigid, no doubt with an eye to lightening the moment. "Time for mush and tears later. Now is a time for celebrating!" She held up her mug in one hand and a half-empty bottle of Bushmills in the other. "Come and have a nip!"

August, relieved for the respite, looked at her mother and the sheriff, which Brigid interpreted as a bid for permission to drink something stronger than ale.

"Oh, don't mind them, Red—you're allowed. Isn't that right, Sheriff?"

Two Feathers, arms crossed, gave a small smile. "Must have forgotten my badge today."

Maybe some whisky would help loosen the knot in her stomach, but hard liquor was the last thing August wanted right now. "I'm good, thanks," she said, her lips a little tight.

Sylvia piped up, "I think it would be good if everybody finished off these snacks. I don't want to have to wrap them all up." Brigid and Sorcha took to jostling each other in mock competition while Linda began tidying up the cake and Abel gathered the dinnerware for washing. August turned to Faolan and still couldn't make words.

"It's okay, darlin' girl, you don't have to say anything just now. It was a lot to spring on you, and I'm sorry I didn't think it through a bit better." He bent down and kissed her on her forehead and squeezed her shoulder. "Why don't you spend some time with Lainy before she has to leave?"

"Okay, thanks," was all she could manage. She gave Faolan a strong, sincere hug—she knew whatever he had in mind, he was thinking of her—then took Lainy's hand and led her out onto the porch, where they could thaw out from the air conditioning and breathe easier in their momentary privacy.

True to form, Lainy started with the small stuff before getting to the big issues on her mind. She talked about the songs on the mix tapes ("This first song from Queen is about this whole fairytale and it's inspired by a real painting") and what the campus at UC Berkeley is like ("Everybody is so cool there and, omigod, the library is amazing"), as well as the town itself ("You would freakin' love the old record and book shops there") and the California weather ("We have these great foggy mornings, but it hasn't actually rained since February").

Eventually they got around to the part where she wanted to talk about how the whole Archer family dropped off the face of the earth for months. August didn't know how much to tell Lainy. She didn't want to drag her friend into the drama and possibly even risk her life. Plus, she knew how crazy it all sounded. But she also wanted to have somebody to share it with, outside of their little clan of werewolves and hunters and other magical things. Somebody her own age.

Lainy seemed to sense August's hesitation. "They told me everything."

"They did?"

"Yeah. I came by last week and you weren't here."

"You did?"

"Yeah, they told me you stay at Faolan's most of the time, now. And about how you guys were at the cabin because there was a woman who was murdered in the Blue Rook. Murdered!" Lainy's eyes were huge. She could get herself worked into a frenzy pretty easily, and often had to be reminded to take a breath. August just nodded. "I mean, I heard about the murder. My mom sent me a letter. I guess it was all over the local news. I was surprised it wasn't on the national news. Usually something like that would be on the national news, ya know?"

"Yeah." August just nodded slightly.

"I guess you guys went to the cabin to get away from the heebie-jeebies and the bad juju for a while? I mean, seriously—poor Abel, too! His arm? Your grandmother? It's lucky they didn't all die."

"Lainy, why didn't you come see me after you talked to them? Like they said … I was just up the hill there."

"I ended up talking with them for a while and they mentioned your surprise party, so we figured we'd surprise you a little extra."

"Well, good job. It totally worked. What else did they tell you?"

Lainy cocked her head and knitted her brow. "Good lord! What else is there?"

August looked off and then back at Lainy. How much was safe for her to know? Did it even make sense to drag her into all of the craziness? She'd trusted Lainy with all of her other deep dark secrets and the girl had never let her down. But being a werewolf's girlfriend—being part werewolf herself—that was a hell of a lot to ask of anybody. She knew Lainy could feel her holding back, but all she could do was shrug.

"I am a bit surprised that you and Faolan are basically living together, August. I mean, he's got to be more than twice your age." She was using her most non-judgmental voice, but August knew that it did look odd. Or at least ill-advised.

"Lots of rock stars have eighteen-year-old girlfriends," August teased.

"Yeah, and that always ends so well," Lainy said, one eyebrow arched high.

"Look, it's not really any of your business. I get enough stares from people. My family is cool with it, why can't you be?"

Lainy's round freckled cheeks went bright pink and she looked down. Even her braids seemed to take on a dejected sag. She picked at the edge of her frayed cut-off jeans and swung her military boots over the edge of the porch, away from August.

August immediately felt sorry, but also a little frustrated with her. She knew that Lainy always felt like an outsider—that was one similarity they had bonded over—and suffered a lot of small criticisms at home. So any tone that seemed harsh would sometimes send Lainy inside of herself. Her usual bubbly energy would fizzle out and she would sit quietly, like now. Usually, August tried to tip-toe around potential conflicts with her, which she was glad to do for the sake of making their friendship a safe place. But it also meant never being able to be irritated around Lainy, and what kind of friendship was that? It's hard to be yourself with somebody when they're so afraid of catching blame that you can't even vent.

"Lainy ..."

Lainy sniffed.

August walked to the edge of the porch and hung her feet over, too. She sat next to her friend and handed her a cold lemonade from the cooler.

Lainy took it but didn't sip. She hiccuped and tried to explain through tears. "You know, it's hard to be nice all the time. I feel like I have to be perfect around you ... like I ..."

"And I feel like I'm not allowed to be upset around you."

"Well, shit."

"Yeah, shit."

"I'm only worried about you. I mean, you've only just turned eighteen and you're shacked up with some guy in his forties. You have to admit it's kind of ..."

"Yeah, I admit it. And you're my friend. It *is* your business."

Lainy sniffed again and pulled the neck of her Star Wars tee-shirt out to wipe her eyes.

"Damn straight," Lainy said, then took a sip of lemonade.

"You've got four braids today. That's new." August gave a gentle tug to the little marbles at the ends of Lainy's braids.

"My mom was trying to do it like when I was little and I wouldn't let her do as many. She's been missing me since I've been off at college."

August nodded and put her arm around her friend.

"I'm in love with him. We fit. We're from the same place."

"New York?"

She gave Lainy a look that begged her not to be ridiculous.

"What? Maryland? I thought you said you were from New York."

"Scotland. But it's more than that. It's hard to explain, and I'm not sure you'd believe me anyway."

"Well now you have to tell me!"

"First, I can tell you we haven't slept together yet."

"Wait … Come on …"

"No, it's true. Not all the way yet. Not that I haven't wanted to."

"If it wasn't for your family knowing about it, I'd be really creeped out and worried about you."

"He's a good guy. And an old family friend. We'd have done it already if it had been up to me. My hormones are making me crazy and I'm so fucking attracted to him. But he … well, he kind of wants to take it slow."

"Well, that's new. Or at least it's not typical. I mean, it's not, right? Not that I have a lot of experience in that area. Sounds too good to be true."

"I don't know. I mean it's not like I've never had sex; I've had some boyfriends before. But they've all been close to my age. I don't know what's normal for a guy his age. And is normal the best thing? And what *is* normal anyway? Who the hell decides these things?"

Lainy looked skeptical. "This conversation got deep quick, didn't it?"

August nodded. "He wants to have this big talk about something. Probably his past. He says he wants to have an honest place to start from." August paused here and gave Lainy an opportunity to

23

interject. Lainy remained thoughtful and silent. "It's important to him, so it's important to me. Honestly, when he seems like he might start to talk about *it* ... whatever *it* is ... I kind of feel like I'm going to throw up."

"This sounds like a serious relationship."

"It is."

"You could probably date just about anybody you want to. You probably should at least date a few other guys your age."

"I don't think I could. I'm very focused on him. Some kind of switch that flipped on, or connected me to him."

"Chemicals. You know it's chemicals, right?" Lainy raised her brows in challenge.

August shrugged.

"Imprinted like a goose," Lainy replied, tossing a bit of jeans fray onto the grass.

August screwed up her face with the most incredulous look she could muster. "What?"

"You know, imprinted like a gosling—a baby goose?"

"I know what a gosling is! I just ... a goose ..."

"Oh, never mind!" Lainy started to giggle.

They both laughed.

"I imprinted on him like a goose, muthafucka!"

"Okay, never mind. I said never mind!" Now the deep belly laughs were rolling out—the kind that make you lightheaded in the best way possible. The kind that always used to make August feel like she could tell Lainy anything.

"This would only be funny to us," Lainy snorted.

"Well that's all that matters," August gasped.

They settled down and the warmth of their friendship grew comfortable again, and they basked in the sun for several moments.

"Where's Snow? I wanted to pet her."

"Probably getting her ears scratched by Gran. She loves that cranky old lady to pieces. Are you going to be around for the rest of the summer?"

"Yeah, but there isn't much of it left. I have to head back to college in a couple of weeks."

"We should spend some time together. I'll teach ya how to use a bow."

24

"Ok. August Archer the archer?"

"Well, yeah, actually. I found out a couple of years ago that my family's name is literal. We come from actual archers."

"That's pretty damn cool."

"Yeah. Lainy, I'm sorry I snapped at you. I know you're only worried about me."

"It's okay. I know that I can be overly sensitive, a little, maybe."

"Shit, we have a lot to talk about."

"I have stuff to tell you, too," Lainy said as she half smiled. "Nothing so wild as murders and dog attacks and mysterious cabins in the woods."

"I'm totally looking forward to hearing about all of your adventures."

Lainy grabbed the porch railing and hoisted herself up and offered a hand to haul August up too. They hugged and went back inside to help clean up the rest of the bacchanalia. Luckily for them they'd managed to miss all the mess and everybody was settling around the big room to play games. August surveyed the room and exchanged an air-kiss with Faolan. He and Linda and Sorcha were standing over a table scattered with jigsaw pieces, turning them this way and that, testing a spot and moving on. Two Feathers and Abel were at the chess table, while Brigid and Sylvia played nine men's morris.

She looked expectantly at Lainy, "Do you want to play something?"

"Do you have Connect Four?"

"Hah! We have the original version of that plastic toy!" Sorcha crowed in the direction of the girls. "Over there, on the shelf. Wood, with little slots to slide the balls."

August and Lainy looked at each other.

"That's right! I said it! Slots! Slide! Balls!"

The young women laughed and poked through the collection of old games until they found the most likely candidate and sat down to figure it out. August won the first game, but Lainy beat her three in a row. This made August a bit churlish.

"You can be mad," Lainy said, "I don't blame you! I kicked your ass three times in a row. I'd be mad too."

"I'm going to practice this goddam game and kick your ass next time."

August began clearing away the game, with the click and clack of game pieces rolling and dropping into the wooden case. Lainy pulled her feet out from under Snow's furry white backside.

"I think I'm gonna head out, August. My parents are taking me to see *Buckaroo Banzai.*"

"Oh, cool! Let me know how you like it. I haven't been to a movie since I moved to Maryland."

"Seriously?"

"Yeah. Let's go see *Red Dawn* this week!"

"Yeah, okay. Sounds great."

August trailed Lainy as she made her goodbyes, hugging and shaking hands and thanking people. August saw her to the door and watched her drive away in her buttercup-yellow Volkswagen Rabbit. Lainy had decorated the edges of the rear windows with rainbow stripes and there was a big bumper sticker on the tailgate: "My other car is the Millennium Falcon." Lainy gave a little honk as she pulled away and Snow answered back with a bark.

Red Night

Faolan and August made their way up the hill to his house as the sun dipped below the tops of the full summer trees, bathing everything in lavender and apricot. Faolan had a sack over one shoulder with all of the birthday loot and she held her bouquet close. They clasped hands and walked slowly, Snow circling them and pausing to sniff various trees and rocks. Occasionally she would lock her body and cast searching looks into the woods, smelling the faint breeze, then shake her ears with a flap and trot onward up the path along the creek.

August was feeling restless, but also pensive. She was quiet and yet bursting with questions she wasn't sure she wanted the answers to. Mostly she wanted to spend all night in bed with Faolan celebrating her birthday and bonding over their love. She'd had the thought that she would don her red cloak, with nothing underneath, and re-enact their meeting. Then she thought that maybe she would prance around the house in something short and sheer. She felt parts of her body warming and a low ache at the thought of him looking at her with want, with hunger, and then putting his hands on every part of her. But she knew that The Talk had to come first, and she wasn't sure she wanted that to happen tonight. But soon—it definitely needed to happen before their trip to Scotland. The idea of jetting off somewhere with him, just the two of them, made her stomach flutter.

"Did you have a nice chat with Lainy, then?"

"I did. I'm kind of dying to tell her about me."

"Oh?"

"Well, she is my best friend."

"Aye."

"Well, I think she suspects I'm not telling her something."

"Oh."

"I don't want her to think I'm hiding something from her. It might hurt her feelings."

"Aye."

"It's not about her, you know that."

"Aye."

"You're no help."

"What would ye have me say?"

"That I should tell her. Or that I shouldn't tell her. Something besides 'oh' and 'aye,' thank you very much."

"I'm afraid I can't help you with this one. You're going to have to decide all on your own."

"Yeah. I guess so. I just wish there was a clear right answer."

"The world is full of unclear answers, love. You might want to settle on that idea."

"Nope."

"Well then you're going to be awfully tired by the time you're my age."

August sighed. She knew some things couldn't be changed, but she couldn't help but burn to change them. She was still too young to recognize how many threads might be woven into any given situation, though she understood all too well that if you pulled or snipped the wrong ones, the fallout could often be the opposite of what you were hoping for.

"Are you trying to tell me I shouldn't try to change some things?" she challenged him.

"I'm trying to tell you that some things cannot be changed," he replied matter-of-factly.

Snow was already on the back deck, panting in the dark shadows by the glass doors. August slid the door open and stepped into the cool of the air conditioning—a refreshing reprieve from the oppressive summer heat that emanated from the rocks and hung in the humid air, even as the sun faded.

"It feels so good in here!"

"Aye. Though not quite as arctic as at the Rook."

"Yeah, Mom and Gran really like it penguin-friendly. Though a little chill is fine—I wouldn't want to get a rash on anything delicate."

"Indeed not," Faolan said with a grin and a gentle swat on August's bottom. She laughed and did a little sidestep away from him. She loved his playful way, and the private games they invented. Her greatest reward was making him let out one of his all-too-rare belly laughs, which for Faolan were rumbly and deep, with just the tiniest hint of a bark.

August tip-toed like a ballerina to the kitchen and grabbed a vase from the windowsill, filling it under the tap and then tucking the flowers in.

"These are so beautiful, Faolan. Scottish flowers. I love them."

They both looked towards the other side of kitchen when they heard the scraping of Snow's water bowl on the floor as she nosed it towards the sink.

"Ah, the beast is thirsty," Faolan said, scooping up the bowl and filling it for her.

"Poor baby. It's got to be miserable with all that fur in this heat."

"It's not as bad as you'd think," he gave her a look over his shoulder.

"Yeah, I guess you'd know." They stared at each other a long moment. August did a twirl, allowing her skirt to give a seductive peek of her panties again. "I'm glad you like my dress." Coy, she tugged her hem back down in front, which then brought her neckline down low enough that her breasts were half-bared.

He grinned, dried his hands and took a step towards her. "Indeed I do." And she saw from the front of his kilt that he did, and she smiled.

She took another step towards him and spun once more and put her arms around his waist, looking up at him. Her long dark curls cascaded down past her bottom, tickling his arms as he put them around her.

He smiled, slight and soft. "Whatever could be on yer mind Red?"

"Oh ... I was thinking ..." She paused here, hoping he'd fill in the blank with, say, something that indicated he wanted to take her upstairs and ravage her.

"Aye ... ?"

"Well ... now that I'm eighteen ..."

"And ..."

"And ... we're all alone here ..."

Snow looked up from her water bowl and gave a wet bark.

"Except for you Snow," she soothed, "we're all alone ..."

"Darlin' girl, let's go sit down, so I can hold you."

He kissed her on the top of her head and she jumped up and wrapped her legs around his waist. He carried her to the couch in the great room—a mere twenty paces, but she enjoyed the ride, pressed close to him. Before she hopped down she kissed him in the crook of his neck. She grabbed a pillow in the corner of the couch and tucked her legs beneath her, sitting sideways, and hugged the pillow. Okay, this was it after all, The Talk. Her stomach was jumping and she tried to focus on the beautiful scenery outside. The wall behind the couch was mostly glass. Nothing remained of the sun but a red glow off to the west that faded into dark blue jeweled tones as the half-moon waited in the wings for its cue. She could just make out the creek flashing with glints of fire as it flowed down the hill. She tried not to look at Faolan as he settled in on the next cushion. He didn't try to touch her or put himself in the way of her averted gaze. He simply paused there in the silence and inhaled slowly, waiting for her attention whenever she was ready to give it.

"Okay, you're freaking me out," August burst out, finally looking at him and holding her pillow a bit tighter. Snow stood up from her curled position on her dog bed and nosed her head into the crook of August's arm. "Sit!" Snow nudged her, then sat, putting a paw onto the couch.

"What?" Faolan asked it quietly, but insistently.

"You're freaking me out."

"There's no need for your worries. Set them aside." She was looking at him now. He looked into her eyes and she relaxed her grip on the pillow.

She swallowed her anxiety and searched his face for his affection. She found it there, around the corners of his eyes and that curve just below his bottom lip. She wanted to lean in and kiss him on those places, but was still feeling protective of her own heart.

"Just tell me please. Get it over with already. It's probably not even that big of a deal. I've just built it up so much in my head because you're Mr. Reluctant all the time."

"I'm sorry I've been so mysterious. This whole process of bringing you in on all of our family and clan secrets has been uncharted territory for me. I didna want to overwhelm ye. But I can see that waiting to talk about this has made you more anxious."

"Yes, excellent assessment, now just tell me." August knew she sounded irritated, but really it was fear. Faolan probably knew that too, she thought.

"I need to get something, I'll be right back." He headed into the study and emerged with a wooden chest. She'd seen it before, sitting in the area behind his desk. She'd never wondered what was in it, but now she burned.

"What's that?"

"It's a trunk, lass. Just a moment." He situated himself back on the couch again and set the trunk down facing the couch.

"I *know* it's a trunk, darling." She was a little exasperated. Faolan never lied, as far as she could tell, but he had a way of sometimes answering a different question.

He worked the latch and lifted the lid, and August fixed her gaze on the contents. She felt a chill, and setting the pillow aside, she wrapped a knit throw around her shoulders and slid down to the floor next to the trunk to peer inside. Snow curled up next to her and let out a great sigh. August felt safer with her hip half-buried in Snow's fluffy white coat.

"What is all of this?" She started to reach into the mound of what appeared to be journals and small keepsakes, then stopped short and looked to Faolan for permission.

He nodded and she picked up one of the newer-looking ones on the top. They were Moleskines, like the ones her father always sought out, and there must have been a hundred of them in the trunk, all of varying colors and conditions. Some were fat with items tucked inside, others were flat and looked almost unused. Or so it seemed.

On the cover of the one she held, she read "1984" printed in blue ink. She held her breath and opened the cover slowly.

January 1, 1984.

It's a new year, love. I'm realizing how much I've held on too tightly to the memory of you. I suppose I knew it before, but now there is so much more at stake. I know you would want me to be happy. That's why this will be the last book. The final goodbye that has been a long time in the making. I couldn't do it for Brynn, or Omolara, or Madeline, but I can do it for August. And truth be told, I must do it for myself.

She looked up at Faolan, who was rubbing his hands and looking a bit anxious himself. Brynn, Omolara, and Madeline. Names she'd never heard him speak before. She wondered if there were many others and these were just the more important ones. She gave him an awkward and skeptical smile and turned her attention back to the journal. She flipped forward a bit and landed on a page that started with March 2:

Goodbye bluebells
I will forget you not
There is a new wild rose
And this is how it goes
And this is how it goes

The poem was short and there were some sketches of flowers around it. There were two more entries on that same page.

March 3
It's hard to let go of something that has become a meditation. Reinforced each day with worship and memories that are so easy to conjure. This day is worship of a new Goddess. This pilgrim has a new temple.

March 4
Iseabail, today I thought of you only once. I will mourn something intangible when I go a day without a thought of you. Today was all books and flowers and sandwiches and hiking. Some belonged to me alone and some belonged to August. I think it's good for me to have quiet time in my mind that isn't crowded by the love and desire of a woman. I can't say if this is good for you, but I suspect your spirit is restless at the haunting of me all these years and now you are able to rest my old friend, my true love.

August's mouth went dry. She flipped ahead a bit more and noticed a flower pressed in on May 16:

I will miss the son I never knew with you. I regret that I was not there with you when it happened. So many years ago, on this day. Such fear in the heart of your family for what could have been a beauty. You must have been so afraid. Today will be the hardest to set you aside. I went for a walk this morning. There was dew on the grass and the flowers were already out. I thought of the life we might have had as a family. I thought of your pale ginger hair. I saved this forget-me-not for our babe, like I used to save them for you. We never even named him. I wish we had done that. It is time to lay these things to rest, Issy.

Snow whined a little. August felt a lump in her throat. Sadness enshrouded her like a suffocating fog, but there was a prick of hot jealousy inside her heart. Forget-me-nots belonged to her and Faolan. How could he share them with somebody else this way? He had been giving her second-hand romantic gestures all this time. What else had he said that made her feel special, but was simply recycled offerings?

Faolan seemed to detect her mood shift. "I'm going to get a glass of wine, would you like something?"

"Water. My mouth is very dry," she said flatly, trying not to let her voice tremble.

"Alright." He stood and stretched his legs. He kissed the top of her head, but she did not melt into it, or appreciate it like she had hundreds of times before that moment.

He walked across the expanse to the kitchen. She watched him pulling out glasses and pouring liquids and focusing a bit too hard on what he was doing.

She turned her attention back to the notebook, flipping until she found the most recent entry.

August 18

I am coming to Scotland, Issy. To say goodbye. I want August to see where I am from. I want her to know I am serious about putting you behind me and focusing on her. It's time to give her songs and flowers that are all hers, without reservation. It's time for me to have a part of myself back that I lost when you died. I think I can find it in a farewell.

August felt awful. She couldn't help but be resentful, however irrational that might be, that she isn't the first girl he ever gave forget-me-nots to. But how could he help that? One thing was for sure, Faolan was right, it is tricky to talk about these things. Strong emotions were rising in her and she wanted him to say something clever, like he always did, to calm her nerves. She wanted to know that whatever he

33

said was something he'd only ever said to her.

He handed her the water and sat on the floor next to her.

"Are ya angry, lass? Because you seem upset."

"Maybe you'd better tell me about this trunk."

"This trunk is full of all the journals I've written in since Issy ... Iseabail died. Like a daily meditation I have written in these journals every day, sometimes pages at a time, sometimes a few sentences. Some days it was just one or two words. I've held her closely a long time. Too closely."

"How did she die?"

"It's a bit of a mystery to me. I was told it was childbirth."

August gave an empathetic nod.

"She was buried on a rainy Tuesday afternoon in the spring."

"Were you there?"

"I was watching from a long way off. It broke my heart that so few had come out to pay their respects."

"I thought she had a big family. I mean, that's what I was always told."

"Her husband Angus was an abusive arse. He didn't go, nor did he let any of the kids or kin say over her. Her parents showed. Brigid. Brigid had heard about it through the midwives network of gossips."

"Brigid didn't tell you how she died?"

"Brigid didn't have any details. None of the midwives did. The reason they knew about it at all is because the woman who delivered the babe was a kitchen maid who was sister to a local midwife. I guess that was enough of a qualification for Angus, who was said to be miserly and felt a midwife too dear. When Angus found out that Iseabail and the babe had passed, he didn't blame himself for being cheap, he blamed the girl. He beat her so savagely that she nearly died. Never fully recovered her mental faculties. She lived out her days with her sister, I heard."

"It makes me sick that I'm related to this guy."

"Oh. Right." He scratched his chin, "I should have been more diplomatic I suppose."

"Why? It's the truth isn't it?"

He nodded, "Aye, it's the sad truth."

"That's a horrible story. I suppose I need to write all of these things down for future Archers. Just so that they don't have to find out

34

all of these things the way I have."

"I'll help ye with that." Faolan swallowed, and his jaw briefly clenched. "So, Iseabail and the babe died. They were buried together in the cemetery of her home church."

"You must have really loved her."

"Aye, I do—I did."

"Well *do* you, or *did* you?"

"Iseabail's name is engraved on my heart, August. I hope you can live with that." He paused and looked at her. She remained silent. "Do you know why I call you August instead of Red or other pet names when I am having a heartfelt discussion with you?"

"Why?"

"Because it is your oldest and truest name and that is the name I want engraved on my heart. Each moment we are together, and I say your name, it traces over the groove and makes it just a bit deeper."

August nodded. It was unfair how he always seemed to know the right thing to say to melt her. Even if it was an illusion fueled by hormones and his ability to push the right buttons, she didn't care. Isn't everything an illusion of perception anyway? Isn't that the very basis of love?

She let out a great sigh and one from Snow followed.

"Ugh. Stop being so amazing. Can't I have just a minute to be jealous and wallow in my other less evolved feelings?" She reached out and grabbed his hand and held the notebook up with the other. "Are you wanting me to read all of these?"

"I want you to do what you need to do in order to move forward with me. I have been bonded to Iseabail for a long time. I've never even tried to set her aside before. With other relationships she existed alongside. Which I now realize wasn't fair, not just to the women whom I professed to love, but to myself. I could never really love them the way they deserved, or form proper lasting bonds with them because of this."

"You were stuck on some girl—"

"Your great-grandmother," he reminded her.

"Oh, yeah. I forgot that part. Doesn't that make this," she waggled a finger back and forth between them, "doesn't that make it kind of creepy?"

"Does it?"

"I don't know. I kind of look like her, except the hair … and I'm kind of skinny. Do you only like me because I remind you of her?"

"Other than your familial resemblance, there is no lover I've had that you remind me of. You are truly one of a kind."

She pondered, then let go of his hand and dug through the box while he watched patiently and with not a little concern.

"I didn't write those with an audience in mind. I don't even know what all is in there. You can look if you want, but you do so at some risk."

"What does that mean?"

"There is 88 years of deeply personal notes of love, longing and growing. Some things I wrote in there may not represent much at all who I am today. Or might make you feel as though you'd not measure up somehow."

August nodded and tried to think of the right thing to ask, but she'd had no experience with delving into the uncensored mind of a man. Or even a boy her own age for that matter.

"There are any number of ways that reading those journals could change the way you feel about me. All I'm saying is that we should both be prepared for that."

August was pretending that she absorbed the full weight of what he was saying. Her face was set as though in stoic concentration and consideration of the wisdom he was imparting to her, but her mind was racing and curious. She wanted to read all of them, that moment, starting with the first and to not move until her legs were numb and she'd passed out from hunger.

"But I can read them if I want to?"

"I don't want you to get hurt."

August remained pensive for a long pause. "Could you order some pizza? I want to at least read some of this."

Faolan sighed and stood up, he kissed her on top of the head once more and gave her shoulder a squeeze. "Aye. Mushrooms and onions?"

"Well, if you didn't want me to read these, Faolan, why did you even show them to me?"

"I told you, I'm just worried about hurting you. Mushrooms and onions?"

August hesitated a moment, thinking how badly she's been

craving meat lately, especially after her tiny transformations. She wanted to tell Faolan to pile it up with sausage and pepperoni, but Abel had certainly been influencing her with his vegetarian ways, and she hated seeing any animal hurt. And the nostalgia of a simple mushroom and onion, like she and her mom and dad used to eat all the time, was an even more powerful hunger. "Yeah. Thanks," she said finally.

She dug down into the trunk while Faolan called in their order. She set aside mementos, including a lock of strawberry blonde hair fastened with a faded green ribbon. She recognized it from the day Faolan first transformed for her to reveal his secret. He'd laid out a number of mysterious artifacts, including this lock of hair and a large painting of a huge white werewolf that looked like something from the set of a Vincent Price movie. It turned out to be Faolan's father, Ban. He had tried to kill her gran Sorcha, but Ban himself ended up dead, setting off a feud between the Archers and the Veritas that left most of Sorcha's children, who were August's aunts and uncles, dead. It also left Faolan's brother Ciardha with a thirst for vengeance. August was proud of how far she'd come in accepting her father's death at the hands of Ciardha. Now all of this, it brought the stinging memories and realizations to the surface again.

"Do you think we'll ever find your brother?"

Faolan took a few paces across the open space from the kitchen to the living-room, two plates in one hand, forks in the other, a dishtowel over his shoulder.

"What's that?"

"Do you ever think we'll find Ciardha?"

"Yes, I do. Even if it means he finds us, first."

"He thought he killed Mom, and he tried to kill Gran. Won't he come back at some point when he finds out he failed?"

"He may not know. About your mother, I mean. He may have assumed Sorcha would die soon anyway. As far as I hear he hasn't left Scotland since last November."

"But why hasn't he come back for *me* yet?"

Faolan stepped back and put the dishes on the table with a clunk and a clang and came to squat in front of her.

"My relationship with my brother is … complicated."

"Yeah. I already knew that. But he wants all of the Archers dead. He thinks I'm the only one left. Shouldn't he be stalking me or something? He knows where you live. Just because you marked the property doesn't mean he can't get me when I'm not here. You can't be with me all the time."

"I'm thinking along a different line. It's hard to put into words—you're going to have to use your more lycan instincts about family and mates. Ciardha knows you are my mate, so it doesn't matter that you're mixed."

"Except that it does!" August could feel her face getting hot. Anger rose up in her throat, thinking of her torn family and dead father. "That's what all of this bullshit is about!"

"Lycans … werewolves … we imprint on our mates, love."

The word *imprint* startled August and her conversation with Lainy snapped into focus. She put the notebook back into the trunk and focused her full attention onto Faolan. "What?"

"We bond to somebody, our hormones, our brains, our ancient animal nature. Once we do, it is very difficult to let go of that bond. And should that bond be broken, it is very difficult, almost impossible, to remake it."

"So that's why you had a hard time bonding with new mates?"

"Partly. Some of it was because I didn't want to let go of my bond with Iseabail."

"But she died. What good would it do to hold on to that bond with her?" She saw a pang of something cross Faolan's face. "I'm sorry, I didn't mean to make that sound so heartless."

He looked thoughtful and gave a nod of forgiveness. "I knew that I would have to mourn it and go through a sort of withdrawal. And I didn't want to lose what I had left of her. Mostly, though, I didn't know what I would be without her. So instead of letting go I did this." He waved a hand over the trunk.

"You wrote about it?"

"I wrote to her, as though she were alive. I wrote about my day as if I could share it with her. This is 88 years of me trying to have the wife I wanted, of keeping my bond with Iseabail intact. It's as strong as any drug addiction and it feels just as terrible coming away from it. Brigid helps with some teas, and I'm doing rituals that help me let go and move on. You help—more than anything else—because I can feel myself bonding with you."

"So that's why 1984 is going to be your last journal like these?"

"Aye. It's also a large part of why I'd like to take you to Scotland. I am going to bury this trunk next to Iseabail. I'm going to show you the places I ran when I was a child. I'm going to introduce you to hunters and lycans who are not prejudiced against each other. I'm going to show you where we come from, August."

August nodded and began to tear up a little and swallowed the lump in her throat. She gave an encouraging smile she hoped didn't look too schmaltzy or forced.

"This journey to our homeland, dearest girl, is so I can say goodbye to Iseabail. And ... well, if after all of these things you still want me, I can bond with you ... Proper."

August felt a flush of love and passion for Faolan, and though accompanied by flashes of fear warning her heart that there was more difficulty ahead, she was undaunted. They were just journals. *What could a pile of journals do to make me feel differently about this man who turns me into a pile of mush? Who always wants what is best for me?* He was so unguarded and trusting with her—how could she doubt that her bond with him would survive any shock?

"I don't think these journals can change my feelings about you."

"Likely not. You have imprinted on me pretty fiercely it seems. Even if it were bad for you, you'd probably love me anyway."

For some reason it had not occurred to August that what Lainy said might be true, and she startled at the revelation. "We really do imprint? I thought I was going crazy. I think about, well you know—think about *stuff* all the time. I kept thinking I was losing my mind, or weird or something. Mom said that my hormones, that they were why I am always ... Well she said that there were reasons, and that it was hormonal, and that she was going to explain and I kept putting it off, but she knew—"

"August ... love, slow down. Your body is awash in chemicals that are determining not just who you'll bond with but how you'll develop as a mature being. In fact, I've come into your world at one of the most vulnerable, impressionable times of your life. For us lycans, anyway. In the folklore it's called *eagal-ainmhidh*, which literally is a monster, or a bogeyman, but they've a term for it in dog-training as well: the fear impact period."

"Actually, you could slow down a bit yourself, Professor Wolf. It's been a long day for this little monster."

Faolan brushed a curl from August's forehead and leaned over to plant the gentlest kiss there. "Sorry, love. I'm only trying to say that you're forming ways of seeing and understanding the world that will be with you a century or more. If something hurts you or traumatizes you at this stage, the fear of it could influence your outlook for the rest of your life. You'd never completely get over it. Which is another reason I take things slow with you."

"I don't think that's true."

"What, am I not going slow enough for ye?"

She looked at him in disbelief, then caught on that he was teasing, and peered at him ruefully. "Wise guy. I mean that I couldn't work through things. Like if somebody hurt me, attacked me or something, for instance."

Faolan shifted and furrowed his brow. "Maybe you could, at first, or so it would seem. You might not even realize how it was working in you. Or it could show up when you're older."

"Look, I was attacked by Tanner and I worked through that. I'm not afraid of all stupid jock guys or going into the woods."

"Is that true?"

She pondered deeper. Was it true?

"Not long after he attacked me I walked through the woods in the dark. That was the night I met you."

Faolan nodded. "Aye, there's that. Perhaps you're past it, then. The fear impact stage, I mean. Or your hunter nature is stronger." He winked. "Then again, I suspect the full moon and the pheromones from my bit of the hill made you restless that night, though you didn't realize it at the time. Not knowing your nature."

"Oh, yeah, there *was* a full moon that night. You were doing that thing with the bowl. Chanting and burning torches and stuff."

"Yes."

"And you wouldn't introduce yourself to me." She crossed her arms and pretended to be miffed.

"An auspicious beginning, indeed."

"Okay, first of all, I know you won't hurt me. Not on purpose anyway. So that fear impact stuff is a moot point."

"I would never intentionally hurt you."

"Moot. Moot, moot, moot. That's a funny word, isn't it?" She uncrossed her arms and picked up the journal she had set aside.

He nodded and smiled. "Aye, 'tis."

She held up the journal. "And because … well, Iseabail."

He tilted his head in a very canine way.

"Why you want to take things slow with me, I mean. You still love … or loved, her."

He nodded. "That's true as well. And since you're only part lycan, it's hard to know which parts of you will be more wolfish."

"How do you mean?"

"I mean, just because I'm over a hundred years old and I've had other lovers, doesn't mean I'm going to know everything I'm doing when it comes to you. It doesn't mean I won't make mistakes, or that a young lover has nothing to teach me, or any influence over me."

"Most people like having young lovers, don't they?"

"Evidently not." He grinned at her and raised a brow.

"Touché. I guess I meant men. Men prefer young lovers."

"There are lovers of all types. Very young men and older women. Couples and triples with only women, or men. Harems, both ways. If you can imagine it, it is being done somewhere. Perhaps not openly, but it is being done."

"But men prefer younger women, isn't that kind of a known thing? That's why they trade in their older wives in for newer models. That's why there are so many rock stars with teenage girlfriends."

"Some men, sure. But you being so young actually makes all of this a bit more treacherous for me. Many times I've wished you were older, but then that seems disloyal to who you are, since your age is part of who you are. I wonder, do you find comfort in our age differences? Do you feel you have some upper hand by being young?"

"Upper hand?"

"Over other women. A competitive edge. Does being young make you feel you're more secure with me?"

August contemplated that one for a long while. "I guess my first answer is yes. But when I really think it out, I realize that means I can't ever age, or I'll lose my competitive edge, right?"

"And this is when I tell you, lass, that I am in love with the whole of you. Not your age, or that gorgeous mane of yours. Or the way you have that crooked smile when you're feeling a little shy. Or the way we can talk about books and music and dreams and love. It isn't any one of these things that keep my bond to you vigorous and alive—

41

it is all of them together that make you so amazing, unpredictable, inspiring, and entrancing."

"Inspiring, really?"

"Did I mention adorable?"

"I wish I was older, Fe. Just so it wasn't a problem. Also, I thought it was the main reason we haven't been to bed yet."

"It's part of it, aye."

"I don't want it to be weird for people. I don't want to hide. My mom has been fine with you the whole time. I thought she'd flip out. And Gran finally made peace with you. I didn't think that would ever happen."

"Ah, will wonders never cease? Your mom and your gran are well aware that you've been an adult for several years now, in our world. The rest, you and I needed to work out. So, here we are."

"Having the Talk." August opened her eyes extra wide and staring, turned down the corners of her mouth and put out her hands like a staggering zombie. "The Taaaaaalk ..."

"Scary, huh?" He grabbed her hands and pretended to eat the ends of her fingers, complete with snarls and gobbling noises. "I'm going to eat your braaaaains!" He gobbled at her neck and head.

She laughed and pulled away, though she kept hold of his hand. "I want to read all of this right now. Like, I don't want to move or breathe until I've read every last page."

"Oh lass, you are trouble, ya know that?"

"Let me just read some of the first one?"

"Go to it then."

She eyed him for a moment, to see if he was sincere, then picked up the oldest journal, marked 1897. It started with heart-wrenching rawness.

June 12, 1897

Issy, darling, I don't know what to do, so I will write to you here. Another returned letter and I am devastated. I know you still love me. I feel a darkness come over me and hatred fill me for those who keep you from me. I can't control my transformations. The rage just swells inside of me for my mate, my love, and it cannot be quelled. I hunt every night, spilling the blood of deer and rabbit and fox, devouring them whole. I dare not go near a hunter village for fear of what I will do.

I will continue to send letters for as long as I feel our connection. For as long as you are alive, I will be here for you, waiting. I must know what has become of our babe. Did you bury him? Where is he? Tell me won't you where his wee body lies? They will not say. I wanted to see his face just once before they put him in the ground. I dream of a world where he grew inside of you, strong and ready to be born. A world where I could hold your hand and comfort you and sing to the babe at your swelling navel. I would tell you both stories—new ones, where the world wasn't so cocked up. I heard that you are to be married to Lord Angus Archer today. All the world is black.

"Faolan?"

He called back from the kitchen, "Yes?"

"Is there any ale?"

"Yes."

"I am going to need some."

"Aye."

There was a knock at the door, and a minute later there was pizza on the table along with two glass bottles of home-brewed apricot and elderflower ale. August tucked the journal in the trunk on the top of the pile and ran over to Faolan to hug him.

"It's emotional stuff, I warned you."

"Just be quiet and hold me."

He wrapped his long arms around her and put his lips on the top of her head, inhaling her—lavender, vanilla, pheromones. She inhaled him—spices, woodsmoke, pheromones.

"Why don't you eat something?"

"My stomach is a bit in knots."

"Come, sit."

They went to the kitchen and sat at the table, sipped on ales and divvied up pizza. Faolan piled stacks of roast beef next to his and gobbled them between slices. August nibbled on some of the beef and felt a little guilty.

"Why is it that, now that I know I'm part wolf, I feel like all I ever do is suppress my appetites?" she grumped, only half joking.

"The price of greatness," Faolan retorted.

After dinner she climbed into the corner of the couch with Snow taking up the length of the rest of it. She picked up the first journal and

43

continued on. It was full of rage, pain and longing, carried on in one-sided conversations with a girl August was beginning to feel like she knew. The way Faolan described her, she couldn't help but root for the two of them, but the sting of jealousy was still there. And there was a slight sense of losing something she'd never had, and had no right to, either. But it was also a blessing of sorts, getting to know her great-grandmother this way. She read until she fell asleep.

Rainy Days and Mondays

August woke to the sound of rain pelting the window behind the couch. Snow was half laying on her legs and half falling off of the couch, her canine body too warm and heavy. August tugged her legs out from under the giant sleeping mound of white fluff and wiped the sleep from her eyes. The beast barely stirred. Faolan was on the floor on a pile of sleeping bags, breathing deep and slow. *It must be early morning*, she thought. But it was grey and wet, so it was hard to tell. It matched the melancholy that clung to her from reading the journal entries. She had grown accustomed to emotional hangovers by now, but that didn't make them any more pleasant.

As eighteenth birthdays go she imagined that hers had been unusual. She went to the kitchen and started up some coffee and dug out a package of treats that Linda had given her as a gift. She plucked out a ginger and lemon scone and picked at the corners of it while she watched the coffee brew.

"I smell coffee!" Faolan called out, his voice still thick with sleep.

August wandered over, straddled him on her knees and bent forward and kissed him. She could feel his hardness through the sleeping bag and gave a little wiggle.

"Ahh, darling girl, that's going to cause trouble …"

"That would be such a shame," she smiled a little wickedly, and kissed him again, this time he put his hands on her arms and kissed her deeply. She rocked back for a moment and he let out a slight groan, then she stood.

"I will get you a cup, just as soon as it's done."

"Oh, girl! Woof! You make it hard for a man to stick to his principles." He stood up and rolled all of the bags, tied them and tossed them in the corner. Still with a bit of a crooked walk, he padded over to the half-bath to pee and finally joined her in the kitchen.

"Did you sleep well, lass?"

"Did you?"

"I confess, I'm an old dog with a bit of a crick in my back. Other than that, just some restive chatter in the noggin." He walked over and held out his arms, and they wrapped each other up. She tilted her face up and he kissed her again.

45

"You taste like scone."

"You can't have any. This one is mine." She teased, holding the scone out in front of him. She ran towards the living room.

"It smells of lemon and ginger. I'm going to gobble it up!"

"No! You big bad wolf!" Her feigned terror dissolved into unrestrained giggling. She waved the scone about. "No! No! You can't!"

By now Snow was up and barking, though with only a little concern.

Faolan managed to grab August's wrist and brought the scone to his mouth. He took a big bite and made ridiculous gobbling and chewing noises, letting bits fall all around.

"You hairy beast!" she squealed, breaking free of his grasp. Snow barked again.

"Not you, girl! Him, with his big eyes and big paws. Here, you can have the rest." She held out the scone and tried to pout while still laughing. "I wanted apricot and ginger, anyway. I think there is one in the box."

August and Faolan looked at each other and then at the box sitting on the table. She flung the less desirable scone at him and bounded toward the kitchen in two leaps, making it to the table first with him right on her heels.

She laughed manically and flung open the lid, fishing out the apricot and ginger scone and taking a big bite. She laughed and then coughed on inhaled crumbs.

"Graceful," he smiled.

"You're just a sore loser!" she managed to reply through a mouthful of scone. Crumbs flew everywhere.

"Oh, very ladylike!"

She felt so bright and full of life with him. Something as simple as coffee and scones could be beautiful, a moment long remembered, and the gray weather just made things cozier. She knew damned well he could have beaten her to the box if he'd tried, and that too made her feel loved. No pangs of jealousy for his long-ago love were troubling her this morning, and as she watched him eating breakfast and sipping his coffee, she wondered what he must have looked like as a lad of eighteen.

Would they have liked each other so much if they had been born

46

at the same time—would their views have matched up so well? Would the attraction have been the same? His hair was probably jet back then, without all the steel and pewter strands woven into his curls. But each mark of age on Faolan only endeared him to her more.

She knew too that his heart had been hurt badly, yet here he was, trying again to love, and love well. It made her warm and full for him, and she ached to take him to bed, to cover him with kisses and fill herself up with him. She knew that day was probably still months away, when they would take their romantic trip, letting old loves go, and weaving themselves together in a true soul bond. Until then, she would embrace every other intimacy with Faolan. She would melt into his kisses and his touch. She would soothe her aches alone, until he could soothe them for her. With her.

"Well, it's work for me, love," Faolan reminded her as he got up from the table. "I've been putting things off too long, and there's some hands-on business that can't wait, so I'm off to Baltimore today."

Her reverie broken, August stood up herself and began clearing the breakfast away. "I did wonder if you were just taking a permanent vacation." She kissed his romantically scruffy cheek. "Well, good. Maybe I'll actually have a moment to myself around here!" she teased.

"What will you do with yourself, actually? Probably just lay about pining for me, I imagine." He winked.

"Hah! Don't flatter yourself, Romeo!" She snapped him with the dishtowel and laughed. "No, I'll probably see if I can't help out down at the Rook."

"I'll only be a few hours, I think."

"Don't worry, I can amuse myself. You go get ready."

Though August thought little about money herself—her parents had always given her whatever she needed, and she'd never had much interest in fashion trends or status symbols—she understood that it was a serious, even crippling concern for most people, and she made sure Faolan knew how much she appreciated his generosity with her and her family. She'd enjoyed having a little spending money of her own when she'd worked at Brigid's old shop, and she wondered sometimes why her parents seemed never to worry about having enough. As she'd mentioned to Faolan, she'd always assumed that her father and mother were well-paid for what they did.

"It's more likely they had a good deal of family money," Faolan had surmised. "Most of the otherkin clans have become adept at keeping the money in the family. And living as long as we do, we tend to favor long-range investing."

Faolan himself had fallen fairly naturally into the imported antiques business, having an eye for beautiful things and firsthand knowledge of much that had become trade-worthy in the British Isles over the past two centuries—goods that always seemed to find a ready market in America. The trick for Faolan had always been hiding his tracks, or breaking his trails, as he put it. Like most otherkin, and lycan in particular, he preferred being a bit hard to find, and so had set up a number of businesses under various company names. He apparently had a dozen or more, though most of the companies had no knowledge of each other, and he would operate as a silent partner; usually that meant he bought into a successful antique shop or supplier, made a number of educated purchases himself to boost the quality of their inventory, and collected a percentage, which is why he could go for weeks or even months at a time without actually having to interfere. A couple of his shops specialized in repair, and he was involved in a shipping business as well, so that he could have easily converted his small stable into a high-profile empire, but that was simply not his way.

"I get that, about being off the radar," August had told him. "I mean, I enjoy the attention of the people I love—as you well know, lovah. But most of the time I'd rather be invisible."

"Aye, it's our habit. Generation after generation of being different from others, as I reckon it. We're generally very good at not being noticed."

"So I suppose this means, if you and I spend our lives together, I'll never have to work."

He had winked at that. "You know, and I know, you're going to have to find something to concern you, else you wish to go gently mad. And it's an important part of your education to understand how economy works. More than once I've had to start over myself. The world changes." He squeezed her hand. "But in practical terms, yes, you can live the life of a pampered poodle if you wish it."

"I'm sure I'll find something that'll get me out of bed in the morning. Besides chasing you around, I mean."

<------«»------>

Having cleared the dishes and tidied the counters, August headed upstairs as well to see if she could catch Faolan in time to watch him dress. To her surprise, he was still in pajamas.

"Would you like to get a shower with me?" he asked as he pulled towels out of the closet, offering one out to her.

"Are you kidding?"

"Not at all." He smiled that devilish crooked smile of his. "This is my abysmally transparent ploy to see you naked, of course."

"But I thought we weren't going to … That you wanted to, you know … wait."

"I think a shower and a little soapy touching would be not too out-of-bounds. If it's okay with you?"

And for the first time, August had second thoughts about having sex with Faolan. As exciting as it seemed to her most days, it was a little scary too, all of the unknowns. What does one do in bed with a werewolf, anyway? *But weren't you just saying you wanted to enjoy whatever sensual touching might come along?* she chided herself. Maybe it was the just the unexpectedness of his offer that knocked her off-balance. At any rate, whatever reservations she had were rapidly being drowned out by the thought of putting her arms around Faolan's naked hips, and the sound of her hormone-driven heartbeat whooshing hard in her ears.

"Okay with you, Red?" he double-checked. She seemed less enthusiastic than he'd expected.

"I'm sorry—yes, of course! After all of the emotions last night, and our lovely morning, I'd love to be close like that with you. I guess I'm just a little … nervous, all of a sudden."

He put a hand on her shoulder and kissed her cheek. "No pressure, love. We can save it for another time then."

She took the towel he offered and kissed him, gave him a little come-hither jerk of her head, and went into the bathroom. He grinned and followed close behind her.

The master bath was an expanse of beige and brown tiles—most of them plain, though several were embellished with art nouveau designs—with plenty of room for two. There was a window wall of glass blocks that made the whole room feel light and open; the upper blocks were clear, allowing a slightly ripply view down the hillside toward the trees and the Rook beyond, and just now they were letting in the sun that had started to peek through the clouds. The lower

49

blocks were textured, making the world beyond them look like an abstract painting. The shower itself was also built of glass blocks, with a return wall to contain the spray rather than a shower curtain.

"They sure loved these glass walls when they built this."

He laughed. "Aye, and be kind. You're seeing the pinnacle of mid-century house design, there."

August watched as Faolan took off his shirt, pulling it over his head.

"Do you want to watch me, Red? Or shall I undress you?" His voice was low and seductive, and the question gave her gooseflesh and sent a tingle down her spine.

"Can we do both?"

He smiled. "Aye, we can."

He turned his back towards her and lowered his pajama shorts revealing the well-toned and nicely shaped backside that August had only gotten to see on rare lucky occasions. There was a delicious dip in his low back, just before his bottom curved outward, where she'd rested her hand many times. She wanted to walk over and cup his bottom in her hands, kiss it, bite it. Instead, she watched as he turned around, his erection long and exciting. She couldn't stop staring at it—this was the first time he'd ever showed himself to her this way. No quiet games of leaving a door cracked and a light on, or a half-obscured glimpse in low light. Here he was, naked, in front of her. Complete intention.

Her pulse quickened as she took in the sight of him. Squared shoulders, tall, lean and a full chest of dark and pewter hair. He was pale, with tan lines here and there, and beautiful, and she couldn't wait to touch him.

He walked over to her, cradled her head in his hands and kissed her mouth, gently. A shiver ran through him and she felt it shake him. Her hands went to his waist, she ran them down the low part of his back and pressed against him. Their kissing quickly grew more passionate, lips parted, tongues dancing. She could feel the heat of his body coming right through her thin dress. After what seemed like forever, and yet only a second, he pulled away and looked at her, holding her eyes with his, searching her face.

"You are so beautiful."

Her hair was a tangle and lopsided. Her dress was wrinkled from sleeping in it all night. What little make-up she had on was smeared. Yet she couldn't help but believe him. She felt beautiful. Maybe because he came right out and said it when she was feeling less than put-together. Or maybe because she felt loved by him, even when she was sure she was being a disaster.

She smiled and put her arms straight up, and in one smooth motion Faolan swept the dress up over her head and tossed it towards the hook. She felt the rush of cool air bump up her nipples, she could see their excited bodies in the large mirror. She heard him inhale and felt his warm hands slide up her torso, then he cupped each breast gently in his hands. August tilted her chin upwards, eyes closed, feeling all of her skin prickled and electric. She moaned a little and he knelt down in front of her.

He kissed her belly and edged the lace panties down over her hips. Her black shock of downy soft hair revealed itself and he nestled his nose there, breathing her in as he squeezed her to him, the tips of his fingers sinking into the softness of her bottom and her thighs. August's knees quivered as he lowered the lace to the floor where she stepped out of it. She heard her voice make a low moan that she'd never made before. It just escaped from her—she couldn't have stopped it if she had wanted to.

Faolan ran his hands up and down her thighs and over her bottom, pressing and caressing into the crease of her thighs with his face. She twisted her fingers into his hair and watched him as he stood up. Her head came to his chest and she put her face into the center of it. The curls of hair tickled her and she inhaled. Spice. Skin. Salty. Delicious. She slid her mouth over to a nipple and kissed it and reached down to touch his cock, wrapping her hand around it. He gasped and moaned as she gently stroked for a moment, then let go.

"We should probably turn the water on," she said and kissed his bicep. She looked down at his cock and grinned.

"I can't seem to take my hands away from you," he said.

Still holding each other, they moved into the alcove and turned on the water. A large shower head sprayed rain from above. A sunbeam cut across the water, sparkling like diamonds with hundreds of tiny rainbows. August felt outside of herself, as though she were in a movie. Everything was so perfect.

They kissed as the water ran in streams and rivulets down their bodies. Her hair clung to her in dark swirls and seaweed strands against her peachy flesh. The sight of her own body pressed against his in the wet excited her. Watching her nipples press to his ribs and his hipbone press to her belly was electrifying.

They stood under the water, kissing and soaping each other up, letting bubbles and foam trace their contours. Sliding slick hands over necks and shoulders and thighs. She watched as he worked the bar in his hands and set it aside, then ran his hands over her torso and down her legs all the way to her toes.

Once the film of soap had washed away the previous evening, leaving them both feeling fresh and new, they kissed and touched until they were both weak in the knees. He reached around her and turned off the water, then shook off the wet like a dog and grabbed a large fluffy towel to rub her body pink and dry. She remained silent, watching the erotic film of her life play out in front of her own eyes. He wrapped the towel around her and scooped her up, and she put her arms around his neck. He carried her down the hall, leaving damp footprints on the carpet as he made his way to the bedroom, his breath heavy and deep.

"Yes," she whispered into his ear.

He laid her in the bed and then climbed in beside her.

"I want to kiss you, lass. Everywhere."

Her breath caught and she wiggled closer to him.

He started at her forehead, like feathers across her face, then her earlobes, down her neck to her collarbone, where he hovered a bit longer, tracing the bones with his mouth. He cupped her breasts, kissing and teasing her nipples, then worked his way down toward the center of her. He nuzzled her soft fur, her tender folds, his tongue slipping down, pushing gently in, urgently kissing and sucking at her until she felt like ripe fruit, thin skin bursting, exploding, and juices running down as she heard herself calling out his name. She spun into the heavens and fell back to earth, where she lay in a mound of blankets, with Faolan resting his head on her belly, kneeling over her hips as if in worship.

She tangled her fingers into his hair again. "Why don't you lie down?"

He gently rose. "I don't want to take my hands from you."

She moved with him, his hands on her hips, as he lay on his

back. She kissed his eyes, his cheeks, his mouth and neck. She buried her nose into his chest hair, rubbing, tickling, and bowed between his legs, taking the base of his shaft in her hand and guiding him into her mouth. She had had other lovers want her to do this, but this was the first time actually felt a deep desire to have a man in her mouth this way. No awkwardness or strange smells, no pushing on her head. Spent yet still aroused, she was feeling tendrils of energy vibrating and entangling between the two of them, and she couldn't help but want to taste him. Please him. Hear him sigh and catch his breath while she dipped and swirled her tongue over the firm pinky-purple flesh. Vulnerable, trusting, pulsing, waiting, sexy and filling her mouth and her want. She found herself swelling again, her belly aching low. He petted her head lovingly, and stroked her hair, his hips moving in a slow dance between him.

"Yes, love, yes ..." he whispered hoarsely. "My beauty, my love, yes ..."

The sounds of his pleasure and affirmations of his desire encouraged her until she was moving faster, hand and mouth working together until she felt him surge and he yelled his love for her. She moved her mouth and her hands as he climaxed, she kissed and sucked the tip of him, his seed warm and almost sweet on her lips. His thrashing, his explosion, and then his body glowing as he lay there spent and absolutely beautiful, the years faded from his face. She licked her lips and then inched up to his face, and their hot mouths touched. He curled an arm around her, his breathing still heavy.

"August, love, that was amazing."

"I love you, Faolan." She felt it more than ever in that moment.

"I love you, August."

She cuddled into the side of him feeling at once satisfied and also oddly off-kilter. She looked at his hairy chest and stroked his arm, his fingers. She rubbed his protruding hip with her thumb. He rested his chin on top of her head and stroked one of her stray curls. It had all seemed so natural, and yet what did she really know about this man? What kind of future could she have with somebody who is in such a different place in his life than she is? With someone who wasn't even human? She was overwhelmed to be finally lying naked in bed with him, as lovers. But before she could contemplate cold feet and what the future might hold, she drifted off to a deep and peaceful sleep.

Pizza and Beer and Folklore

When August finally woke enough to get up, all of the clouds had cleared away and it was past lunch and well into the afternoon. There was a note from Faolan on the bed table, promising to be back before dinner. She couldn't believe how long she'd slept, though it wasn't quite so surprising once she realized her period had arrived. She wondered if Faolan had noticed while he was down there, and felt a momentary flash of embarrassment. If he had, it certainly didn't seem to bother him any. She imagined he would be in Baltimore still, but she found him downstairs in his study, on the phone with a very businessy sort of voice. She slipped into the room and kissed him as he was saying, "Just let it go for two-thousand, that's fine."

August had dressed and was feeding Snow when Faolan finally came into the kitchen to announce his dealing had ended for the day. They were headed down to the Blue Rook for a big family meal with the clan—essentially, everyone who had been there the day before for August's birthday, with the exception of Two Feathers, who was looking into a series of burglaries in the area. The topics that night were Scotland, gardens, movies and where to get a good jigsaw puzzle. Mostly they talked about the upcoming wedding on September 15th, now less than four weeks away. August watched Gran and Abel together, and she couldn't tell who was more excited.

It was like this now: comfortably hot days in the garden or the kitchen, and long evenings on the porch with the rhythmic whirring and chirping of summer, the fear of Ciardha and his possible reprisals reduced to a shadow in the corner somewhere. Snow and Smoke kept watch, patrolling their territory and alert for any strange smells or sounds, though they'd never turned up anything more threatening than a squirrel, and usually ended up chasing each other or getting their bellies rubbed. Ever since those winter months hiding out in Faolan's cabin, as Sorcha, Brigid, and Abel healed from Ciardha's surprise attacks in November, the family had grown accustomed to sticking close and breaking bread together often. It seemed only natural then that the Rook became the family home for all of them. Sorcha was the first, officially ending her residence at Sunnyvale Nursing Home to move back permanently to the house where she had raised her brood in the States. Not long after she and Abel announced their engagement, he moved many of his things to the Rook as well. Initially Brigid had lived there too, after closing down Leigheas Apothecary, her herb and tea shop. But now she was occupying Abel's house, a gem of a bungalow in the 1920s style, with gardens he'd been tending for years. She was doing him a favor, he told her, since he didn't want to let it go to seed, or sell off the house, so Brigid's being there made it possible for him to keep it. With all of the herbs, vegetables and fruit growing on his half acre, it was like a mini Eden, and Brigid was happy to tend the plants and experiment with brews and potions in the kitchen.

For two weeks Faolan spent most of his time between D.C., Philadelphia, and Baltimore, sorting out business deals and deciding what he wanted to sell off, so August didn't see much of him, and when she did he was tired.

The upside for August was that she could spend more time with Lainy, before she had to go back to Berkeley. They went to the arcade and played *Space Invaders* and *Centipede*, then window-shopped for home video game consoles. Lainy said Atari would be the best to get, but Intellivision was the one with *Dungeons and Dragons*, so she wasn't sure which way to commit her resources. August made a mental note to send both of them to Lainy's college address, and hoped she wouldn't be providing too much distraction for a girl who seriously wanted to graduate with honors. She knew this time with her wouldn't last long, but it was still a blast just to talk to somebody her age about such dumb everyday stuff. It felt blissfully normal—something she didn't realize she missed.

They spent time at Faolan's house—which August had taken to calling the Den, since she got tired of calling it "Faolan's house" all the time. They watched a few movies downstairs in the game room and listened to tapes and LPs together while they played chess and gin. Lainy was particularly impressed with Faolan's high-tech compact disc player, though her favorite activity was poring over his collection of antique books—many of them first editions and several of them signed.

The day before Lainy was to leave for Berkley, they took in a matinee showing of *Red Dawn* in town.

"Do you think that could really happen, August? An invasion like that?"

"I can't imagine it. Though I guess if it happened here, the kids would call their resistance group the Marauders. That'd be funny."

"Well, I didn't really like it. I mean, did they have to kill everybody off?"

"I think that was the most realistic part. It might have been a fantasy but it wasn't a fairy tale."

Lainy just nodded.

"I mean, in a fairy tale, there's a lesson or something. But real life just sucks sometimes, and the good guys lose."

"I know. My mom says the same thing. Just kind of a bummer, is all. Dude, I'm gonna miss you when I go back."

"Yeah, I was trying not to think too hard on that either. Hey, let's go home and crack open some beers and order pizza, huh?"

"'Y' know, that might just about work."

When they got back to the Den they dug into August's stash of Newcastle ales and she popped one and handed it to Lainy.

"You're staying over, right? Faolan's gonna be in Philly 'til tomorrow."

"Shoot, that's means I'll miss him. Y' know, he's a lot cooler than I thought he would be. I think you two make a good team. Hey, wait—where's Snow? I definitely wanted to say goodbye to her."

"She's with Smoke at the Rook. She gets lonely if I leave her here. I'll call my mom after we get some pizza and have her send her home. She'll just say 'Go home Snow' and she will run right up the hill to the back door."

"No way!"

"She's a smart girl."

"She's huge too! I remember when she was just a little fluff ball."

"Hang on, lemme call for pizza before we do anything else. We have them on speed-dial on this fancy Inspector Gadget phone."

August picked up the receiver and hit the code for Al's Pizza. "It's not Nino's, but it'll do. Hey. Is this Pat? Hi. Yeah, that's me. On the hill. Mushroom and on—yeah, onion. The usual, you got it. Oh, okay. Yeah, that's fine. Thanks." August hung up the phone. "It might take a while. Friday night, everybody wants pizza I guess. Pat's been hiring extra drivers 'cause he heard they're gonna put in a Domino's."

"That's cool, I can wait."

After a couple of beers they were giggling and talking about

Lainy's college adventures.

"Oh my God, August, I had this preppy roommate first semester named Tiff who's kinda racist, but in that way that isn't overt, y' know? She plays it low-key. But I swear, it's like she has no idea I'm part black and part Pilipino! She asked me what suntan lotion I use because she, 'like, totally thinks my tan is, like, seriously awesome to the max'." Lainy could hardly talk she was laughing so hard. "Oh, and she kept saying, 'where do you get all of your cocoa butter from,' and asking how I get away with only washing my hair every two weeks. I mean, clueless!"

"You think she was trying to be sly with you?"

"Maybe, but I really don't think she's that smart. She also thinks I'm straight. She kept trying to set me up with guys from her sorority brother fraternity whatever—I don't know. I don't do that Greek life shit, so I don't even know. Anyway, she says, 'I guess you don't have time for boys since you're just, like, totally into academics.' Lord help me!"

"Wow. That is ... clueless."

"Yeah."

The conversation hit a lull. They sipped. August was turning over in her head how a talk about werewolves and hunters would go, but she couldn't figure out how to even start it. She got up and put on the radio—some Top 40 call-in show with dedications. A guy named Ed wanted to "send this one out" to Bella and the deejay put on "a number one hit, from Air Supply." Being true rock fans, Lainy and August looked at each other and rolled their eyes, groaning and making faces over the syrupy tune—neither one guessing that the other one knew all the words, and had secretly sung along more than once, "Here I am, the one that you love."

The doorbell rang. August glanced at the clock. "Hey, only thirty-five minutes. Must be because we're such good customers."

They went to the door together, Lainy digging in her pocket for cash and August waving off her offer, while Air Supply crooned in the background. But when the door swung open all conversation stopped.

Standing there on the porch was a tall, muscular young man in a red Al's Pizza cap, looking down and reading off the order from the bill taped to the box. When he looked up, August and Lainy both recognized Tanner, the former wrestling champion of Mahigan Falls

High School, who two years before had pinned August to a tree in the woods behind the school and tried to rape her. It hadn't ended well for him.

Lainy's eyes went wide and August crouched back, prepared to spring, her ears and fingers tingling like they were on fire.

"What the ..." she began, but she saw Tanner's eyes bug out and his face go paper white.

"Oh Jesus! Oh Jesus! I'm sorry, I'm sorry, I'm sorry! ... I didn't know you were here!" He reflexively bent to cover himself, and shoved the box at Lainy. "Here! Take it!" he shouted and began to sob. As soon as the pizza was out of his hand he bolted from the porch. "Free! It's free! No charge! No charge!" He was back in his car in seconds and a spray of gravel flew up as he gunned it in reverse.

The girls stood there, stunned. August broke the silence.

"Holy shit."

"Yeah. I guess he learned his lesson," Lainy said, peeking in the box. "Hey—free pizza."

August bolted the door and checked the other doors and windows while Lainy dropped the pizza on the table. They both looked at it like it might be poisoned.

"Think maybe I'll have a sandwich," Lainy said and then slid the box away from her.

August popped another Newcastle and chugged almost half of it down. She felt for the tips of her ears and Lainy gave her a funny look.

"Hey, Lainy ... So ... Fairy tales, right? What if I told you fairy tales are real?"

"Like unicorns?" Lainy sipped her beer and laughed nervously. She wondered what this had to do with the unexpected appearance of Tanner, and why August wasn't talking about it.

"Like mermaids and hairy people living in cottages in the woods," August went on. "Like ... werewolves."

"Werewolves?"

"Yeah."

They both sipped their beers and eyed each other.

"Aren't you a little freaked out about what just happened at the door, August?"

"Well, not as much as you might think. I'm kinda getting to that."

"Okay, so what are you trying to say? You've seen a mermaid?" Lainy scrunched up her forehead and looked at August sideways.

"Oh god, that'd never happen. Mermaids are incredibly rare."

"Right. Hah! Of course, my mistake."

"But maybe ... a werewolf."

Lainy stopped, mid-sip. She stared and waited for the gag, but August just stared back.

"Oh, come on."

"Remember when I told you that you wouldn't believe me?"

"August ... a werewolf? Come on." Lainy studied her friend, who didn't look like she was about to slam a punchline. "Okay, okay. Let's pretend for a moment that werewolves were even remotely possible, where did you see a werewolf? Oh, hey, *Young Frankenstein*! Werewolf? There, wolf!"

August tilted her head and arched a brow. "I'm serious."

"Fine, you're serious. So tell me then, where? ... Wolf?"

August huffed. "Lainy, I mean it! I'm trying to tell you something ... Ugh! Never mind!"

"I'm sorry! Sorry, sorry ... C'mon, don't be mad. Look, no more playing. I'll be serious."

"No ... It's me. I'm sorry. I don't mean to be so weird, I just ... I don't know how to say it."

"Dude! What is it?"

"Here, is where there are werewolves. Here in Mahigan Falls."

Lainy blinked. There had to be a punchline coming.

"I know. I sound crazy. Did you know that Mahigan is an Algonquin word for wolf?"

"I think I heard that once. Our school mascot makes more sense now."

August nodded. "And the wolf sightings around here. Which, I believe, you're the one who told me about them."

"Okay, so that's wolves, not werewolves."

"I'm getting to that." August squared herself and took Lainy's hands in hers. "Before I tell you this, you have to understand, this is some serious shit. Being too close to me could put your life in danger."

"What? Girl, you've had too much beer on an empty stomach. You're cut off."

"Really, Lainy. I've wanted to tell you about this stuff for a while, but I was worried about you being in the wrong place at the wrong time when something bad happens."

"Okay, now you're scaring me a little. And I don't mean 'cause I'm afraid of werewolves, but you sound like you're losing it."

"Man, there's just no way to make this sound real. I'm gonna have to show you."

"Show me what?"

"Just watch."

August thought of Tanner and then Ciardha, letting her ears and fingers burn, and then pushed the burn harder until she could feel her aspect emerging. Her ears began to point and fur grew around her neck and jaw. Her teeth stretched out into spikes. Lainy watched in amazement and confusion, while August regarded her quietly with now black-rimmed eyes. Lainy reached out to touch one of August's ears.

"What the fuck, August? These feel like real ears. What are you?"

In a moment August's wolf aspect slipped away and she soon looked like her regular self again. She sagged against the table, then took a seat. "Water, please."

Lainy backed away and grabbed a glass, not taking her eyes off of August. She filled it from the sink and handed it to her.

"What the hell was that? What are you?" Her lips curled and August felt the sting of making a huge mistake.

"Shit." August couldn't find the words to explain what had just happened. Too many beers clouded her judgment. "I thought I could trust you."

"What? You can! Fuck—of course you can trust me! I just ... Well, could you maybe explain what the hell you did just now?" Lainy was a bit frantic but she wasn't running away. That at least was something.

"I've been trying to tell you. I'm not normal. I'm not like most people. It's like in the fairy tales. I'm a werewolf."

"I guess this is where I do some movie-scene freakout and tell you I don't believe it."

She and August stared at each other for some seconds.

"But damn ... you just had dog ears and pointy teeth a minute ago, so I guess there's that. But you didn't, like ... Not all the way"

August shook her head. "I can't. I might never be able to. I'm only part werewolf, really. It's inherited."

60

"August!"

"I have to eat something first." August grabbed the abandoned pizza and pulled off a quarter of it, folding it over like a taco and nearly inhaling it while Lainy went to the fridge and started putting together a sandwich for herself. "Could you make me one too?" August called. "Like with a big pile of the roast beef in there?" She crumpled the pizza box and tossed it in the trash.

"Are you going to tell me what this is about?"

"Hang on. I need my girl here." August picked up the phone. "Mom? Hi. I know—sorry. Listen, can you send Snow up here? Lainy wants to play with her. Saw a movie—mostly we've been catching up a lot." August shot Lainy a side glance. "Tomorrow. We will. Okay. Love you too." August walked over to the back door and in moments the big white dog bounded through.

"Wow, that was fast. C'mere Snow!" Lainy squatted down and the wolfdog almost head-butted her off her feet. She gave Snow a hug around the neck, told her to sit, and got her a giant chew bone from the pantry—the third one she'd given her in as many days.

August helped put the sandwiches together and the three of them crossed the living room to the long couch by the window wall. Lainy did more staring than eating as August powered down the huge sandwich with a tall glass of milk. She saved a big bite for Snow, who curled up close at her mistress's feet.

"How is this even possible, August? None of it makes sense."

"Honestly, I don't really know. I don't know how it works, and I don't know all of the story, but we just have werewolf blood in my family."

"Your parents?"

"Yes. My mother is part werewolf."

"Holy shit. This is un-fucking-believable."

"Tell me about it. I mean, imagine—I had no clue I was different from anybody else until last year. I can't fully change. I mean, maybe someday I could, but what you saw is about as far as I've been able to."

"August, your mom is part werewolf?"

"Lycan, they call themselves. Yeah. Can you believe it? A werewolf in a hot pink pantsuit? Not that she can transform at all."

"What about your dad?"

"He's something called hunter. My mom's part hunter too. She's

61

both."

"Like a hunter? Like these rednecks in their trucks? That's it? There's nothing magical about that. We're hip-deep in hunters around here."

"No, no, no. His people are from Scotland and there is this clan of hunters—they protected everybody from the werewolves. They aren't really human, either. Or, they're superhuman. They can heal quickly. They can hear and see very well. They're fast."

"So wait, you're part werewolf and part what hunts werewolves?"

August nodded.

"How does that even happen?"

"My mom and dad fell in love. Lycans and hunters aren't supposed to get together, there's a lot of prejudice. Gran and Pop Archer moved to this little town when my dad was a baby. He pretty much grew up here. Then he was back and forth between here and Scotland for some years, studying folklore and stuff, and he was over there giving a lecture when he ran into my mom, who was also just visiting, and they instantly connected. It's a long story. What happened was there was a feud among the lycan and the hunters back in the 1960s and a lot of people died, including my dad's brothers and sisters."

"Wow. August, I have so many questions."

"Then my parents moved to New York and pretty much went into hiding. They never told me what I am. They wanted me to have a normal life. Then my dad died and me and my mom moved here and this is where we're at."

"At least it worked."

"What worked?"

"Your having a relatively normal life."

August bit her lip and played with the piping on the corner of the pillow.

"Don't you?"

"Not exactly. It's a lot to talk about. It's only been a year since I found out, and I'm still learning things. Mostly, I wanted to just tell you because you're my best friend. I kept feeling like I was hiding this big part of myself from you, but I didn't want you to be in danger, but I wanted to share—I couldn't figure out what the right thing was. For both of us."

"So what do you think's gonna happen to me? Should I be worried you might attack me or something?"

"What? No! Good grief!"

"Then why would I be in danger?"

"Yeah. The people—well, one guy really. The bad ones from Scotland? That my family tried to get away from?"

"Yeah?"

"They found us. They found my dad. That's how he died."

"Oh no! Oh my god! I'm so sorry! That's horrible!" Lainy scooted in a bit closer to August and gently petted her shoulder.

"We know who did it. He's the same one who attacked here last year, and why my family all disappeared last winter. He hurt Gran, Abel, and Brigid, and they needed a safe place to heal."

"That's fucking scary."

"Now he's the one hiding. But it's been so long since anybody's seen a sign of him, things have settled down a bit. Maybe it's a false sense of security, but whatever's happening, I can't walk around in constant fear. Anyway, now you know. That's the danger—that this psycho may come back."

"I don't even know what to do with it."

"Me either."

"Does Faolan know?"

"Actually ..." August averted her gaze again and fiddled with the pillow.

"What?"

"Well ..." August hesitated and squinched up her face.

"What!?"

"Faolan ... is a full-on, furry, pure bred, big bad werewolf."

"Oh my god! August, your boyfriend is a werewolf?! How many of these things are there around here?"

"Actually, that's a good question. I don't know either. But this is why our age difference isn't such a big deal. Not that it should be if we were human. I mean, young people date older people all the time, right?"

"Not all the time. Mostly young women and old dudes. But yeah, it happens."

"Well, evidently I went through my moon phase—which is kind of like puberty—when I was about eight or nine. So I've been physically mature for ten years, according to lycan culture. And he's, like, way older than his forties."

"I thought he was like forty-five or something."

"Yeah, not quite."

"Okay, how old is he then?"

"You won't believe me. I need another sandwich. It's the transforming—makes you famished."

"I will make you another sandwich and you tell me how old he is."

"Deal."

"Roast beef again?"

"Yeah."

"Okay." Lainy made a sandwich super-fast, tore off some paper towels and handed it to August. She settled in next to her again with the last Newcastle as August began devouring her second big sandwich.

"Thanks," she managed through a mouthful. "Why don't we get comfy in some pj's? We can finish the beer and watch movies until we pass out."

"Don't forget I have to leave early tomorrow."

"Boo. Okay. We won't get too crazy."

Lainy looked at August as she got down to her last couple of bites.

"What?"

"You were going to tell me how old your boyfriend is."

August gave her a sidelong glance as she chewed. She knew the number of course, but how was she going to make it something Lainy could relate to?

"Okay … When Faolan was born, nobody had heard of H.G. Wells yet."

Lainy's ale stopped in midair, halfway to her mouth. Her eyes went wide.

"No cars. No airplanes. No records. No telephone."

Lainy slowly placed her bottle down on the coffee table.

"And, um … Jules Verne had just written *Around the World in Eighty Days.*"

For a few seconds there wasn't a sound in the room, other than Snow groaning in her sleep. Lainy just stared at August. Then the corners of her mouth curled up and a slow, sly smile spread across her face.

"Ho-ly fuck. August … holy fuck! That guy that I've been hanging around the Rook with? Your totally gorgeous boyfriend? He's a real, live time traveler! Like, he was there! When all that stuff was new. He was there!"

August nodded as Lainy began reflexively patting her on the leg.

"Holy crap! Did he meet Wells? What about Darwin?"

Lainy stood up and almost shouted.

"His library! Oh my god—all those first editions! He got them new, didn't he?"

She sat back down, put her hands on August's knees, and looked earnestly into her face.

"This is all real, right? I mean the werewolf thing, the history. It's the real thing, right?"

August smiled and shook her head, marveling at her friend. Then she nodded gently.

"Yeah, Lane, all of it. We celebrated Faolan's 109th birthday last March."

"Wow. I … wow. I wish I'd known all that the last time I talked to him."

"Don't worry. I'm sure we'll have another visit soon."

Lainy was quiet again, lost in thought. She sat back with her Newcastle and looked at August like she'd never really seen her before.

"It's kind of weird, isn't it?"

"Which part?" August laughed.

"Finding out that this fairy-tale folklore stuff exists, then just going on with the night like it's perfectly normal."

"Yeah. You get used to it, though. At least I can tell you stuff now. Stuff I couldn't say before. And you'll be in California, so you'll be safe from anything dangerous. So long as you don't tell anybody."

"Who would I tell?"

"Your weirdo roommates?"

"Right."

August smiled, a little sadly, and spread her arms to embrace her friend. "I'm sure gonna miss you," she said, wrapping her up in a hug and laying her head on Lainy's shoulder.

Lainy patted her head. "I'm gonna miss you too, weirdo."

Green-eyed Monster

Faolan floated back and forth between home and the cities the rest of the next week, leading up to the wedding. August was more and more a bundle of hormones and sexual energy, frustrated and missing Faolan but having little opportunity to do anything about it. Only once did he arrive home before she was asleep, and that was when they took some time to catch up with each other. They cuddled close, though the conversations weren't exactly romantic. She told him about letting Lainy in on their huge secret, which he didn't seem too surprised about. She told him who delivered the pizza. He studied her carefully during this story and held her tight while she let the lingering memories of her helplessness that night two years ago wash over her.

"I actually felt powerful this time, standing there knowing I could protect myself. Or Lainy."

"You're not invincible, August. You still have to be careful."

"But aren't you proud of me? I totally handled it, this guy who nearly raped me once, and he didn't scare me at all."

"I am exceptionally proud of you, actually. Always have been." He pulled her in closer and kissed the top of her head.

"I wonder why I didn't transform at all before? You know … when he attacked me?"

"It's hard to say, love. Fear can immobilize even the strongest person. More likely, your body simply hadn't matured enough yet. Even among pure lycans, the ability can come late. Sometimes not at all."

She nodded. "It just felt good not to be afraid. And if I'm being honest, it felt really good to see him cower."

"I imagine it would."

Even that night together was so full of practical things that needed to be taken care of that only a little kissing and cuddling took place before they both fell asleep. August started to feel like they were an old married couple—like maybe Faolan was losing some of his interest in her. But he hadn't even been inside her yet—how could he possibly be bored with her? Then she wondered if people just get bored having sex with each other after a while. Or was it something that could stay exciting for the rest of their lives?

These things plagued August more in her dreams than anywhere, and manifested in awkward near-nightmares of missed chances or saying the wrong thing at the wrong time—or watching Faolan fall for another woman and pretend he never knew her. Those were the worst, standing there talking to him, or yelling at him, and him blandly replying, "I don't know who you are."

The women in the nightmares were always more mature, sexier and curvier than August. Several nights that week she woke up in a sweat, and then they only had twenty minutes together at breakfast before he was out of the door. "I promise love, once this is wrapped up we'll have all the time in the world," he had reassured her, but she was beginning to have her doubts.

August spent her days that week at the Rook, helping make wedding decorations for the back yard, finding wedding rentals, looking at stacks of linens, dishes and glassware. Once they'd gotten most of the preparations done, the final bit was shopping for Sorcha's dress, which Sorcha kept putting off.

"I've gone too soft," Sorcha would say. "I'm not a young bride! This looks ridiculous on me." It was a bit unnerving for August to witness such insecurity in her usually confident grandmother.

Sylvia would say, "Stop. Nonsense. You look lovely."

But there was little convincing her that she belonged in a bridal gown. So Sylvia, Brigid and August banded together to find something they thought would work and take the pressure off of the constant hunt. Eventually the three of them piled into Sylvia's old Bonneville and ended up at a boutique with vintage and antique clothing in Frederick, where they found a lovely silk gown of pale gold with champagne pearl details. It was floor-length with an empire waist, flattering and airy and showing off a little bosom. The small sleeve was perfect for warmer weather, but would be enough to make Sorcha feel comfortable. It was fancy, but not extravagant—a dress a person might wear for afternoon tea in a scene from *Sense and Sensibility*.

They arrived back at the Rook in the afternoon with the gown, now so close to the wedding.

"Sorcha?" Sylvia called out down the hallway. Snow and Smoke came running, getting underfoot and clogging the entry way.

"Hi babies!" August dropped to a knee to pet the dogs, then pointed to the main room and they energetically bounded off. They found Sorcha in the kitchen with Abel going over the menu, distracted and agitated.

"These really must be topped with raspberry! That cheese needs to come from the place I heard about in New Market, that imports specialty cheeses. I don't know who is going to drive all the way out there and get it. Hell, it's probably too late anyway. I wonder where the caterer thought they were going to get that?" She was waving the card and talking to Abel who quietly watched her wind up. August saw him breathe with what she recognized as one of his calming exercises, then take the card from Sorcha, set it aside and place his one hand on her shoulder.

"Sorcha, darling, the caterer did get the cheese from New Market. And those tarts will have raspberry. Please, you're fixin' to give yourself a heart attack. Look, your granddaughter is here now. Didn't you have something you wanted to ask her?"

Everybody looked at August and suddenly her face got hot. "What?"

"Sweetheart, I just wanted to ask if you would be my … maiden of honor, I guess you'd call it. Seems strange to have your granddaughter be your maid of honor, doesn't it? But it seems strange to be my age and getting married, too, so I suppose I can do whatever the hell I want."

August flushed again. "Wow. What an honor, Gran. Yes, of course I will!" She hugged her frazzled grandmother and smoothed her frizzy hair down. "We have something for you."

"Oh?"

August looked to her mother and Brigid, who gave a nod and handed August the box.

"Here."

Sorcha took the box over to the dining table. Once she freed the dress from the layers of tissue she shook the garment out full-length and held it out in front of her. Everybody in the room held their breath as she regarded it.

"Oh my. Oh my, my!"

Finally she pressed the dress to her and did a spin, like a little girl.

"Oh my, this is just beautiful! It feels so soft, and this muted gold … Oh, it's lovely. I love it!"

Everybody breathed again and laughed and clapped. Sorcha took turns hugging everybody and thanking them.

"Wait. Won't gold look bad with my gray hair though? I mean, it might look a bit like mutton dressed—"

A chorus of "No's" came back to her and they all assured her it would be gorgeous with her silver and black hair.

Sorcha looked around at all the loving faces in her family. "Thank you, all. This will do just fine," she concluded, and took the gown back to her suite to hang.

"Shit, I need to figure out what I'm going to wear," August muttered. "Gran?" she shouted after Sorcha. "What do you want me to wear?"

Sorcha came back in and dusted off her hands. "Something green, darlin'. I've always loved green."

"Like, what kind of green? Peridot? Sage? Emerald? Grass? Forest?"

"Oh, you artsy types! Let's say a medium or sage green would do it. Oh, why don't you wear that gown that was your mother's wedding gown? I remember it as a very light velvet and no sleeves, and a bit medieval. Shouldn't be too hot, you think? You wouldn't mind, would you Sylvia?"

"Oh no, Sorcha—of course not. I think it'd look lovely. I think your father would have been very pleased to see you in it, August."

August nodded and felt a little rise of emotion in her throat to think of her father being proud of her in her mother's gown, a grown-up woman. She also had a slight twinge of alarm, realizing the wedding was not even a week away, but at least now she had her outfit at the ready. She thought about how she would be wearing her mother's gown to a wedding with Faolan—that must be good luck. She would also wear the Conall Pearl necklace, and maybe make some flower wreaths for their heads.

When Faolan finally came home Tuesday night, announcing that he had largely dissolved his empire, August forbade him from talking about or doing any business whatsoever, and he was only too happy to comply—though apparently one of his shop managers had made for him a flaming rum punch, so he set about duplicating the drink for her. They sipped the heady, bittersweet elixir as they cuddled on the couch and watched *Terms of Endearment*. By the time Jack Nicholson was letting Shirley MacLaine drive his Corvette on the beach, August was asleep on Faolan's shoulder, her fingers tangled in his chest hair.

By Wednesday afternoon, most of Abel's kin had arrived in town, and August was excited to finally get to meet some of the people she'd been hearing about, including two daughters, Frida and Alfrie—one quite lean and long-limbed and the other very full-figured, but both beautiful women—and his son Zeke, who could have been a model, all up from Atlanta. August also met Abel's brother Imari, whom he sometimes called Cal, though Imari didn't seem to acknowledge it. He looked every bit as distinguished as Abel but had a completely different style, speaking in a carefully cultured accent and wearing brightly patterned red and yellow clothing cut long and straight, with a cap in the same colors.

But August was most fascinated with Abel's sisters. His younger sister Hannah had been the baby of the family, and she looked little older than Abel's daughters; her elegant features always seemed to be lit with a gentle smile, as though she were radiating peace. And indeed, she had a calming influence on everyone, most especially on Abel's other sister, Afia. From the outset, August could tell she was not happy being there, standing in the main room at the Blue Rook, sucking her teeth and clucking her tongue and muttering under her breath to Hannah.

"What's wrong with Afia?" August asked Brigid.

"She doesn't like your gran."

"Why not?"

"She thinks she takes advantage of Abel's good nature."

"That's fair."

Brigid's eye twinkled and the corner of her mouth twitched up ever so slightly. "Aye, 'tis."

"Gran seems to be going out of her way to be nice to everybody."

"Well, tha's the fun part, wouldn't ye say?"

August had to dip her head a bit so Sorcha wouldn't see her laughing.

The next night, Faolan took Abel out for a men-only celebration (he wouldn't let Faolan call it a bachelor party) with Two Feathers,

Imari, John, Zeke, and a young friend of Zeke's named Alvaro that August suspected was his boyfriend. Their destination was supposed to be secret, but August already knew they were headed out to this roadside jazz bar halfway between Mahigan Falls and the middle of nowhere. Faolan described it as an odd, smoky little place like something out of *The Twilight Zone*, and surprisingly classy considering it wasn't surrounded by much. The owner was an old sax player named Shakey Lonesome, and the shows often featured beautiful women in tight sequined gowns singing sultry ballads. Patrons could sit at the bar, get a table up front by the stage, or drink good whiskey and smoke cigars on red velvet couches in the back, if they were so inclined. August figured Faolan was a couch man, and he agreed.

It had occurred to her that some woman might approach Faolan—he was gorgeous, charming, and an absolute gentleman, after all—and it made her stomach hurt to think of him flirting with some sultry and experienced jazz club seductress. But Faolan was utterly faithful, she reminded herself, and utterly bonded to her—well, her and Iseabail, but she wasn't exactly around anymore. August had nothing to worry about, and she couldn't really do much about it anyway, so she decided to focus on the hen night that Sylvia and Brigid were planning as a surprise for Sorcha.

The pair of them had been scheming for two weeks over it, and made August their cohort. They had rented a couple of limos, complete with champagne on ice, and had a DJ and open bar set up at the lodge that the sheriff's department frequented. Sylvia used her pull with Two Feathers to get a whole room for the night. August expected it would be ugly dropped-tile ceilings and a lot of tippy metal folding chairs, but it was actually quite cozy, with a rustic flavor, plenty of wood details, leather seating, and a full bar with a rail and a big mirrored backsplash. It reminded her of an oversized saloon, and they had the smaller of the two rooms there decorated with balloons and streamers. In attendance, besides the three plotters and the Woman of the Hour, were Linda from the bakery, about six women from the Sunnyvale home—some of them patients and some of them staff—and the four women from Abel's family.

August was determined to try and make friends with grumpy Afia, and started by offering to get her a drink. When Afia gave her a little side-eye she looked exactly like her brother, and August had to keep from smiling. But she accepted the wine with thanks, and August felt like she had at least accomplished one small thing by managing to earn a tiny smirk out of Afia. After she finished the glass, August noted, she seemed a little more ready to have some fun.

"So what we gonna do in here?" Afia asked the crowd.

"Whatever we damned well please!" Brigid replied, hoisting a pint in a frosty glass.

"Well in that case, I'm gonna have a lot of that wine and tell that DJ to play some music." Afia strolled over to the DJ and within moments Donna Summer was singing "Hot Stuff" over the speakers and Afia was kicking off her shoes and shaking her queen-sized hips on the floor without spilling a drop. She motioned to her family to join her, but only Hannah came out on the floor. August was mesmerized, watching how she seemed to glide so gracefully, while Afia spun her profound curves as though she weighed nothing at all.

It seemed like no time at all had passed, but the hors d'oeuvres they'd set out had gone cold, the pale blue and white cake was cut and served—"Not one of mine, but hey, not too bad," Linda had commented—and a pile of presents lay open on the table. What had started as genteel wine-sipping during the toilet-paper bridal gown contest turned into chardonnay chug-a-lugging, and the DJ packed up the easy listening and re-started the disco and funk groove. Soon all of them were laughing, swaying and spinning on the dance floor. People from the other room were milling over to see what all the commotion was about and ended up toasting the bride, while one of Sorcha's friends from the nursing home was doing doughnuts on the dance floor in her wheelchair and yelling, "Bring me a hunky fireman!" It had all turned into a glorious kind of chaos.

Fortunately they'd hired somebody to clean up, because they were leaving quite a trail of streamers and empty plastic wine glasses behind them as they all piled out into the two long black cars from Bill Nader's Luxury Limos waiting to drive them home. They gave their drivers an earful as they popped open the champagne they'd saved for the end of the evening. "To new family," toasted Afia, "May we love them as much as the tired old family we can't get rid of!" Then she busted out with a big belly laugh and slapped her thigh as everybody joined in the hooting and cheering "Hear, hear!" swaying loudly and trying not to spill their drinks as "Dancing Queen" came booming out

72

of the speakers.

Some were headed home, some were up for more dancing, as the cars dropped everyone off at their various destinations. August opted to ride out with the Sunnyvale group and see them home. After they were dropped off, it was only August left in the car with Bill Nader himself. She knocked on the partition and he rolled it down.

"What can I do for you?"

"Could you drive me out to Lonesome's?"

"You've got me until 6 a.m."

"Is that a yes?"

"Natch."

"I'm drunk."

"Yes, I know."

"You're a gentleman aren't you?"

"I like to think so."

"Good. Lonesome's please."

Bill started to roll up the partition and August shouted, maybe a little too loudly, "No!"

"What?"

"Sorry, I didn't mean to shout. I just … It's lonely in here now that everybody is gone. Could you just leave it down? Do you mind, Bill? You are Bill, right?"

"Yes. I don't mind. Do you want some music?"

"Yeah, but no more disco."

"How about some rock?"

"Do you have any jazz?"

"Sure." He dug through a box of cassette tapes sitting on the seat next to him and popped one into the player. "How's this?"

Billie Holiday's voice floated through the speakers. August closed her eyes and nodded. She grabbed a shot bottle of Jack Daniels from the mini-bar and sucked it down. "Yeah. That's perfect."

She then grabbed another whiskey and downed it.

"You might want to drink some water, miss. There's some Perrier in that mini-bar."

August opened a bottle of the fizzy water and drank it. It tasted a little weird to her without much flavor, but she guzzled half of it down and immediately let out a big burp.

"Whew! Excuse me!"

"Yes. Very ladylike."

"Are you making fun of me?"

"Maybe just a little."

She laughed and felt things go a little tilted. Her face was warm. "I will forgive you. Just this once!"

He laughed. She told him a story about her dog Snow being able to grab food off of the kitchen table without even rearing up on her hind legs. "But if you catch her doing it, she gets so embarrassed, she will go sulk in her bed for an hour," August concluded. So Bill told her a story about how he has a cat that sits on the floor in front of the couch like a person and watches TV with him and his wife.

"You have a wife, Bill?"

"I do."

"You are very clever, to mention her so cleverly."

"Right."

"Were you afraid I will get … the wrong idea, and tell you what a nice man you are?"

"Not at all, miss."

"How long have you been married? Can I ask you?"

"Six years next month."

"Six years next month." She let out a sigh. "Do you like it?"

"I adore her. I hate having to be away from her at night, but I meet a lot of interesting folks in this line of work."

"Oh, gosh, I hadn't thought of that! I bet you do." She waited a moment, but it seemed no stories were coming. "Is your wife pretty?"

"She is."

"What does she look like?"

"Well, she's short and curvy. She's got hair that is almost gold. It used to be long when I met her, down to her waist almost."

"What happened?"

"We had a baby a few years ago and it was just easier for her to cut it short. Plus I think she was ready for a change."

"Do you hate it short?"

"I miss the long hair. But she's still beautiful."

"Are you one of those guys that makes a woman feel bad when she wants short hair?"

"Well I hope not. Never meant to. She looks cute with it short and I tell her so. I only miss her long hair because I'm a sentimental fool and that's how it was when I first fell in love with her."

"I have long hair, Bill. It is often a pain. But this is what I look like, a long-hair girl, so I don't cut it off. So you wish she had long hair?"

"Long, short—as long as she's happy. Either way, I have the privilege of calling her my wife, and the mother of my child."

"Wow. That is so … deep. Bill, you are out of JD back here, buddy."

"Miss, do you mind if I ask if there is somebody meeting you at Lonesome's?"

"Kind of. My boyfriend is going to be there. He doesn't know I'm coming."

"I just want to be sure somebody is there. For your safety."

"Oh, that's so sweet!" She laid her head on the top of the headrest nearest the opening of the divider and started to get a little weepy.

"You probably want to drink some more water, miss."

August drank the water and felt the car sway and tilt, maybe more than it actually was. But her skin was so alive and she was crackling with the warm summer night, the stars visible through the moonroof, the wind whipping by and her heart full to exploding with love. The smell of the whiskey on her own breath and the sound of soft jazz made her feel sexy and grown, even though parts of her face felt numb.

"I am! Drinking the water," she answered him a minute later.

He startled a bit. "Alright then."

"Alright then," she replied, but it came out breathy and a bit slurred.

"We'll be there in about fifteen more minutes."

"Why is it so far?"

Bill laughed and shook his head. "You're something else."

"I am. Yes, I am. Okay, I'm just going to relax here for a minute and watch the sky."

"Good plan."

She lay there, listening to the different jazz arrangements until the tape clicked and rewound. She finished off her water and felt the car slow to a stop.

"We're here!" Bill hopped out and opened the back door. "Shall

I escort you to the door?"

"No, I'm good," she said as she oozed out of the car, her skirt rolling up her thighs and her spaghetti strap hanging off of her shoulder. "Oops!" She tried to stand by herself, but ended up taking the hand that Bill had offered.

"Let me walk you."

"Okay, fine."

He brushed her skirt down and steadied her to walk towards the entrance, which was flanked by purple and orange neon and said the word "Jazz" and "Piano" and had a couple of music notes floating around. When she arrived at the door she showed her ID to the bouncer, who studied her and finally said, "You ain't allowed to drink. Soft drinks. That's it."

"Oh boy," she huffed and rolled her eyes and turned to Bill. "Ya hear this guy?" She mocked his deep voice and accent, "You ain't allowed."

"We ain't gonna have trouble with you are we?" The bouncer eyeballed Bill who responded with, "She's just looking for her boyfriend. No trouble. They get along just fine."

"Thanks Bill … Gosh, you're so nice." She pushed her hair aside and petted him a little too hard on the shoulder. "Just so nice."

"I'll be waiting here, miss. On duty 'til 6."

Bill and the bouncer watched August wobble into the bar. Inside there were very grown women, with lots of curves in clingy dresses, expertly striding around the room in six-inch stilettos. Some of the dresses were so short you could almost see the globes of their bottoms. She suddenly felt like a child in her long sundress and slightly heeled sandals. She straightened up and tried to walk like a not-drunk person as she peered around the room, while men and women who were ten to twenty years older watched her go past. It wasn't until she got to the big room in the back, loaded with couches and curtains of velvet, that she found the men she knew. They were smoking cigars and laughing—even Abel—but Faolan was missing from the pack.

She went a bit further into the room and fixed her gaze on the woman sitting on a piano, her red dress sparkling and her ebony skin tight and glistening, her hair in natural curl, short with sparkling barrettes. She was singing about how girls were made to take care of boys and there were couples swaying. There was one of Abel's family

76

members on the floor and then she spotted Faolan, his arms around a tall redheaded woman in a green spandex mini-dress that dipped so low down her back you could see bottom cleavage, yet it was so short she was in danger if she dropped anything on the floor. She might as well have been wearing an elastic headband instead of a dress. August felt her face get hot and her mouth go dry.

She watched them, swaying, the woman shifting her weight on high heels that made her almost eye-to-eye with Faolan. She looked him in the face and said something, then laughed and, much to August's chagrin, laid her head in the crook of Faolan's neck. Right where the collarbone protrudes and makes a nice spot to kiss. August felt anger wash over her as she imagined this woman kissing him there, on *her* spot! Faolan's arm was looped around the woman's small waist, which seemed even smaller when coupled with her flaring hips and the round bottom that made her into the perfect hourglass. Something August would never be.

August steeled herself and marched over towards the dance floor, straight towards them. People seemed to part like the Red Sea for this angry woman-child, wearing a play dress in a nightclub.

"Excuse me!" she called out as she came. "Excuse me!" Faolan's back was to her, but she knew he would be able to smell her now, and he turned around.

"August." He said it simply and blinked. He let his arms fall away from his dance partner's waist.

"Oh, hi honey," the woman said to her and looked her over. "You're cute." She turned to Faolan. "Is this your daughter?"

"No! I am not his goddamned daughter, you redheaded hoochie!"

"Look, I don't know what your problem is, little girl—"

"I am not a little girl! You know what? If I wanted to I could come right over there and tear your—"

"August! August, it's okay. Why don't we go have a seat?"

The woman cocked a hip out and put a manicured hand on it. "Faolan, who is this?"

"Who am I? Who are you, lady!"

"This is my … This is August."

The woman pulled something out of her clutch and wrote on it. "Here. My number. Call me when you've sorted out … whatever this is."

Faolan just nodded to her and said, "Bye, Trish."

"Yeah! Bye Trish!"

Faolan seemed to watch her walk away, and that pissed August off, too.

"Take a picture, it'll last longer," she sniped. She knew she sounded bitter and jealous but she didn't care.

Faolan turned towards her and took her by the shoulders. "August, what are you doing here?"

"Looks like it's a good thing I showed up. Wonder what would have happened next. A little trip behind the velvet curtains maybe?"

"You are not yourself." He regarded her for a moment and sniffed about her a bit. "How much have you had to drink?"

"I've had a little. But no matter how much I drink I won't look like Trish, with her big boobs and her tiny tight dress."

"August, what is this about, lass?"

"Don't you lass me! Why not go find Trish? That would be a braw night for you, aye?" She mocked his accent and for a half a moment he looked angry, but then he laughed.

"You're jealous."

"Am not."

"You are. You're seething with it."

"Shut up."

"Look, you've got nothing to worry about."

"Then why did you have your hands all over her?"

"She asked me to dance, so I did. It certainly wasn't going to go any further than that."

"She gave you her number."

"And I don't need it." He crumpled the paper in front of her and turned his hand over and let it fall to the floor.

"Oh."

"Oh, indeed. There's nothing wrong with me dancing with a beautiful woman."

"Beautiful!"

"Aye, beautiful. She's beautiful, and so are you, and you're being a jealous child, so leave it. Nothing bad has happened. I'm still your man and all is right with the world. Except that you're drunk."

"I'm not a child. I can prove it." Her tone turned flirtatious.

"There is a limo out there waiting for me. Maybe you'd like to join me in it?"

"I'm not sure that's—"

"Oh, you'll put your hands all over a strange woman, but you won't make out with me in a lim-o-sine? Come with me to the limo and kiss me." She tugged his hand and he followed her out to the car.

August was filled up with so much emotion, desire, longing, passion—she was starting to feel overwhelmed. She wanted to make out in a limo while buzzed on wine and Tennessee whiskey, and the man she wanted to do that with was Faolan. She tried not to think about her childish sundress and her smallish breasts while they climbed into the limo.

"Found him! Roll it up Bill!"

"Yes ma'am."

Bill rolled up the partition. Faolan helped himself to a small bottle from the bar—Scotch whisky, no surprise to August. She pulled her dress up to mid-thigh and straddled him in his sexy grey suit.

"You look so sexy right now, I want to kiss your goddam face off." She bent to him and started to kiss. He allowed her to kiss and wiggle around in his lap, unbuttoning a couple of his shirt buttons and kissing his neck and collarbone.

He put a hand up in a half-hearted protest, "Sweetheart, you might want to—"

"Shhh," she put a finger to his lips and stared at him a moment, then traced his lips with her fingertip. Then took his hand and gently kissed the tip of his index finger and put his hand on her breast.

"You like my breasts, don't you?"

"I love every part of you."

She continued to kiss him, pulling his arms around her and wiggling in close. She felt powerful and beautiful and warm from the liquor. His breath was honeyed and delicious. She kissed and pressed against him, kissed and sighed, until she finally settled in next to him on the seat. She put her head in his lap and he petted her hair.

In a faraway voice she asked, "Do you think I'm pretty?"

"Yes, I do."

She smiled in a dreamy way and looked up at the stars through the moonroof.

Faolan pressed a switch. "Bill?"

79

The chauffeur rolled down the partition. "Yes, sir?"

"Would you go in and gather up our party? Let them know we're headed home."

"I could radio John and have him come wait."

"Oh, thanks. That's great. Could you take us to my house then, please?"

"Sure thing."

"Thanks."

"Oh, *you* got the limos," August mumbled. "Should have known. You're so sweet Faolan. So sweet. Taking care of everybody."

Faolan took off his jacket and covered her with it. He petted her hair the whole way home. August inhaled his scent and cuddled down into the jacket, feeling beautiful and loved. She dozed off with his warmth and his spiced scents surrounding her.

The Hair of the Dog

August woke up in Faolan's bed in a nightshirt and panties with a tray next to her head—fruit, toast, juice and coffee. There was even a bud vase with some forget-me-nots in it. She smiled and sat up, and that was when her head felt like somebody had filled it with lead and her eyeballs were going to pop out.

"Shit."

Faolan appeared from the bathroom buttoning his jeans.

"Holy shit, Faolan, do you have to come out here looking like that when I'm too gross to even kiss you? And that steam coming out of the bathroom …"

"What about it?"

"It's too loud," she whined.

"Love, eat some toast, drink that juice and then have some of those aspirin there." He pulled a tee on over his head and ran his fingers through his hair.

"Ugh," she said, fingering the toast. She picked up a strawberry and bit it.

"Seriously, take them. You've got a long day dealing with your gran. And don't forget to get out your dress for the wedding, in case it needs any attention. That's my suit there. Do you think it will go?" He pointed at a suit hanging on a hook at the far end of the bedroom. It was pale grey and had a mossy colored shirt and a tie with several shades of green separated by diagonal gray stripes.

She shrugged. "Looks good to me. You're the one with the fashion sense."

She bit the toast and swallowed a little coffee. Then felt slightly nauseated. After waiting a bit, she sipped some juice and took the aspirin.

"I have some errands to run for your mother. Canopy and caterer and the like. I'll be back in a couple of hours."

She sighed, as quietly as she could. "Fine."

What seemed like five minutes later Faolan was gently shaking August and she woke up feeling thirsty, but free from aches.

"Fell back asleep I see." He bent over and kissed her forehead.

"Crap! What time is it?"

"Your exclamations are full of excrement this morning."

"What?"

"Nothing. Bad joke. It's 11:30. Not so bad."

August got out of bed, slowly.

"I guess you put this shirt on me last night."

"Well if I didn't, you have some kind of magical elves that help drunk women."

"We actually need that in the world."

"I didn't figure you'd want to sleep in your dress."

"I probably wouldn't have, just for comfort's sake, but I'm likely never going to wear that stupid dress again."

"Why not? Looks lovely on you."

"Because it makes me look twelve."

"Does not."

"Does too."

"Doesn't."

"Does too!"

He grinned at her until she caught on.

She laughed and said, "Okay, fine! Dresses twelve, acts five. You're so clever. Jerk."

"I've never seen a twelve-year-old in a dress like that. Nor make it look as good. Maybe you were just feeling self-conscious in the nightclub?"

"Why, that would just be ridiculous."

He chuckled. She smiled and shook her head. It was comfortable. Reassuring.

"Would you get me some water please, while I put on some clothes?"

Faolan disappeared to the bathroom while August stole a glance of herself in the mirror. Yuck. Circles. Crazy hair. Smudged and flaking make-up.

"Here." He handed her a tall glass.

She gulped down the water in a few seconds and dug a pair of shorts out of her set of drawers—right side of the dresser, all three. Little things like Faolan making room for her in his home made her feel special, even if it was mostly just practicality. He'd done it gladly, and just for her. She pulled her mother's wedding dress out of the closet, hung it on the door and smoothed it over.

On her way down the stairs to the living room she was already buzzing with thoughts of the day. What needed to happen and where. "I think we ought to take the Jeep, in case we have to run more errands," she said, and he nodded.

"Ok."

"Where'd my sandals go?"

"They're over there." They both headed across the living room when August suddenly stopped and turned towards him and blurted out, "Are you getting bored with me?"

"What? You're joking. Where is this concern coming from?"

"I just feel so … routine."

Faolan looked down into her face. "I love you, August. Truly and deeply. We're simply adjusting. There has been a lot going on, with my business and your family. We've both just been busy and tired. That's all." And with that they kissed slow and deep, his hands tangling in her hair and her hands finding their way up the back of his shirt. He shivered, and then she did too.

They gasped and kissed again as he scooped her up and carried her over to the couch, where he sat down hard and she straddled him. She came up for air long enough to peel off her tank top and unhook the front of her bra and allowed it to slip to the floor behind her. She put her hands around Faolan's head and guided him to her chest where he nuzzled her in the valley of her cleavage, cupping her breasts, inhaling her skin, and teasing her nipples with his hungry tongue. She felt his cock grow hard inside of his jeans and she pressed harder against it, feeling the friction of the fabric and the seam of her shorts against her until she was moving faster and moaning louder, it wasn't long before she crested. She was pulsing in her low belly and between her legs. Release—she had needed it so badly!

"I want you in my mouth again, Wolf!" she breathed. She pulled open his jeans and yanked them down just enough to get to him, kissing the tip and then taking him into her mouth, one hand at the base dipping, rubbing, kissing all over it until he was growling and near to howling, his hands caressing her shoulders, his hips moving upwards in restrained thrusts.

"Oh, love, love, yes! Yes!"

She felt a surge and she knew he was about to crest, she pulled back, rubbing him, her hand tight around him, until he exploded onto her breasts, warm and sexy and worshipful as an offering, and she felt a tiny quake shudder through her and then relax. He collapsed against the back of the couch, eyes closed, lids fluttering, his lips parted and his breath in pants.

"That was so sexy!" He traced her shoulder with a finger and then squeezed her arm. August watched him, peaceful and pleasured and felt satisfied that he could want her as much as he does. And that she wanted him so much, too.

"I love you, Faolan."

He leaned forward and kissed her.

"I love you, too. Here, lay down love, while I go get something to tidy you up with."

She smiled serenely and lay on the couch. He returned with a warm, damp washcloth, kneeled next to the couch and gently wiped her chest while she watched. He would wipe, then kiss her forehead. Fold the cloth and wipe, then kiss her cheek. It was a sweet little ritual she hoped would become part of their lovemaking. This taking care of her afterwards felt like love. It was a little strange to not consider this really lovemaking, because it was in so many ways to her. She wondered if it was more werewolf stuff, or if Faolan just wanted things to be right for the moment he was inside of her.

He pressed his lips to her temple, "You are so amazing, lover."

August wasn't sure she could love him any more than she did in that moment. She lay there and reveled in it until it felt decadent.

"Thank you."

"My pleasure."

"Mine, too." They both laughed softly. "I guess I should put my shirt back on so we can get going. People are probably wondering where the hell we are."

"Well, they'll get over it." He handed her the bra and her shirt and they both had some water, hopped in the Cherokee and headed down to the Rook.

A Monet

The few errands of Thursday somehow managed to expand and fill the whole of the day. Abel's sisters and daughters dropped by, and August felt honored to receive a warm rocking hug from Afia. The room was filled with powerful female energy and at times August closed her eyes and let the music of all the voices flow through her. She was very much hoping there would be more family gatherings before too long. Imari and John remained scarce, perhaps exploring the town a bit, but Zeke came by later with Alvaro, and August was even more sure they were together; maybe one day they would feel safe enough to express their affection openly, at least in the safety of the family. She couldn't imagine anyone there making them feel wrong for it.

By Friday, the Rook was looking particularly spectacular, with flowers at the gate and in garlands on the porch rails. Abel, Sorcha, Sylvia and Brigid were in the kitchen worrying over the to-do list and putting pale green satin ribbons on a couple dozen small boxes of homemade shortbread.

Sorcha and Abel were getting married in the garden and then heading off for a honeymoon across Alabama, Georgia and Louisiana, both to visit Abel's extended family and so Sorcha could see Abel's old stomping grounds.

As Sorcha had told August a couple of months before—over a long breakfast with plenty of Irish coffee—she thought about how most women her age, had they been through what she'd been through in her life, might just be ready to sit in a rocking chair. But ever since she'd woken up from her long catatonia at the nursing home, she'd opted for a life fully lived, taking the risk of pain over the certainty of nothing. "And at the moment it seems things are going pretty damn well," she'd declared. That wolf-spawn Ciardha was nowhere to be found; she was forging a relationship with the remarkable young woman who was her granddaughter (August had flushed a bit at her gran's rare show of sentiment); and she finally felt free enough to love the kindest, smartest, sweetest man she knew. And now she was going to marry him. Sorcha had confessed that she'd often wondered why Abel would have a grouchy old bitch like her, but then she reminded herself that she once saved him. And he'd saved her, too. "Plus I look pretty good for my age," she'd declared, "even if I don't look quite as young as I feel. And Abel looks damned good, too. Sort of Sidney Poitier, if he were sixty." She'd laughed then, and told August how Abel had pointed out to her that Sidney Poitier *was* sixty, or thereabouts.

August and Faolan were to get the cake at Wynda's and pick up Abel's suit from the haberdashery in town. Other than flower crowns and directing the guys where to set up tents and chairs out back, which Sylvia had under control, things were pretty well set. This provided more calm in August than she expected.

She had never realized all of the planning that went into even a small wedding. You needed chairs and tables, you needed enough plates and cups and trash receptacles. You needed little tokens of appreciation and a guest-book and special clothes and, of course, good food and pretty flowers—and as far as that goes, Abel's abilities with plants of any kind were incomparable.

The Blue Rook was about the finest place a person could have a wedding in Mahigan Falls. Abel's gardens were nothing short of the work of an artist, and the house was a grand painted lady in a complimentary cacophony of colors: a deep royal blue with gingerbread trim in canary yellow, coral pink, powder blue and white. The flower beds around the porches and foundations echoed the trim colors in the same bright colors and in muted hues, like a Monet garden painting. Add to this an arch in the backyard covered in wild roses and ivy, and bunches of sweet woodbine at the ends of the chair rows. August was feeling a little giddy seeing the backyard looking like a fairy wonderland, and watching her gran marry a man she was proud to have as a member of her family.

"Gran, how are you doing?"

"Oh, I'm fine dear. Just a little nervous about the wedding night." Wink. Nudge.

August just grinned and chuckled. "Okay, Gran."

"I'm teasing."

"Oh, I know."

"I feel surprisingly alright, sweetheart. Everything seems to be going as planned. The flowers and the tent and such will be here in about two hours. I'm just trying to stay out of the way and let your mom handle it all. You know the way I can lord over something."

August nodded. "We're going to head out and get the cake and Abel's suit. Be back later."

"Okay darlin'."

"Gran?"

"Yes, dear?" She tied a ribbon onto a small box.

"Gran?"

Sorcha stopped and looked up at her granddaughter.

"I love you. I'm really happy for you."

"Ah, you are a dear girl." Sorcha kissed her on the cheek and went back to tying ribbons on shortbread presentation boxes.

August and Faolan retrieved Abel's repaired suit first and then stopped to grab lunch at the little diner that now occupied the old train station. "A decent reuben and an outstanding cup of coffee. Can't beat that," as August summed it up.

When they arrived at Wynda's to pick up the cake, August was stunned. It was two tiers with a simple pale yellow buttercream frosting, but it was covered in real edible flowers, decorating every inch of the top and spilling down the second tier and around the base. Linda had really outdone herself.

"Wow! I didn't know a cake could look like that. Amazing."

"Oh, thanks, hon. Me an' that gal Brigid dreamed this one up together, couple o' months ago. I tell you, she is a hoot. An' I'm glad it came out so special. It's only the best for Abel and Sorcha."

"Aww, that's sweet."

"Well, it does a heart good to see such nice folks gettin' together. You know what I mean? Now you keep 'er refrigerated 'til tomorrow—not too cold, now, just cool—an' I'll take 'er out when I get there."

Faolan had already prepared a stable platform in the back of the Cherokee for the ride back, and he and August carefully lifted it together.

"Now don't you drop it, hon!" Linda called after them, laughing.

Once back at the Rook, August couldn't resist showing it off, laying it on the dining room table and pulling away the box as they all gather around to gush over it. August hoped she had not just ruined a big reveal, for Linda's sake.

"Wait, what is that smell?" August turned around to see her beautiful white wolfdog happily wagging her tail and streaked with the remnants of a day of mischief in the woods.

"Oh, you dirty beast! Away from the table! What am I going to do with you, young lady? Snow—go to the porch." August sighed. "Well I guess I know what we're doing next, Faolan. We'll see you guys later."

They made the climb up to the Den, Snow frisking around them and obviously quite pleased with her accomplishment. She was less than happy about what came next, however, and sat whining like an annoyed child as they gave her a bath in the big Jacuzzi tub. When finally freed from the Horrible Bath Monster, she made puddles all over the floor as she shook out her once-again beautiful white coat. They rubbed a little scented oil on her and bid her to go lie in her bed, which she eventually did, after about fifteen more shakes along the way, despite being mostly dry.

"Ugh. I'm covered in matted, wet, smelly dog hair. My turn." August peeled off her clothes while Faolan watched her, admiring her soft flesh, the beckoning curves of her hips. The shy beauty of her small mounds, pinky here and peachy there. Her black hair in waves and loops draped across her back and cascading over her shoulders. He wanted to cup her and kiss her, but instead just watched.

August was so tired she didn't much note his presence as she stripped—or she pretended not to, as if this was just how they do things, and have always done them, for years. She really did just want to hurry and get under the water because she was smelly and gross and her muscles ached. Once she was soaped up, however, with the smell of mint bubbles waking her senses, she realized that she felt a little slighted that Faolan didn't react to her nakedness. She watched through the textured glass blocks as the tall blob of peach moved across the bathroom, tossing off clothes. Her mind restlessly started inventing reasons why he made no flirtatious remarks or flattery, each more ridiculous than the last. She knew he loved her—why was she so plagued with doubt over this man?

Faolan's head popped around the corner of the glass wall. "Mind if I join ye?"

Her heart leapt. She held out the bar of soap for him.

"Ah, you favor the mint one."

"I do when I'm kind of beat."

He stepped in under the water with her and began to lather up

88

his chest and shoulders. She watched him, her arms sort of half-crossed, her hands cupped at her chest, catching pools of water then dumping them with a sloosh, while distracted thoughts churned through her mind. *What do I really know about this man? He's attractive. Very attractive. But his feet are a little strange, especially his big toes. And his scratchy stubble grows in so fast. He also has one weird fleshy bump just inside his hairline at the back of his head above his right ear. Why doesn't he have that thing removed? It's not like he can't afford it. What am I doing here? I should be in New York. I should be heading to college. I should be dating a guy closer to my age. He's in love with somebody else. This is just going to end up hurting me. This all looked better when I was further away from it.*

"Red? August?"

"What?"

"Is anything wrong?"

She blinked. She watched the water run down his tanned skin. Tiny rivers curling this way and that, hugging his cheeks, dripping off of his chin. She shook her head.

"Here, turn around and I'll wash your back." She didn't really want him to wash her back, but she turned around anyway and let him. Despite her feelings folding in on themselves, she liked the comfort of his hands on her, if not as much today as she usually did. She turned around and put her hands up and he washed her front, too.

"Are you sure you're okay?"

She nodded.

"There. All clean, silly girl."

"I'm not a girl."

"What?"

"I'm not a girl. I mean, I *am* a girl, but I'm not a *girl*." She huffed. "You know what I mean."

"Are you angry with me?"

"I don't know. Maybe."

He shut off the water and got her a towel and wrapped it around her.

"I'm not a baby, you know."

"Of course I know. What's this all about?"

"You do everything for me. You don't think I can do anything."

"That's not so."

"You don't even think I can wash my own back, or get my own

89

towel."

"August, I do those things to be sweet to you, not because I don't think you can do them." He contemplated her churlishness for a moment. "Don't you like it when I do them?"

She looked down and felt like sticking her lip out, but held it together. "Yes."

"Then what's bothering you?"

"I just don't want to be seen as an incapable child."

"And I don't see you that way. You said you like it when I call you girl."

There was a long pause as she stood there, sad and dripping, struggling for the right words. "I just don't know if I'm supposed to like it."

"I see. Well, I'll stop callin' ye girl if you want me to. I'll stop fetchin' your towel and makin' ye breakfast in bed. Will that make you happy?"

August heard how ridiculous it sounded. Of course she loved all of those things, and she loved him, too. But she had felt so lonely lately. Disconnected from him. Perhaps it was nothing more than that.

"I love it when you call me girl. And lass. And you get my towel and make me breakfast in bed. I think I'm just overwhelmed from wedding stuff and I've hardly seen you. I'm a little nervous about Scotland, too."

"No need. You don't have to do anything you don't want to."

"Also …"

"Aye?"

"Also … I'm still kind of jealous about you and that woman, whatever-her-name-was that night. Did you like dancing with her?"

"You won't believe me if I tell you."

"Yes I will."

"I was bored. She was boring."

"With a dress like that? Give me a break. I'm not stupid."

"Well, I think your objection is more to what was in the dress, and that it was hard to ignore."

"Hey!" August half-heartedly slapped his wet shoulder. It made a sharp smack sound and he regarded her.

"She was very sexy. I shan't deny it!" He grinned and peered at her, teasing.

"Shan't?" She mocked.

"Yes, shan't. We've reached the ridiculous part of this conversation now. She was sexy and not my type. Except for the sexy part. The rest of her wasn't my type."

"If you call her sexy one more time I swear—"

He laughed a full, deep belly laugh and then she laughed, too. This conversation was indeed ridiculous. And vital.

"I'm really tired, Fe. Can we just go to bed and you can hold me?"

He wrapped a towel around his hips, scooped her up and took her to his bed. She toweled her hair and slid under the cozy layers. She watched as he dried himself and crawled in next to her. Skin to skin. Despite being exhausted and a little uncertain about her future with him, she felt her skin call out to him. Her nerves crackled and buzzed to touch all of her to all of him. She rolled over to him and kissed his cheek, and then his mouth. Deep, soft, slow kisses, and soon she was aching for all of him.

"Touch me," she whispered.

"Turn over the other way," he prompted, and then he spooned himself around her and enfolded her body in his arms. When he lay back again he brought her on top of him, her back pressed to his chest, her bottom to his pelvic bone, his big hands cupping her breasts from behind while he licked and gently bit her neck, rubbed his nose into her damp locks. As she lay on Faolan his hands moved all over her body, making her gasp and moan. She felt strangely possessed like this, and it was intoxicating.

His cock rose up between her thighs and she reached down to grab it, holding it firm against her ache so she could wiggle and rub him while he nuzzled her and petted her from shoulders to thighs with his long, powerful arms. His breath caught and gasped as she rubbed him against her and she felt herself swelling, lost to everything but his touch and his breath. She heard herself saying, "Yes … yes … yes …" and soon he was saying it with her and she moaned and shook and then felt him erupt in her hand and on her mound and her belly. She rubbed the slippery seed over the firm tip, relishing the feel of him in her hand, so warm and passionate. She rubbed it into her skin and sighed. She turned over on top of him, pressing the whole front of her now to the whole front of him, and they kissed tenderly.

"I love you Faolan."

"I love you August."

"I'm sorry I get so wound up. I don't know why that happens."

"But how I treasure the unwinding."

Vows

Faolan was up ahead of August, turning over conversations in his mind. He fed Snow and made a quick meal.

August woke up to sounds of Faolan dusting off his suit. There was a tray of toast and tea next to her and forget-me-nots in a bud vase. All a little too perfect. Or borrowed. She wanted to simply enjoy the flowers, but now they made her think of Iseabail. She felt a cloud surrounding her mood.

"I'm a terrible person."

Faolan turned around and squinted an eye. "Well good morning, sunshine. What did you do this time?"

"I just ..." She couldn't find the words. If she had, they probably would have been ridiculous.

"Yes?" He waited patiently.

"Good morning."

"We have to be at the Rook in just over an hour."

"Guess I slept in."

"You could say that."

"Well, that was a pretty nice lullaby you sang to me last night," she flirted.

"My pleasure, love." He gave a little growl.

She ate the toast while she watched him and enjoyed the quiet domesticity of the moment. Sun streaming in, floral tea, crispy toast, and a beautiful man.

"How old were you when you met Iseabail?"

"Are you sure you want to talk about that subject, love? So close to wedding time?"

"You're probably right. I suppose this is one of those days my mom warned me about."

"What days are those?"

"She likes to warn me about insecurity. She says I can choose the way a day goes. Though I don't know that's a hundred percent accurate. I mean, I guess I can choose to focus on good instead of bad. Doesn't make the bad go away."

Fancy hair was out of the question now, so August opted for a quick shower and hoped for the best. As she came back into the bedroom Faolan had finished the ritual of tying, zipping and tucking and was putting on his belt. As far as August was concerned, the sight of a man putting on or taking off a belt was one of the sexiest damn things in the world. Same with ties—although she admittedly thought that the taking *off* of ties and belts was a skosh more titillating. Faolan looked in the mirror, tilted his head, made a grunt and undid his tie and pulled it over his head. Then unbuckled his belt and pulled it out of the loops—which gave August a bit of a shiver.

"What are you doing?"

"I'm gonna wear my kilt."

"Why didn't you just plan on that in the first place?"

"I haven't been to a wedding in a long time. When I've dressed up the last twenty years or so, I've worn suits. I'm just used to it now I guess. But a half-Scottish wedding calls for a kilt." He dug out his boldest tartan from the back of the closet and started sorting through a drawer of various leather accessories.

"I guess I'd better put on Mom's gown."

"I can't wait to see you in it, actually."

"Yeah, I know you're fond of women in green dresses."

"With green eyes," he responded evenly, looking steadily at her until she caught the meaning.

"Ah. Yes, green eyes." There was a hint of a smile at the corner of her lips.

"No one holds a candle to you in my eyes, lass. Whatever it is that's eating at you, I'm sure you'll overcome it. We can talk about it tonight if it's still gnawing. Fair?"

She nodded. That was fair. Today was about love and coming together. She thought of the names of his bygone loves—Brynn, Omolara, and Madeline—and how the beginning of the end of their relationships might have started. Was it like this? Women older and more experienced than her have grown cold in the particularly long shadow cast by his past.

"Do you still love Iseabail?" She couldn't help it.

Faolan was thoughtful.

"Do you?" The words caught in her throat.

"I never stopped loving her. But I am ready to let go now." Perhaps that would be gentle enough for August and still honor Iseabail.

94

"She died in childbirth."

"Aye, she did. Red, These are things that aren't the best to set off on a wedding day. I can see you're having a hard time setting this down, though. Medicine wasn't as good or as available then as it is now. Even with a good midwife things often went wrong in those days. Particularly with mixed bairns."

"In time, do you think you could love me the way you love her?"

He was flummoxed. Up until this past week most of their communications had been vibrant and flowing, sparked with excitement—not these jags of hazard and caution. Though he could write her question off as a symptom of her age and inexperience, he knew it was a reasonable concern, and the undercurrent of insecurity was one that anybody could suffer from, whatever their age.

"I already love you, August." There was a taste of metal in his mouth. This had happened too many times already, with too many other lovers. Each time the response was different, but it was never good and always ended in ragged feelings, misunderstanding, and tears.

"She's not here, August. She can't be here." Faolan saw her breathing deepening and quickening. She was close to being overwhelmed with hurt and he didn't know how to stop it without lying. He had a flash of panic that he might lose her, that it would all be too much. Though if he did—if even August couldn't love him as he was—he knew he would never have to answer such questions again, because he would build a wall around himself that was impenetrable.

"Nothing bad has happened, darling girl. I love you. I explained the bonding—it's not something you can just set down."

He came to her and sat on the bed and took her hands.

"August, I want to live the rest of my life with you. I love you so much I am willing to let go of a bond I've had for almost a hundred years. For right now, I want to have a nice day with you. I want to watch Sorcha and Abel get married. I want to enjoy music and food and I know you're looking forward to cake. Right?"

She nodded like a sullen child.

He put a finger under her chin and lifted her face and leaned in for a gentle kiss. August felt the warmth of his lips and his love flow through her.

"I love you, too. Sorry I'm being so awful."

"You aren't being awful, but you are spoiling what could be a perfectly lovely day."

"True."

August took a deep breath of wisdom and hope, hopped up and looked at herself in the mirror. Her hair was a huge wild bush of curls. She just smiled at how crazy it was and grabbed the forget-me-nots and tangled them into her hair.

She stepped into her sandals, but the middle of the dress was a bit tight and made it hard to bend over to get them buckled. She put a foot up onto the stool next to the reading chair and Faolan slid over and knelt to buckle it.

"I don't need you to buckle my shoe!" She said it louder than she meant to.

He stopped and looked up at her. "I know you don't *need* me to, but do you *want* me to?"

Now she really understood how foolish she'd been behaving, on what should be a nice day together.

"Yes, actually. Thanks."

He buckled them both and stood, patted her bottom and kissed her on the cheek. "You're welcome. Now let's go." He held out his hand and she took it and off they went to the Rook.

The house was bustling with activity. People were tying cushions to chairs outside, putting up bunting, and decorating the arch with finishing touches. The day was sunny and mild with an occasional gust that would send folks scrambling after escaping napkins. The tent would shudder a little, but it seemed pretty sturdy. The Rook looked amazing, with wild roses everywhere. August busied herself with making head wreaths out of the remaining rosebuds and wildflowers. One for Sorcha of mostly roses, and two of mostly wildflowers for herself and Brigid, who were to stand with the bride during the ceremony.

August was doing ten things at once and could feel her face getting hot, then she realized she hadn't even seen her grandmother yet. She found Zeke and Imari and put on their boutonnieres. Alvaro was helping the men tidy up. She put flowers and ribbon around Snow's fluffy white neck, then took the rose crown to her grandmother in her suite off of the kitchen.

August walked in and Sorcha turned around, her pale gold silk draped from just below the bosom. The fabric had a soft glow. Her hair, mostly white but with a black stripe, was done in a low roll in the back, and her make-up was flawless. Her face, though lined with age and experience, twinkled like a girl's, full of wonder and trepidation.

"Wow, you look amazing." August gushed.

"Do ye think? No ..." Sorcha brushed the front of her dress and gave a crooked smile.

"Yes, you look amazing. I'm going to let you do my make-up from now on."

"Oh, hell child, I didn't do my make-up. Alvaro did it. And my hair, too. Evidently I now have an in at a rather good salon in Atlanta." She admired herself in the mirror. "I do look nice, at that."

"Yes, you do. Here I made this for you."

"Oh, it's lovely, darling girl. Here, put it on me."

August pinned the halo of wild white roses to her grandmother's head and gently fixed the wreath in place.

"I feel like a giddy girl."

"You're going to take his breath away."

August felt a little outside of herself as she walked down the aisle behind Snow, towards the arch, towards Brigid, who was officiating, and towards Abel, waiting for his bride.

Abel had his good hand folded over his artificial one. It occurred to August that his ring must be going on his right hand.

Once in her place August searched for Faolan's face sitting in the row up front with Sylvia. They were both softly smiling at her. Her mother mouthed, "Beautiful," and August felt it. Faolan's eyes were full of love and she let it wash over her. She turned her attention to her grandmother who was beaming and August felt her heart well up when Abel, who often was quiet and stoic, showed a huge white-toothed grin that spread across the guests as they all lit up and smiled as well. The joy was palpable.

Brigid's vibrant purple robes and floral crown made her look like a goddess. She read something about love and family that she had written, but August was so overwhelmed by the moment that she was viewing it from above, and the words kept going fuzzy. Feeling the sun on her bare neck, she was thinking of her mother wearing this same dress, marrying her father. Any trace of jealousy she had been feeling earlier had receded and all she felt now was an eternal connection with everybody around her.

She stood quietly in her revelry and felt the sweet vibration of all of that love, and through a haze she saw Brigid bind the hands of Sorcha and Abel. She watched Brigid's mouth move, the sun making a halo around all of them, folding and winding the long green ribbon around their hands.

Sorcha said, "You are my family now. And my heart remembers what my soul sometimes forgets when I look into your eyes. I promise to keep your secrets and be kind and accept your beautiful love, as though I deserve it."

Then Abel said, "You are my family now. My heart cannot forget what my soul insists each day, and that is that I am meant to spend my days with you. I promise to keep your secrets and be kind and accept your love and love you when you think you don't deserve it."

They kissed.

Then Sorcha and Abel jumped over a broom laid on the ground in front of them, adorned with ribbon, roses and tulle.

"You are now married!" Brigid pronounced and threw a handful of white rose petals over the bride and groom. They tried to turn around, but it was awkward with their hands fasted together, so they did a sort of circle and faced the guests. The small crowd stood and clapped and made hooting sounds.

Brigid announced that food and music would be happening under the tent and everybody began moving in that direction. Caterers bustled around and readied the food. August was actually surprised at the number of people there, considering her clan was such a secretive bunch. But with Abel's family and some of his gardening friends, as well as some of Sorcha's nursing home friends, it was a decent little crowd.

The string quartet started up and Brigid announced that Sorcha and Abel would be dancing and that everybody else should join in. August stood in a corner watching as the newly wedded couple leaned into each other and slowly swayed to the music. Faolan came up behind her and slid a hand around her waist.

"Did I tell you how beautiful you look?" he whispered. She smiled to herself.

"Only about twenty times. But you can say it as many times as you like, it never gets old."

"The dress suits you. And the pearl. You look like a goddess of summer."

She leaned her head to the side, an invitation to kiss her neck. He gave a soft slow inhale, then kissed. She felt little electric waves reach out to him. And every doubt she'd entertained earlier totally vanished. She knew he was the man for her.

She relished the neck nuzzles and watched as her mother and Sheriff Two Feathers walked onto the dance floor and started to sway together, too.

"Wanna dance?" Faolan asked her.

"Yeah?"

"Yeah."

"Okay."

August had only ever danced with a couple of boys at school dances; mostly she held down the wallflower post. She had danced with her father a number of times at fancy balls for his department, or for charities. This gave her another pang, for her father, but she let it go quickly enough as Faolan led her to the dance floor. He turned to her and they too were soon swaying to the strings. Nothing had ever felt this good, she thought. So much love and light. She felt like she belonged here, in his arms. Here, dancing and connecting and celebrating family. It filled her up.

When the slow music ended and they started up what sounded very much like a happy Celtic tune, August stood back and looked around and noticed the floor was full of people all smiling and hopping, some shuffling—depending on age. There was so much joy. She wanted her someday-wedding to be like this. People who knew her best. People who loved her best.

The rest of the night was a blur of speeches, dancing, food, wine and then the cutting of the cake. Sorcha and Abel fed each other bite-sized squares of cake delicately and respectfully, though there was a twinkle in her gran's eye that made August wonder if she wouldn't surprise them. Then the toast and the goodbyes as Sorcha and Abel climbed into their limo to head off to a hotel in Baltimore, where they would stay a few nights and then head down south for a few weeks. It was a long break to be sure, but they didn't have anywhere else they had to be and Sorcha wanted to meet all of the grandbabies.

Soon the guests were filtering out and the caterers began cleaning up. Then it was quiet. The sun had set and the temperature dropped.

The tent was now outlined in white twinkle lights and glowing green and gold lanterns, making it look like a magical mini-kingdom on the back lawn. Faolan threw his jacket onto the ground and sat next to it. He held his hand out to August who sat down next to him on the warm jacket.

"Am I a wuss if I take the laces out of the back of this dress?"

"Hardly."

"Good, would you please take the laces out of the back of this dress?"

He laughed and loosed the laces a bit.

"Is that better?"

"Yes. Thanks." She let out a big sigh. "Hey, I have a bottle of champagne. Want some?"

She took a swig and offered him the half-empty bottle. "What an amazing wedding. What an amazing day."

"It was a beauty," he said, and took a swig off the bottle, too.

She laid back on the jacket and looked up at the twinkle light chandelier.

"Do you ever turn wolf while you're doing it?"

Faolan was startled. "What?"

"I mean, you're doing it and you get all excited and lose control and next thing ya know, claws! Snout!"

"Uh ..."

"Don't wanna answer huh? I guessed you might not want to answer." She tried to take another swig while laying down by just tilting her head up a bit and champagne ran all down her cheek and neck. She inhaled some and started coughing hard and sat up, then took another big swig. Faolan reached over and took the bottle and tossed it outside the tent.

"Alright, yes. But not by accident. It can happen by accident with younger lycan, when they are less ... When they are more hormone-driven, I guess you could say. Hair trigger, if you will."

August laughed loud and hard at that. "Hair trigger! Good one!"

"It's also an individual thing," Faolan went on, bemused. "Some lycan have better control in general, but it helps to take the herbs and meditate on the ... matter."

"Did ya ever do it on purpose?"

"Do what?"

"Go wolf on somebody you were doing it with."

Faolan didn't want to lie, but this line of questioning was deeply personal. Although, he had invited her into his past, and even gave her the journals, which probably mentions what he and Iseabail used to do. What Iseabail liked.

"Iseabail liked me to turn when I was with her."

"Why?"

"Why? I don't know …"

"I think you do."

"I suppose it made her feel like I couldn't control myself with her. It made her feel more desirable maybe. I don't know. It's not like I can ask her." Faolan could feel himself become a little irritated with the question, though he wasn't sure why.

"That's exactly what it did. If a woman can make you lose control like that, she knows your passion for her is endless. Boundless. Timeless. Bottomless."

"I suppose being young had a lot to do with it."

"Are you calling me immature? Because it sounds like you're calling me immature."

"I did it because she wanted me to. Not because I couldn't help it. I think it had more to do with her feelings about me, than mine about her."

"I feel like I'm second best. Consolation prize. Cheap imitation."

"Don't be angry August, but I do think some of this is your inexperience talking. And I don't mean you're immature. But these things you're focusing on don't have to be a problem, if you don't let them."

"This from the guy who's been burning a candle or holding a torch—whatever you call it—since the turn of the century?"

"That's a fair point, I suppose. But we could be having a nice time right now."

"Take me home and make love to me."

"I would, but you're drunk."

"I don't care. I want to."

"I will take you home and read to you."

"Ugh. Never mind!"

"Come now, let's not end the night like this."

"Then take me home and make love to me."

"If you still want to make love once you've sobered up, I vow that we will. That's my final offer."

"Fine. Old poop."

And then August grumpily snuggled in next to Faolan and they looked at the lights in the tent until she fell asleep, and Faolan lay close to her all night.

The Light of Day

"I need some water. And some aspirin. Faolan, wake up."

Faolan made a grunt and shielded his eyes against the sun. The tent rental workers were standing over them.

"We need to remove the tent, sir."

"Yes, of course. Sorry. We'll get out of your way."

Faolan and August rolled unsteadily to their feet, brushing off grass and blinking in the morning light. They shuffled into the kitchen and found Sylvia there in a robe, along with Two Feathers in boxer shorts and a tank tee, both of them making breakfast.

"Hey honey, want some breakfast?" Her mother asked, a bit too cheery for August's mood.

"Yes, but I need aspirin."

Faolan went to the cabinet and got August some aspirin and a glass of water.

She gave him a meek "Thanks."

"Sylvia, I could eat about a dozen eggs." Faolan said. "Can I help?"

"Nope, they'll be done in a jiffy."

August sat at the island and buried her head in her folded arms on the counter. Her voice emerged, muffled and repentant. "Mom. Mo-o-om."

"What honey?"

"I was being a jealous little bitch last night."

Sylvia looked at Faolan. He just raised his brows and shrugged.

"I see, sweetie. Well, how are things looking in the light of day?"

"I don't know. I think I'm having a crisis of some kind."

"Let's have some breakfast," Sylvia coaxed, petting her daughter's back. "The crisis will still be there when you're done."

"Okay."

Two Feathers slid a plate of toast over to August. "Here young lady. Try some of that."

Her head stay glued to the counter. "Thanks." She slid her arm out and grabbed a piece of toast and curled it back into her little hiding place and munched.

"It's alright, love," Faolan said, then petted her back gently.

"Are those leopard-print boxers?" she asked Two Feathers, spying them out of the crack between her elbow and the countertop.

"Cheetah."

"Oh."

Sylvia served up a heap of scrambled eggs to everybody and the conversation paused as people chewed and drank and smiled at each other. Snow whined once, and Faolan fed her some bacon.

"I can only eat a little bit. God, I'm never drinking again," August said as she tentatively forked a bit of egg.

"So long as you eat something," her mother replied, her long coral fingernail nudging August's plate closer. "And drink lots of water."

Before long August's headache was gone and she was feeling more like being social. The group spent the day tidying up and sorting gifts and saying goodbye to Abel's family, who were headed back south, but not before leaving some moonshine and some home-canned peaches.

The weather turned, with gray skies and wind bending the treetops. Before it could get too crazy, Faolan and August climbed the hill home, where August spent the rest of the day digging through the trunk of Iseabail journals. She read through fifteen of them, only stopping long enough to stretch her legs and use the restroom. Faolan mostly paced and brought her food and tried to suggest they do something else for a while, but August wanted to get it behind her.

"You could choose not to read every last one."

That thought seemed impossible, considering her insatiable curiosity, not only about Faolan's inner workings, but also it was like getting to meet him before she was ever even born. It wasn't until the seventeenth journal that his first girlfriend after Iseabail showed up. *Almost seventeen years,* she thought to herself. *There's something sort of terrifying about that kind of intense dedication.* She wondered if she wanted to be that stuck on anybody, though she had to admit she probably already was. The journals with Brynn were full of passion and torment. Faolan had clearly been lonely and in need of affection. He found Brynn fascinating and clever, but too obsessed with material possessions and status. She didn't like wildflowers, only decadent bouquets would do. These things comforted August, mostly. But the descriptions of Byrnn's body, and what it was like making love to her,

104

were hard for August to read. For the first time since reading the journals she realized that these things were going to stick with her, long after this trunk was buried. They were making her insecure. She put the journal down.

"Maybe I don't need to know everything about you right away. Maybe it's nice to have you tell me the important things you remember."

"Did something hurt you?"

"Well … yeah. But it's not your fault. I probably should stop reading this stuff. It's too much. And even though you told me I could read them, it feels like an invasion of privacy." He nodded and closed the lid.

They popped a big bowl of popcorn and went down to the game room—"It's like a cave for the fanciest lumberjack," August had once commented—and they curled onto the big sectional couch and tucked in with Snow snuggled between their legs. It was sweet and comfortable, like warm apple pie for the soul. Faolan wrapped a blanket around August and she leaned into his chest as he tuned in some light entertainment on the big screen. *This is where I belong*, August thought to herself. *It just feels right*. Before *Ripley's Believe it or Not* was over, she was falling asleep.

Conall Keep
October 17, 1984

It had been an awkward ten months of romance at Conall Keep. Ciardha did his best to woo in his clumsy animal ways. He continued to try buying Blair's affection with his dwindling fortunes. Silks, gowns, flowers, extravagant dinners and desserts. Wines that any oenophile would die to get their hands on. He even tried to be sweet at times, though it didn't last long. The sex was frequent, powerful, bonding, and yet lacking any tenderness. In time it was little more than a distraction for her, like eating cake, or going for a horse ride. She would go outside of herself and watch them going at it. He was undeniably a sexy man, physically, and his skill with the female body was intoxicating. But none of it touched her the way lovemaking was supposed to. He would pass out and she would roll away, staring out of the window into the night sky, feeling empty and used.

She had settled into a routine of pretending to be madly in love with him, hoping he would become the man she imagined he was when they met. Intelligent, strong, a leader with passion and vision. Then in September he arrived home from a Veritas conclave and she was pacing. Angry.

"You said you were going to end the Veritas now that you have had your vengeance. You have become more obsessed with that group of close-minded lycan purebreds than ever! How can you preach about purebreds, and being the chosen ones while you are married to me? Me—a hunter? Not even a mutt, I am pure hunter. What do they think of that in your pathetic, small-minded group?"

"They know you are with us. That's all they need to know. I'm their leader and what I say goes."

"Is it true they're going to start hunting down mix-breed babes and offer them up for sacrifice?"

"I'm making changes. Important ones. We have to move into the twentieth century. We are dying out, so don't be givin' me this gobshite! I have to do this, for my people!"

"You're a fraud, Keer. How can they not see that?"

"They all loved my father as I did, and they still want vengeance for his death. Anyroad, I don't think we're getting somewhere with this. I'm not letting anybody kill any mixed-breed babes. I swear it."

"So it's just that simple, is it? You're insane. I can never be around them, Keer. They'd have my head on their walls. What kind of life is that for us?"

"They aren't after you, love." His tone softened and he turned so earnest she almost believed him. "They'll do what I say, and they will come to love you as I do. For your strength and your spirit."

Blair crossed her arms and eyed him.

"Look here. I've written this up for the next meeting."

He handed her a folio and she read. Her eyes narrowed and her mouth twisted a little here and there. She looked at him, "This advocates for mixing blood. I mean, it's subtle, but it's there."

"Aye."

"They aren't going to buy this. They believe in the Veritas shite, the code of true purity."

"It's a wee nudge in the direction of mixed breeds."

"But why would you do this? After all this time? And it's against everything your father taught you."

"Did ye no hear? We are dying out. There are only two clans left with full-blooded lycan. We won't survive if we don't mix. Every remaining female is less than a third lycan, Blair—and none of them can transform."

Blair's mouth now agape she was at a loss for words. Her mind was racing—she could think of a thousand things and nothing all at once, and all of it was stuck in her throat.

"Nothing to say? This is rare." He raised a brow and grinned.

Blair could feel her heart beating hard. She wanted to smash his smug face with her fists. She was so angry she thought she might grab her knife from its sheath and slash his throat. She saw him in her mind's eye, spurting his wretched, hateful, selfish blood all over the floor stones.

Calm and measured, through her gritted teeth, "After so much damage? Why did you scorch the earth with your black vengeful heart before deciding that mixing blood was going to save your precious superior race?"

"I don't think I need to explain myself to you, woman."

"You cack-handed blaggard, I'm fed up with your disgusting broken morals, your incessant childish need to bend everybody to your will and your way. It's foul and stinks of rot!"

He regarded her, at first his face growing red and concerned, but when she was done he only laughed heartily and walked over to the bar and poured himself a whisky.

"I'm going to Perth tomorrow," she said.

"What for?"

"You know what for."

Several moments passed, yet he did not look at her. "You're not," he said while pouring himself another whisky and tossing it back.

"You cannot stop me."

He poured another whisky and swirled it around in the glass, looking into it as if studying the liquid. "I will call in a favor. You'll arrive at HMP and find you've missed the body by moments. No long romantic goodbyes. Just a report from the prison."

Her stiff chin now quivered and her eyes welled up. "You wouldn't."

Ciardha still did not look at her. "Are ye goin' to Perth tomorrow, lass?"

Tears now traced rivers down her cheeks and dripped onto the stone. Blair turned to walk away.

"I need an answer. It'd be a pity if something happened because you didn't speak up. So … Lass, are ye going to Perth tomorrow?"

She stopped, her frame sagged. She whispered, "No."

He knew her answer before she said it. He smiled and downed the whisky, walked over to her and patted her on the bottom, and went out the door.

All In
Mahigan Falls

Faolan had wanted to wrap up all of his business dealings before they left for Scotland—he talked about loose ends and money trails and other things August was vaguely aware she would have to learn about someday soon—and so he'd spent most of the past few weeks hopping from Baltimore to Philly to DC. By the third week of October Faolan had sold off most of his imported antiques and warehouse businesses, although he decided finally that the small Baltimore store wasn't ready to be sold. Liquidating his holdings, particularly in the rapidly recovering economy, created a huge influx of ready cash, and he let August know that she could spend some if she liked.

"How much are we talking? Like a car?"

"More."

"A fancy car?"

"About a thousand fancy cars."

"Ah."

"Aye, it's quite a penny. I can't say why I didn't sell the businesses sooner. I suppose I liked to keep myself occupied."

"Why didn't you sell the Baltimore store?"

"Well, that one's a good bit smaller. It was my first business when I moved here—really just a small neighborhood storefront, and I'm somewhat attached to it."

"Oh. Can I see it?"

"You want to see it?"

"Yeah. It's got sentimental value, right?"

"Aye."

"Okay, I'd like to see it. You are taking me to Scotland to show me all of your old haunts, after all—let's start here in Maryland. In fact, let's go today. Now. You've barely been home for weeks. I miss you. Let's spend a day together." She thought he would jump at the chance for a day trip with her, but instead he seemed stoic, almost hesitant.

"What's wrong?"

"I'm just tired," he assured her.

"Well, we don't have to. I just ..."

"No, it's alright. It's near the Inner Harbor. We'll walk around and get together some things we need for our trip. Maybe a new outfit for you? Dinner to celebrate?"

"Sounds great! It's such a beautiful day, too." She hopped up and pulled on her cowboy boots, twirled her dress for him, and grabbed her favorite jean jacket. "I'm ready!"

"You look adorable."

She walked over to Faolan to kiss him on the lips. "Thanks lovah!"

August drove on the way to the city. Her skill and confidence had much improved over the year—she said the way Faolan taught her to maneuver in a flowing way made her think of swimming—though she still didn't like the Baltimore beltway, and sometimes Faolan chuckled at the passion of her curses over various driver offenses. Once they reached the Inner Harbor he encouraged her to park near the spice factory, and the gloriously scented air was almost magical. Hand in hand they walked to the waterfront, where they stood at the edge of the pavement and looked out over the water.

"I feel almost normal in moments like this, Faolan. Look how beautiful it is. The tall buildings, the blue sky, the sound of the water and the gulls, the old sailing ship over there. The buzz of the city. I miss New York sometimes."

"We could go for a visit when we get back from Scotland," he suggested. "You could show me where you lived. We could eat at some of your old favorite spots."

"Mom has to come, too. We need pizza from Nino's. We need to watch a Broadway show, too."

"Not *Cats*, though."

She laughed at that.

"Cats and dogs, it's a bad scene," he said, completely straight-faced.

She nodded, still smiling. "Absolutely."

They walked lazily down a road of old shopfronts, gazing in the windows at art books, vinyl records, smoking accessories, comic books, bohemian fashions, and home furnishings. Faolan slowed as they reached an intersection, and diagonally across August saw a corner store done up in bright fresh trim. An old-fashioned signboard hung over the door with the silhouette of a woman—above it was the name "Iseabail's," and beneath, "Antiques & Imports."

August's stomach tightened and her cheeks grew warm. She dropped Faolan's hand.

"I guess that's it."

He nodded.

She crossed her arms. "You could have warned me." She would have glared at him but she couldn't look away from the apparition across the road.

Sheepish, he rubbed near his ear with an index finger and studied the ground. She turned to him finally and he gave her an apologetic half-smile.

"I want to go inside," she declared.

"Are you sure that's best, lass? Given your reaction just seeing the sign?"

"I don't care. We're going in."

"Aye, then. In we go."

The store was, in a word, charming. The big bow windows at the front were trimmed with gleaming wood moldings and panels, drawing the visitor into a recessed glass door with a big brass bell above it. Just inside was a rack of gorgeous antique gowns in velvets and silks, with feathered hats set above them, and across from them was an oak table with stacks of books and journals from a hundred years ago. Two elegantly petite roll-top desks displayed ebony and silver pens, crystal ink wells, and other writing accessories, beside a small hill of at least a dozen picnic baskets overflowing with hankies and linens. A huge carved oak wardrobe full of silk underthings stood proudly, flanked by a matched pair of cherry wood vanities with pink marble tops, each arranged with purses, compacts, hatpins, brooches, and other, more mysterious items. Toward the back of the store was a tiered sideboard piled with packaged Scottish goods—shortbreads and tinned biscuits, jarred preserves and sauces, soups and honey, teas and whisky cakes, and even canned haggis—all of it with labels she recognized from Faolan's pantry.

There was a knot in August's stomach now, and she was glad she hadn't eaten. The whole place was some kind of shrine. She couldn't decide if it was scary or sweet—maybe a little of both. If Faolan ever bonded to her, was he going to be like this? Was it loyal or obsessive? Endearing or just creepy? She couldn't decide. The only thing she did know was that this level of devotion both comforted and frightened her. Was she really ready to commit the rest of her life to him? August realized that her hunter side might be more pragmatic about love than her lycan side and that, maybe in her case, that was a good thing.

She was fingering some gowns hanging in a travel trunk when she looked up and stared straight at a photo of Iseabail in an oval frame. She turned and looked at Faolan, and he squinted a bit and averted his eyes.

"I've seen enough."

He nodded and reached out for her hand, but she pulled away. He stepped aside for her to pass, and she pushed her way through the door and out onto the sidewalk. She stood there, arms crossed tight in the bright sun, her face set with irritation, and looked away down the street.

"I apologize for not telling you, August."

"I thought you were letting her go!" she shouted, startling herself almost as much as the passerby who turned to look at them. August lowered her voice. "You said you were letting her go, Faolan. So you could move on. For me. For us."

"I am."

"This ..." She waved her arm at Iseabail's silhouette. "... does not look like moving on to me, Faolan!"

"Could we go somewhere else and talk about this? I am trying, August."

"I am not going to be some sad second-best love."

"Come on, lass. Please don't take it on that way—it's not like that. You know I love you."

She paced a few times.

"I'm starting to feel like maybe you love me because I don't have a lot of relationship baggage, Faolan. Nothing like what you have. So how could you suffer by comparison? Me, I'm stuck with this legacy, being compared to the magical and perfect Iseabail. Who can compete with your sunshiny glowing perfect ideal of that woman?"

"That's unfair, Red."

"And you know what?"

"August ..." His brow was deep and sorrowful. He reached out again to her.

"Don't."

"I feel terrible I've hurt you. What can I do?" He looked

haggard, but this only made August more uncertain of their future together. Did he look like that because he was sorry, and pained at the prospect of losing her, or was it for losing the last vestige of Iseabail he could retreat to?

She shook her head and kicked at a loose stone. "I'm sorry she died, that's what. I'm really sorry your dreams of raising a family with her were ripped from you. Believe it or not, my love, I feel for you, for both of you, when I read those journals. It's terrible and sad and there is so much that you will never know, but that's just it, isn't it? She will always be young and beautiful in your mind. She was ripped from you at the height of your joy and it left so many threads dangling. Your romance will always be perfect and sad. You never had time to have problems. You imprinted perfectly when she was perfect and she stays perfect. No woman could compete with that, Faolan, and it's not fair to expect anybody to!"

"You're not second best. You're not." He put a hand on her shoulder. August had an impulse to shrug it off, but she couldn't do it to him when he looked so abject. She wanted to tell him that he had to get rid of that store, for both of them, but she was the last person who could say so, and she resented him for putting her in that position.

"I'm not going to tell you what to do. I think you know why I'm mad, and what you need to do if you're ever going to be free to love anyone."

He nodded and sucked in a deep breath. "Could I take you for something to eat?"

"I'm not hungry."

"You're upset Red, and you haven't eaten for hours. We'll go have some noodles. Once you smell the food, you'll feel like eating." He eased in closer to face her, and his hands all but covered her shoulders. "I will sell the store."

She hesitated to look up. She was mad enough in this moment that she could let him go and say goodbye to this problematic courtship. Find somebody without so much of that baggage, and maybe create a little of her own with someone else. But there was an alarm in her heart that warned her not to walk away. She saw herself lying in her old bed in her old room, staring out of her window seat with no Faolan in her life, and it didn't feel like freedom. It felt like grief. And worse, what if she did walk away now, and he gave up any hope of ever moving past his imprinted lost love? She couldn't stand the thought of that. She loved him enough to stay for him, as much as for herself.

"I didn't ask you to sell it, Faolan."

"I want to. And I need to."

"You didn't want to yesterday. Why today?"

"Because you're right about moving on. Because I can't stand the thought of losing you. I'll do anything it takes to keep your heart close."

She felt her soul reach out and wrap around him. She leaned her head into his warm, cotton-covered chest.

"Let's not wait anymore, Wolf. Let's go home and make love."

"Red ... you know that won't solve this difficulty between us."

"I just want us to bond. I want to know what it feels like to be that connected to somebody." Then, unexpectedly, she laughed.

"What?" He looked down at her, his hands holding hers.

"This is starting to sound like a soap opera. Or a bad romance novel. *I Married a Werewolf.*"

"I do want to take you home and ravage you, love—you know that by now, lass. We can go, right now, if that's what you want. I just want to make sure that we are both in the right place in our hearts and our minds when it happens. That we aren't doing it out of some sense of desperation."

"Faolan! It's like you're trying to set up this perfect situation. Isn't the sex we've been having helping us to bond?"

"Emotionally, aye. It does. But it's not full mating, love, so not really—not like you mean. Not for a lycan." He read her perplexed expression. "I know—it sounds daft. But if you're rushing it because you feel urgent about us—well, that urgency can be dangerous. It makes for bad decisions in love that you're then beholden to, or might put you at odds with your own family, so we resist it. It's entrenched in our culture, even; *Romeo and Juliet* is a tragedy from the off to us. We know it's going to end in blood."

August just smiled and shook her head. There was a whole other world standing there in front of her that she knew nothing about. *But it's my world too*, she thought. *Might as well start learning to be a part of it.*

"Five days and we'll be in Scotland, Red, putting my past where it belongs and looking ahead at our futures stretching out in front of us." His eyes were searching her for understanding, for acceptance, but she had reached an emotional impasse. Fortunately, more practical matters came to the fore.

"I'm hungry, Fe. And I want a pin for my jacket."

"Ah—well that's a glimmer then. Let's get some food. And a pin. If I remember, there's a record shop near the noodle place. And their sushi is outstanding. The restaurant, not the record shop."

In spite of herself, she smiled.

The noodles helped. And sushi was a new experience for August; she delighted in seeing how hot she could make her soy and wasabi dip while Faolan talked about a sushi restaurant he remembered in Osaka. When they left the record store they were holding hands and there were three new buttons on her jacket: one with the lips from *Rocky Horror Picture Show* and two metal lapel pins—a letter F and letter A. Faolan had offered to help her pin them on, but August wanted to do it herself. She jabbed her fingers twice, but only bled a little and was happy with her tiny haul. She marveled at how such small things can make a person happy. Then she wondered what small things filled Faolan with that simple sense of joy, and she took his hand as they walked up South Charles.

"I wanted to see the Domino Sugar sign lit up across the water," she reminded him.

"We'll come back. I have to anyway, to sell the shop. You want to come with when I do?"

"Yeah, actually."

"Alright then. First order of business when we're back from our trip." They paused to smell the late roses entwined in an iron gate. A painted plaque read Scarborough Fair Bed & Breakfast. "We can even stay here. It looks a sweet little cottage." A man with a beard and a warm smile looked out and waved at them. August waved back as they moved on.

"We'd better get back to the car before we get a ticket."

"Thanks, Faolan."

"For what?"

"For everything."

"You're welcome, love. Hey …"

"Yeah?"

"I'm all-in, Little Red. Don't you worry."

She smiled, and despite the nip in the air, she felt warm all over. They reached the car as the sun was going down.

"Can we stop at a mall on the way back? I'd like a few new things to wear for the trip—is that too girly?"

He laughed. "I'm rather fond of your girliness, girlie."

Half an hour later they were looking at a big illuminated directory pylon in search of women's fashions, and August led Faolan by the hand into the first store. She grabbed an armload of dresses, pants and tees, as well as a few underthings, then pulled Faolan into the dressing room to watch her model them. She was delighted to see his pants bulge as she brushed against him and bent over in front of him, wiggling her bottom out of whatever slacks or jeans she tried on and winking at him over her shoulder. She occasionally sat on his knee as she slipped her legs into another pair of pants—usually with a little extra wiggling—and there were gentle kisses and much playful touching. She knew they would soon be making love, and it would bond them the way their kind should be bonded. And though she didn't know everything she should expect, she was sure it would be beautiful.

Summerblynd
Conall Keep
October 27, 1984

Blair had been sneaking into Ciardha's folio all week to peek at the speeches he was planning. Each speech would advocate for mixed-breeding in clearer terms, and each one rubbed her wounds raw. She felt her physical bond with him withering, despite the frequent sex. She'd been drinking more, particularly when he was home and likely to bed her. The more emotionally numb from the alcohol, the easier it was to untangle her feelings and remove herself from her body when he was pawing her.

He was clever, she would give him that. Maybe as clever as she had thought he was when they first met. He had slowly and expertly switched positions from pure breeding to mixed, but with otherkin, not with the cumanta. The idea he was trying to sell now was that all of the otherkin are superior to the cumanta, so therefore they should breed to make a stronger race, combining their special abilities and powers.

She knew that arguing with him would do no good, but she was so enraged and frustrated at his waffling that she argued with him in her head all day, trying to reason with him. But just as in real life, in her head he was never reasonable and always blameless. It never occurred to him that some of his misery, if not near all of it, was of his own making. In their earlier years, she found this almost endearing, like a wound she could tend to. But no matter what she did, it festered and seeped, angry and infected. Unfortunately, it was also contagious. His hate spread like a virus and she could do little to stop it.

By the time he was at the keep again, she was ready to argue—reason with him about his quest to find ways to inflate his own ego by making others less than him. Though she did admit that cumanta were inferior in many ways to otherkin, she also knew they had many wonderful strengths—something Ciardha would never understand, let alone admit.

As soon as the door swung open she was on him.

"Keer, I want you to let this go. I want you to abandon your Veritas vendettas and let us just live our lives. You promised once you got your vengeance it would be different. You promised." Blair smoothed a flutter of yellow chiffon ribbon at her cleavage and crossed her arms in frustration. She stared at him, demanding.

"Can you not see that I am angry, woman?" He said it low and through his teeth, like a growl. She hadn't noticed that he was partially transformed. She rocked, and took a step backwards. But her head was still spinning with the arguments she'd had with him inside of it all day and her resolve was renewed.

She uncrossed her arm and jutted out her chin. "I don't care if you're angry, Keer. I want you to keep your promise. You don't get to break your promises every time you get angry. What's the point? An easy promise is a worthless one."

"They're alive."

She knitted her brows together and re-crossed her arms. "Who?"

"That filthy mix-breed Sylvia, and your mother."

Her heart surged. Her mother was alive. Blair felt relief wash over her. It was the first time in a long time she'd hoped for anything, but now she felt herself hoping she'd see her mother again someday. She had to hide her relief under arguments.

"I thought you liked mixed-breeds now." She cocked her head to the side, challenging him. She regretted it almost instantly as his hands became paws with razors sticking out of the ends. His snout pushed forward with crackling and drool dripped all over the stones. His ears pointed and he let out a blood-curdling howl that shook the windows and sent hounds all over the property tuck-tailed, whining and running.

"Shut your hole you hunter whore! Their heads will be over my doorway! I want their bodies in a thousand bloody pieces scattered across the islands. I want the sea to eat their souls!"

"Perhaps they aren't meant to be dead." She was afraid, but standing her ground. She was so out of practice with her skills that she couldn't have protected herself from even an old, weak lycan.

"My vengeance is incomplete!"

"Your vengeance? Your vengeance!" She laughed with no joy. "Most of our lives have been about your vengeance. Your father! Your pain! Your suffering! Your selfish crusades have crowded out any love and happiness we once had. Why can't you see that, Keer?"

She was feeling sorry for her mother and her little niece. For her dead brother, whom she betrayed so long ago. None of this had turned out the way she planned. Love blinded her and made her do foolish things.

She felt duty-bound to derail him. To save what was left of her family. To undo some of the harm she has done. "Come Ciardha, don't be a fool. Whoever told you that is lying. They are trying to usurp your power and distract you from your new mission of mixing otherkin. How did you find out they are alive?"

He looked away. His snout retreated and his paws were becoming more manlike. He made a show of reviewing the buffet she'd laid out on the table anticipating his return. Piles of meat and bread and cheese. Without looking at her, he answered, "Liam."

Blair was momentarily stunned at the name. She put her hand to her heart and her eyes welled. "You saw ... You saw my son? You saw my son and you didn't tell me?"

Ciardha grunted and picked up a turkey leg from a pile of food on the table and took a bite.

She rushed close to him and tried to look into his face, but he turned and bit the turkey leg. She put her hand on his shoulder. "When? Is he here in Summerblynd?"

"Aye. He's heading to Perth tomorrow."

"Why didn't you tell me?"

He picked up another turkey leg and tore in.

"Keer, please. He's going to be thirteen this winter. I want to see him. It's been so long."

Ciardha seemed to quietly contemplate for a moment, then tore another bite from the turkey leg. "You can see him when his father is dead."

Blair felt her knees go weak and she knelt onto the floor, gasping and feeling the pain in her chest in waves. "Please, I want to see my son!" She keened his name, "Keeer-ya! Keeer-ya! Please!"

He tossed the bone to the floor, just missing Blair's splayed fingers. Bits of bird and grease sprayed onto her. She stared at the glistening bone. The ripped tendons and the white cartilage, and felt sick. She'd been feeling so sick lately. She thought she'd vomit, but the nausea passed and another feeling came over her that hadn't in a long time. She felt her hunter aspect rise in her. She didn't fully understand it, but she wasn't afraid, or maybe she was so full of rage that fear was crowded out. She watched him climb the stairs and listened as he headed to his study. She dried her face on an elegant silk sleeve, her pale red hair stuck to her tears, her cheeks ruddy. She didn't know if Ciardha had won, or if she was just done fighting. She put on her cloak and walked into the woods and towards the loch's edge, pulling her knife out of its sheath.

Farewell
Mahigan Falls

August started awake in her own turreted bedroom in the Blue Rook in the wee hours of the morning, with a bit of an ale headache. Faolan had left a note on the side table: "Back soonest, Sleeping Beauty." She had spent the evening with Mom and Brigid, drinking Scottish brews, eating junk food, playing cards, and talking about Scotland, Ireland, love, and men until after midnight. They made a little ceremony, and Sylvia transferred a small amount of Fletcher Evan's ashes into a vial to keep, while the rest were placed into a lidded box to be tucked into August's luggage. August was happy to know that another little bit of her father's ashes were already interred in her locket, safely stashed away in her jewelry box—though she wished now that she had made one or two fewer toasts to all the generations of the dearly departed.

She was also regretting that she had vowed not to read the rest of Faolan's journals. In those quiet days when he was gone, she'd had so many burning questions about Iseabail, and his thoughts about her. And she now felt less than prepared for him to destroy them all. What if, one day, she needed to read those words to gain some precious insight into this man she loved? Still, August knew he was right about how his memories and confessions would change the way she saw things; ever since she'd read about Iseabail's love of forget-me-nots, for example, and then saw a number of her favorite books turn up in the shop in Baltimore, August felt like those things were claimed by her, like territory that that had been staked out by a romantic rival—who it turned out was her own great-grandmother. She laughed out loud sometimes at the ludicrousness of it all—a part-werewolf, part-hunter, superhuman teenager who has a way-older werewolf boyfriend who has been in love with her great-grandmother for almost hundred years. Literally unbelievable.

But the day held too much promise to let missed opportunities and a little throbbing slow her down. The journey that she and Faolan were about to take was one that would set her on a path to her future with him, and with her lost kin and heritage. Through good and bad, August knew now, she would stand by Faolan. Ever since that troubling visit to the shop, he'd been very attentive, setting aside business dealings to fully inhabit their relationship and his adopted family. She hadn't even realized how distant from each other they had become until she found herself feeling on the verge of turning away from it all. But his affirmation of love and his determination to move on with his life gave her back that sense of belonging with him that had so electrified her the year before. It was like finally coming home after a long voyage; maybe that little shake-up was what they had needed to remember what was important in their everyday lives.

Faolan knocked and came in as she was tugging on her boots. He was wearing a wool jacket and kilt, and it was all August could do to stop herself from running over and lifting it up for him. Apparently, not long after she tumbled into bed, he had left her sleeping and went up to the Den to finish packing their bags, then came back to the Rook and put some breakfast on the stove, which accounted for the delicious smells that had followed him into the room. All that remained was to call for the car that would take them to the airport. They held hands and made small talk as August munched bacon and ketchup-drizzled eggs. She was actually a bit nervous, despite being sure that this was what she wanted. She opted to pretend that hopping off to Scotland with her werewolf lover was something she did all the time, and that airplanes never dropped into the sea. No big deal.

From Baltimore to Glasgow was a long flight over a lot of water, and August watched with childlike glee as the sparkling lights of the city and then the coast dropped away behind them. At first she was able to ignore the fact that there was nothing beneath them but deep and chilly ocean because she simply couldn't see it. Once the sun came up however, her tactic for beating the jitters was not working as well as she'd hoped, though she tried not to let it show. Faolan recognized her growing agitation anyway, and whispered assurances in her ear while the clouds piled around them and the ocean hung below them for what seemed like forever. She was at once thrilled by it and also increasingly convinced that land would never appear again. When Ireland and the Scottish isles were finally in view, she breathed a sigh of relief and regained her excitement. Towns and ships swept into view, and then her ancient homeland was finally under their wheels.

The airport was full of life. People came and went in clumps and streams, hugging, laughing, talking on payphones. The bustle and international chatter of it all reminded her of New York.

"I like it here already," she said as they stood waiting for their luggage, and watched as fancy oiled-leather cases and beat-up, much-traveled luggage chugged along the carousel. Faolan had bought her new red luggage, and she spotted it easily as it came into view. He handed her the wheeled bag and shouldered the hanger, grabbed his own buckled leather and tweed, and together they headed out to look for their ride.

In spite of the late afternoon sunshine, it was no more than forty degrees outside, and August was glad she'd kept a sweater in her shoulder bag. They were collected by a driver in an old-fashioned, fancy sort of limousine—Faolan called it a Daimler—and it gave August a distinctly unsettled feeling to watch the cars going past them on the other side of the road, like they were swimming in the wrong direction. The driver skirted the city itself and soon they were riding through trees; they had arrived in time to see the leaves turned, and it all seemed so beautiful that August felt a lump in her throat. The rest of the scenery was a gorgeous landscape of rolling fields and distant fells, like something from a fairy tale. After an hour riding through this magical countryside, August's jaw dropped as they pulled up at the gates of what looked to be a castle. Above the entrance was a wrought iron arch with a wolf's head in the center, painted white.

"Faolan ... where are we?"

"White Wolf Manor. It's where we're staying tonight and tomorrow, then we're off to Edinburgh." She watched through the sunroof as they passed through the gates and under the archway.

The place was immaculate, with ceilings in the main hall that must have been twenty feet high, and miles of polished wood, marble, and brass, punctuated with crystal and tapestries. August took in the ornate furniture and fine artwork—most of it landscape paintings filled with varieties of creatures, rendered in luminous oils. There were also several portraits of buxom women or men in kilts. She watched Faolan talking to one of the staff, looking so handsome in his kilt, and she realized how easily it could be him standing proudly in one of those paintings.

Their bags were whisked away, and after another minute a gray-haired fellow led them up the sweeping center staircase to their room—a huge, high-ceilinged chamber with a mix of old stonework and new walls. August went straight to the balconied windows that gazed out over the gardens on the southern side of the property. Trees like watercolors stretched as far as the eye could see, still showing orange, red and yellow in the fading light, and August felt much like she did the first time she arrived at the Blue Rook, sitting in her window seat looking out at the new world that was her home. *After all, this is home, too, in a way*, she thought. And just as it had been at the Rook, though she longed to feel connected, she had a sense of being apart from it all. It was too perfect to absorb—this place, this man, this beautiful countryside. It felt like something she was hungry for, but hadn't known it. She wanted to stroke it, pet it. Or eat it—consume it in some way. But all she could do was sit there and look at it in wonder and sense some ancient yearning. She felt her ears pointing a little, and her fingers were tingly, like they might sprout claws, but the feeling passed quickly.

"This place is incredible," she declared, and then took a running leap for the bed and dove into it, causing a great floof of pillows and blankets. "This is amazing! I feel like a princess! No—a queen!"

"As well you should, Lady Archer." He walked over and gave her butt a swat and they both laughed.

"I can't believe I'm here. Look at this room." She ran over to the bathroom and flung open the doors, revealing pristine white wood, white marble floors and a huge window behind a tub draped with a gauzy curtain. She flung the curtain to one side. "Look at the size of that tub. You're giving me a bubble bath in that. You realize this, don't you?"

"Aye, I'd had a suspicion. I think you'll find a bottle of something bubbly in there." There came the squeak of a handle and the sound of water rushing into the tub, and Faolan smiled. "I'll order us some supper. Even though it's barely past lunchtime back home, I'm needing something. You, lass?"

"Yes!" August appeared again at the door. "Oh my gosh, yes. Please order us some amazing food. I bet this place has amazing food."

She soon had filled up the tub with bubbles, peeled off her clothes, and hopped in while Faolan waited for the food to arrive. Which it did, in very short order. He rolled the cart into the bathroom and extinguished the lamps, so that all that remained was the soft glow of fading twilight and a few lavender clouds across the sky. He pulled the chair next to the tub and watched her dunking in and coming up, blowing bubbles from her hand and laughing. It did his heart good to see her so happy. He wondered if he could continue to keep her happy, once she'd bonded to him. It was an honor and also, he had to acknowledge, a bit of a burden, knowing it would be his responsibility first and foremost to be a good mate—and knowing how often he had fallen short of that.

"Would you like something to nosh?"

"Whatcha got?" She folded her arms on the edge of the tub and rested her chin, waiting.

"I have strawberries, blackberries, melon, some cheeses—Scottish cheeses, mind you—cold beef, sliced quite thin it seems, and a very nice brown bread. Also, chocolate and whisky mousse—Pot de Creme, I think they called it. Look, they come in these fancy little pots with dainty spoons—apparently for hedgehogs or wee fairies. What would madam like?"

"Holy hell, Fe—I want all of it!"

He lit a pair of candles on the tray and fed her nibbles of everything. She watched his hands as he put bits of cheese and mustard on the small slices of bread and brought them to her mouth. She fought the temptation to think about the next hour, the next day, the next thing she wanted to do, so she could just be in that moment. She reveled in the decadence and allowed herself to feel all of the love in her heart filling the rest of her up. Right here, right now, she had no doubts about her love and commitment to this man.

August took the little Pot de Creme and leaned back against the tub, dragging the tip of the tiny silver spoon through the creamy confection, licking the tip and repeating the process. Faolan made short work of what remained of the food and pushed the cart aside.

"I'd climb in with you like they do in the movies, clothes and all, but that'd make a pretty big mess."

"It would, and you'd have to take the time to yank off all of your wet clothes and hang them up to dry. The floor would be flooded. And you'd probably get soap bubbles in my delicious mousse. I vote you wait until I'm out of the tub to put your arms around me."

He nodded. "I'll second that motion then. I'm going to go put on some music."

"Yes, do that."

He left the bathroom and she soon heard a gentle sound drifting in, a bit like classical music but with a definite Scottish lilt. Despite her preference for electric guitar, August could certainly appreciate the faintly magical charm of a harp in this setting. She listened intently, studying the melody and imagining what other instruments she was hearing. Faolan walked back in and pulled off his shirt. She watched with mounting fascination as he unbuckled his belt and tugged it from his waist with a leather-on-wool *schwoop*, leaving him in nothing but his buckled kilt. He wrapped the belt around his hand several times and set the scrolled leather on the counter—a ritual she had seen him perform many times, and which now made her feel both turned on and also cozy and domestic, as did watching him brush his teeth. Finally he grabbed a fluffy towel and held it out for her.

She just smiled and sighed. There in the glow of candles at dusk, enfolded in the warm caress of cotton and Faolan's arms, she pressed against him and nuzzled into his chest. So strong, smelling of skin and spice. Safe. Sexy. *What more could there be to forever?* she thought. *How could it be better than this?*

August put on panties and one of Faolan's tees, wrapped herself in the large blue and green shawl Gran had made for her trip—"To match your eyes, love"—and curled into one of the tufted chairs by the window.

"Wish I had a hot cocoa right about now."

"See that tall silver pot over there on the cart?"

"Yes." She looked at him and blinked expectantly.

"What do you suppose is in there?"

"You're awful!" She laughed. "You think you know me so well."

"That pot of hot cocoa over there proves it, lass. Quod erat demonstrandum."

She chuckled and held her hands out. He shook his head with a wry smirk and pushed the cart her direction. "Shall I pour for you?"

She straightened up and assumed her best posh manner. "Do you wish to pour for me, bare-chested ruffian?"

"It is my pleasure, Your Majesty."

Now she was the one shaking her head. Her damp curls were getting some spring back and no doubt were headed straight for frizz. Plus, she knew she had a few dots of acne on her forehead and cheek. No bosom to speak of, no great education, no elegant airs—nothing

126

about her suggested royalty. So why, she wondered, was this man so taken with her? *It couldn't just be wolf hormones, could it? This couldn't all just be chemicals? Is that all love is? Chemicals and a few things in common?*

"Why are you so sweet to me?"

"Because you deserve sweetness," he replied, without even a beat of hesitation, and somehow it made complete sense.

She sipped cocoa while Faolan browsed the wall of books across from her. She watched him in his kilt, no shirt, his curls pulled back into the world's shortest ponytail, high on the back of his head. The soft light made him so beautiful. She noticed a few pale scars marking his body. A rake of them across his right shoulder, only noticeable by a silvery sheen when he flexed.

"What happened to your shoulder?"

"What?"

"The back of your right shoulder, Faolan." She got up from the chair and leapt across the room to him in one bound.

"Fight with Keer when we were kids. It was deep. Took weeks to heal."

"So he's always been an asshole?" She gently touched the faint scarring with her fingertips.

"He felt terrible about it. Did my chores for a month," he went on, still reading spines.

"You had chores?"

"Sort of. Mostly practicing with weapons or hammering something together in the field. But we did have responsibilities." He turned toward her. "Father said work was for peasants, not the sons of a laird. But mother argued it would give us character. Sometimes he let her have her way because she was Primary."

She watched his sage green eyes recount his childhood. He would smile and creases would appear next to his mouth and eyes. He hadn't shaved in hours, so he was already getting a shadow on his chin.

"What does Primary mean?"

"Ah. Lycans often mated with more than one bitch."

She looked sharply to him. "Excuse me?"

"Mate, then? The Primary mate is the one they have bonded to, and typically the one they have children with—legitimately, anyway. In terms of passing on heritage and estate. The others, other mates, sometimes lived on the premises as well and serve as ... I guess you'd call them concubines."

"What. The. Hell."

"Och, aye. And it gets wilder. After our numbers started to thin and the men started fighting more over the most fertile—um—female mates, they would turn instead to otherkin of various sorts, and even the occasional cumanta, to keep as extra mates. Often the pregnancies there ended in miscarriage, or sometimes death for a cumanta, so they saw that as a problem that worked itself out. And should any of the non-primary females bid for a better position in the estate, the lady of the manor could challenge them to combat. To the death. Which was more a fair fight when the rival was lycan, I suppose. But a cumanta was no match against a lycan primary, nor most any otherkin, for that matter."

"This is your world, Faolan?"

He nodded. "The one I came from, at least. But that's generations past." He pulled a book from the shelf. "And not as different from human culture as ye might imagine. Deadly rivalries are something of a specialty among the cumanta."

"I never heard you use the word bitch like that before. I don't like it."

"Aye, it's an old word. I forgot it's not as common in the States. But it is the traditional terminology."

"I don't care. It's not the dark ages anymore. I don't like it."

"Then I shall use it no more. Anyroad, my mother was beautiful, gracious and quite powerful. She didn't take any of my father's shite. She definitely had a hold over him the way only a true primary could."

August nodded and softened a little, "You never told me about this extra mates stuff before. You don't expect to take on any concubines do you?"

He looked at her incredulously. "August!" He re-shelved the book and shook his head. "I'm a one-mate wolf." He smiled at her, his eye twinkled. "Set your mind at rest on it. It's not happening."

"It's a lot of sexist crap anyway. Do they even do this stuff anymore?"

"It's very old-fashioned, aye. And some have always done so. But it hasn't been common for centuries."

"Fe—where do you think Ciardha is?"

"I've been pondering that. I think maybe Conall Keep."

"Conall Keep?"

"That's what we called it, at least. It's a bit of an old fortress in the woods, out in Perthshire. A sort of a mini-castle. It was built as a watchtower, to spot hunters or anyone else approaching Summerblynd. That was our village, in the heart of lycan territory. It's mostly hunter now. The tower must've had a view for miles, once. It's rather overgrown now, and it was in disrepair—which is why I hadn'a kenned to it afore. I thought it was uninhabitable. But it is on Conall land, and I probably should have checked it first—it had been a favorite place for us to play as lads."

"You think he could be there?"

"Aye. It'd make sense. There's also a chance …"

"What?"

"Your Aunt Blair may be with him. Last I heard she was spotted in Summerblynd once or twice last year."

"Oh my god, I completely forgot about Blair. You mean they're together? Like a couple?"

"I don't ken it fer sure, but it would seem."

"But—Faolan? Her brothers—her sister? How could she be with that murderer?" August spluttered. "He tried to kill her own mother!"

"I dinna ever see them together, Red. And Sorcha still loved her, even after Blair left the family."

"Gran still doesn't know she's alive. We should tell her."

"I'm not sure that's a good idea, love."

"I would want to know if I was her. I feel terrible knowing."

"It would depend on Blair, if she was ready to reunite with her family or not. If Sorcha knew and Blair wanted nothing to do with her—think how that would hurt her. Best to let it alone for the time."

"But it's so hard keeping it to myself. I feel like a liar."

"Aye, and that's one o' the things I admire about you, since you were asking. I've never met a more honest soul. But for the burden— that's about you lass, isn't it? Sometimes we carry the load so our loved ones don't have to. Best to do what's best for your gran, no matter how uncomfortable it makes you."

"I'm going to defer to your wisdom here," she smirked at him. "Just this once! But shouldn't we go to the keep and check? Ask her right out?"

"I suppose if they are living there, the news of our presence will soon make its way to Keer in any case. So, we've got quite the itinerary," he laughed. "Which would you like to do first, risk our lives at Conall Keep, or rip open emotional wounds at the cemetery in Meikleour?"

"Is that near Summerblynd?"

"It's on the north side of the Tay, just south of Blairgowrie."

She blinked at him.

"Right. Summerblynd is about an hour drive from the cemetery."

"Are we staying in Meikleour?"

"Aye. We could go make a day of it in and around Meikleour. After Glasgow and Edinburgh, I mean—we'll head up to the Tay and spread Fletcher's ashes. Then on to Meikleour. We'll take care of our business at Iseabail's ..."

"Are you ok?"

He nodded. "Little bit of a pang, thinking of her grave. I reckon it'll pass."

"I'm not making you do this." She noticed the bit of defensiveness that crept into her voice.

"Hush, love. I know. Set your worries aside. I want to do this. I want to move forward." He took a deep breath and transformed his attitude, "Anyroad, there's a fine little inn we'll be staying at. I'll say my goodbye and finally lay it all to rest. We'll walk away. We'll have some ale and some bloody good pub food and bed down in our quaint inn ... make love ..." He looked to her, an eyebrow raised.

"Yeah?"

"Aye. I think I will be ready to take the plunge, so to speak. Care to be the plungee?"

She laughed and then sighed. Indeed she did care to, and he knew it. Besides, once they had finally consummated their relationship—*say it, August*, she chided herself: *our marriage*—it could stop being such a thing between them.

"How dangerous do you think it will actually be—going to the keep? Should I tell my mom we're going?"

"I don't think that Keer will do much on his own turf. We'll go and look around first. To assess the situation."

The small feast and the big bath had made August sleepy, despite the fact it was only mid-afternoon back in Mahigan Falls. She was anxious about the next few days, but even that was not enough to ward

130

off the exhaustion catching up to her. Brigid had warned her about jet lag, and had given her capsules with an herbal blend she and Abel whipped up, though Faolan himself rarely felt lagged for longer than a day. August took them now, determined to enjoy every moment of their trip—*because we never know when things will suddenly change*, as she had said to Lainy.

She climbed into bed next to Faolan, their arms and torsos entangling. He stroked her hair and her back and she petted his hip, and it wasn't long before she felt him stirring against her. She imagined that, if they were the last two people on earth, at the last day before the sun winked out, she would still want him to consume her, as she did him. In moments, they were reeling in the joy of their intimacy, her hands devouring him, his tongue caressing her, both of them driven by the want of each other's love and comfort as much as desire, and then they were spent and sound asleep.

Parnie & Osborne

Over the next couple of days, Faolan's whirlwind introduction to her ancestral country nearly made August forget what lay ahead. Sunday was Glasgow, and after a bit of a drive, when the spires of the city came into view, she felt a thrill flash through her. Faolan had the driver let them off near the university, and a short time later they were sitting down in a bustling little cafe to share a proper Scottish fry-up of tattie scones, baked beans, mushrooms, fried tomato, egg, and no less than five meats: back bacon, black pudding, bangers, haggis, and squares of lorne sausage. August had never seen so much on one plate, and she was glad Faolan hadn't ordered one for each of them. Honestly, she'd barely been able to understand what he asked for. She'd been delighted to hear his accent come on stronger since they'd arrived, but the local lingo he spoke to the man behind the counter was nearly unintelligible. "Glasgow patter," Faolan called it. Fortunately, he had no trouble polishing off most of the plate himself, even after the big bowl of porridge that started the meal. She couldn't help but think how Abel would have shaken his head.

They spent the next two hours in the Kelvingrove Museum, where Faolan pointed out to her the many subtle influences of otherkin culture that could be found in everything from medieval carvings and Renaissance portraiture to the architectural details of the building itself. August was beginning to feel her true connection to her heritage, and her homeland. She liked this city, at once cosmopolitan and gritty, and as they walked through the streets she realized that it didn't really trouble her whether or not they were in a good part of town. Faolan, in fact, seemed to be a bit more interested in the rougher parts. "Should have brought a camera," he commented at one point. "This place has changed so much. That gaping hole there used to be St. Enoch's Station."

They walked along a Victorian-era viaduct that had once carried the railway, as Faolan told her, and August was fascinated by the little shops that had been built into the arches underneath. "Aye, they use every scrap of space in an auld city like this," he noted. A little farther on, the road made a hairpin turn. But as they were passing the shop at the end of Parnie Street—or maybe it was the beginning of Osborne—

132

Faolan stopped and seemed quite intrigued. "Red, have a look at this window, with its antique cloaks on display."

She turned to the half-round storefront, made of the same red limestone that was everywhere in the city, with big wood-framed windows wrapping around the curved end of the building. "Wow— looks like they've been here a while. Or at least making coats a while."

"Aye, look at this one." He half-smiled and pointed to one just past her view. She took a few steps and saw a long red cloak, not very different from the one her father had given her.

"What?"

"Owned by hunters, this shop." He smiled and watched her reaction.

"Wow. This is so weird. Totally awesome, but weird."

"Do ye want to go inside and meet them?"

"You know them?"

"I do."

"Did you tell them to do this?" She waved at the huge red form in the window.

"I plead the Fifth."

"We're in Scotland."

"Right. Look how American I am now. Have pity on me and come meet them."

"I'm nervous, Faolan. I've never met your people."

"They're *your* people, lass!" He stifled a laugh. "They won't bite."

She rolled her eyes. "That was terrible."

"As was intended."

"Would've worked better if they had been lycan."

"Well, we can't all be so blessed. Let's go in and say hello."

Faolan held the door and they went in. There was a couple standing there behind the counter, as if waiting for them—both with dark hair and fair skin. The woman was lithe and short and had a band of freckles across her nose. She smiled, revealing a slightly gapped set of front teeth, which somehow made her instantly adorable to August.

"Faolan!" She rushed around the counter and threw her arms around his middle. "I misst ye sae muckle!"

"Misst ye sae muckle, aye!" Faolan replied.

The man, nearly as tall as Faolan and a good bit beefier, came around the corner and stuck out his hand. "Awreet, Faolan! Damned good to see ye!" The burly man grabbed Faolan and pulled him in for a bear hug.

"Aye, you as well! You as well!" Both men laughed and pounded each other hard on the back. "It's bloody brilliant to see ye both." Faolan turned to the woman and gestured towards August.

"Kenzy, this is August," he panted, and Kenzy threw her arms around August so joyfully she nearly toppled her.

"So grand to meet ye, August! Ah, yer a sight! Y' favor your da, y' know. A'm sairy 'bout your loss, dear. Fletcher was a fine man."

"You knew my father?"

"Aye, what's left of us, we all knew him. Here's my husband, Angus."

August smiled and shook his hand. "I guess I was bound to meet an Angus eventually."

The two exchanged looks.

"Never mind," she said, feeling a little foolish. She looked to Faolan but he seemed to be avoiding her gaze.

"You're so American, dear, I dinna ken what yer sayin'," Kenzy said, and they all laughed. "You need to meet our son Adair. He's been in America many times, visiting our kin in the States. He almost sounds American."

"Oh, where is he?"

"He'll be down in a moment," Angus said, in his deep booming voice. "He'll be heading to Summerblynd, though. Training." He sounded proud of his son.

"What's he training for?" August asked. Kenzy and Angus both looked over at Faolan.

"Hunter stuff, love, much the same as you and I have done. The Veritas have been rumbling of their dissatisfaction with our hidden role in the world. Which they've certainly done before, but it's been bolder of late. So the hunter clans are taking steps, in case they want to stir up trouble. It's just … precautionary."

Angus lowered his voice a bit, "Aye, he's already been trainin' a couple o' years. We thought it best he be able to protect himself, and the cumanta, if necessary. He's small, our Adair, but he's strong and swift. He'll get stronger as he gets older."

August wondered why people would let their children train to fight, but then again, she wished she too had started earlier. She realized she was still thinking like a cumanta, a regular human, which she had believed herself to be up until last year. At least this boy knew what he was. Didn't matter if he was a kid or a grown man, it pays to know how to fight in their world, she'd certainly learned that.

"I've heard you have one of our old cloaks," Kenzy said.

"I do. I have my dad's old cloak."

"Grand!" They said in unison, both fairly beaming with pride.

"They do last, don't they?" Angus asked, and patted her shoulder. "And tha' one wasn't new when it came t' your da neither. He had an eye for the classics, even at a young age."

August nodded. Then she heard footsteps descending the staircase toward the back corner of the store.

A young man emerged from the archway, and August felt her heart slow and thud harder. His close-cropped hair was thick like Angus's but chestnut brown, and he was surprisingly tanned to be part of the pale clan she'd just met. And if this was their son, he was also definitely *not* a child—August figured him for twenty, maybe twenty-one, and his eyes seemed to belong to an old soul. Nor was he "small," at least not to August—though she could see how his enormous father might think him so.

The young man smiled warmly at the crowd. "Welcome all of ye," he said, nodding to Faolan and August.

Angus put an enormous hand on his son's back. "Adair, this is Faolan." The two men met eyes and shook hands and nodded to each other. "And this is August. Though, I've heard tale that she might be called Red as well."

August blushed as the young man extended his hand to her. "August is fine." She took his hand and felt a warm surge shoot through her body. She released his hand quickly and folded her hands in front of her and nodded.

"Pleasure to meet ye," he said politely, though he seemed a bit bewildered, with his hand still mid-air.

She took a step backwards and put her arm around Faolan. "Sorry, I'm just a little overwhelmed." She then reached up and pecked Faolan unexpectedly on the cheek. He gave her back a gentle, reassuring rub. Then he asked if the family cared to meet again for something to eat in a couple of hours. They agreed on fish and chips at The Coronation.

"Under the bridge on Gallowgate,"Angus confirmed.

"How could I forget?" Faolan replied.

They bid their farewells and Faolan and August resumed their walk around town, this time heading down toward the river. August held Faolan's hand tight as they peeked in little shops. He offered to buy her any little thing she wanted, but she didn't see anything that really called out to her. She clung to him as they strolled through a broad grassy park toward a glittering building in the center that was half castle, half greenhouse.

"Love, are you okay?" He asked her.

"What? Yeah. Why?" She tried to sound totally okay.

"You've been a wee bit close, is all."

She dropped his hand and stepped back. "Well, I'm just feeling romantic I guess. Sorry. I won't be so clingy!" She marched off ahead of him.

"Come now, Red. What's the problem?"

"Nothing. I guess I'm just a wee too close for you these days."

He caught up to her in two long steps and put his hand on her shoulder. "Stop. Red! Stop, please."

She stopped, her back to him, she crossed her arms and studied the ground with a scowl. "Ok. I'm stopped. Are you happy?"

"Thrilled," he said flatly.

Then her shoulders started to shake a bit.

"What is the matter, lass?" He rounded her and looked down at her, putting his hands on both her shoulders. "Come here, come … It'll be fine. Whatever it is, it'll be fine."

She stood there, in the heart of Glasgow, halfway across the world from everything she knew, and most of what she loved, and sobbed like a seven-year-old.

He held her as she let it out. "There, there," he said softly, lips pressing to the top of her head, arms wrapped snug around her.

She took in his smells. His warmth. And she felt ashamed for having noticed Adair the way she did. She couldn't even bring herself to tell Faolan about it.

By the time she was done crying it was time to head to The Coronation and meet the others.

She tried to wipe her face, her tears, her running nose, but she didn't have anything but the shawl her grandmother had given her. Her

136

small bag was devoid of anything resembling a tissue, nor could she have crammed even a penny in the pockets of her skin-tight jeans. Faolan saw her need, untucked the tails of his shirt and held it out to her.

"What? No!" She said in protest, her face wet and red.

"Here, just have a blow and I'll tuck it right back in. It'll be fine. Lemme be gallant, won't ye?"

So she crouched a little and wiped her tears and nose on his shirt, "Ew. I'm so gross."

"Yer not even close to gross."

"Stop being so cute." She smiled a half-smile and snuffed. "I'm so hungry, but I don't know if I want to meet them for dinner."

"We're supposed to be there in ten minutes."

"Can't you call them from a payphone and tell them we can't come?"

"Lass, what is this all about?" He searched her face for some small clue.

She grabbed fistfuls of shirt and pulled him in close for a hard, deep kiss. He kissed her back, holding her close and stroking her hair until they both heard a loud whistle and somebody hollered something at them from a long way off.

"If you want me to cancel, I will. I just don't understand what this is all about."

"Let's just go and get it over with."

"Was there something they said that bothers you, Red?"

"Not exactly. Mostly I'm worried about going to the keep. I'm scared your brother is going to ruin what we have ahead of us." None of these things were lies.

"I can't promise you it won't go off, but we can't have it hangin' over our heads either."

She nodded. "I know. But, we're so happy right now. We're so close to …"

"We're close to being married souls."

Her features softened and she felt bliss at that idea. "Yes, married souls. Your brother isn't going to like that. And really Faolan, even if he doesn't try to kill me, I might try to kill him."

"Yer worried about what you'll do, aren't ye, August?"

She was startled for a moment, wondering which of her concerns

137

Faolan was really speaking to. "Yes," she said simply. "I'm worried about what I'll do."

Fried

The restaurant was tight—only a few tables and a long bar. Kenzy, Angus, and Adair were already sitting in the corner where they'd pushed two tables together.

To her consternation, as soon as Adair turned around and smiled, her heart did another round of those hard thuds, and she chided herself for not being able to control it. He and Angus both stood as she approached, and Adair pulled out the chair next to him for her. "Lass," he said.

"Oh, um ... thanks." She looked around and, since she couldn't imagine a scenario in which telling him she preferred not to sit there wasn't going to sound rude, she sat. When she tucked in her chair, she tried to move it imperceptibly further from him, and closer to Faolan. Instead she ended up leaving a good foot of air between them, while being crunched right up against Faolan and his long sharp elbows, which she regretted as soon as the wrappers hit the table and he tucked into his fish and chips like he'd found a lost love. She gave him a little more room, scooting back toward Adair a bit.

"Faolan tells us you're good with the bow," Kenzy said, vigorously shaking vinegar over her plate. "That's me as well."

"Oh ... oh, that's cool. Maybe you can show me some stuff sometime. "

Kenzy nodded. August was trying to be engaging, but she was trying harder to ignore the heat of Adair's arm so close to hers. She wanted to crawl into Faolan's lap for safety, but part of her also hoped that Adair's forearm would soon brush hers. *God what is wrong with me? Horrible, disloyal girl!*

"Ever shoot from a horse?" Angus asked. "That's a fine skill to have."

"No. I don't have any horses."

Angus and Kenzy nodded in unison.

"I'm sorry, I'm afraid I'm not very interesting. I'm worried about some things, and I'm a little homesick."

They both let out a small laugh and Kenzy patted her hand, leaving behind a grease smudge. "Oh don't you worry on it lass, you'll feel at home soon enough," she encouraged her. She and her husband nodded again and dug into their suppers.

Despite having been starving a little earlier, August found her stomach in a knot and she picked at her food, even though it was the most delicious fried cod and potatoes she'd ever tasted. She tidied up her filets into a little pile and pushed the chips around. Then Adair leaned across her, close. Only to grab some napkins, but he ended up extending his bare neck just inches from her face. He smelled of lemon, sage and pepper. She closed her eyes and felt his scent rush through her. Her skin started to tingle and prick, particularly at her ears and fingertips and toes.

People were talking, but it all sounded muffled and far away. She heard the word "Fletcher" but it didn't shake her from the spell.

"She asked you if you know where you're going to spread your father's ashes," Faolan said from a mile away. "August," he said louder this time, giving her arm a squeeze and she snapped back to reality.

Everybody was looking at her now.

"Are you okay, love?" Faolan asked her.

"I'm just so tired. The jet lag, I guess. You've all been so nice, but I really need to get some rest, I think—I might be a bit lightheaded."

"Don't you worry about it," Kenzy said and stood and held her arms out for a hug. "I wish we had more time when you're feeling like yourself. I have so many stories to tell you."

"Would it be alright if I wrote to you?" August asked. Her brain was still swimming.

"Of course, of course."

"Nice to meet you, young lady," Angus said as they all stepped away from the table into the tight aisle. He gave her one of the warmest hugs she'd ever had. And then Adair stepped in and said, "I hope we meet again."

She nodded awkwardly. "Nice to meet you. Adair."

They all spilled out of the doorway onto the sidewalk and waved as they went their separate ways.

"What is their last name, anyway?" August finally asked once they had turned away.

"Hunter."

"Oh. Well … That's going to be easy to remember."

"Aye. Let's get you to a bed. We've got to get up early and head to Edinburgh. It's going to be another long day."

Wild Parsnips
Conall Keep

"Dè tha thu a' dèanamh?"

"What's it look like, husband?" she said with an edge of exasperation.

He jutted out his chin.

"I'm makin' some dinner, Keer." Blair chopped at a pile vegetables beside her in the kitchen. She was slowly sorting and washing and dicing them neatly. She filled a large tub with water, salt, garlic, and paper thin slices of small wild white parsnips. A marinade for the meat.

"We have people to do that, woman."

"Oh, I know. I just wanted to make something special for you, my love." She pulled a large leg of lamb out of the icebox and slapped it onto the butcher block.

Ciardha's ears pricked at the sound of wet meat hitting the wood. His nose twitched at the iron smell of blood. Blair sharpened her cleaver on the stone and began hacking at the leg, then expertly used a long thin knife to flay the bits closer to the bone. She cut the meat into large hunks and dropped them into the marinade.

"Well, you might want to make enough for our guests."

Blair stopped cold and stood there thinking of what to say.

"Did ye no hear me wife?"

She nodded. "What guests?"

"I hear Faolan is in town with his mixed-breed bitch."

She pulled her gloves off and turned towards him. "Faolan and August are here, in Perthshire?"

He grabbed the giant bone from the block and ripped the sinewy bits off, chewed once and swallowed.

"What makes you think they're coming to the keep?"

"I know my brother."

"What are you going to do, Ciardha? You're not going to hurt them?"

"I don't know yet. I haven't told the Veritas either. They have scores to settle with Faolan. They'd love to tear into that little Archer bitch, too."

"Don't you think it's bloody stupid for the Veritas to kill anybody with a trace of lycan? Isn't mixed breeding your new angle?" She swung the cleaver hard and the tip stuck into the worn butcher block. "How do you know they're here?"

"They will be, soon enough. They're booked at Meikleour."

"Oh, your slimy minion … that bartender Tommy Huntar? He told ye, did he? Why would ye trust somebody from a hunter clan anyway?"

"Why would he lie about a thing like that?"

"I don't know, to get you to give him some money?"

"He knows I'll kill him if he lies to me."

"If he doesn't kill you first. He's otherkin. He could, if he wanted."

"Och! Woman! Yer gon' t' mak me bust a gut!" He let out a wail of laughter.

"You're an arse."

"I like your arse!" He laughed and smacked her butt. Blair stiffened and fought a wave of rage. She didn't want him to even talk to her, let alone touch her.

She turned around and held up the knife, waving it at him as she said, "If your brother and his lady come here, you're going to act like a laird of this manor and a host to your family. You'll be lucky if that hunter girl doesn't put an arrow through your heart. If you still have one."

He grunted and threw the bone across the kitchen. "I do as I bloody well please."

She curled up her lip and wrinkled her nose and turned away. "Why don't you go piss around the property? Animal."

"Better than your kin. Stronger. Better. Smarter."

Blair bit her lip and fixed a glare into the void. She loved this man once. She gave up her family for him—everything she was. She hoped that Faolan would kill him.

Written in the Stars
White Wolf Manor

Restless, troubled by insistent thoughts, August rolled out of bed as quietly as she could. But her man was a light sleeper.

"You okay, lass?" Faolan asked, his voice thick.

"I am," she whispered. "My brain is just busy. Go back to sleep."

She crept over to the minibar and pulled out an apple juice and drank half of it down. It was too cold and it immediately made a small knot in her stomach, but she finished it anyway. Not having food in so many hours had left her feeling woozy. She crept over to the bathroom and started the water to fill the tub, sat on the toilet to pee, then kicked free her panties and peeled off her tee and got into the hot bath. The water felt safe. Warm and comforting. She slipped all the way under and came back up, leaned back with her eyes closed, and tried to relax.

Too many things were coming to her mind: flashes of the New York City apartment she grew up in, Dad reading to her in the study, Halloweens and birthdays with Mom and Dad both smiling back at her. She thought about the urn in her luggage and what she might say when spreading his ashes ...

More flashes: Tanner putting his hands on her—waves of nausea and the smell of iron. The faraway sound of his screams as Faolan ripped into him. Her mother's sadness. Her mother's happiness with a man who isn't her father.

More faces: Faolan, before he would give her his name. Ciardha—his terrifying, grizzled, yet handsome face, so full of hate and vengeance. The vengeance she herself felt when the hatred for her father's killer took her over.

What was it going to be like at the keep? Would he make an attempt to hurt one of them? Would he succeed in taking away any happiness she could have? Could he wipe the remaining Archers off of the face of the earth? Even Blair?

What about the cemetery? The trunk of journals? She was truly sorry that Faolan was having his pangs. It made her wish Iseabail hadn't died—that Faolan had the love of his life and his baby, and they were living happily ever after. If August had never met Faolan, she wouldn't know what she was missing. She would have found somebody, someday. Somebody less … complicated.

Her brain tried to trick her into thinking about Adair, but she kept changing the channel to other worries, drowning it out. She didn't want to think of what kind of person it made her to be attracted to this other man while on a vacation with her intended—a honeymoon, really, if they did indeed complete their bond.

Maybe she should tell Faolan. But what if it worried him? Or hurt him? She couldn't do that to him now, not while his oldest feelings were so close to the surface.

But he isn't a child; he would understand simple attraction, right? That's natural, and normal, right? After wrestling with it a bit more, she decided it had just been a surge of hormones, combined with stress and maybe cold feet. It would be pointless to tell Faolan, because it would pass. And she wanted to convince herself it didn't make her a bad person … or bad hunter … or lycan. Whatever she was.

When she finally climbed out of the tub the water was tepid and her digits were prunes and Faolan was knocking gently at the door asking what she wanted for breakfast.

They sat on the balcony overlooking the forest, bundled up in decadently fluffy robes, and ate more manageably-sized fry-ups without much conversation. She was going to have to sort out her feelings about eating meat later. She shook her head and smiled ruefully at herself. A vegetarian werewolf—she just had to make her life that little bit more complicated, didn't she? In any case, she was in Scotland, so she was going to eat fry-ups. *When in Rome.*

"We have another fancy car coming to get us today?"

Faolan sipped his tea and nodded. "Same one, but yes."

"Cool. I like sitting with you and cuddling and talking while we ride. I also like sitting with my back to the windows so I can go sideways."

He let out a small laugh and smiled. He took the last tattie scone in what had been a sizable pile and bit it in half, then offered her the last piece. She opened her mouth and he tucked it gently in, and she felt a rush of joy as she ate it. Moments like this were what life was about. This place. This man. Quiet comfort and good food. Sunshine and blue skies. It felt right. Being with him, it felt so right.

They dressed for the cooler weather. Faolan wore jeans and a

145

cream colored cable-knit that was gorgeous, though it looked a bit itchy for hugging. He noticed her admiring it.

"Like me jumper? Sorcha made it for me. For the trip."

"Oh, I didn't realize."

"Aye, at the same time she made you that shawl."

"Guess she doesn't hate you anymore."

"I'm irresistible, it seems."

"Is that it?"

"Something like that." He pulled her into a hug—it turned out the sweater was not nearly as itchy as August had imagined. When she gave him a quick peck on the cheek and wriggled free, he swatted at her bottom, but she tucked it in and scooted away, laughing.

"Missed me! Missed me! Now ya gotta kiss me!" She squeaked when he made a grab for her, but she didn't run farther than the other side of the bed, where he quickly caught her up, and she curled happily into his embrace and sighed.

"I'm looking forward to Edinburgh, Fe," she said into his neck.

"Me as well."

Nose to nose. Little kisses on the mouth. He nuzzled her behind her ear. She felt her flesh go all bumpy.

"Any surprises like yesterday, Mr. Wolf?"

"Not really. Just your standard tourist stuff. Is that okay? Maybe a waltz around the castle?"

"Yes. That sounds awesome. You may spank me now, if you want to."

"If you're a good girl."

August giggled.

The ride out was lovely. They didn't talk much, just held each other, kissed and petted a bit, and watched the scenery go by the window on the far side of the limo. August prickled a moment when she thought about how easily these things—money and privilege—seemed to come her way. Was it a reward for coming through the horrors of the last two years? *But other people live through whole lives that are horrible.* She realized there was no order to it, no fairness. All she could do was embrace the good and remember it with gratitude, and endure the bad with grace and hope. And right now, it was wonderful not to have to worry about things like shelter or food or being cold. Or alone. If her life ever settled down and she and Faolan got married, maybe she could find a way to give something back to the world for the good fortune she'd been given.

Married. That word again—the weight of it. Was she really ready? Was being married more than being bonded, the way she wanted to be with Faolan? And what would marriage mean to him? She realized she didn't know; for him the bonding seemed to be everything. But this was nice. There was no reason it couldn't be like this for them, always. Always?

Ugh! Could you possibly stop worrying about stuff for five minutes, August?!

She picked up Faolan's hand from where it lay on her chest and tenderly kissed his palm.

They came into Edinburgh from the north side, the whitecapped waters of the Firth of Forth on their left and the ancient towers of the Old Town to their right. Where Glasgow was a red city that hugged the banks of the Clyde, built for shipping and commerce, Edinburgh stood tall and gray, with stone skyscrapers hundreds of years old—a capital built to impress.

"It's so beautiful, Fe! It looks like something out of a dream."

"Aye. A dream of a sovereign land."

"This is where Mom and Dad fell in love."

"Not too surprising, actually. D' ye know who else fell in love wi' Edinburgh? Your friend Jules Verne. It's why there's so many Scotsmen in his adventures."

"Ooh! That castle—that's it! Edinburgh Castle!"

"I wonder if ye have any idea how adorable y' are at this very moment?"

"Stop." August made a crooked little smile and elbowed Faolan gently in the ribs. "You only like me 'cause I'm so easily impressed."

"In fact, we'll be staying right in th' shadow of that castle. Step out in the morning and walk uphill a couple o' doors and yer there. How's that, then?"

"Oh yes, you are impressing the pants off me." She stretched and put her arms around his neck. "That was your plan all along, I'll bet."

"You're missing the scenery."

147

"Just kiss me already."

⟵————《 》————⟶

Their rooms were in the heart of the Old Town, and Faolan asked the driver to drop them off on High Street and tipped him to take their luggage on to the inn, so they could walk up the Royal Mile together. They peered into shop fronts and restaurants, holding hands and navigating the irregular cobbles. The tall windowed walls rose above them like a canyon, punctuated by the spires of Tron Kirk, St. Giles, and Tolbooth as they climbed the hill, while the castle gradually revealed itself between the buildings at the summit.

"It's like a city of hills, Fe."

"Rather a city nestled in the hills. Like ancient Rome."

"What's that big one, with the ramp around it?"

"Arthur's Seat, love. We can climb it if ye wish, though it'd take the better part of the day."

"The only place I absolutely want to see today is the castle. We'll be back though, won't we? To Edinburgh? We don't have to fit all of Scotland in one trip?"

"Aye, we'll be back, as often as ye'd like to. Assuming we work everything out in Summerblynd."

Faolan squeezed August's hand and pointed to an old-fashioned sign hanging out over the street.

"The Witchery? What's that, Fe?"

"That's where were staying, love."

It didn't look too promising to August from the outside—just more Edinburgh stone with a few arches at the base. Once they were inside though, she could understand why Faolan chose this place for their romantic little trip. Opulent was the only word for it, but with rustic touches that made August think of fairy tales. Indeed, if fairies needed a vacation, they would come here, she was certain of it.

"This place is full of otherkin history, salvaged from all over town. It's tucked into every corner," Faolan whispered to her, and August wondered if she'd ever see it as naturally as he did.

But once they reached their suite she ignored all cultural lessons in favor of taking her ceremonial running plunge into the huge four-poster at the far end. "Man! This never gets old!" she proclaimed, her voice muffled in the downy bedcover. She rolled over with a flop and a satisfied sigh. "I could live here for the next ten years!"

Faolan laughed. He kicked off his jeans and belted on his kilt, as August watched from the pillows, the many tangled thoughts of the morning now beginning to clamor once more.

"Faolan ..." She traced squares on the soft plaid duvet with a fingernail. "Do you ever think about marriage?"

He looked up from his buckling and tilted his head, as though the question didn't make sense.

"I mean, do you ever think of being ... What it would be like to marry me?"

"Of course I do, lass." He said it so easily, like it was simply understood.

"You do? Because you never talk about it."

"Marriage, as in the legal sense? That's only the final, official step in the direction we've been headed, love. Once we've consummated our bond, we'll live as husband and wife, and as far as I'm concerned we will be. Then the marriage ceremony is largely a way to celebrate the joy of that bond, and establish us in all eyes as a household." He came to her, tenderly put a hand to her cheek, and looked into her eyes. "Is that not what you were expecting, lass? To be married to me as well as we two people can be?"

August touched his hand and held his gaze as she contemplated this revelation. It really should have occurred to her that this was the road they were heading down. But why was it that the word *marriage* scared her more than the idea of some fierce, bordering on obsessive emotional bond? Perhaps she didn't yet understand everything that marriage is, and what it means—or how it can change things, and people, for good or for bad.

"Och! Ye'll be wanting a proper proposal then, I reckon. Ring and all."

"Aye," she said and laughed. "I love watching you put on your kilt."

He gave her a flirty head tilt and grin, "Do ye now?"

She put on her best Scottish accent, "Aye, I do lad."

"You can be quite mercurial, ye ken that?"

"I know. Is it too much?"

He narrowed his eyes and looked to the ceiling in thought. "Well

. . ."

August smacked his arm. "Stop! You're going to give me a complex."

He laughed and sighed, then petted her upper arm, then her hair. He leaned in to kiss her and she received it tenderly. The sweet kissing deepened. Breath mixed with breath. Tongue danced with tongue. They pressed into each other as he stretched out alongside her on the downy platform. His kilt rode up on his lean muscled thigh; she reached out to stroke it and he sighed. They tried valiantly to keep their lips pressed together as they pulled off each other's tops. Once she had his shirt off of him she caressed his torso and nuzzled into his neck. He reached down and unzipped her long black boot, then the other, and August kicked them onto the floor. Their bodies were twisting and swaying together, pressing, warm. The scratch of his stubble rubbed against her soft cheeks in a thrill of friction. He pulled down her jeans and panties, his hands caressing her legs as he went, and she kicked them to the floor, then guided him to lay back down. Starting with her hands on his bare knees she massaged his thighs, his kilt riding higher with each stroke. The tartan curtain was finally pushed to his hip, revealing Faolan's urgency to her, and she took him in her hands, thrilling to his firmness, the pulse of his heat and desire.

"I want you so much!" She straddled his right thigh and pressed herself firmly against it as she took him into her mouth. He moaned and his body arched to her. He reached to touch her shoulders and her silky curls as she rocked on his thigh, taking her own pleasure as she stroked and sucked him, until they were both sweating, swollen to bursting. With a howl Faolan erupted for her, and she shuddered and gasped with her own release.

They lay back in each other's arms, blissful in their afterglow, softly touching each other and talking quietly about what they should do with the rest of their day.

"I want to save the castle until sunset," Faolan said. "Does that suit?"

"Yeah. Actually, my darling wolf, that's how my parents met. Right up there. Some purple twilight sky, as they told it, back in the sixties. It's funny to think of them here, in this city. Or me, here." She rolled over and gave him a kiss on the cheek, and looked into his eyes. "Edinburgh was always their place, and now I'm here too. All that separates us is twenty years of sunsets."

They both inhaled deeply and sighed, and rolled off of the bed to go tidy up.

"Holy shit, these towels are amazing!" August proclaimed, burying her face in one much like she would with Snow. Faolan nodded in agreement and gave a satisfied grunt as he dried his face. They pulled on their clothes—Faolan switching back to jeans—and straightened their hair.

"I thought you were wearing your kilt. Faolan … did you put that on just to tempt me?"

"I'll never confess," he answered with a devilish grin.

"I see. You've been peeking at my playbook, Mr. Wolf." She pulled on a boot and imperiously held her leg up for him, and he strode over to zip it.

"Thanks, lovah!" She swatted his behind before digging under the bed for the other boot.

"My pleasure. You know, I too met your father in this city."

"You did? How?"

"Well … actually … I was supposed to be having a date with your mother."

August straightened up instantly and spun to face him, hair flying. "Oh my god, what?" She spit out a stray curl. "What?!"

"Relax, Red."

"Get on with your story, please."

"It wasn't that kind of date, anyroad. I'd already met your mother, in Summerblynd, where she was staying, and we knew right off we were never meant to be lovers."

"Oh my god, Faolan! Could you please not use that word when talking about my mother?"

He sighed. "Right. Sorry. We immediately realized there was no chemistry between us."

"That's a little better, at least."

"But I had wanted to know her better, since I could tell right off she had a bit of lycan in her blood, and we became friendly over a week or two, to the point where we shared views on mixed blood and lycan culture and cumanta and the politics among otherkin. So she made some sort of school trip to Edinburgh and I was going to accompany her. As a friend," he was careful to interject. "But some bit of family business kept me home and she went alone. She came back to Summerblynd a few days later, completely besotted with your da."

"But how did you meet him in Edinburgh, then? You said you met him here at the same time."

"No, actually. It wasn't the same time."

"But you said …"

"I dinna say, but no worries."

"I think you—"

"Love, how much time would you like to spend arguing the point? Because I'd actually like to take you out into the city and have some fun."

She made a petulant grumble and peered at him. "But you said …"

"August."

"Fine." She crossed her arms.

"Alright then. She came back and told me all about Edinburgh. She had found some clear indications of lycan culture, specifically, throughout the city, but even more exciting to her was that there seemed to be a rather significant settlement at one point of mixed-bloods. She wanted me to see some of what she'd found."

August nodded, impatient but quiet.

"She'd managed to find out when Fletcher was speaking at university again and we scheduled a trip to go together. They were already exchanging letters by then and he was excited to see her. And it was during that trip that your da and I first met."

"Wow. It really makes me wonder how many stories I haven't heard yet."

"Thousands, no doubt."

She walked over to him, put her arms around his waist and looked up. "How about thousands of kisses? A kiss for every story. Here's the first." She offered her lips and he was only too happy to taste them.

"This I could get used to," he murmured.

"A story for a kiss. It's our new thing."

"I will certainly be thinking up the next. And the next."

"Let's go get some Edinburgh sights."

"Let's do." He offered his elbow and she hooked her arm into it. They strolled back down the Royal Mile, snacking as they went, and August was surprised to see how much of the foods and goods for sale were more international than particularly Scottish. "We've missed the festival season, I'm sorry to say," Faolan noted. "This street would be wall-to-wall people, some outrageously costumed, and there would be vendors and street performers and sudden eruptions of theatre and any number of remarkable things to see."

"Oh, that sounds awesome! Yes, we have to come back. When is it?"

"In August, actually," he winked.

They also did a bit of an otherkin tour. If one knew what to look for, one could find hints of a race of spider-like people scattered across ancient tomes in the library. Also, being so close to the North Sea, the *morrough*—mermaids—were a theme hidden throughout. Some of the otherkin influence was less subtle, like the unicorn perched atop the column of Mercat Cross, and now that she was looking at the world through wiser eyes, August couldn't believe she never saw before how folklore is made from something real. Giants, dwarves, trolls, mermaids, wolfmen—all of them were real in some way, living right alongside humans.

They walked and wandered for miles, poked into promising doorways, ate chocolates and fish and chips and more chocolates and kebabs and still more chocolates. They kissed by a small loch behind Holyrood House, and dreamed about their life together, before heading back up the hill toward Castle Rock.

The sun had dipped low when they reached the castle grounds, and it seemed that God, or Gaia, or Mother Nature—whoever was in charge—had deliberately painted the sky for them. The view of Edinburgh was breathtaking, with lights coming on all across the city, while the long autumn twilight made it easy to still see individual domes and spires among the buildings. August and Faolan stood on the stones near a huge and ancient cannon, leaning against a low wall that looked out over the city, exchanging stories and kisses. The place was getting quiet and empty and the stars were finally showing themselves.

"Ye can't see Canis Major just yet, but ye can see Venatrix, there." Faolan pointed into the darker part of the sky. "It's hard to make out in the glow of the city, but there's some of Andromeda as her head, bits of Pisces. What the Greeks named Pegasus—see the square, there? Aye, he's a little different here; ye can see the bow for Venatrix, with that bright star—Ailbeena, as I remember—as the tip of her arrow."

"Mom and Dad did a lot of constellation spotting. I wish I could say I remember better which were which."

"That's partly why I'm telling you. Is that a kiss-worthy story? That may be the other reason I'm telling you."

She felt her face get warm and her heart fill up. She leaned over and kissed his mouth, lingering for a few moments, until they both turned their heads back to the stars again.

"I've never heard of Venatrix. Did you make that up?"

"No, but your people did. The story is that Canis Major, literally the Great Dog, who possesses the brightest star in the sky, is being chased for all eternity by Venatrix, the Huntress. Some say she has no pity for him, and she will never give up her pursuit until she puts her arrow through his heart. I say it's more metaphorical—like Cupid's arrow—and that they are chasing each other around the year. Without the other, in fact, neither would be whole."

August made a thoughtful hmm and took a deep breath. "You always have such beautiful ways of looking at things, Fe."

"You do inspire a bit of it, ye ken? D' ye think we ought to head out for a bit o' supper?"

"I want to say something about my dad first."

"Ah, that's good. Go on then." He stood up straight and folded his hands in front of him.

"I'm going to say it to the sea."

He nodded. "Awreet. There to the north ye can see the firth."

August turned and faced the deep blue pool of ink that was now the Firth of Forth, opening to the North Sea. She gathered her windblown hair and smoothed it as best she could behind her shoulders.

"Dad ..." Her voice cracked and she cleared her throat. Faolan gently petted her back, then folded his hands again.

"Dad, I really miss you. I guess here they'd say 'I miss ye sae muckle.' I miss sitting in your lap in the study, reading big fat books together. I miss playing Old Maid and walks in the city, holding your hand and you making all your observations. I miss your voice telling me about the world. I'm glad I have those memories ..."

She sniffed and was silent for a moment.

"Also I want you to know that I'm not just here this week because of Faolan, even though that's a big part of it. I'm here to learn who I am. I'm here because I wanted to do something for you, so I came to bring your ashes to the earth of your homeland ... our homeland. I'm sorry that you, your family, had to leave this beautiful place. It must have been the right thing for your parents to do. I know a Scot doesn't run, but also family is everything. I want you to know that even though I wished you had told me who—or what—I am, I understand why you never did. I know you wanted to leave the fighting and keep what was left of the family from falling apart. And that you thought we'd have more time for you to show it all to me. But I'm grateful for the time we did have, and I promise you this, Daddy: I promise to be the best I can be, because I want you to see me, if you can, from wherever you are. I want to make you proud. I love you."

She turned to Faolan and buried her face in his chest and cried gently for a good few minutes.

"Thank you for bringing me here," she sniffed into his wet shirt. "I really do love it."

"I'm sorry this trip has brought so many tears for you. I'm afraid these might not be the last."

"Probably not. But maybe it's kind of good for me to get it out."

He squeezed her tighter. "You ready to go?"

"Yeah," she sniffed a bit. "I need to start carrying tissues."

Faolan pulled a handkerchief out of his pocket, "I should have had one of these for you yesterday. I'm going to lose my gentleman card."

"How old-fashioned."

"I'm kind of an old-fashioned guy."

She let out a wet muffled giggle through the cloth.

They listened to sounds of the autumn evening and the clop of their heels on the stones as they made their way back to their rooms.

Ashes to Water

August and Faolan had intended to rise early and head out for the Tay, but the opulence of their chamber, the luxurious comfort of their bed, and the soft warmth of each other's faintly soap-and-spice-scented bodies made it all but impossible to contemplate ever rejoining the rest of the world. Breakfast too ended up being more leisurely than rushed, and before they knew it, it was nearly noon.

Faolan had rented a Range Rover—"A bit less spartan than the old Type Two, eh?" he bantered with the grizzled fellow who'd brought it to the hotel—and piloted the big vehicle out of the city toward Perth and Meikleour. They spent the next hour talking and taking in the painted foliage, the fallow fields, the sparkling rivers, and the gray buildings slipping by under the blue afternoon sky.

"Ya know, I'm getting kind of sick of all of this beautiful scenery."

"Is that a fact? Well, I wouldn't worry," he grinned. "It's been uncharacteristically sunny of late. Before ye know it there'll be mist and damp and rain. We're about to pass Perth, love. Your pearl necklace is from there. And the boxes."

"Our wooden boxes?"

"Aye. One made for me and one ..." he stopped, forgetting himself.

"The other was for Iseabail, wasn't it? The one with the wolf on it?"

"Does that upset you?"

"I think I had it figured out a while ago. The keys fitting either box. I'd guessed I had Iseabail's, since she was family."

"Aye, that's it. Does this count as a story? Do I get a kiss?"

"I suppose." She leaned over and he presented his cheek for a peck. "I'll give you a proper one when we've made it to the river."

"Deal, then."

"Deal."

They crossed over the Tay to the north shore and drove on a bit further until they found a secluded area to park where they could approach the bank for the small ceremony they intended. Fletcher Evan's remains were in the back seat, in a small urn that August had insisted on buckling in. She felt her chest filling up with emotion as she pulled it from the car. The sky had turned grey, as Faolan had predicted, and August thought it fitting.

They skirted the sandy mud and dodged two clouds of midges to arrive at a spot near a grove of beeches at the water's edge. The grass was lush here, emerald green and soft, and August sat down and hugged the urn against her.

"The river's smaller than I thought it would be, Fe. Almost like a stream."

"It's bigger down by Perth. We crossed it on that big bridge with the arches under. Do you recall?"

"This is the same river?"

"Aye, it's the longest we've got."

August held the urn for a good long while before standing and holding it out in front of her.

"Ashes to water. I love you, Dad."

She opened the urn and swung it out from the bottom, scattering what was left of him into the Tay. She didn't cry this time; she felt all cried out. She was actually glad, in a way, that she could return her father home. For a moment, her heart pounded harder and her lips went a bit numb, but the feeling faded quickly, to be replaced by a deep sense of closeness to the place, and to her father—as if he were there in spirit, all around her.

"May I say some words?"

"Of course. Oh, I'm sorry, Faolan. I should have asked."

"Don't fret." Faolan stepped to the edge of the grass where it met the sandy sediment.

"Fletcher, whit ye hae tae go and die fer? A'm gonna quote a bit o' Rabbie Burns for ye. 'Farewell to the mountains high covered with snow; Farewell to the straths and green valleys below; Farewell to the forests and wild-hanging woods; Farewell to the torrents and loud-pouring floods.'"

They both gazed into the water for a moment, and Faolan went on.

"Fletcher m' lad, I miss the sound o' yer laugh and the smell o' yer pipe. I miss the long talks and the dreams we shared for a better world. You were a better man than most an' the best I ever knew. So I want to thank you, Fletcher Evan Archer, for seeing in me more than I saw in m'self. For letting me close to yer family, and for trusting me with their welfare. I only wish you were here so I could ask ye myself for your daughter's hand. I love August. I promise always to keep her best interests t' heart. 'Til my own dyin' breath. Farewell my friend. We'll have some whisky and toast you tonight. *Mar sin leat.*"

"That was beautiful," August whispered to him as they embraced, there on the banks of River Tay. Tears were brimming in her eyes. They breathed in unison and squeezed each other tight. By the time they let go August felt like a weight had been lifted from her.

"I feel a lot better."

"Brilliant. Let's go to the inn and check in, then celebrate with a toast to your da."

"Yes!"

Hand in hand they turned from the bank, and Faolan paused. He'd spotted a little patch of blue just a few yards away, and led them both over.

"Looks like your father left something for you," he said, bending to pluck a patch of small blossoms.

"Forget-me-nots."

"Late season, too. Kind of miraculous."

"It's been a miraculous kind of week."

A Parting Glass

The drive to Meikleour took them through a patchwork of fields and low hills with little cottages, on lanes hardly wider than their Rover, while dense stands of trees almost like rivers of autumn crisscrossed the road. August imagined it was places like these that had inspired the Hobbit holes of Tolkien's Shire, as adorable as dollhouses scattered on a bedspread quilt. They drove along a hedge of tall beech trees that had grown together into a towering wall; in their fall foliage, they seemed to turn the air itself lemony yellow. Moments later they were pulling in at the hotel. To August, Meikleour was a magical little place, and her heart broke a little for her family having to leave such a home behind, assuming Summerblynd wasn't much different.

"Whoa," she said quietly once they got inside the old inn. She'd had no idea one place could hold such potent levels of charm, and half-wondered if someone could die from an overdose of it. There were old-fashioned Halloween decorations all around the room, both handmade and store-bought, from any number of past decades. Her favorite was a straw witch sitting on the front desk by a bubbling cauldron, oozing the mist that August's father had dubbed "fauxg." The desk itself had to be three hundred years old, and it was scattered with what seemed to be carved vegetables glowing with candles inside them.

"What are those?" she wondered aloud.

"They're turnips made to lanterns. Tradition." Faolan explained, and rang the call bell.

"Oh." August tightened her lips and puffed out her cheeks—so many things to learn in her rediscovered homeland.

A middle-aged man with dark hair and a round belly appeared. "Welcome to the Meikleour Inn. What'll I do for ye?"

"We have a reservation. Conall."

"Aye, have it here." He gave Faolan a sidelong glance. "Haven't seen a Conall 'round these parts in mickle a year."

"There en't many of us left."

"Well, thank …" The man stopped mid-sentence and cleared his throat.

Faolan squinted at him, but said nothing.

Apparently the Conalls aren't particularly revered in these parts, August mused.

"Well, good to have ye at the inn, Mr. Conall. Honeymoon, is it then?" He glanced over at August.

"Of a sort, aye," Faolan replied.

The clerk nodded and eyed August a bit more closely this time. August smiled, a little awkwardly.

"Well, if ye plan on visiting around a bit, we have some brochures here …"

"Oh, we'll do awreet. I'm familiar with the place. Anyroad, we'll be visiting the cemetery at St. Bartholomew tomorrow midday. Perhaps you can arrange a packed lunch for us?"

"Aye. Have it for ye here at the desk around 9, if that suits."

Faolan nodded. "Thanks, brother."

"Ah, yer welcome, sir. Here's the key to Cottage Tay, the furthest out, near the row of trees."

August and Faolan retrieved their bags from the back of the Rover and shouldered them down the cobblestone path to Cottage Tay, crossing a tiny bridge over an even tinier stream along the way.

"Fe, this place is so cute I can't stand it."

"I'm glad you're pleased."

"Do you think you should have given them a fake name? What if Ciardha gets wind of us here?"

"I wouldn't worry, love. The keep is very secluded. And as the gentleman put it so candidly, they haven't had a Conall around in a while."

August watched Faolan as he changed into his kilt and a lighter-weight sweater. His chin scruff had come in quite thick by this time in the afternoon, and she felt herself getting warmer thinking about how it would scratch her tenderest skin. Could she be more smitten with this man?

"You belong on the pages of a 'Hot Scots' calendar or something."

He winked. "Who says I aren't?"

"It's too late to take care of the chest tonight, isn't it?" she tried, fairly sure of the answer but unable to put aside a prickle of unease. Burying the chest would have been the milestone in their relationship that would let them take the next step together in their little cottage this very night. But, truth be told, August didn't feel quite ready at this moment. The ceremonies for her father had been quite enough letting go for these past two days. As unlikely as it seemed, she realized she'd rather wait to do all of that tomorrow—the trunk, the moving on, the preparing for Summerblynd and the keep.

"Aye, lass—it is getting late. We wouldn't have enough light even if we started right now. Does that make you unhappy?"

"Honestly, I think it's a good night to toast my dad and rest. How do you feel about it? It's your farewell."

"I'm happy to spend the night drinking to your da and resting up. I can tell you some stories and collect a few more kisses." He flashed her a dashing smile.

"That smile will get you no—oh, who am I kidding?"

She peeled off her boots and jeans. "I think I've had enough boots and jeans for the week."

"We ought to get you a kilt."

"I'd like that. So, hankies and kilts on our way back through Glasgow?"

"Aye, I think so."

She stood there in her bra and panties, pale and beautiful—nothing more than wisps of nylon between the two of them—and she reveled in his obvious appreciation.

"Put on my necklace, Fe?" She held out the pearl necklace he'd given her—the Conall Pearl, an antique from the long-ago time when the Tay itself gave up pearls—and lifted up her heavy curtain of hair, exposing the back of her neck. She could see herself in the wall mirror and watched his face as he leaned into her neck and placed a gentle kiss. He took the necklace as he put his arms around her, brushing sweater sleeve to bare skin. She gave a little shudder of delight.

"Chilly?"

"No."

"Ah."

He fastened the clasp and she turned around for one more kiss before pulling on a kelly green sweater dress over her head and sliding her feet into comfy short boots. The pearl was framed quite fetchingly by the V of her neckline.

"You look incredible," he murmured, eying her as she moved in the body-skimming dress. "Incredible."

August felt herself blush. She stepped in close, pressing her upper arms against the sides of her breasts to deepen her cleavage. "Do you like the necklace?" she asked coyly.

He nodded slowly, appreciatively. "Aye, I do." He put his hands on her waist and slid them up to her bosom. "You look good enough to eat."

She shivered again. "Ooh! A little later, Wolfy. Right now you need greasy pub food, and fast."

The pub took up half of the ground floor of the main hotel building. It was bigger than August imagined it would be, but it felt close and cozy with low ceilings, rough-hewn wood beams and electric lighting in old gas fittings, turned down low. She was glad there were no jazz women in micro spandex dresses to arouse her jealousy here, which only reminded her that she still had a bit of growing up to do about that.

August had a look around at the rest of the patrons in the room as she and Faolan stepped up to the bar. There were locals and travelers mingled—she felt fairly confident she could tell which was which—and the place had gotten fairly crowded. From snippets of conversation she overheard that at least one other American was visiting a relative from the town, which seemed to her an odd coincidence in such a small location. Her eye was caught by a very old couple who looked like they might have held down the same table every other night for last fifty years, and it gave August a little pang, thinking about love and growing old. And how it often didn't work out that way. There was a woman at the corner of the bar that August caught sight of a couple of times, though her shawl was blocking most of her features. It seemed like she was checking out Faolan. *Not that I can blame her for that, because damn, he sure does look amazing tonight.* August also noted one of the smaller tables had three chairs and three plates of food, but after a few moments she realized no one was actually sitting there.

"That's weird," she pointed to it. "There's no bags or coats, just food at an empty table."

"That's for All Hallows Eve, my love. For the dearly departed who might come to sup."

"Ah, interesting. But isn't that tomorrow? It's only the 30th."

"Aye, you're correct." Faolan looked thoughtful. "Well, for some it begins at sundown the night before. And having a gander at the rest of this place, I think Halloween is rather a specialty here."

The bartender, Tommy, was the same man that checked them in at the desk earlier. They let him choose the whisky, which seemed to make him feel honor-bound to get it just right.

"Here, this is the one!" He said, handing them tumblers with two fingers of amber liquid. It was smoky and peaty, and they took the drinks, along with a bowl of Scotch eggs, back to a table in the corner.

"This smells like a bonfire."

Faolan sniffed his glass. "Indeed it does, lass. Isn't it wonderful?"

August shrugged and threw hers back. "Warm."

"I smell something familiar," he said, scanning the tables for something.

"Like what?"

"I don't know, a flower maybe. It's hard to tell with all of this pipe smoke and whisky."

He shrugged and they both looked into each other's eyes and smiled. He waved Tommy over for a refill and ordered bangers and mash for the two of them. They sat there, sipping, getting warm on whisky and love. August told Faolan New York and Halloween stories. She told him about her old boyfriends and the stuff she kept locked in her wolf box—the box that had once been Iseabail's. The realization did not give August the jealous moment she might have expected. She smiled at that.

They toasted Fletcher Evan Archer at least five times before they headed back to their room, drunk on fine Scottish whisky and sleepy from heavy pub food. They didn't notice the woman under the shawl was still keeping her eyes on them as they nearly closed down the pub.

They peeled off their clothes and tucked under the covers in their underwear.

"I love you, Faolan. Do I say it too much?"

"It's impossible for me to hear it too much."

"Good. This was a good day."

"Aye."

"You will owe me some kisses tomorrow for the stories I told."

163

"Oh, I didn't realize it worked both ways."

"Of course it does, silly man."

He smiled contentedly, took her hand and kissed it, then kissed her gently on the lips before settling back down into the pillows.

"I love you, Faolan." Her head was spinning gently, like floating. She could smell the alcohol as she breathed out, and heard herself say "I love you," one more time.

She fell asleep as Faolan replied, "I love you, August."

The Watcher

She had been watching for the couple in the pub. She'd heard last week that Faolan Conall was coming to town, as she knew he had before, but she had to see it for herself. There was only the one inn in Meikleour, and none in Summerblynd, so for the past two days she'd parked herself in the breakfast room, with a clear view of the desk, and drank tea all through the midday, hoping to catch him.

Making her way to Meikleour alone would have been impossible just last week, with her ever-watchful brother still controlling her every move. Both of her brothers had, for so many years. But with James gone last November, and Bruce finally following him only days ago, she was now able to move about, a free woman. She couldn't remember the last time she didn't have some man telling her what she could and could not do. She didn't really believe she would see Faolan; the timing just seemed too improbable. But in case he did show, she had a satchel with her to give him.

She had been shocked to see him enter that afternoon with a beautiful young woman. Her plan to approach him when he arrived was dashed then, and she was left unsure what to do. She had slipped to the shadowy side of the doorway to listen as he talked to Tommy at the desk.

Tomorrow he would be at the cemetery, she heard. She knew why. She also knew he wouldn't bring that girl with him. Not to visit the grave of his long lost love.

All Hallows Eve

Just beyond the fields of Meikleour stands a small church, little visited today, made of ancient stone and delicate stained glass. Faolan and August pulled into the dusty lot to the side of St. Bartholomew and stopped in a dewy puddle of shade. The whole area was dotted with mature trees and sleeping rosebushes, beautiful and serene—a place somebody would come throughout their whole life, from baptism to consecration to wedding to funeral, and all else in between.

"This place is just so beautiful, Faolan. Truly."

They wore practical clothes today. They looked like an ad for Scottish pants and sweaters.

"You should stand there like a Ken doll, and let me take a picture. You belong in a catalog photo."

He laughed, but dutifully posed, head slightly cocked to the side, his fingers all together, hands stiff, elbows slightly bent—a frozen smile on his face. August snapped a photo with her pink Le Clic camera.

"That's some camera you've got there."

"I know. My mom gave it to me as I was leaving. It looks like something a six-year-old princess would use."

"I can't imagine why she thought of you. You got the shot?"

"Yeah. Smartass."

"You ready to do this, love?" He stepped in close and looked her in the eye and waited.

"I think so. What about you?"

"I am."

He pulled the trunk out of the back of the Rover and August

166

grabbed the shovel. She followed him toward a hedgerow and a surprisingly large cemetery beyond; as they rounded the back of the church they walked right past a small car tucked in the shadows without realizing it was there.

"Wow. That's a lot of dead people ..." Then she thought better of the remark. "Sorry."

"This is an old church, an old town. The faithful have to go somewhere."

"Did you go to this church?"

"I didn't. This is a hunter church. This was Iseabail's church. We imagined we were going to be married here."

August felt a stab in her stomach. In her heart. "What?"

"I'm sorry, lass. I should have thought. Does that upset you?"

"I guess it should have occurred to me." Her pangs at that moment were for Faolan rather than herself. She could feel his loss. This beautiful little church and the quaint town—the generations of family, tradition, history, all denied him. She felt a lump rise in her throat. "I'm really sorry. Are you sure you want to do this?"

He kept walking, "I do. I want to do it, and to move on. The closer I get to it, the more sure I feel about it."

The day was brisk and she could see his breath when he talked. His nose was a little red. She wanted to throw her arms around him and take away all of the pain he'd ever suffered by hate and prejudice and grief. He wasn't what those hunters—well, her own family, her great-great-grandparents—he wasn't what they thought he was, some disgusting beast. It was all so much to take, as they wound their way between the gravestones of her now-silent kin. She had the blood of his first true love coursing through her veins. She had the blood of those who would take Iseabail from him and let her die. August felt the shame of these things, even though she could do nothing about them.

"I'm sorry for what my family has done to you."

"Fear and hate are all the same, no matter the family," he absolved her.

Their serpentine trek came to a halt. She set down the shovel, taking her cue from Faolan setting down the trunk. He stood gazing down at a headstone that didn't look eighty years old. It hardly looked weathered, carved from a pearly blue granite with Celtic knotwork and flowers around the edges.

Iseabail Ayrshire Huntar
Daughter, Wife, Mother
Beloved
June 1878 – April 1903

"You put this here, didn't you?"

"Aye. The one her husband put here was thin and cheap. I couldn't bear it."

August nodded and pulled a red knit cap that her gran had given her tight over her head. She held herself and watched Faolan in his contemplative sorrow. She felt utterly helpless to do anything useful.

He squatted and ran his hand over the headstone. He tidied up stray leaves and twigs, then stood back up.

"Well, nothin' to it but ta do it." He grabbed up the shovel and put the spade tip into the dirt, stood his foot on the blade and pushed it into the earth next to where Iseabail lie.

"Faolan?" A soft feminine voice came from behind them. Both startled, they spun around, the shovel hitting the ground and August almost losing her balance on her twisted legs.

A pale woman was standing behind them, no more than twelve feet away. Short, but very feminine in her figure, she was cloaked in a gray shawl, her long dress a gray-blue.

Faolan stared and thrust his head forward. He then tipped his nose into the air, and in seconds he was partially transformed. He howled, first tentative, then deep and long. It startled August. She had never seen Faolan lose control that way, and she soon felt her own aspect shifting, her ears and fingers and toes starting to tingle, her mouth and gums hot and starting to pulse. An animal instinct was rising within her that she didn't understand, and she drew a deep breath and took a couple of steps forward to get a closer look at this woman. Far from frightened, the woman was smiling at Faolan's transformation. Then she looked directly at August and lowered her shawl from her head.

Her eyes were an unusual, almost ghostly pale blue-gray. Her ginger-blonde hair bore subtle streaks of white. She looked familiar. August looked over at Faolan, who was now less wolf and more man again, but his breathing was deep and fast. His eyes were glowing.

"You were at the pub last night," August identified her, and waited for some kind of reply. But the woman only stood there, hands folded, and smiled and returned her attention to Faolan.

"Come!" She called him like a dog. Her grin wide and her arms opened to receive him.

He started towards her, but hesitated when he saw August looking at him.

"Who is this, Faolan?" August asked in confusion. "One of your exes? Is this Brynn from your journals? She looks like a Brynn." She stepped towards the woman and put her hand out.

"I'm August Archer."

The woman grasped August's hand warmly. "I'm Iseabail Archer."

August's mouth went dry and fell open, and she dropped the woman's hand and stepped back. She looked to Faolan, who was now fully man again, and she could only watch as the two old lovers embraced each other with joy and passion enough to make August uncomfortable. She felt almost like she was invading their privacy, but she was also afraid to turn away, thinking she might never see Faolan again if she did. She thought she could hear the entire rest of her life falling in pieces around her.

After the emotional and physical intensity of their reunion started to wind down a little, Faolan stood back and took in the sight of his long-lost Issy, his eyes wet, his hands not leaving her.

"How is this possible? I don't understand how this has happened, love. Where have you been?"

"It's a bit of a story, Faolan, but I'm happy to spend the time tellin' it to ye. And your young friend there."

Faolan seemed to come back to earth for a moment realizing that August was still there.

"Oh, August, love," he said, and waved her over. She felt rooted into her spot, but managed to pull one boot free, then the other, and soon she was standing in a tight circle with them.

"Iseabail—you're going by Archer?—" he titled his head in question. She nodded. "Iseabail Archer, this is your great-granddaughter August."

"My great-granddaughter? That canna be! But lookin' at her now, I see the family resemblance. Green eyes instead of blue, the dark hair so dramatic, but almost the image of me at that age."

"Well, not really, my brows are way different, and my chin, well I got the chin from my mother's side …"

August did not like the idea that she looked too much like Iseabail because it made her think that was why Faolan was with her. It made her stomach hurt now, looking at the middle-aged version of herself. The two people in front of her were all smiles, but for August everything was coming apart. This was supposed to be the moment Faolan was going to let go and move on. Why was it that every time something amazing happened, something shitty was soon to follow? Why could she never escape the shadow of this woman?

"Well come and let me put my arms around my great-granddaughter."

"You look like you're not even fifty years old. This is so weird." She could feel jealousy sucking her into its murky blackness, resentment suffocating her like a hot, wet blanket. This was not a happy reunion—it was a fucking disaster.

She did not want to hug this woman, but she did anyway. Half-heartedly. Iseabail only continued to smile, placid and patient as the grandmother she was.

"This is for you, Faolan," she said and held up a rather large doeskin satchel.

He took it by the strap and regarded it. Wiped away some more tears, and felt the outside of the bag. "What is it?"

"Letters."

August felt her face get hot and her heart start pounding hard and fast.

"Letters?" He lifted the flap and reached inside and pulled out an envelope addressed to him, from her. He pulled out another, and another. He squatted and she did too, smiling at him as he laughed and cried and dug through hundreds of letters that were still sealed.

He held a fistful of letters and looked into Iseabail's face, "I don't ken, why dinna you send them?"

"I did. They were always intercepted. I only discovered them last week after James and Bruce died."

"Your brothers?"

"They'd been hiding them. I don't know why they didn't just throw them away. Gods, you look fantastic." She reached up and touched a loose curl beside his face, twirled her finger into it, then touched his cheek. "I've missed ye."

He reached up and touched her cheek and looked into her eyes. "Blue as I remember. Fair. So fair." His smile was soft now, and his eyes full of thoughts.

"What's that?" She pointed to the chest of his tortured journals. "Why've you brought that to my grave, love?"

He hesitated, wondering how to explain it all in just a few words. "It's a goodbye."

"A goodbye?" She tilted her head, not understanding.

"See, Issy, we came here … August and I, we came here to say goodbye."

She looked over at August. August gave a weak smile and tried to hide the fact that she was so nervous she wanted to puke.

"Did you bring the child here to show her the history of her people? A goodbye? To the departed?"

Was she simply being obtuse or did she truly not understand the subtext of her presence? "I'm not—" August began, a little too loudly, then swallowed hard and softened her tone. "I'm not a child."

Faolan leaned over and took August by the hand and gently pulled her to his side. "Iseabail, I am in love with August." He put his arm around her. August felt jittery and her body shook, despite the affirmations. "August is to be my primary—my only—mate. I came here to release my bond to you."

Something flashed behind Iseabail's eyes, but what it was August couldn't guess. She remained quiet and still, even as tears welled up and slid down her cheeks. Without even a quiver in her voice, she said, "Of course. It's been … what?"

"Nine—" Faolan began.

"Ninety years almost since we last saw each other. Our constellations forever chasing 'round the earth." August thought Iseabail might laugh. "Now I ken how she wore your pearl last night."

She regarded August with a steady gaze. "It looked lovely on you, my dear," she said with a gentle smile, before turning back to Faolan.

"Please, Faolan—keep the letters. Maybe someday we can talk about them."

August folded in on herself, wanting to be as small as possible.

She was the one between them now—between Iseabail and Faolan, just as Iseabail had been between her and Faolan. She wished she could slink away, hide in the hole in that tree trunk over there, and just stay there until this was all resolved.

Iseabail fixed her shawl back over her head. "Granddaughter. Take care of him. He's worth the effort." She nodded a goodbye to August, turned and walked away.

"Issy!" Faolan called out to her. "Issy, where can I find you? For someday."

She turned around. "Raven's Loch. It's mine now."

Then she was gone.

A thick fog hung in the air between August and Faolan. She had no idea what to say, and hoped he would say something first.

"Well, what do ye know about that?"

August could hardly look at him. The weight of what just happened was settling on her now—what it could mean for the future of her and Faolan. What it meant for her family. What it could mean for Faolan, or even whether it was good or bad, she didn't know. It was a lot to process.

"I just met my great-grandmother … And my rival."

He turned to her and chewed on his next words, "August, I know this is terrible timing—"

"Oh? Is there some time that this would have been good? Like after we'd slept together? Or after we got married? Or had babies? Would it have been good for the one true imprinted love of your life to emerge from the grave at any of *those* times?"

"August …"

"No, I think it's better now. Before I'm fully imprinted on you and you haven't sorted things out with your ghost lover. God, I can't believe all of the things I know about her from your journals, and she's here … alive. I am totally creeped out right now. It's like watching somebody step out of some old sepia photo and into real life."

Faolan listened to August go on, his brows knit with concern and looking utterly sick over the idea he was hurting her.

"Don't look at me like that, Faolan. It makes *me* feel bad for *you*. I get to feel bad for me right now."

He took in a long deep breath, unknitted his brow as best he could and nodded.

"I think it's going to be alright, lass."

August crossed her arms, more from a sense of self-protection than indignation, and threw a glance at the trunk of journals. "What are you going to do with that?"

He looked at the trunk, and then at August. He had nothing to say.

"Yeah. This is gonna be awesome. We'd better go back to the inn, I have a lot of journaling and thinking to do."

The ride from the cemetery was cold and lonely for both of them. August looked out of her widow and watched the edge of the road go by, the grass a blur, then looked off into the distance where things were nearly still as they passed. Perspective is illusion, she thought. The car was going the same speed no matter how quick the scenery seemed to go by, near or far.

Faolan went in to the office and set them up with another couple of nights at the inn. Summerblynd itself was only forty minutes away, and the keep another twenty deep into the woods—if you knew where to look—but Summerblyd itself had no inns. "People visiting Summerblynd are vistin' kin," Faolan had told her. "So they stay with kin." Whatever kin either of them had in Summerblynd, Faolan had suggested that he and August needed time alone to sort things out. Which probably was true. She felt herself resenting Iseabail anew. Even though she had no idea how or why the woman had reappeared, she wished her back in the grave, kin or not.

They were too grim to eat in the pub, and their packed lunch had gone bad, except for the fruit, crackers and wine, so Faolan ordered something more substantial from the pub to bring back to the cottage. He was drained from his brief transformation and needed plenty of food.

Before she could even consider talking to Faolan about what would happen next, August needed to sort some things out in her journal.

October 31, 1984
This has been the most exciting week of my life, romantically. This has been the most upsetting week of my life, romantically. Both of these sentences are true.
I don't know what to do with all of these feelings I'm having. They're all

mixed up and confusing. I love Faolan and he makes me so happy, so I want him for myself. I love Faolan and I want him to be happy, so I want him to be with Iseabail.

Why are so many of my journal entries about conflicting feelings? I suppose because that's when I need to write them down the most. To sort it. To make sense of it all.

Right now I feel angry and jealous and selfish. I want him for myself. I want her to disappear. That's what my heart wants. My gut is jealous and lashing out. I want to push her. I want to scream at her. Why couldn't she just stay dead? Why did she have to come in and step on my moment? Why did she have to tread on my landscape? This is mine now. He's mine now.

My more evolved self, the more intellectual part of me is informed by the part of my heart that is sad for Faolan's losses. She could tell him so much about what he has been wondering all these years. Where she's been. Where the baby is buried. How sad is that?! He could tell her how long he'd held tight to his bond with her. Why do I even care if she gets that from him? Aren't I supposed to hate my rivals? Isn't this a competition and I'm supposed to want to win? Ugh! I hate this!

Today was simple—we bury the trunk. We come back to the cottage. We eat, he gives me a bath, we make love. He fills me, and I engulf him. I imprint, he imprints. We are bonded. Our souls married. This was MY wedding night and she ruined it. She's always there, floating around like a ghost, ruining things.

I don't even know what to do with all of this anger. I want my better self to prevail. I want to be more philosophical—love him without expectation. But that's just an ideal isn't it? To make us appreciate what we have, when we have it? I suppose if you've no expectations, you've no disappointment. In love, this is a big benefit. But love is full of expectation. Or is it? Is that not really love? Is love really the part where I want him to go off with her and be happy, and the other part—the possessiveness and resentment—are those something else that just comes along with love if you don't grow it the right way? Or if I don't grow the right way?

If I'm being totally truthful with myself, I'm also curious as hell what the deal is with her being alive. Why? Why is she alive? How could she do that to Faolan all this time? Maybe she couldn't help it. I don't want to know if she's had a hard life or if something bad happened because then I'm going to have to feel sorry for her, and I just want to keep hating her.

That goddamned trunk is in the car. He's going to want to read those letters she gave him. I'm going to be burning to know what they say. It feels like disloyalty for him to read them now. He should only be reading letters from me. ME! I sound like a spoiled child. Maybe I am a child. Maybe I'm too young for him. Maybe he's too old for me. Maybe they belong together and that's why this happened, before he and I had lives that were too combined and too hard to pull apart without losing too many vital pieces of ourselves.

Can I find a way to see this as something good? Can I find a way to not be afraid of what's coming? Even more than what will happen when we go to Ciardha! I'm more afraid of her than him. Can I make myself see this as a beautiful intervention of fate? A chance to grow? I don't know. It doesn't seem that way now. Right now I just want to tear her heart out and scream at her. How grown up is that?

Ghosts. Halloween spirits. Tomorrow is All Saints Day. Go back to your grave Iseabail, you ruin everything.

August couldn't write anymore because her fingers were tingling and her mouth was burning. She dropped her pen and doubled over. Everything hurt, all the way down to her bones. Her ears pointed, her face made a sick cracking noise, like celery being snapped. She could see a snout growing between her eyes and tasted blood in her mouth as teeth pointed and elongated.

Faolan swung open the door with his arms full of boxed dinners, when he saw her on the floor by the desk, bent over and moaning. He set the packages aside and ran to her, "Lass, are ye alright? What's the matter? Are ye sick?"

She fell to her side, groaning and shaking and he reached for her hand and noticed it was almost fully changed into a paw. He rolled her towards him to better see her. "Lass! You're transforming! It's alright, I've got you. Don't worry, I've got you." He stroked her hair and slipped the knife from his waist to cut her clothing loose. Within a minute she was not just a werewolf but fully transformed to canine—a magnificent red wolf, with sable ticking all through her coat and a dark sable back from forehead to tail. She sat up, then stood on all fours, and let out a fierce long howl. Faolan felt everything she was communicating in that cry—a shared language of rage and sorrow. His heart near to burst at the pain and beauty of it.

He put his arms around her and petted her. He gazed into her copper-green eyes and whispered into her ear, "August, never worry. I love you, always. Whatever happens, I love you always."

She whined and hopped up onto the bed and curled into a ball, shaking gently. Faolan removed his clothes and transformed himself into a wolf of shining pewter and black streaks, nearly twice her size. He hopped up onto the bed with her, their bodies making an interlocking circle of fur, limbs and tails, until they both fell asleep.

Inns and Outs

August woke before daybreak, naked, looking human and feeling famished. She lay awake in Faolan's arms, letting powerful and conflicting emotions flow through her unhindered and unexamined. However much she was a hunter—and she laughed at herself to realize how briefly she had known even that part—she was a werewolf. She remembered glimpses of dreams: an ancient world, where no human civilization yet existed; werewolves sitting at a long table, with roasted bodies piled on platters; people with snares and ropes, so many people, dragging dead wolves by their necks. And she had dreamed of running—faster than thought, trees blurring as they whipped past her—and leaping as though borne on the air. She wanted to inhabit this moment for the rest of the day, for a month, for a year, just processing all the impossible feelings, with Faolan wrapped warm around her.

August thought of a hundred different things to talk out with Faolan, mostly questions about his feelings, and about how his perspective had changed. But whenever she tried to imagine where the conversation would go, it all fell apart. What could he say about his lifelong-bonded lover reappearing, just as he was ready to let her go? What could he possibly tell August about what he would do next? How could he even know? And how could she trust that anything he told her would hold up?

With her emotions so at sea, August's practical side came forward to take the controls for a while. Not only was there Ciardha to deal with, she was also going to be meeting her kin soon—hunter clans, all of them—and she knew she would have to prove herself, if only for her own satisfaction.

She rolled out of bed and looked for yesterday's clothes to put on, finding them shredded where Faolan had cut them away from her. "Shit. I liked that shirt," she said simply, and the outlandishness of the situation registered as hilarious, though she was not interested in laughing right now. She headed for the cube fridge, took a few swigs from a bottle of milk, then gulped down the rest of it. She walked past the bed again, kissing Faolan on his forehead as a thank-you for being there for her last night, and went to the long case they'd had shipped to Edinburgh. She snapped the latches open, picked up her bow and hip quiver, and headed towards the door.

"Where ye goin' with that?" Faolan was awake, and leaning up on one elbow.

"Practice. I'm nervous as hell about meeting the family."

"Clothes, Red? Right now ye look like Diana herself."

She looked down and let out a short laugh. "Ah. Right. Didn't seem important."

"Let's both put something on, and I'll come with ye."

August grunted in reply and dug in the other bag for the only pair of shorts she'd brought. She was glad Faolan hadn't tried flirting with her, despite their both being naked. Right now she was holding him in a kind of limbo. She knew somehow, from their being wolves together, that she would always be kin with Faolan Conall. What she could not guess was where he would decide to call home, and who his bonded mate would be, and so she put those feelings in a box, for the time being. And she was very glad she could. Right now, she felt like she could do anything.

They hiked through the morning mist into a secluded spot at the edge of the river as the sun was rising. She ran along the banks, hopped over rocks and let arrows loose into trees. She loped through the high grasses, crept alongside fallen trees, and galloped through shallow parts of the water across slippery river stones. She didn't lose her footing once. The arrows struck in bridge pilings, mossy logs, the P in a no-trespass sign—one even pinned a falling leaf to its own tree trunk—and all of them exactly what she'd been aiming for.

Faolan followed, arms crossed and eyes watchful, like a proud but nervous father. When she'd exhausted her quiver, Faolan came forward to help her collect the arrows.

"Don't! I'll do it."

He rooted himself in his spot, and re-crossed his arms. At some point he kicked a stone into the water.

Without bothering even to brush their hair, August and Faolan sojourned to the pub, wrinkled and rough-looking. The other guests and pub denizens who were enjoying the morning's scones and tea elbowed and whispered to each other at the sight of them.

They sat down at the table near the window and ordered five fry-ups to split between them. The waiter wasn't sure he heard right. He walked off shrugging and muttering.

They'd each drained two cups of coffee by the time the food began arriving and the both of them cut and speared and downed the meats and tatties as if they hadn't eaten in a week.

"Folks are starin'," Faolan said low, and with a hint of amusement. "I reckon they've not seen a lass your size tuck in like that before."

"Can't look. Eating."

By the time she was three-quarters through her second breakfast she was feeling less urgent and slowed down a bit, picking at her tomatoes and dragging them through the baked beans.

"They took the plates away from the ghost table." She pointed her fork over her shoulder.

"Aye. The ghosts are supposed to go back to where they came from today."

"Huh," August grunted. She watched Faolan swallow a banger whole. "I know some guys who would pay to watch you do that."

"Yeah? Well, they can watch, but I'm a one-wolf man."

"Are you?"

"Aye, lass."

They held each other with their eyes for a moment, then August looked away, out of the window.

"Why didn't you bury that trunk?"

"I don't know. I think perhaps I wanted to be able to let her know I honored her memory." He pushed away his third plate and folded his arms on the table and watched her staring outside the window at nothing in particular.

"I don't think there's a way around it, Faolan. I think you have to see her and talk things out."

"I'm not going to pretend I don't have a thousand burning questions for Iseabail, because of course I do. My body is sick with want to talk to her, but, I'm not sure it's a good time for that."

"I think maybe I need you to do it, for me. Well, not for me, for you for me."

He tilted his head and dipped a brow. "Eh?"

"You just said you're sick with want for her—"

"That's not—"

She raised her voice, cutting him off, "It doesn't matter, Faolan! I know and you know that you're dying to talk to her and figure out what

179

happened. It's here, it's already happened. There is no escaping it!" Some of the patrons turned and looked their direction.

"Could you lower your voice, lass?"

"Don't tell me what to do!" August shouted. Other conversations stopped. People were looking nervously around the room for the waiter. Faolan remained unruffled.

"I asked you, and I'm asking you again, to lower your voice. Please."

He reached a hand out to take hers. She started to pull back, but let him envelope it. That spark that always came from him went right through her and she softened enough to let him talk.

"I'm here with you by choice. I could have chased after her. I wanted to …"

A sharp look from August.

"I wanted to, but I didn't. Because I don't want to lose you."

"We'll see how you feel after you read a hundred of her letters."

"Let's get ourselves together for Summerblynd and the keep, and worry about the rest of this later. It's waited this long, it can wait a bit longer."

August couldn't understand how Faolan could suppress his urgency. Was it his love for her, or was it more a sense of duty to be where he thought he belonged? She didn't want to win him that way. She was nobody's duty. As little as she knew about being in love, she knew she would not be happy that way for long. He had to love her, and only her, or it wasn't going to work—not as a marriage.

She wanted to lay it all out in her journal—try to figure out where the real meanings were to be found. But if she wrote for three days straight she couldn't cover the emotions going through her right now. She wanted Faolan to go find out if he was supposed to be with Iseabail, but she also didn't want him to leave her side. How was she going to let him go if she lost out?

It also occurred to August that Iseabail might not be the woman that Faolan had idolized all this time. And the more she thought about it, the more she settled on the idea that Iseabail couldn't possibly be so perfect. Nobody could. He'd built her up in his memory as some golden angel, but she just can't be. *Because she's been alive all these years, letting him think she was dead.*

So which was the wisest path to take: protect their relationship from this invasion from the past by covering it over and calling it irrelevant? Or let Faolan test his bond with Iseabail to see if it really was as vital as he'd imagined all this time? Hormones and pheromones were powerful chemicals, August had learned already; they can make you see things that aren't there, or exaggerate the things that are. Would Faolan ever see Iseabail as she truly was? Then August wondered if everything holding her and Faolan together was just chemistry. Her faith in love was well and truly shaken at this point, and she had not one clue how he would proceed—though honestly, how could anyone be expected to know what to do in a situation like this?

Faolan put a hand on her shoulder and gently stirred her from her reverie. "Lass, whatever it is can wait."

"That's easy for you to say—you're not going to lose your love, no matter what happens."

He knew he couldn't argue that inequity away—August was the one who stood to lose the most in this mess. And even as he swallowed down his urge to see Iseabail—to hold her and kiss her again, not just in memory but in reality—he understood that his commitment to August was precious, and to strangle it while still so new would haunt him just as Iseabail had done all these years. There was nearly nothing in the world more valuable than loyalty, and he would not abandon August. She was the first to love him in a way that made him want to save him from himself, or believe that a lasting relationship was even possible. And, he realized, she was the first one to make him seriously think about raising a family since he had lost Iseabail all those years ago.

He got up and tugged her arm gently, and she stood. He put his big arms around her—he could have hugged two of her—and she tentatively squeezed back.

"That's not a hug," he said into her tousled mop. "Surely you can muster more strength than that, lass."

She had already wanted to hug him—she just wanted him to ask for it. Little noting or caring at this moment how often she got in the way of her own happiness, she squeezed him tighter and it did make her feel a bit better.

They went back to the cottage and showered together, though rather platonically, and August didn't know if that should make her feel more or less secure about the whole Iseabail thing. But she was sick of analyzing everything and instead closed her eyes to all but the process of washing up, and then restraining her unruly hair. She pulled on clothes that were comfortable and practical for trespassing and sneaking about in the woods: snug-fitting brown pants, dark green long-sleeved shirt, and her favorite brown doeskin boots she wore to practice shooting. They were tight, quiet, flexible, and comfortable—a sort of moccasin that her mom and Two Feathers had given her as a gift.

"I need to call Mom. I can't go off to this place without talking to my mom first."

"Awreet."

Faolan coached her as she arranged the call through a transatlantic operator; her mother picked up after the fourth ring.

"I wasn't sure you were going to answer. Sorry it's so early. Did I wake you?"

"August? Oh my gosh! Good morning sweetheart! I woke up half an hour ago. I had the strangest dream."

"Why are you whispering? Is Two Feathers there?"

"Well, yes, sweetie."

"When he wakes up, tell him I said hello."

"August says hello," Sylvia said, her voice sounding muffled for a moment. "He's waking up. Little bit of a bear before he gets coffee." A giggle, muffled again.

"Mom, I wanted to let you know that the trip has been going fine. I've learned, gosh … really just so much since I've been here. It's been kind of amazing." Despite her successful emotional distance, the sound of her mother's voice had gone straight through August's heart, and she could feel the edge of tears creeping in. She pushed them back hard. "Anyway, I am about to do something … kind of dangerous, and I just wanted to let you know, and tell you I love you."

Sylvia blurted out, "Dangerous? Like what?"

"Oh, no big deal, Mom. We're going to snoop around this little castle in Summerblynd and see if Ciardha the murderer is there. You know, just a typical day." *Nothing like I might never talk to you again. Or that you would be utterly devastated—nothing like that*, she thought, but kept it behind the wall of bravado. She shot Faolan a look, and his face seemed to say *Don't frighten the poor woman over nothing*, which was actually very reassuring to August at that moment.

182

The other end of the line was silent and August thought perhaps the persnickety long-distance connection had dropped her call. "Mom?"

"August, I know that you and Faolan need to do what you need to do. Just promise me that you will be careful and protect yourself. If you do run into Ciardha, don't trust him. He has no honor. And, please call me tonight, so I know you're okay?"

"Okay," August said a little flatly.

"What?"

"I guess I expected you to be more bothered by it."

"Oh, Button … I'm plenty bothered by it. But would you listen if I told you not to go?"

"Well … no."

"Your father wouldn't have either, if he was decided he would do something. August, I don't really think Ciardha wants to kill you, or he would have tried harder. There is a chance here, for a truce."

"How can you want a truce with him, Mom? He killed Dad!"

"I actually want him dead, August. Hell, I'd do it myself if I saw him again. But any fight between lycans and hunters just brings more fighting. Maybe we'll get lucky and somebody will cut his throat. Maybe Faolan will finally see his way past his loyalty to his brother and do what we all want him to do."

"That's not fair …"

"I know, and I'm not proud of it. But you asked, and these are my answers, August. A truce would stop the further killing of any more hunters. And it would let you rest easier and start your life. If it was a choice between a truce or more death, I'm sure your father would choose the former. He was a man of empathy and patience, not vengeance. He always chose diplomacy whenever it was possible. If you are able to negotiate a peace, then do it."

"I understand what you're saying. And I wouldn't want to disappoint Dad. If that's what you think he'd want, I'll do what I can. Faolan will, too."

"Just make sure there aren't any of his Veritas buddies around, August. That would be a trap. Where is it exactly you're going?"

"The Conall Keep?"

"Ah, I've never seen it. I think it's somewhere in the forest in the far northern parts of Summerblynd."

"Do you miss it?"

"Miss what?"

"Scotland."

"Eh, I would miss America more. My mother was Scottish, but your Grandpa Jaeger was German. And he was a diplomat, so we moved around a lot. I really only know Scotland from vacations there."

"You were a diplomat's daughter? Why did I not know this?"

"What? You're kidding."

"I can't know what you don't tell me. I don't think you ever told me how they died, either."

"I think when you get home I'd better catch you up on all of that history. I'm sure I told you that Grandpa Jaeger was a diplomat."

"Well if so, I was a kid. I didn't know what all that might have entailed."

"Touché. Isn't it funny? You tell somebody something and you have the full meaning in your mind of what you're saying, but you only really convey a small portion. Like you expect people to just know what you mean."

"It's been a bit of a bane to my existence, lately. So yeah, it's hilarious."

"You know what I mean, silly girl. What? You're not an empath?"

"Not that I know of. Yet."

They both laughed.

"Mom, I love you. I promise to be careful. I'll call you when we're back to the inn tonight. Try not to worry."

"I love you too, August. So much. I know you and Faolan can take care of yourselves."

"Bye, Mom."

"Bye, sweetie." The line clicked and clicked again before it went silent. Then the dial tone resumed, and August hung up the handset.

"That was encouraging," Faolan said as he laced up his boots.

"She's more worried than she's letting on, but she's right, we have to do this, and her asking me not to wouldn't change it."

"Aye. Ye got yer strength back, then? Had enough t' eat?"

"Aye." Tiny smile.

"August ... your new changes? Your ability to fully transform? Let's keep that just between us for now."

"I don't want anybody to know about that, Faolan! I don't even know what it means."

"Exactly right. It's something we need to explore, but when there's time, and not so much anxiety in the air." He sought her gaze and held it. "But it's important, I can tell ye that. By rights, you shouldn't be able to at all, but I had an inkling there were hidden depths, just from the small changes we'd seen."

"But I went straight to wolf. No half-change like the were-form. I couldn't even talk to you."

"Aye, and I reckon that'll take some training before ye can go to the fighting form. But this is important: Ciardha can never know. None of the Veritas. I have a feeling you would suddenly become much more interesting to that lot if they guessed at your abilities."

"I'm actually glad you brought it up. I'm still kind of in shock about it I think."

"Aye, love—but let's say no more now. Just this: if you feel your wolf aspect coming on, think of heat. Imagine it's a broiling hot summer day—really feel it, the heat on your skin. Usually that'll calm the transformation."

August nodded solemnly, and leaned forward to give him the gentlest kiss on his scruffy cheek.

"So, to more practical concerns Red, I put your cloak and bow in the car. Our weather luck has passed us; there's more mist rolling in, and dark clouds behind. It's gunna be wet."

"This is some way to learn about the ins and outs of Scotland. Sudden fangs, ghost girlfriends and murderous brothers."

Faolan strapped his dirk to his waist, tucked another smaller knife in his boot and pulled a leather box out of his larger suitcase. "I've got somethin' for ye," he announced, holding out the box and assuming the look of teen boy offering a prom corsage.

"What is it?"

"I suppose there's a remedy to that question, innit?"

August perched her bottom on the edge of a wooden cottage chair and flipped open the little case. Inside was a rolled-up length of leather with buckles and a short sheath, in which was a small knife.

She took it from its bed of suede, wrapped her fist around the stubby black handle, and pulled it from the sheath. It was beautifully carved and fit her hand perfectly. A small thing, maybe six inches from butt to tip, but exquisitely shaped and balanced. The blade was half its length, simple and utilitarian, but it gleamed with a fine sharp edge. Now she looked more closely at the handle, tracing the carvings with her finger—the silhouette of a wolf on one side and a girl on the other.

"Not to sound cliché, but … I don't know what to say." Her hands held the blade reverently, like an offering, and her eyes searched his for an explanation.

"It's a *sgian dubhs*. A thrust weapon, for stabbing in very close quarters. Here, stand up."

She stood, sheathed the weapon and turned it over to him.

"Arms up." Faolan wrapped a strap around her shoulder, across her back and to her other shoulder, leaving a loop under her left arm. He took the sheathed dagger and affixed it to the loop so that it was tucked into her left underarm, the handle angled somewhat downward. "Put your jacket on."

August did as she was told, grabbing her brown and cream houndstooth blazer and shrugging it on.

"See now, you reach inconspicuously inside with your right hand under yer arm an' you can pull it out with haste."

August did it after an encouraging nod from Faolan. Then re-sheathed it.

"Thanks?"

"You don't like it?"

"I do. It's beautiful, just … unexpected. Is it even a real weapon?"

"Aye, and as trusty a blade as ye'll ever have. It's small enough to be unnoticed but deadly efficient if you use it in the right spots. Look, here …" he indicated the side of his neck; "and here," toward his eye; "and go here," he pointed to his kidney, "if you can't get to the head. And lass …"

"Yes?"

"Use all your might."

She nodded, a bit sullen. "This isn't the best way to spend a vacation, is it? Preparing for deadly combat." She watched her boots as if they might jump on their own.

"I reckon that depends on how it all ends up."

"I reckon it does," she said, feeling a bit anxious.

It wasn't enough she had to be nervous about dealing with

somebody as unpredictable as Ciardha. That, she could endure. But she also had to be nervous about the steadfastness of Faolan's love. She didn't have any reason to question his sincerity, but she felt something. She didn't want to give it a name or call it to the front of her mind, because then she'd have to admit that even if Faolan chose her, he would always be wondering what could have been with Iseabail. But even if she was wrong about that, one thing was for sure—he was still going to be in love with her. The question was, could she live with that for the sake of her relationship with him? If he could set aside his deepest desire of wanting Iseabail, then couldn't she set aside her desire to be the only person he loves?

"Let's go get this over with. If we die, then at least I don't have to worry about us anymore."

"You don't have to worry about us."

She stared at him, willing him to say a thousand different things. Shower her with affection and affirmations and assurances. She knew he had some doubts and she wanted him to deny it. Swear it. Beg for her to believe him. Instead he was calm and thoughtful—and not saying any of the things she thought would help her. Even though she didn't make him aware of what those things were, she expected he should know them. And since he didn't, she was going to allow herself to harbor a little resentment.

She nodded. "Okay." It wasn't very convincing, but it was all she had.

She caught sight of her long dark hair in the mirror. It was a bush of frizz. She wondered why she hadn't inherited Iseabail's pale red hair, and if Faolan dreamed of red hair on his lover.

She sighed and pushed through the door.

Finders Keepers

The ride to Summerblynd was a bit longer than August had anticipated. With the lingering tension between them, they drove on with little to say. Conversation used to be so easy with Faolan—it seemed there was always something they couldn't wait to talk about, ever since they first started meeting for tea and books on the banks of the creek that ran through their properties in Maryland. Was it really only a year ago? In this moment, August longed for the innocence of those days, when she didn't know about any of this—when Faolan was just a heavy crush she wanted to know everything about. Now it was all so complicated.

The day turned wet and gray as Faolan had promised, only letting up slightly as they reached higher ground. Occasionally the sun peeked through the heavier clouds, leaving only a veil of haze, but the sky would close back up again. It was only after they rounded a perfect little mini-mountain (which August said looked like the flocked landscape of a toy train set) that the clouds parted and the sun shone over the little valley they were dropping down into. The village below was clustered at the foot of a mountain by a pretty little loch, while several tree-lined lanes wandered off from it in various directions, including toward the woodlands—roads that might take you to any number of mysterious locations.

August took in the beauty and tried to ignore the pulsing knot in her stomach.

"It's so perfect. This is where my family is from?"

"Many hunters lived here. We passed that castle back a wee bit? That was the Laird's. He ruled not just Summerblynd, but most everything in Perthshire and a bit more north, too."

"But did my father come from here?"

"Aye. This is where it all started. Hard to believe it now to look at it."

"It looks like a postcard. Where is the keep?"

He pointed toward the densest part of the forest. "In that way, abouts. It's been decades since I've seen it, and there's no road. Some go in by horse."

"Um … I can't ride a horse. Neither of us can, because we don't actually have a horse."

"Seems we'd better turn back then."

August smacked him playfully on the arm. "Well, then?"

"We'll go as far as the road takes us, then go in on foot. I'd reckon it about half a mile from the road to the keep. The woods around it are near impenetrable, full of mature trees, bushes, brambles and devilishly thorny thickets."

"Sounds like fun."

"That's the spirit, lass! Other than tha' part about my brother possibly wantin' to murder us, at any rate. Ah, I used t' tear through those woods like a mad dog."

They continued on until the road got so narrow that branches were brushing the sides of the Rover and the canopy was all but blocking the sky. Fortunately the mists had cleared off enough to at least make the road somewhat visible.

"I'm glad you know where you're going, Fe. I feel like we're driving into a nest."

"Following my nose, actually. I couldn't begin to tell anyone else how to get here."

They pulled off between a couple of trees and behind some bushes to clear their vehicle from easy sight of the roadway. They pulled some leafy branches from smaller trees and covered the bits of metal and glass that were still visible on the side facing the road.

Faolan handed her the bow and quiver, which she fixed to her hip. She felt a rush of adrenaline as she strapped the cord to her thigh. Images of her father's smiling face danced around in her mind. She wished that he was alive to teach her more about archery, and to teach her all of the things about being a hunter that her mother didn't know. Once again her heart filled with anger. Ciardha had stolen so much from her. He tried to destroy her whole family—all for the sake of his stupid vendetta. She wanted to remember all the evil he'd done, and she hoped he would give her a reason to put an arrow through his throat. She wanted to put a final nail in all of this, though she also understood what her mother had said about hunters and lycans at war.

August stared into the forest but still saw no sign of the keep—nothing other than trees and leaves and bits of sky. Luckily the air was still, and would not give them away as they approached. The damp of the undergrowth was held back by her sturdy boots and cloak, though her bow tangled in the brambles a few times as they headed uphill. Whenever they approached a thicket that seemed impossible to penetrate, Faolan would yank on something and the knotted vines and thorny branches would part or lean away. After fifteen minutes of walking she could make out the top of a small tower that must have been the tallest part of the keep. Then a few moments later a small gust of wind puffed out of the west toward them, shaking dewy drops from the leaves and giving the forest a ten-second rain shower, followed by a stink so rank and foul that they both winced.

"Holy shit! What the—"

"Piss, actually. He's marked this area, to keep lycan from crossing."

"Isn't he friends with all the lycan around here?" August said through a pinched nose. "He must have marked this twenty times, it smells so bad."

"These lycan are never truly friends. Just allied by a mutual cause. He probably comes out here and pisses every day. Just to keep it fresh."

"Well, what are we going to do? We can't cross that right?"

"If we were only wolf, no, we couldn't. But since we are more than wolf, our intentions matter. And we are not here to harm him."

"He might think our weapons say otherwise."

"They're for self-defense. We're going in to negotiate peace."

August swallowed and thought of how dark her heart had become ever since that night she thought that he'd killed her mother. Even knowing he'd failed, she had been struggling to not nurse that hate into a monster.

"Also, technically, this is my territory too. We both inherited it."

"But, he's the laird isn't he? Since he's the oldest?"

"Aye. But it's more complicated than that. In Scotland we have blood tanistry, which doesn't always end in the oldest male taking the position. And in lycan culture I'm the alpha between us, even though he is older."

"You're saying we can cross then?"

"Aye. Unless you can think of a reason we can't?"

August knitted her brow and shrugged. She wasn't going to admit she intended to hurt Ciardha if he gave her any excuse.

"Alright. As soon as we clear these thick branches we're going to

190

circle around to the back side and see if we can't get a look at what's going on in there. You should take off your cloak. Even in all this fall color, he'll spot it for sure if he's in human form."

She shrugged the cloak off, awkwardly handling her bow from one palm to the other, unwilling to release it. She rolled up the cloak and Faolan tucked it under his arm.

"August …"

"Mm?"

"I love you."

"I love you, too."

"Now, follow me." He stooped a bit, stepped sideways and started padding from tree to bush until they were facing the mossy back of the keep. As they got low and crossed the open field she could finally see the keep, unobstructed. It looked like a simple building of ancient stone, the main part of it looking like a big square bunker with castle-like parapets at the corners and a single stout tower that rose above the rest of the roof. It seemed more imposing the nearer they came, and August began to feel rather small next to those old stones, but she trusted Faolan and held onto her grit.

Raven's Loch

Iseabail returned to Raven's Loch Manor after confronting Faolan at the cemetery. She didn't know whether to rejoice for having finally seen him again, or to weep for a hundred years. She had imagined their reunion in her head so many times, she was shocked into silence when it didn't go any of the ways she'd expected.

She stripped down to her sensible beige silk underclothes and stared at her body in the mirror. She traced the stretchmarks on her stomach with a finger, then tugged at a white and ginger curl, regarding the color before letting it bounce back into place. She walked over to her vanity and slathered on a handful of silky body butter, smoothing over every part of her that wasn't young and fresh.

She took her glass of mead over to the sun rays beaming onto the vibrantly tiled floor, and gazed out at the hills and the rocks, the trees and the brook, all framed in the manse window. The loch in the distance winked and sparkled as cloud shadows rode in and broke away with the breeze across the landscape. Now that she was finally free of all of the men who had controlled her life for so long—her father, her husband, her brothers—she wanted to share the rest of it with the one man she couldn't forget. The only one, of the few that had ever been good to her. This place was now hers. The future was hers to decide. Anything could happen. In fact, she imagined she could make all sorts of things happen, if she wanted to.

She sipped the potent honeyed drink and then abandoned the view for her desk. She peeled a sheet of letterhead from the stack in her drawer and lay the smooth ivory linen on the blotter in front of her. She gulped down the last of the mead and wiped her lips with the back of her hand, picked up her pen and started to write.

Dearest Thom and Maggie,

I know it's been a long while since my last letter to you. It was hard to get word to anybody with my brothers controlling my every move and overseeing my mail. I am forever in your debt for what you've done. Now that James and Bruce are gone I can write whomever I like, whenever I like. What a relief to know that the danger posed to Reade by their hands has died with them.

Faolan is here in Perthshire. I mean to tell him all, but I wanted to give you the benefit, so you were not caught unaware when Reade *comes asking questions.*

Please think of coming to Raven's Loch to visit. I have plenty of space here and all of the rooms have just been redone. It would be lovely to have some company and to meet the great-grandchildren. I miss the sounds of wee ones, it's been so long. We could picnic by the loch and we can practice our rusty archery skills. It would be such a grand thing to see friendly faces here to brighten up the place.

You have been family to me. I treasure you always.

Every blessing to you,

Iseabail

She paused over the epistle for a few moments, satisfied it was the right thing to do. She dug out an envelope, addressed it, sealed it and posted it. She slipped on a sweater and tweed slacks and took the letter downstairs to the maid, who was ordered to take it to the post office right away. Without argument, the girl threw on her shawl and headed out, letter in hand. Iseabail watched her, smiling to herself. She gave herself a hug, poured another glass and soon was lost in a whirlwind of possibilities.

My Brother's Keeper
Conall Keep

They could both smell food cooking as they made their way, low and half-crawling, to an open window from which the fragrant smoke billowed. But before they could even stretch high enough to peek into the window, a door flung open and a bucket of mop water flew out of it onto the stones beside them. The woman who did the tossing was more startled then they were, and she squealed. She looked almost like a frightened mouse, with little bead eyes and a long pointy nose that seemed to twitch.

Faolan and August straightened up and looked at her, and then at each other. Faolan sighed and August rolled her eyes.

"Who are ye? What d' ye be wantin'?" Her voice was squeaky and she spoke through slightly bucked teeth. August almost laughed despite her agitation.

"I'm Faolan Conall. This is my land and my keep."

"Laird Ciardha is master of Conall Keep. You best be watchin' yer back, too. He don't take to strangers."

"Ciardha is my brother, therefore I am not a stranger."

"Brother, if ye be, ye best go around to the front. He won't like ye comin' in the back like common servants. Go on now, I'll meet ye there."

Faolan and August looked at each other, and she was surprised to see embarrassment in his eye. She'd never seen him mess up this badly, and it threw her a bit. She had always been sure he knew what he was doing, and any plan he had would work out. Was there anything more he might have miscalculated about coming to his brother's lair? But the die was cast—what else were they going to do, just up and leave? Ciardha would know now they're in town and he'd have the upper hand, should he wish to take action—they'd never see him coming. He could attack them in their sleep; he could fly back to Maryland for the rest of her family. No, they needed to end this now, even without the element of surprise. Maybe it would even be better—maybe Ciardha would give August the fight that part of her still wanted.

Faolan handed August her cloak, and she fastened it around her throat. They then strode around the side of the keep, watching for anything unexpected to happen. When they reached the front gate, the ten-foot-high double doors heaved open to reveal not the mouse woman, but a tall, red-haired woman, striking if somewhat gaunt, dressed in what August thought must be riding clothing.

Faolan dipped in a bow, leaving August with no idea what to do other than to stand there clutching her bow and feeling stupid.

"Lady Blair," he greeted her. He straightened himself and stepped forward to take her hand, kissed it, then bowed his head again.

"Faolan, what a surprise. I would have thought this is the last place we'd ever see you."

"I didn't think much surprised you, m'lady."

She peered at him. "I don't ken yer meaning."

"Oh I think ye might."

If she did, she let it pass, and turned instead to August. "And you, child, step forward."

August approached slowly, but not before giving Faolan a glance, and he returned it with an assuring nod.

"You must be my niece," Blair concluded after a moment's inspection.

Faolan raised one eyebrow and tilted his head like a cocker spaniel. "Ye see, Blair? Naught is all surprises ye."

August remained silent, too stunned to speak, which didn't matter because Blair looked over at Faolan as if she wasn't there, and continued on the conversation with him. She took a step back and pursed her lips.

"I am surprised you showed up here. You know what he's like."

"Is that a new gift from my brother?" Faolan indicated a pair of visible bruises around Blair's wrist. She tugged her sleeve down.

"Nothing I can't handle."

"You've been saying that a long time."

"Aye, and I'll keep sayin' it until it's not true, so if you would, shut yer hole, brother." She turned back to August. "Stop making a puss, child. You two come in. I've got a meal ready for you."

Faolan put his hand out and took August's and they crossed through the wide doorway together.

"Ye know it's tradition to leave weapons at the door, when visiting a friend."

Blair held her hands out, and August looked up at Faolan, who reached over and took her bow and quiver. August had a slight look of panic on her face, so Faolan gave the bow a gentle stroke and whispered, "It'll be fine."

Faolan took off his dagger and handed it to her.

"And your boot, brother."

He reached into his boot and pulled out the smaller dagger and handed it to her. Blair walked over to August and grabbed her wrists and felt her sleeves up to the elbow. With a satisfied nod, she said, "Welcome to our home. You are guests here and there is to be no violence. You have my word. Do I have yours?"

Faolan gave a single nod.

August stared blankly, waiting for any further instructions and feeling relieved that her sgian-dubh had not been discovered under her arm. She understood better now the value of such a tiny weapon, and her faith in Faolan was somewhat restored. But she was still trying to process the fact that standing before her was another ghost in the family.

"So where is Keer, Blair? Is he also aware there's to be no violence?"

Blair folded her hands together and looked at them for a moment. "Ciardha is ill today. He's been ill since last night, I'm afraid. He's in no condition to be fightin' anybody."

"Ill?" Faolan frowned at her, skeptical.

"Aye, tossed up his dinner and his breakfast this morning. He's as sad as a weak pup at the moment."

"Well that's got to be the first time in this century."

"Aye, 'tis. He's a strapping and stubborn beast. He's been in his cups more of late. A lot more. I suspect it's catching up to him."

Faolan nodded again, still looking skeptical.

"Or perhaps the Veritas fledglings are poisoning him," she laughed. "That Engres Laithenskye never did agree much with Keer's leadership and … well … shifting philosophies. Always warned him he was too soft—too friendly to the mixed, ye ken?"

"Too soft? What the hell!" August had finally been shocked out of her silence. She hadn't meant to shout, but her aunt gazed mildly at her as though she were a spoiled child, and she shut up once more.

"Aye, niece. I'm standin' here, aren't I? Keer loves me and the

Laithenskye lad burns about it. He would love to take Keer's place as Chieftain of the Veritas. But so long as Ciardha is breathing, it won't happen. He has too many loyal friends. Keer is the alpha, and you won't find anybody stabbing Caesar, even in that raggedy group."

"Shall I go up and see my brother, then? Did he know I was comin'?"

"He knew. Ye can see him, but not with her."

"Fine."

"He's in the master's chamber, at the end."

August turned to Faolan and took him by the sleeve, and whispered harshly, "Don't leave me down here ... alone."

"Blair will be here. She's your kin, she'll take care of ye." Faolan shot Blair a look and Blair tipped her head to him.

August couldn't do anything but go along. She watched him ascend the sweeping staircase and head off to the left, his boots echoing down the hall of naked stone. She turned back to Blair and gave her a face that implied she had nothing to say to her aunt—though that didn't last long.

"You're the only one of my father's brothers and sisters that's still alive."

Blair's arms were crossed, her body language was guarded. She held her head high and straight and looked August up and down. "Aye. I ken that. Take off yer cloak."

August didn't want to, but she swept off the cloak, being careful not to let her jacket flap open and reveal her dagger holster.

Blair took a step forward and snatched the garment from August. "Ye ken you ought to put some grey and green fabric in the lining. Goose never was good about keeping up with those things. This thing looks like it's never been mended or updated.

"Why would I ..."

"Because when you don't want 'em spyin' ye in red—you know, when they are not their beastly form—you want to be the color of the forest. Greys, greens, browns. Isn't that why it was under Faolan's arm? So nobody would see ye comin'?"

August nodded. "I didn't really think of that."

"No shite. Let me tell ye, you've got a lot more to learn about being a hunter, and that's the least of it. But a proper cloak lining is a start, even if there's not much a need for that kind of thing anymore.

There hasn't been a battle in decades, despite the best efforts of the Veritas. Most otherkin don't want any such thing."

Not all the killing has been in battle, August thought bitterly, but she decided to pursue a different topic with her aunt for now.

"I thought only Gran called Dad 'Goose.'"

"Well I reckon there's a lot of things ye thought that are wrong, lassie."

August might have been irritated with the way her aunt was speaking to her, but she sensed that it was false bravado. She had the distinct feeling that her aunt would actually have liked to hug her and regale her with family memories. But August didn't really know this obviously proud woman. After all, Blair had chosen a homicidal, speciesist maniac over her own family. *She's let her own mother think she was dead all this time. That's pretty fucking cruel.*

"Yeah, I reckon you're right," August finally said, without much emotion.

"Dinna ye want a tour of the keep? It's Faolan's too. If you do marry him, I reckon that'd make it yours as well."

"No, I'm not the least bit interested in the keep, Blair."

"Well, young lady, ye don't have to be an arse about it …"

"I'm not being an arse," August said in a mocking tone, summoning her artificial Scottish accent. "I'm just not good at standing here and pretending like your husband didn't murder my father, who happened to be your brother, too, by the way—and the fact that Gran made herself numb to the world for years because she thought she lost all of you, violently. She just withdrew. She couldn't handle all that pain, and you're just traipsing around this stupid little castle like a princess and you don't even fucking care!" August heard herself getting louder as she went, so she shut her mouth and glared at Blair, who glared back. Both remained silent for a long while. Blair seemed almost wounded, looking down at the ground and then at the wall. August thought she saw a tear well up in her left eye.

"So you've a tongue after all. You and I, niece … we have a lot to talk about. When the time is right."

"What's wrong with now?"

"I don't have enough hours in the day to answer that."

August's lips tightened into a line and she rolled her eyes to the ceiling.

"May sound like excuses to you, girl, but it's hard life."

"I know a little something about hard life."

"I'm not gunna have a pissin' match wi' ye over who's had it harder. I've been livin' a hard life for longer than you've been alive."

"Maybe your life wouldn't have been so hard if you hadn't betrayed your fam—"

"I did not betray my family!" Her ferocity stunned August into silence, her mouth went dry and she swallowed hard. "I was a child, in love. Ciardha imprinted on me and I'd never felt so adored—so loved and cherished. My mother may seem like a nice old lady to you now, but she was a hard woman t' please and she always favored the boys. My father was a thoughtful man, but he was distant, and not especially open with his affection. A girl needs that—ye know, I'm sure—and Ciardha was the only one t' gie it, and so much of it. It was *Romeo and Juliet*, August. My hormones were wild. My bonding with him eclipsed everything else I knew. Ye must ken some of what I'm talking about, niece."

August inhaled deeply and let it out, uncrossed her arms and nodded. "I do."

Blair shuddered. It had been years since she'd even let herself remember, and she said much more than she'd intended. "Another time. I tell you all of it, another time."

August nodded again. By now they could hear the door to the upstairs room creak shut and Faolan's boots making their way to the stairs. They both looked up at him and he looked like he'd gotten a little older in the last ten minutes. He was slow coming down the stairs, as though he were dragging boulders behind him.

"What is it, Faolan?" August asked.

"He's in bad shape. I wouldn'a believed it was so bad if I hadn'a seen it. He's pale as a sheet, and his hands are shakin'."

"Aye, it's hard to see anybody like that, let alone your husband."

"He's asking for some meat. He felt like he could hold some down."

"I'll get him some, brother."

"I'll just cut off some of what's on the table and take it to him."

"Aye, good idea, Faolan. It's so rare it's near to still alive."

August followed Faolan through a large passage into the main hall, with heavy wooden beams under twenty-foot ceilings and a long table in the center, piled high with food—all of which August imagined was Scottish. He sliced huge pieces of lamb and beef and took them upstairs while Blair described everything on the table for August.

"Here we've got some fine local cheeses, ye'll find no better. Bannocks."

"Oat cakes, right?"

"Mm-hm," Blair nodded. "And here smokies—smoked herring. Also, some Irish brown bread, which Brigid gave me the recipe for so many years ago. I make it every week. I do miss her. Here's some macaroni pies, much like yer basic mac and cheese. In the tureen is Cullen skink—sounds wicked, but it's fantastic. And of course lamb, beef and ham, as rare as it can be."

As the lesson was wrapping up Faolan was back in the dining hall. "I'm famished," he announced, and rubbed his hands together in anticipation of filling his fists with eating utensils.

Blair looked away from him. "Is he eating the food?" she asked, as though she were mentally preparing herself for the answer. Faolan and August exchanged a look. They both had noticed how Blair acted a bit odd every time Ciardha was discussed.

"He is. He looked like he might finish it off without much trouble. Maybe the malady is passing."

"Perhaps. Let's tuck in."

Faolan pulled out the chair at one end of the table for Lady Conall and then he pulled out August's, and they all sat in a clump at one end of the table. Faolan passed the food to the women, then took portions for himself.

"Ciardha always takes his portions first."

"Well, that's not very gentlemanly of him."

"He is the Laird."

"I suppose he never lets you forget it."

They chatted on, and August sat there feeling outside of herself, as though she were floating above the table listening to a pleasant dinner conversation that might happen at any family table anywhere in the world. But for August, this conversation was tinged with resentment. She wanted to go upstairs and stab Ciardha in the neck for what he did to her father, but the man was weak and helpless, and though she didn't have much experience as a warrior, August knew somehow that was wrong. She had to force herself to stop thinking

200

that he would do it to her if given half a chance. She wasn't like him. She would never let herself be like him. She thought some more on what her mother said, about diplomacy and peace, so instead of stoking the fires of her hate, she focused on the mundane task of getting through dinner. Despite the fact that her stomach had been upset, she felt it grumble at her and grabbed an oat cake and a macaroni pie and picked at both. Faolan was tearing through everything on the table in great portions. It seemed that Blair was used to accommodating lycan appetites, so there was plenty to go around.

"Whatever meat you lot don't eat I'll put in the stew tomorrow for Keer. He loves my stew."

"You ought to have favored us with some, sister. That would have been bonny."

"It's especially for Keer. He'd be cross if I shared it with anybody else."

"Well this is a fine meal anyroad. I meant no disrespect."

"I ken, brother."

And the conversation went on like that—about food, and recent weather and small hints of family history in passing comments about wedding gowns and couples who'd paired off.

"Also, there seems to be a lot of otherkin who are suddenly keen on buggery," Blair said, her eyes on Faolan, as if waiting for an explanation. "But who am I to say what love is?"

"What, outright? Seems that would be a dangerous thing to admit. Especially with the likes of the Veritas and some other pure-blood fanatics railing about the thinning of the stock. They don't take to any sex that isn't resulting in proper otherkin bairns. Well, I reckon they're brave for coming out of the closet. I know what, let's have a toast." They all lifted their goblets.

"To love, however it may find you," Faolan said.

"To love!" the women echoed him, and they all clinked their glasses together and drank.

Despite having ultimately eaten three servings of macaroni, August could feel the effects of the second glass of wine warming her arms and cheeks. She started to relax, despite being among a murderer and a traitor. August couldn't help but stare at her aunt and imagine her as a child, playing with her father when he was a little boy. What did they look like then? And the twins, Tom and Tavish, older than both of them—did she play with her brothers at all? Or did she stick to spending her time with her older sister Ceana? She thought of them all, kissed by summer sunshine, running around the Blue Rook, eating from the garden and practicing their archery. She imagined Sorcha, nobody's gran yet, standing at the kitchen sink, looking out the window at her brood safely outside enjoying a hot Maryland summer day while she washed and cooked. And how it must have felt to Sorcha when all of that was shattered—the cruel beast upstairs being responsible for so much of that suffering. August flexed her left arm and felt the reassurance of the hard handle of her sgian-dubh against her soft underarm flesh. She felt her jaw set and flex as the images that danced in her mind went from children rollicking to blood and tears.

"August?" She finally heard Faolan's voice from somewhere distant and looked at him, still sitting right across from her. Both Blair and Faolan had a look of concern.

"What?"

"You alright lass? I said your name three times."

She shook off the funk and picked up her water goblet for a couple of gulps. "Guess the third time was the charm." She looked at her plate and around the room, then back at her plate. "It's been a very weird day."

Blair and Faolan both let out a sound that said they found some humor in her comment and tipped back their wine.

"Aye!" Blair said and then tipped it back again, finishing it off.

"So, what do we do now? Just sit here and pretend we're one happy little family?" August was having a hard time stomaching the role of diplomat.

"The happy little family is a myth, niece."

"It might be for you, but it wasn't for me."

"I think it's about time for us to go," Faolan wiped his mouth with a linen napkin and set it on his plate, now clean of everything. *Even the bones*, August thought, with a slight shudder. *At least he didn't waste anything.* It made her a little sick to think of herself that way—part of her newfound heritage that she didn't much care to contemplate, though she wasn't going to deny it either. She certainly didn't find listening to Faolan grind bones particularly appealing. She made a mental note to ask him later if that kind of thing was supposed to be good manners for lycans.

Faolan bowed toward Blair, "Thank you for your hospitality."

Blair stood. "*Se do bheatha.*"

August couldn't make herself thank her aunt, even though she knew it was what her mother and father would want.

"It was a pleasure to meet you, niece. Perhaps we will meet again soon and we can have that talk."

Faolan regarded the women with curiosity, but asked no questions.

Blair took them toward the door but detoured to a large knotty pine desk against the far wall, where she pulled out a small card to hand it to Faolan. "This is the number here. Call first next time."

"Fair," he acknowledged, and bowed, taking her hand for another kiss. August said nothing and walked out of the door ahead of him. She didn't relax, or speak, until they had uncovered their pointlessly hidden car and got rolling again.

Seeing Things As We Are

We don't see things as they are, we see them as we are.
—Anaïs Nin

"Well that was … something." August watched the trees blurring by, her arms crossed to help stop herself from shaking.

"Are ye cold?"

"No, I think it's just jitters. From realizing I'm not going to die today."

"Aren't ye supposed to get the jitters before something?"

"Well maybe that's the wrong word. I'm all shaky now that I'm not focused on mere survival. Maybe it's a kind of shock."

He reached behind her seat and pulled her cloak forward and laid it on her lap. "Best to keep you warm, then."

"So, what did he say when you went up there? Please tell me he looked like he was going to die."

"Well. He did look to be on death's door. I've never seen him look so sallow—weak as a kitten and drooling all over the place. I was surprised he asked for meat. I think it was more for show than hunger. Or perhaps he is on the mend."

August turned towards Faolan, "Are you actually worried about him?" Her tone was accusatory.

"I think worry is the wrong word."

"I don't know how you can be worried about his murderous fucked-up ass!" August croaked out the last bit as her throat tightened with rage and salt tears. She turned away from him again, focusing on the blur of brown and green and yellow, tightening the cross of her arms as if to emphasize how much he'd just let her down again.

"Lass, I'm mourning the brother I used to have. The Ciardha you know is not who I grew up with. Not exactly, anyroad. When we were young, what some might call a cruel streak seemed like youthful lycan mischief. Though now he has the power to do real evil. You're right, I shouldn'a mind if he dies, he's hurt so many people I care about. Nor can I know all he has in mind, no matter how … hopeful I might be about him changing."

August shot him a look.

"Love dies hard for our kind Red, for better or worse. I should be willing him to die, but I canna muster more than wishing his fate to be whatever is best for this world in the end."

"You are never going to have the guts to do anything about your brother, even if he tries to kill me. He wants to kill me!"

"We don't know that, love. He wants to avenge our father's death."

"If it ends up with me dead, then what difference does it make why he did it? Think about it, Faolan! How could I ever be in the same room with him?"

Faolan nodded. "I take your point, August. You want me to wish my brother dead?"

"It's either him or me, it seems. I don't think you can have both of us."

"If I don't wish my brother dead, or kill him myself, are you going to hold it against me? Is that going to come between us?"

"Honestly?"

"Of course."

"It could."

Faolan inhaled deeply. "I have a lot to consider, I suppose."

"I suppose you do." She didn't look away from the window for the rest of the ride back to the inn, where she climbed down out of the car and walked zombie-like to the cottage through the downpour that had started, drenching her hair and her clothes, her cloak fallen in a puddle behind her. Once inside she went straight to the bath to fill the tub, and soaked for a long while. Faolan hung her cloak over the radiator and set her boots next to it to dry. He then paced around the front room waiting, hoping to be summoned for the usual reasons—forgotten towel, or a snack, anything to make the evening a bit more normal. August emerged, mostly dry though still looking sullen and colorless in her big grey tee. She walked over to the bed, crawled in and curled up under the covers, facing the wall away from Faolan. When he tried to walk around to the other side and kneeled to look at her, she rolled the other direction and pulled the covers up tight under her chin.

"You're angry with me."

She didn't answer. She didn't know how to answer. Or maybe she was embarrassed to admit she was willing to punish him for not wanting his brother to die. How could he possibly not want Ciardha to die after all of the murders and fighting and the fact that he still is trying to spread his hate?

She huffed and tossed the blanket off and sat up straight, arms crossed, brow deeply knitted.

"Your brother, Faolan—he's a bad dude. He's just bad. Whatever good that was ever in him isn't there anymore. I mean, every living thing deserves a life, I get that. We can't just go around killing people we don't like, even if they do some really bad shit. But what if we know that some monster is going to keep doing bad shit unless they are stopped? What then? How many people have to suffer or die because of him before it's too many?"

He sat silently, enduring the pummeling. Her shoulders slumped and she let out an exasperated sigh and softened a bit. "It's not that I want you to kill your brother, or even wish him dead. I want you to stop him from hurting people. If we're both being totally honest, we know what that means, Faolan."

Faolan, seated on the corner chair, elbows on his knees, studied the floor. "I understand what you're saying, lass. I do. I'm not saying you're wrong, I'm sayin' it's hard."

"I think it makes me feel like you don't love me enough to protect me from him, because he's your brother. Like he matters more. Maybe he should matter more. Is that how this works? Family always matters more, even if they are murdering tyrants with hate like a virus? I mean tell me, because I really need to know if that's how this world works, because if it is, I don't want to be a part of it. Just let me off right now." She was being a little sarcastic, but the edge of frustration was sharp.

"I'm glad you can tell me what you need from me."

"What's the point if I don't? Just live with this thorn digging at me?"

"Many people do."

"I guess. That brings me to another subject, which is not making my mood any brighter."

"Iseabail."

"Yes, Iseabail. I know you've been thinking about her. It just … I mean, how could you *not* be thinking about her?"

Faolan clasped his hands together as though he might speak, but no answer was quick to come from him.

"You are, aren't you?" August was hoping he'd say, No, absolutely not! You're the only woman I ever think of and there are no other women on the face of the earth as far as I'm concerned. Also, you are without a doubt the most breathtakingly beautiful woman I have ever had the pleasure to be in love with. But somehow she knew that wasn't what he was going to say.

He raised his gaze from the floor to her eyes. He had a look of utter anguish on his face. One August had never seen before and it knocked the breath out of her. Whatever he was about to say, it wasn't going to be good. She started to shiver again and pulled the blanket up in front of herself, like a shield.

"Aye. I'm sorry, Red, I have been thinking about her. I can't stop thinking about her."

August felt a slight wave of panic followed by nausea. Her eyes started to well.

"Well that's just fan-fucking-tastic," she said through clattering teeth. Her face now red and sweaty. She fought back the tears and shivers that were wracking her body. She gave a shudder.

He stood and started to pace, his ears pointing slightly. He rubbed his hands, which she guessed were trying to transform to paws. "I dinna want to hurt ye. I also dinna want to lie to ye. What would you have me do, Red?"

A tear traced down his troubled face, followed the line next to his mouth and fell off of his chin. He wiped his face with his hand and sniffed.

August was shaking harder. It was a truth. His truth—and now hers. It couldn't be unmade, it couldn't be reasoned with or forgotten by magic. Seeing Iseabail obviously reinforced their bond.

"I've been trying to put it aside. But I've held on to her for so long. Can you imagine what it is to love someone for almost a century? I have to know at least what happened."

"Why? Why do you have to? What difference does it make now? Why can't you just let it—"

"Can I do nothing right for you?!" He yelled it so loud his face went crimson. His ears almost full-on wolf ears now, and his hands were twisting and snapping, his nose looking a bit longer, his teeth a bit sharper. August was stunned at his sudden show of temper, something she had never seen before.

"Wha … wha …" she stuttered, looking for the right words.

"Hae ye stopped for a moment t' think o' how hard this's been fer me?" he spat, his voice still rumbling with anger.

August awkwardly tried to defend herself. "You know I have. I asked you over and over—"

"Ye dinna though! Ye might a thought it, but all 'at's said has been aboot your feelings, your fears, your needs. Ah'm doin' all I can t' be all 'at you imagine I am, but I don't think I c'n do it."

"Faolan! That's what this is about after all, isn't it? What we imagine people are, not what they actually are? Brothers or lovers or whatever?"

They both sat in the inky silence as the daylight faded from the window, until August quietly reminded him, "This is your own fault."

He pursed his lips, and it was so matronly and unattractive that she hoped it would not become a habit. "How's that agin, Red?"

"You know, you look like an old lady when you press your lips together like that." She sounded exactly seven years old.

"Ah, that's incredibly helpful. Allow me t' make my face into a configuration tha' pleaseth you, m'lady. Should it be th' strong buck?" He straightened is spine and squared his jaw and shot her his manliest glare. "The kindly neighbor?" He bowed and put a hand out. Then he reached in his jacket for his reading glasses and perched them on the end of his nose. "How 'bout the seductively intelligent professor? Would that fulfill yer fantasies, then?"

"Stop it, Faolan! You're not being funny."

"I'm not trying t' be funny! I'm attempting t' illustrate to you tha' yer comments are, frankly, unkind."

She was propelled out of the bed by her outrage. "Unkind? What? What? I couldn't be unkind to you! All I ever think about is if I'm pleasing you or not. Do I look good enough? Do I smell good enough? Do I read smart enough books? Do I remember all of the things you like?"

"Well Red, I reckon 'at's a heavy load t' bear, having t' think all o' the time on what another person likes. D' ye suppose I wouldn't know how that feels?"

"Faolan, I didn't say that. You're twisting my words around."

He bit his lip and squinted at her. Probably trying to avoid the "old lady pucker" she'd ridiculed him for. *Why did you tell him that?* she chided herself. A minute passed, without even a shift in his weight. He wasn't going to respond. She began to pace. She felt the tears coming that she knew would quickly devolve into the ugly crying face. She felt like she had when she'd broken her father's favorite pipe. Her face began to ball up; there was no stopping it. Wet all down her cheeks, and her nose. Between sobs she tried to yell at him.

"I can't believe we're even fighting over this stuff! I can't believe you're making me feel bad when you're the one who has the murdering brother and the cloying ex-whatever, whatever-she-was. You drag me all the way here to Scotland. Show me all of this stuff. Act all in love and romantic, and the minute your ex shows up, bam! You don't want me anymore! What the hell am I supposed to do? If we had made love like I wanted to, we would have had a stronger bond going into all this mess!" She was flailing arms and snot, red-faced and sweaty. "We would have been imprinted and none of this would have happened! This is your fault, Faolan. Go ahead, try and make me feel bad for being upset. I don't care! I refuse to accept the blame for your baggage. No! I won't do it!" She stood there sobbing and grabbed the front of her tee and pulled it up to her face. Her underpants showed, her belly peeked out at him. The smallness of her physical form was only underscored in the oversized shirt and she was sure she looked like a child having a temper tantrum.

Faolan's anger had passed and he tried to settle the energy in the room. He took a deep breath, softening his face, and took a couple of steps towards her. She dropped the front of the shirt and watched him. He took another step and she crossed her arms, but very loosely. She uncrossed then re-crossed them—still loosely and lower this time. He was fairly certain she wanted him to approach. He took one more step and put his hands on her shoulders and looked down at her. She was still shaking with sharp inhales and sniffling. He put a finger under her chin and lifted her face to look into his.

"I am sorry this hurts ye. I don't want to hide anything from you … Ever. But I will if ye want me to."

The hopelessness of it all. She could not move forward into a union with the man she loved, until he could figure out if that was where he was meant to be. More than anything she wanted to be back by the stream, having picnics, discussing books, and fantasizing about kisses. But she couldn't go back to that either. August felt trapped and claustrophobic. Her shoulders slumped and she leaned her face into his chest, and he wrapped his arms around her and held her until she was out of tears.

Into his shirt she said, "Do you love me?" and sniffed, her heart feeling trampled and physically in pain.

"Aye, lass … August I love ye so much. Nothing could ever change that." She inhaled deeply. His clove and patchouli, his musk and detergent. The bouquet of scents that conjured images of him whenever she smelled them.

"Then I guess you'd better go find out what … I guess you'd better see … You should go ahead and …"

"My intention is to just find out what happened, so I can put it behind me."

"I'm so tired."

"Me too, " Faolan said, and pushed a stray curl from her eyes.

"Is it All Saint's Day? We met on All Saints, you know."

"I'll never forget it," he said with a gentle smile and a soft kiss on her forehead.

"What do we do now?" She wanted to erase all of the bad of the trip and curl up in all of the beautiful moments.

"Summerblynd again, but this time, your hunter village. You'll get to meet some of your own kind. Even some hunters your age."

"How long is our trip anyway?"

"I'd planned on three weeks. But we can stay longer."

"I was thinking of shorter."

Faolan looked disappointed. He nodded his head, "I reckon I see why you'd be feelin' that way. I won't see her, if you ask me not to."

August's eyes flashed and she stepped away, pivoted and crossed her arms. "Why would you put that on me? That's totally unfair, Faolan!"

Faolan assumed the physiognomy of a dejected champion.

"I think you'd better go clear things up. The sooner the better. I don't know if I can handle too many more days with this hanging over our heads."

Faolan nodded, "Aye. I understand."

She waited for more. When nothing came, she started to tap her foot and huff, but didn't turn around. "Well?!"

"Lass, I don't know what ye want. Why don't ye just tell me?"

"I want to know when you're going. Why can't you figure that out? Damn!"

"How about tomorrow? I think we need the night here to be together and rest. Then tomorrow I will take you to the village and you can spend the day there while I go see Iseabail."

August felt her stomach turn and her face get hot again. A panic rose in her, but she recognized there was no way around it. If she was going to lose Faolan to her, it might as well be now. It might as well be before she bonded herself to him in a way that made it impossible to get over him.

She turned around and burned him with an accusatory gaze, "So you're just going to go drop me off in some strange village and leave me there all day while you go find your lost love of your life and stroll down memory lane with her?"

"August … Kenzy and Adair will be there. They'd planned on hosting you and showing you around. Lycan are generally accepted, but we're still not especially embraced by the community. You can understand that?"

The last thing August wanted to do was be away from Faolan when things were so tenuous, but she wouldn't have minded seeing Kenzy and Adair. She'd liked them both. Maybe Adair a little too much, but it was totally innocent, she assured herself.

"Fine. At least I'll be distracted by Adair's good looks." She gave him a purposeful stare. She meant it to make Faolan jealous, but if it did, he wasn't showing it.

"Would you like to go to the pub to have a bite, lass?"

Food was the last thing on her mind, but the idea of sitting in a cozy room with other people around and something strong to drink was at that moment the most appealing thing she could imagine. *How is it that now all of a sudden he can read me so well?* she grumped to herself.

"I could use some distraction, I suppose. Something for us."

He took a deep breath and smiled ever so slightly, warm and loving waves coming off of him. She pulled on some baggy clothes and he took her hand and led her to the pub through the mist in the fading light. The place was almost empty. They took a table in the corner and ordered fish and chips and beers. Faolan reached his hands across the table toward her. August uncurled hers from inside her sleeves and put

211

them on the table into his.

"I don't want ye to worry, lass. My heart is with you."

"Are you wishing about now that you hadn't met me two years ago?"

He shook his head emphatically. "I'm only sorry I hadn't done this sooner, is all."

"Isn't All Saint's Day when the ghosts are supposed to go back to their graves?"

He nodded.

"Well, a girl can hope, anyway."

"Let's talk about that night we met," he said, giving her small hands a squeeze.

"Oh, our own, very short little memory lane? Well, I was restless," she said, then a smile spread across her face. She tried to suppress it and looked away.

"The full moon, I remember."

"Well ..."

"You didn't yet know that you were part lycan, so you wouldn'a kenned why you were so restless. I was doing my suppression ritual." He cupped her left hand in his and began petting the back side of it.

She let out a bit of a giggle, then composed herself again.

"What?" He cocked his head to one side and gave her hand a little tug. "Tell me. What are you on about?"

"Well ... that night? I was watching some Skinemax, that cheesy soft porn they have on late at night on Cinemax."

"Oh?" His brows went up and he half grinned. "Do tell."

"Well, this was after what that asshole-you-know-who did to me, and I was still hurting from it. But these people, they were being so sweet to each other. I mean, it was dumb, it was totally dumb, but it was fun, too. They were laughing and having a good time, kissing and touching. Everybody wanted to be there together and they were sexy. Then they were naked."

"And you were hormonal. And with a full moon as well." He nodded in understanding, now suppressing his own smile. One corner of his mouth was tugged down, but the other didn't obey. He let out a breathy laugh, small and warm.

"Well, I ... You know ..."

"No, tell me ..." His grin was getting a little wicked.

"Well, I … touched myself." She pursed her mouth to hold in her smile.

"Go on …" He squeezed her hand a bit tighter.

"I did that, then I fell asleep. Then when I woke back up it was after midnight and I wanted to go shopping or run a race or something. I was feeling so antsy. That's when I wandered up the hill toward your mysterious place."

"And stood upwind, snapping twigs and spying on me from the bushes." He laughed and it was lovely.

She laughed too, a little embarrassed, but not too much. It actually felt like the most loving conversation she'd had with him all day.

"You told me we couldn't be friends. You wouldn't even tell me your name. I wanted you to kiss me but all I could do was go home and 'think' about you … you know … and call you Wolf."

"You used to 'think' about me, huh?" His brow went up, and his voice deepened. It sent a little shiver down her spine.

"Oh yes, often. Mostly I thought of you coming to my room. But, remember that time we ran into each other in Leighas? You walked past me, and it was like a force field stuck us together for a moment."

"You felt it too, then?"

"Well, sometimes I would imagine us right there in the store. You couldn't unstick your energy from me, and you wanted to take all my clothes off. And you did."

"Steamy. Yer gunna make the table rise." She felt herself blush. Her breasts got a little warmer and she was feeling a little swollen below. Their eyes were fixed, each swimming in the other's gaze.

"Ach, here ye go!" The spell was broken by the arrival of their beers, followed by steaming hot fish and chips.

They let go their hands but kept each other's eyes as they munched on their food and recalled the picnics and book discussions along the stream that first year. Then they talked about books they hadn't read yet, but hoped to get to. August tried not to allow in the thought that they may never get to reading those books together—that he may be with Iseabail, reading alongside her in the grass, by some stream, under shady apple trees. Before the thought could bring tears, she looked at Faolan and focused hard on him, on that moment. On the food and the beer and his smile. On the fact that he loved her now, even if some day it would fade into oblivion—a heart-breaking reality she was now wishing on somebody else. But she laughed with him and he recited some poems from memory.

Back in the room she pulled out a small stack of books from her bag. "Let's forget everything else tonight. Let's time-travel back to when we were getting to know each other and nothing scary had happened between us. Could we do that? Would you just hold me and read me a story?"

"Always." He said it and it sounded like a promise. She let it hold her together in one piece, let it wrap around her like a warm blanket on a chilly night. She pulled off everything except her panties and climbed into the bed and held out Angela Carter's new novel, *Nights at the Circus*. She watched as he pulled his sweater over his head, unbuttoned his shirt and tugged the tails free. She found that almost as sexy as when he would unbuckle his belt. Her chest got tingly and she pulled the covers up and tucked them over her breasts. She fingered her pearl necklace while she watched him undress to his briefs. He climbed in next to her, perched his glasses on the end of his nose put his arm out for her to cuddle in close.

She pressed her skin to his, and she felt the heat of their connection and the comfort of his arms. She put a hand on his hairy chest and closed her eyes as he began to read, his rich and gentle voice lulling her to sleep.

Perchance to Dream

A grassy path, heart pounding, feet beating the earth—she was swift as a frightened doe, but chasing, not chased. The greenery, a blur through the mist. A bow in her hands, arrow nocked, ready for flight. What was she even chasing? The path dead-ended at a cliff, she nearly went over, her bow disappeared into the abyss. She felt naked, defenseless. She heard a growl and turned around to see a wolf, huge, with black and white fur and two different eyes. It curled its lip and growled, drooling, snarling. Then an apparition next to it: her Aunt Blair, put a collar around it, leashed it, and led it away. She followed the path back to wherever it was she came from. The mist cleared and she found Faolan standing there, looking at her yards away, surrounded by grass and trees, the sun shining down on him. The air sparkled, but his eyes were vacant. Then an apparition next to him: Iseabail. She put a collar on him, leashed him, and led him away. He didn't even wave goodbye. As if he didn't know who she was. As if he never loved her.

August began sobbing before she was even awake. Her body shook and Faolan gently petted her arm, and her back, whispering, "August, love … love, wake up. It's only a dream, lass. Shhhh, it's alright."

As she emerged from the haze, she was vaguely aware that she had been dreaming. Her heart felt like a big needle had poked it and she was so hurt by Faolan's actions in the dream she almost couldn't separate herself from the mist world of the ether. She spoke through tears, "You didn't know me. You wouldn't even look at me." She panted and sniffed. "Like I didn't even matter!" she wailed, dissolving into more hiccupping sobs. Her ears were pointing a bit and she could feel her hands tingling. She didn't want any transformations so she tried to calm down, tried to imagine heat. But it was hard to tamp down the very real feeling of a broken heart.

"I love you, sweet, sweet girl!" Faolan cooed in her ear. "I love you dearly. I'm so sorry your heart is achin' the way it is. Of course you matter." He kept whispering reassurances into the cloud of her chocolate curls, petting her as he held her tight.

Eventually her sobs slowed and she sniffed. "I need a tissue." She sounded so small and wounded, it tugged at Faolan's heart. He released her long enough to lean an arm back and snatch a tissue from the box on the nightstand behind him. Something about the papery *fwwp* sound reminded her of heartaches past.

"It was just a bad dream, love. I could never forget you. I love you."

She felt reassured, for now. She wasn't looking forward to the awkward and uncertain day ahead—but if there was one reliable theme for this trip, she reminded herself, it was that her days were nearly always uncertain, so maybe she was getting a little used to the rollercoaster.

If after today Faolan still wanted to be with her, then she didn't need to worry about anybody else taking him, ever. Their relationship would be solid and unassailable, she reasoned, since nothing as destructive as Iseabail was ever likely to come along again. If on the other hand Faolan came back and didn't want to be with her—or if he didn't come back at all—well, she'd just swear off men for the rest of her life.

With this fatalistic attitude in place she set aside her anxiety about his visit with Iseabail. August didn't want to ruin what precious time they had together today with jealousy and fear. But she had to admit she felt competitive for Faolan's approval in a way she never had before. She imagined if she showed any sort of whininess or immaturity, Faolan would mentally put a checkmark in the "Cons" column under her name, and tick off "Pros" under Iseabail's. It was as though she was somehow less amazing today than she was two days ago, when Faolan was ready to bond with her for life. She was the same girl she had been two days before, and the whole year before that—but suddenly she was demoted to second chair. Backup. She didn't like it one bit.

Ciardha's Well
Conall Keep

Ciardha was still in his bed, but upright at least. "I'm feelin' better, wife." His voice was shaky, but stronger than the day before. "Whatever it was that gripped me seems to be passing."

"The good fortune of lycan healing, Keer. You're going to live to be a thousand." She wrung out the cloth she had in a basin next to the bed and wiped his forehead. He grabbed her by the wrist and fixed her with a glare.

"What the bloody hell do you mean by letting my brother and that mixed-breed in here? Into our house."

Blair pulled herself free from his grasp, much easier than she ever had in the past. *Still weak*, she thought to herself, and suppressed a grin.

"I lost all the meat Faolan gave me yesterday," he said, obviously a bit surprised that his wife could just now have clobbered him if she wanted to.

"Aye, I noticed." She threw a towel over a large metal basin, turned her face from it and put it near the doorway. "Katie! Kate!" A young woman in a servant uniform arrived quickly at the door, her uniform loose on her slim frame, stringy black hair escaping from the sides of her cap.

"Aye, ma'am."

"Please take that down and dispose of it."

Katie did a little bow and hauled the stinking vessel off.

Ciardha seemed momentarily sheepish. "I'm sorry yer havin' to clean up after me. I'm not used to being ill. I feel like a bloody child."

Blair noted that, though his puppy-dog moments would have made her heart ache with empathy in the past, she now felt nothing when he sounded sad. She also felt nothing when he was angry. Her feelings toward Ciardha had hardened into a rocky wasteland of indifference.

"Perhaps I should make you some bone broth. You seem dehydrated."

"I reckon I could hold that down. Hand me that, would ye?" He motioned towards the case that contained all of the documents he'd been working on for the Veritas.

"Honestly, Keer, do ye ken this a time to be—"

"Just hand it to me woman! If I don't keep up with it, that simpering dog Laithenskye is going to try and take it over."

"He'll never be alpha over you."

"The ways of the past are starting to crack. It's disgusting. Unnatural. Everybody knows he's not the alpha, but he's just young enough and he runs his sodding mouth. He challenges me at every turn. It's not the way of auld."

She dropped the case next to him on the bed. He moaned a bit and the color left his cheeks, but it soon returned and began digging through the papers.

Blair turned to leave.

"Blair." She stopped and looked over her shoulder. "I'm doing this for you. Once the Veritas accepts mixing, we can be proud of our relationship. We can be open with it."

"I was proud of it, Keer. It was you who were ashamed of me." She walked out of the door and back to the kitchen.

It Takes a Village
Meikleour Inn

August was sure she couldn't eat breakfast after exhausting herself with tears, but the sky was blue, the air was crisp and smelled of woodsmoke, and for the moment she felt as though nothing could go too far wrong today. The fact that Faolan held her and gave her so many reassurances didn't hurt. She also realized that she was actually looking forward to seeing the village where her dad and many of her relatives came from. Even Iseabail, she supposed. Somehow she seemed less threatening when August thought of her as a family member.

At the pub, August easily dispatched a full fry-up and asked for some tattie scones to go.

"These would taste better with ketchup."

"Sacrilege," Faolan scolded with a wink.

She laughed, feeling happy and relaxed. She was proud of herself for getting over the nightmare and growing up a bit, after all the blame she'd been feeling and handing out the past two days. Faolan wasn't ready to have sex with her, not because he didn't want her, but because he thought it was the best thing for her. How could she be mad at that? Even as she was feeling it, she knew it was unfair. Maybe life would be a bit easier if she just held everything in check.

"Fe, do you think it would be better if I was more like you? If I didn't, for example, tell you every single time I'm upset? Or tell you why I'm mad? Is it ... manipulative? To tell you when you're doing something that hurts me, I mean. See, I don't always know when I'm supposed to tell you some—"

"August?" He put his hands out across the table, she put hers in them. He rose up off of the chair and leaned forward across the table, and waited for her to do the same. They kissed—long enough so that the other patrons paused, breakfast on forks, to take notice—and then he sat back down. She lingered a moment in the air, enjoying the sweetness of that soft, soulful kiss, then took her own seat.

"One of the reasons I fell so in love with you is for the nakedness of your heart."

August blinked and thought about that for a moment. "It is?"

He smiled, so gentle he was almost humble, and nodded. "It is."

"For some reason I always thought of it as a flaw of mine. I'm just blaaah, you know, out there with it. Especially when I'm nervous."

Faolan listened in that deliberate way of his, and nodded for her to go on.

"I thought that maybe I was giving you too much feedback about heartaches and all of my hopes, dreams, you know—all that stuff. It's *so much stuff* sometimes, I get tired of hearing my own voice. I guess it goes back to self-esteem a little; I feel like maybe somebody wouldn't want to know all of those things about me. Like it's annoying. I'm sure there are times I could go with the idea that sharing isn't always caring."

Faolan smiled so wide it touched the corners of his eyes and he let out a small laugh. "You're something else, Red, d' ye ken it?"

"I guess I ken." She couldn't have sounded less Scottish. Not that she was trying to. "I've gone on a ramble again."

"Aye. A delightful ramble, full of heart and courage and faith in me to hear it. Let's go get the day started, Ramblin' Red, and come back to each other's arms tonight."

The trip out to Summerblynd was just a little longer than their ride to Conall Keep the day before. "It's weird to think that the keep and the village are so close together," August pondered. "What are they, twenty minutes apart?"

"More like thirty, but both are well hidden from the main roads. You'd need a helicopter or some such to figure it out if ye dinna know where they are."

"But each knows where the other is, I'm sure. After all this time."

Faolan nodded. "Aye, that's right enough. There were lycan lands all through here once, though lycan and hunter are both a bit thin on the ground these years."

August marveled at how beautiful the day had turned out to be. "Man, this weather is perfect. A little nippy, but otherwise just gorgeous."

"We've been quite lucky. Maybe you bring sunshine with you wherever you go, Red."

She smiled, and felt her heart do a little flutter. He managed to make moments like that for her every day. Some kind word. Some small flirt. Even on their most worn down and distant days, he would brush her cheek or read her a poem. He always had time for her, even if it was just a few minutes.

Then her feeling of joy caught on a hook of fear and it tore. She remembered that these could be the last moments she would have with him where he was hers. She wondered if she could live with it if he loved both of them. What if he chose her, but couldn't stop loving Iseabail? Can you stop loving somebody, even if you want to? What is love anyway? Is it chemical? Is it being seen, and knowing you matter to someone? Is it time you spend, holding hands and sharing a meal? Is it sex? Maybe it was all of these things, or any combination, or just one of them at a time. She swallowed down the tears that tried to make their way to the surface.

"What was your favorite book when you were young, Fe? Maybe we can read it when we get back to Maryland."

"Well, I was an early fan of Verne's *Autour de le Lune*, mostly because, being a young werewolf, I was naturally very curious about the moon. Never did meet him, Verne—I was only a pup when he last visited Scotland. Anyroad, I had a beautiful illustrated edition in my youth. Back then, the moon was very mysterious. I suppose it's still mysterious."

"I think so, too. I mean, why do we change at a full moon? The moon is always there—the whole thing—it's just sometimes lit better."

He laughed and did a little howl. She joined in and they howled merrily together for a moment.

"Nobody really knows why. Mayhap it's only race memory, since the light of a full moon is enough to hunt by. Generation after generation of hunting by moonlight, resulting in our powerful urge to transform. There is still some magic in this world, and I reckon it'll take science a while longer to catch up to it. My favorite book, though, was a collection of Burns's poetry." He leaned in conspiratorially. "I dinna ken if ye twigged to it, but I'm a bit of a romantic at heart."

"Hadn't noticed." She said it deadpan and looked at her nails. He nudged her arm with his elbow.

"Hah. I've always liked my Grimm, as ye know. Makes a bit more sense now, perhaps?"

"Perhaps. Oh, Fe, I still want to see a mermaid, though. I know they're hard to find."

"Aye, they're slippery."

August let him hang there several seconds before acknowledging him. "That … was terrible."

"Ah know. But you like my terrible jokes, don't ye?"

"I don't know if it's even fair to call that a joke. More like a badly timed half-pun, But, I admit, I might laugh at your terrible jokes from time to time."

"My favorite is when you give me the straight face of silence, then a couple of blinks. Blink, blink. Och, it's the best!"

They rounded a hill and drove onto a small winding trail that was flanked by trees. The road was barely more than two tire tracks leading into a thickly wooded area.

"Are we almost there?"

"Aye, about ten more minutes."

"You weren't kidding. Who would even know to follow this road? It looks like a private drive."

"It's a bit easier to find things in the winter, when the foliage is thinner. But it's thick in parts, with trees doubled and tripled in rows." Indeed, the trees marched along the trail in long lines, no doubt planted long ago as camouflage. Many had dropped their leaves already, and in the clearer spots they could see where other track roads crossed or branched off.

After they drove over a small berm and through a tight line of trees, the view opened up a bit. There was a long stone wall trailing off into the distance on both sides, with tall stone columns where the wall met the road. There was a large iron gate standing open and a carved sign attached to the left-hand column, reading "Hunter's Village." A smaller sign beneath warned of security cameras. "There's no cameras, actually," Faolan noted. "It's just to discourage the curious."

Near the entrance there was a stone tower that reached as high as the tallest trees, though not above them. It reminded August a little of Rapunzel's tower, with windows around the top.

"That tower didn't always have a clock on it. It was strictly for guards to watch over the entrance. Once peace was remade, they set it up as a clocktower, hoping to make things a bit friendlier, I think."

She regarded the ironwork clock face cobbled onto the tower, and it didn't look right—as though it were a friendly mask.

"Does it have a bell at the top?"

"It does, actually. For warning the village in an emergency. They haven't used that in fifty years though. It's phones and radios, now." He chuckled. "Though I suppose it'd do in a pinch."

Moments later they were parked in front of a small general store, situated next door to a tiny pub. The whole place looked like a model railroad set, so tidy and perfect. It reminded August of old western towns, though instead of wood sidewalks and clapboard storefronts, with painted windows and swinging saloon doors, this village was stone and thatch, flower beds and wrought iron. There was a fountain and a circle in the center of the village, and Faolan parked at the curb, opened August's door for her, and led her across the circle to the fountain. He turned around and parked his butt against the low stone wall, crossing his arms and then his booted ankles in a casual attitude.

"Umm … What are we waiting for?"

"Your kin."

"Oh." August looked around at all the windows facing the circle and felt a bit like a fish in a tank as she adopted a similar attitude of waiting. Who was watching them? What would they be thinking of her? She pulled her sleeves down over her fingers and crossed her arms and looked around. The place was so unnaturally quiet it was making her jumpy, and she had the growing feeling that it wasn't a real village at all. There were only three other cars in sight, and an ancient-looking delivery van, pale yellow with a painting of flowers on the side.

After about five minutes of this awkward waiting game, August heard a door creak open and turned around to see five figures exiting the flower shop across the circle. The group walked towards them and Faolan stood and dusted off his bottom. Evidently this was the welcoming committee, though it wasn't nearly the warm halloo they received in the cloak shop in Glasgow. Most of them were older men with pale skin and wispy ginger hair, and there were head nods and a few words like "grand to see ye" but no hugs, and only a couple of handshakes. But among their group was a young woman who had warm yellow skin and a multitude of deep brown freckles. Her hair was in braids—three of them down each side of her head, ending in wood beads—and her amber eyes fixed on August as she gave her a warm smile.

"Hi, I'm Gordania, though everybody calls me Nia." August took her outstretched hand and they shook. "These are my uncles,

Benneit, Barclay, Breac, and Bhradain." She gestured towards them, each one taller and heavier than the last. Benneit actually took August's hand and gave it a kiss. Bhradain seemed to be unhappy to have to greet August at all. She tried not to read too much into it, but she was already feeling incredibly self-conscious and also nervous that Faolan was going to leave her here for the day.

"So, are you gentlemen the local florists?"

Benneit was the first to laugh and, the others followed. He responded, "I suppose we are."

August felt her face get warm with embarrassment. They didn't look like florists, but what did she know about what florists look like around the world?

"So you're leaving her here with us for the day, eh, Faolan?" Bhradain asked, arms crossed. "Not afraid to stick around, are ye?"

Faolan's face said that Bhradain was being ridiculous. "Whatever you like, Bhradain."

"Aye, tha's as I thought."

Faolan inhaled deeply and let out a sigh, as though underscoring how unruffled he was. He took August's hand to say his farewells. "I'll be back around eleven tonight."

"Eleven!" August felt her heart thudding hard in her chest. She wasn't at all sure she wanted to be stuck with these strangers out in the middle of nowhere for all that time. She also didn't much want Faolan hanging out with Iseabail for the entire day and half of the night. It made her a little nauseated just thinking of it.

Everybody looked at her, a bit startled at her protestation.

"Let's give the two lovers some privacy to say goodbye," Benneit said, and led the others away.

"We'll be just in there," Nia offered, pointing at the florist shop.

August nodded, wide-eyed and, if anything, even more terrified than when she went to see Ciardha. This revelation only magnified her anxiety over who would be coming back for her tonight. Would it be the Faolan that was all but ready to be her husband, or the one who realizes he's still hopelessly in love with Iseabail?

"Don't go. You can stay." She sounded whiney, she could even hear it herself. It was not her proudest moment, but she felt like she wanted to fight or flee, and left her worried and clingy.

Faolan's face registered his sympathy, but also determination. "I can't stay for this, lass. It's just not done. You're safe here, you'll have a good time. Go learn about your people."

She could feel tears welling up in her eyes.

"You needn't worry about us, August. I'm going to settle things—to say goodbye, as I always intended to do when we came here."

"But that was when you thought she was …" A tear escaped and rolled down her cheek.

"I love you. Try to be here, with these people, your people, and trust me." He took her hands in his and kissed each of her knuckles, then pulled her arms around his waist and encircled her with his for a tight hug, kissing her on top of her head. She followed him back to the car, where he handed her her bag and cloak and then got in. "Go on now, head over to the shop door. I'll wait."

August looked utterly dejected. She slumped her way towards the flower shop, stopping to look over her shoulder more than once. Each time Faolan winked at her and motioned for her to keep moving and have courage. He didn't pull away until the door was shut and she turned around to wave at him through the panes.

The Hunting Grounds

August watched as the Range Rover disappeared around the bend. She swallowed, steeled her nerves and turned around. The hulking uncles all ducked through a small doorway at the back of the shop. When the curtain closed behind the last giant, she surveyed the shop.

Everything was whitewashed wood, quaint barrels and vases. She noticed that the actual flower inventory was sparse.

"We are at the end of a delivery cycle," piped a small voice from behind the counter. August looked over her shoulder to see a tiny woman, her hair in a silver pixie cut and her eyes as bright as a nymph's. Though her wizened face was a roadmap of lines and creases, her flesh was pink with life.

"I see. Okay." August could barely turn around in the place with her bow, quiver, cloak and bag in her arms. She peered around her bundles to try and figure out where she should go next.

"We don't do a lot of walk-in business. We tend more towards … events. So we don't keep much inventory on hand," she finished brightly.

August puffed out her cheeks and lifted her brows and nodded, an expression that she hoped said, *That's cool*, though she was thinking more along the lines of *Who cares?* She waited for instructions and finally looked to Nia, who was watching the exchange patiently.

"This way," Nia said, with a jerk of her head towards the curtained doorway in the back. August waddled a bit through the narrow aisle and tried not to get caught on the fabric as Nia held it aside.

The back looked unremarkably like the tiny storeroom of any small retail establishment—this particular one with lots of floral wire, nippers, scissors, and vases, along with trashcans, extension cords, and ribbon spools. Nia put her hand up, motioning for August to stay put a moment. She grabbed a vice that was on the side counter and gave the handle a yank, then grabbed a peg hook with a water hose coiled around it. To August's amazement, the whole pegboard panel opened like a door, as if they were in an old spy movie. August took a step forward and craned her neck as Nia turned on a light and grabbed some weapons—a bow, a quiver, a couple of knives—and backed out, closing the secret passage.

"For emergencies," she said, and winked at August, who felt her face getting a little warm. She realized she actually would have liked to kiss Nia, and it left her momentarily speechless. Nia led her out of the rear door of the shop and into a little back lot where three more vans were parked, identical to the one out front. The uncles were standing next to one of them, and Benneit was holding the passenger door open for August. He bowed and waved her in, taking her gear for her as she hoisted herself up into the van. She felt the uncles get into the back, the vehicle lowering more and more with each body settling into place. She hoped that the road they were taking wasn't too bumpy or they were going to be scraping the ground all the way.

Nia offloaded her equipment into the back with the uncles and hopped in the driver side, turned over the engine, and lurched the vehicle forward with not a lot of grace.

"Where are we going?"

"The hunting grounds." She said it as though they'd already discussed it weeks ago.

"Oh. Okay. Only … I … uh … I don't hunt."

"Heh. Not that kind of hunting. It's training. You're a hunter, Archer—yer gonna need some trainin' with yer gear." Her accent was probably the lightest, with the exception of Adair's.

"Are you … Do you live here?"

"I'm from here, aye, but I travel a lot. My father is from here, my mother is from Panama. But I've spent many a summer in the States."

"How old … I mean, if you don't mind me asking, how old—"

"Nineteen."

August nodded.

The road out to the hunting grounds was isolated—even more so than the road out to the keep. After the first five minutes of houses and buildings, there was virtually no sign of civilization, with the exception of one rather large house that was slowly being eaten by the vines and weeds around it. They drove up and up the side of a low mountain and then through some trees to another gated road.

"You all are fond of gates."

"They aren't always enough for keeping out them that are determined," Benneit chimed in from the back. "But they do let a body know that they're trespassing, an' it won't be taken kindly."

They hit a deep hole in one side of the road and the uncles muttered and groaned.

"Sorry! I keep forgetting about that one!" Nia called back to them.

"Yer gunna pop a tire, ye tyke!" one of them shouted. Nia whistled like a falling bomb. Several of the uncles laughed. August could only wonder how many family jokes she wouldn't be getting today.

The gate was flanked by two guards wearing kilts, boots, and shoulder belts hanging with weaponry.

"That's Henry," Nia said as she pointed to the handsome guard on August's side of the vehicle. "He's an Archer."

"An Archer, or an archer?" August asked, feeling a little silly.

"Both."

August nodded and looked close at the young man as they went by, wondering what branch of the Archer tree he was on.

Nia added, "Most here are Archer, Huntar, Blackwood and Hardy. Of course there are some McCabes, the original cloak-makers. Others, too. Some of the lines have joined and lost a name here and there, but there's some'll go to lengths to keep theirs alive. We had a rash of girl births about twenty year back, wi' yours truly. Some have taken to keeping their family name in marriage, or having their bairns outside of marriage, just to pass the name on. I think if you look up some of your history, the names will tell you a bit of what you might wish to ken about your homeland."

August nodded. She was thinking about how she was the last child in her father's line. Well, that she knew of. Which meant if she got married and took on a name, her Archer branch of the family tree would blunt.

"I didn't think there were many Archers left," she admitted.

"There is more than one line, though. It's far from straight."

August nodded again, resigned to the idea she would have more questions than answers after all this.

They parked next to what looked like a small barn, or a big shed.

"That's the weapons store. There's targets and all kinds of weapons to try out."

August was the first out of the van and she watched as the van got taller and taller as each uncle exited the back, until she could finally see the whole of the tires again. She shouldered her equipment and followed the group around to the back side of the barn. There was another building there with the big doors flung wide open, where a half-dozen men and women of various ages worked at old-fashioned pedal sewing machines. When they all went at once it made quite a racket, August noticed.

"Those are mostly McCabes. Terrible fighters, most of them, though some McCabes are legend. They are genius at the needle." Nia walked towards one of the older men in the group. He was working on a pair of doeskin pants. "Gavin, this is August Archer, from the States." Gavin sniffed the air a bit and gave August a little side-eye. Nia smiled, "It's alright, she's one of us."

Gavin grunted and turned his face towards her, one eye was covered with a patch. "Well, so long as she stays lookin' like it." It took August a moment to realize that her ears and fingertips were tingling ever so slightly. She understood that now was no time to be showing her lycan side.

Nia scooped August's cloak right off of her shoulder. "Could you please mend and update this? Make it lighter? Reversible?"

"Ah know bloody well what *update* means, lass. And ye c'n spare me the charm." Gavin stood and pulled out a measuring tape and garment chalk. Nia took August's equipment and Gavin threw the cape around August and began measuring and marking. He then whipped it off of her shoulders and commanded, "Arms up." He looped his arms around her, pulling the tape firm around her hips, then waist, then bust, which made August feel incredibly awkward. She also noticed he was missing a couple of fingers on his right hand. Nobody else seemed to think it was much, so she just looked up at the ceiling. He snapped his tape measure and rolled it up smoothly, then and sat back down and turned towards his machine. "It'll be ready by supper."

"Thanks, Gavin," Nia chirped. He grunted in reply and they left the hall of chugging machines.

"He's not going to ruin it, is he Nia? It was my dad's."

"Don't worry. No one knows hunter garb better than a McCabe. Ye'll love it, I guarantee."

"That's a little weird, isn't it? A whole clan of surnames is only good at one thing?"

"Not all of them, just most of them, and not when you really think about it, August." Nia stopped and turned towards her. It was then that August noticed that the uncles were no longer lurking nearby and she and Nia were alone. As she watched Nia talking, she couldn't stop feeling a little mesmerized by her eyes and lips. *What the hell is up with my hormones?* she wondered.

"Musicians, artists, athletes," Nia went on. "We never think it's weird when the son of a great singer is also a gifted singer. Talent is part experience and opportunity, after all. Along with a natural ability comes the passing down of knowledge and skill to each new generation. It becomes a way of life—a family culture, y' could say. I think we've had two good McCabe hunters in later generations. The rest are great at making clothes, mending traditional cloaks. It just works out that way."

"I see," was all August said, though she was thinking, *I'm glad I don't have to be pigeonholed into some predetermined fate because of where my parents are from.* Somehow, the irony of that thought completely escaped her at that moment.

"Remember the story of Little Red Riding Hood?"

"Of course."

"A McCabe."

"Ah. Okay." August supposed she meant the Red Riding Hood story that Sorcha had told her at the cabin, and not the one in fairy-tale books. She shook off the little daze she was feeling and realized how close she was standing to Nia. She made herself take a step or two back. "Sorry. Late night. What's next, Nia?"

"Practice. Planning. Strategy. We need to be prepared."

"Prepared for what?"

"The Veritas, and others of their ilk. They pose a real danger to the fragile peace between our peoples and the cumanta—and they have no idea what kind of havoc they could wreak."

"I heard the Veritas was small, and dwindling. I also know that Ciardha is ill."

Nia shot her a look and tilted her head. "Ciardha Conall? How do you know this?"

"I saw him yesterday."

"You *saw* him?" Nia narrowed her eyes.

"Well, I didn't actually see him. Faolan saw him. We went to …

Look, he's sick. I don't have any reason to make that up."

Nia crossed her arms and cocked a foot outwards. "I didn't say that you did. But if Ciardha is ill, that's important intel and I would like to know more. You want to help us or not?"

"Well, I certainly have no love for Ciardha. He murdered my father and tried to kill my mother and my gran, and my friends."

"He'll kill you too, ye know. Given half the chance."

"I don't know about that. We're trying to negotiate peace with him. Because Faolan has bonded to me, it seems his brother is less keen on killing me."

"I wouldn't let my guard down, if I were you."

August nodded. "I won't."

"Good." She looked thoughtful for a moment, and August felt as though Nia were weighing her with her eyes. Then she went on. "Ciardha isn't our only trouble. There's some younger blood in the group now, including some who don't like the changes he's been moving toward."

"Changes?"

"Changing Veritas policy. Ciardha has been building the case for mixing otherkin blood."

"Mixing races? I thought that was like, the whole thing the Veritas was about, though—not mixing. Pure breeds."

"That's why this new opposition is so fired up. The whole party seemed to be sagging, and we thought it might just die off altogether, outnumbered by the younger lycan and half-lycans and other mixes who'd rather socialize than rule the world."

"Wouldn't that be nice."

"Aye, but then this Engres Laithenskye came along, spouting that whole 'werewolves are the naturally dominant species' thing, so now all the speciesists and 'true believers' in lycan superiority are coming out of the woodwork."

"Engres Laithenskye? Well, that's a dramatic name."

"Aye, and he's a dramatic bloke. You wouldn't want to cross paths with him on a full moon. Ciardha didn't mention him during your visit?"

"I don't know. He was sick upstairs, Faolan went up to see him. I spent my time with Blair."

"Blair?" Nia seemed confused.

"His wife."

Her face clouded. "There has long been a rumor that he had a wife, but nobody could confirm it absolutely. Just rumors, for years. She must stay locked up in that place."

"It's pretty isolated."

"How did you get in?"

"Through the front door."

Nia took on a determined expression. "We're going to need you to draw us a map of what you saw."

"I don't know … I should talk to Faolan first. I'm not really in a place—"

"You need to do this, August," she said with sudden intensity. "And you cannot tell Faolan about any of this. Not the map, not the hunting grounds, not the training—none of it."

August was stunned into silence. She felt her face get hot and her ears and fingers start to tingle, her mouth agape.

Nia put her hand on August's shoulder. "There is no reason he needs to know. He is the brother of one of our worst enemies. Ye cannot tell him." Nia's plea was urgent and forceful. There was no wiggle room for discussion.

"I wish you had told me I was going to have to lie to my boyfriend before you dragged me out here. He thinks I'm eating a feast and talking about family. It feels like lying to me." She looked defiantly into Nia's eyes.

"And what is he doing today?"

August immediately felt a sense of urgency rising at the thought of Faolan at Iseabail's door, probably this very moment, anxious to connect with her. Not even missing August. Maybe hugging, holding or even kissing Iseabail.

"I … He's … Seeing an old friend," August managed to get out.

"Do you trust him with his brother?"

That hit a mark, too. August felt herself growing cross with these piercing questions. She looked down at the ground and jammed her hands into her jacket pockets.

"You don't know me, Nia," she replied to the grass and dirt.

Nia softened, and gently tugged August's hands out of her pockets. She laced their fingers together and crouched down to place herself in August's earthbound gaze. "Your people need you to keep this secret, Archer. It won't hurt for him not to know about it. It may actually be a burden to him, if you tell him. But if he knows, it could hurt us. Even with just an accidental slip."

"Faolan's too good to make a mistake like that."

"But if he did, he'd feel awful. Especially if it caused more death and destruction. Right?" Nia waited for a reply. "Right?"

"I guess it won't hurt for him not to know. I have to tell him something though."

"You can tell him we did some practice shooting. You can tell him we had a good meal—we'll be doing that. And you can tell him some of the family stories we're going to share with you today. Just don't tell him what we're preparing for. Alright?"

August nodded. "Alright." She supposed that there was no reason for Faolan to know. She could barely admit it to herself, but she didn't always trust him about his brother.

Nia stood, smiling, and let go of August's hands to give her a hug.

"I had a feeling about you, August Archer. I could tell you were made of stronger stuff."

August laughed, feeling somehow lightened. "You can call me Red, Nia."

"C'mon. It's time we were at the rock."

Nia led on at a more determined pace, past the cluster of sheds and buildings and higher up the hill. Once they rounded a grove of fiery rowan trees and a few scattered boulders there was a lovely overlook view of the green and gold valley below, and to the side, some sixty or seventy people clustered around a large table rock jutting up out of the ground. August watched as a long-legged dark-skinned woman appeared, took a couple of strides and leapt effortlessly up onto the four-foot-high rock and turned to address the crowd of pale faces and black and ginger heads. They were turning and whispering to each other, but quickly fell silent when the woman crossed her arms.

August stared and took a few steps forward, transfixed. She had never seen anybody like this woman—limbs long and lanky, her skin the deepest shade of any black person she could remember, but with a difference she couldn't place. Her hair was onyx, hanging in loose fat curls just past her shoulders. Most striking, she had patterns of white dots and lines on her face, and more markings in bands on her upper arms. Her clothing was animal skins and fur, her pants hugging powerful thighs that looked as if they could crush a man's head like a walnut. August thought she was possibly the most stunning human being she'd ever seen, and wondered where she came from, though she was afraid to ask, not wanting to reveal her ignorance or to insult such a proud figure.

The woman looked down from the rock, scanning the crowd with her large, deep-set eyes. Her full lips set firm, her face impassive above her long neck, giving away no sense of her emotion.

"I am Merindah. I am not here to show you weapons. You have your weapons, I have mine. Other masters of skill will teach you to better use yours. I am here to help you expand your awareness. To make visible what surrounds you unseen. We will begin our journey at sunset, over there by a fire." She pointed to a timber pyre that had been laid in the open hillside. "Until then, continue your practice. Do not neglect to eat and drink. Warriors need their strength. No fire burns long without fuel."

Merindah floated back to the grass and strode away. August turned around to find Nia and ran straight into a boy. For a moment she had a flashback to Tanner bullying her, which made her stomach flop and her heart thud. Then just as quickly she felt a flash of delight when she realized it was only Adair, smiling warmly.

"Hello," he said.

"Oh, hi." August's heart sped up again and she coughed.

"D' ye need some water?"

"Oh … er, no. I'm okay. Thanks." She felt her whole body flush.

"Mum sends her regrets. Da was feelin' peaky an' so she stayed to run the shop and nurse him back from the brink."

"Oh, I'm sorry. Both for missing her and for Angus."

"Truth to tell, I reckon he only has the 'Kenzy flu.' Ye should see how pitiful he is when Mum's on an away day."

Adair was looking over August's shoulder.

"So, pretty braw, aye?"

"Wha—" August looked around.

"Merindah." His grin was wide. "She's a legend." He seemed utterly star struck.

August took this as her chance to find out more about her origins.

"Where … How … I mean …" She had hoped to word the question in a way that she didn't sound completely clueless. And it seemed Adair wasn't going to let her off of the hook, or maybe he was just slow on the uptake—either one was a mark against him in August's book. She told herself she could never be attracted to a guy who doesn't understand subtlety.

"Adair, I'm trying to ask you … Well, I don't know what to ask, actually."

"She's Aborigine."

August stared for a moment and tried to grasp his meaning. "Aborigine means indigenous, doesn't it? An indigenous person?"

"She's the kind from Australia."

"Oh …" August had little more to say. She realized her knowledge of Australia was severely lacking.

"Don't get to see many of them," Adair went on. "Mostly they really don't like Scots, though who can blame them?" He squatted to pick up something from the grass, examined it and tossed it away.

"What? Why?"

"Well, you know when the English went to America and shat all over the native people? Stealing their land, killing, raping, bringing disease, defiling sacred places—you know, that stuff."

"Yeah."

"Same thing in Australia, but with we Scots."

She thought at first he meant wee Scots, like in little Scotsmen. Then she realized he meant "we" as in all of them, August included.

"You'd think, after being shat on by the English for so long, we might be a bit more … sympathetic to them that lived there. Nope."

"Why is she here then? I mean … if she hates you? I mean, us."

They both looked over in the direction of Merindah, who was quite far away now, throwing a boomerang at some birds, knocking one out of the sky.

"Damn," August said, feeling equal measures of amazement and sadness.

"She's here because she is part Scot, specifically part hunter. She's otherkin."

"She seems like more than a hunter, to me. What sorts of otherkin is she besides hunter?"

"Nah, I think it's just hunter. The rest is just being Aborigine.

They have their own kind of magic."

"I'm sure there's a long story behind her being part Scottish hunter."

"I'm sure there is, but I don't know much else."

Ever the academic when at a loss, August realized what she really needed was some books, and maybe some *National Geographic* magazines. "I'm definitely going to want to read up on this subject when I get back home. I wonder if Faolan …" She felt a stab in her chest at just saying his name. At the very idea that maybe she wouldn't be seeing his library anymore.

"If Faolan … what?"

She tried to hide her rising emotion, "Just, maybe his library has something. He's got a big library."

"Maybe so. Ye wanna go run and shoot? Wait, they didn't give ye your clothes yet?"

"What clothes?"

"Ye need better hunting clothes than that. They didn't say they had some for ye? I'd swear I heard it said …"

That was when Nia tapped August on the shoulder.

"I forgot to give you these. Sorry. Traditional hunter clothes." Nia eyed the pants and jacket combo August had on.

"How did—?"

"Your mother sent us your sizes."

"Wow. Ok, thanks."

"You can go change over there." Nia pointed to a bush between two large oaks.

"Um …"

"Never know when something is going to go down out in the field, so you can't be shy."

"Right." August took her package and marched over behind the bush, and did her best to figure out the new clothes and pull them on overtop of what she had on, before taking the other stuff off. She was struggling with her new shirt, which was rather awkward to get into because she had to take off her bra, when a spear flew by her head so close she could hear the whistle of it in her ear just before it struck and lodged in the tree beside her.

"Shit!" August yelped, almost toppling over, struggling to keep herself covered. "Who the fu—" At that moment she noticed Merindah standing just inches from her.

"Never leave your weapons," was all she said, and she dumped August's bow and quiver at her feet. August was too shocked to say anything, and imagined that even if she did think of something it would only inspire more terrifying lessons. The woman turned away, then stopped and turned back. She put both hands on August's shoulders and nearly pulled her off her feet.

"What are you—" August tried to wiggle away from her, but Merindah's grip was steel. A gust of wind whipped up and, with a crack, a large dead branch came crashing down in the spot where August had just been standing, breaking into half a dozen pieces.

August shuddered and looked at Merindah in silent awe. The woman released her, tugged the spear out of the tree, and walked away without another word.

"Shit. This is a crazy day."

Adair came running over. "August! Are y' awreet? Um ... you have a little—"

"Turn around!" August yelled at him and tried to tuck her half-exposed breast into the doeskin top. "Why is this so low-cut?" She shouted in frustration.

Adair started to turn back around, "Y' just tighten the la—"

"Turn around! Christ!" He spun back around.

"Sorry. Sorry. A'm just trying t' help."

"Well I don't need your help." Though she had to admit his hint about tightening the laces did help. The top seemed to be designed to accommodate different breast sizes; the bigger the breasts, the wider the gap. August was able to lace it to nearly closed. "I don't have a mirror. Can't they make this out of something other than doeskin?"

"It's traditional."

"I know, but ... did a doe really have to die to make me a shirt? It seems ridiculous. At least the pants are, well ... they're made of fabric." Still, August couldn't deny that the feel of the leather was supple and fitted nicely to her. She imagined she probably looked pretty good, too. She was going to have to settle this battle of conscience later, when less drama was happening.

"Most people just say thank you," Adair muttered. He was now picking leaves from the tree and tossing them.

"I didn't ask for any of this." Luckily she wore her boots—the

237

ensemble would have looked ridiculous with loafers. Then she remembered that she already owned doeskin moccasins, and treasured them. She wondered if she could have slunk silently away in them, from this embarrassing episode of grumpy hypocrisy.

Adair crossed his arms and leaned against a tree, still facing away from her.

"What do I do with this? Adair ..."

"Reckon I can turn 'round now?"

"Yes, you can turn around now."

He had intended to be curt with her, but not a chance. Not looking as good as she did right now, in tight brown leather and snug green britches.

"Wow."

"What?" She felt her heart speed up again and her cheeks go warm as Adair looked her up and down.

"Well, ye look ... Mmh!" He gave a shake of his head.

"What's that mean?"

"It means Faolan is a lucky man."

"Yeah, well ... Could you tell me what this is for? Please?" She held a long plaid scarf out for him.

"That's just your scarf from the Huntar Tartan—we all wear it. See?" He grabbed the edges of his kilt and fanned it out. "That you've got's for unmarried lasses to wear over their heads. When you're single, you wear it over—"

"Yeah, I'm not doin' that."

Adair shrugged. "Suit yerself."

"I will."

"It's cumbersome, anyway. None of the girls wear them the way they're supposed to. These ones are lighter than the winter ones, so they make a nice belt, if ye like."

"What I need is a jacket. How am I supposed to conceal my dagger holster in this cave-girl stripper top?"

"Ye ken you've got a bit of an attitude?"

"Yeah, I ken that."

Adair loosely crossed his arms again and took a couple of steps forward. "Ye don't need to conceal it here." He tugged the straps a little on her shoulders to even them out. The whole ensemble looked pretty badass. "Ye wanna tell me what's eatin' at ye? I'm a good listener."

She didn't want to talk about it; she didn't even want to think about it. But she also felt like she was going to explode.

"I don't want to tell anybody anything."

"Awreet. Well, if ye change yer mind, I'm all ears. I'm happy to—"

"I don't want to tell anybody how stressful it is to be in this place I don't know. I don't want to tell anybody how scary it felt to have that woman throw a spear at me. I certainly don't want to tell anybody that Faolan is ..." She swallowed down tears that were rising up in her throat.

"It's alright, lass. I'm not going to tell anybody."

"That Faolan is at this very moment with some woman—who happens to be my great-grandmother—that he's been in love with since, oh, just about forever."

August snuck a peek at Adair, who had a concerned look on his face.

"I don't want to tell anybody that I am really ..." *way too attracted to you*, she finished the thought in her head. She actually did want to tell Adair, but she didn't want it to be a thing all day, either. So she took a deep breath and used the scarf to dry her tears. She could feel her ears tingling and her gums vibrating. She was very close to slipping up and transforming, at least in part. *Heat—think of heat.* She grabbed the little flask out of her bag and took a swig of the tea Faolan gave her that was Brigid's special blend for suppressing transformation. She took another breath and tucked it back into her bag.

"That you're really, what?" He said it very tenderly and offered out a hand, which she took and he squeezed, sending an uncomfortably sensual chill throughout her body.

"I'm really stressed out, Adair. I'm supposed to have this brave warrior blood or something."

He took her other hand and squeezed them both. August noticed the sun highlighting the red in his dark brown hair. His eyes hazel with flecks of yellow. She wanted to kiss this boy. She wanted to kiss him very badly. It made her forget for just a moment how hurt she was by Faolan. It made her forget Faolan altogether for about a quarter of a second. Then she chided herself for wanting somebody else, when it hurt her so badly that Faolan wanted somebody else.

"How's this then—why don't I get you acquainted wi' some of the others and we can all have a go shooting and stabbing and hiding together? It's the best sort of thing to work off nervous energy. Besides, I heard yer pretty flash with a bow and arrow."

She realized she'd been holding her breath, and she released it with an audible sigh. It did sound like a good idea—she could burn off some of this nervous energy. She also didn't hate the idea of getting to know Adair better. She would probably never see him again after today, so she might as well just enjoy the time she had with him.

She smiled and nodded at him, and he was visibly relieved. She belted on her hip quiver and donned her glove and bracers.

"Let's do it."

The Dreamtime

August met at least thirty clan members there at the hunting ground that afternoon. She discovered that some of them were older, if not as old as Faolan, but most of them were between seventeen and twenty-five. Some of them were genuinely happy to meet her, though it didn't escape August that many of the girls had only social smiles and greetings. She guessed that pretty much all of the single women had their eyes on Adair, and she couldn't blame them. Whenever she could, she informed them that she was only in town for a couple of days, then it was back to the States. She dropped the word "boyfriend" several times when talking about Faolan, but none of them seemed to buy it. She guessed the imbalance of females to males was partly to blame for the aggressive competition she sensed, and though she was experiencing her own desperation over men in a different way at the moment, she could relate. It also didn't help that Adair was sticking to her like a combination watchful chaperone and hopeful pup.

When she wasn't distracted by sexual politics, August focused on what she was actually there for, and observed her kin as they practiced their skills. Everybody she saw seemed to be well-skilled—the Archers and Hunters mostly used bow and arrow, and as she watched them her fingers itched to pull her bowstring. Other hunter clans stuck to daggers and close hand-to-hand combat. Adair himself showed her several ways to use her sgian dubh in close quarters. Neck seemed the most likely strike to her, but most importantly she knew now that if she ever found herself in another bad situation with a man trying to hurt her, he was never going forget the encounter—assuming he survived it.

Finally, she took the opportunity to work her archery skills, and all thoughts of boys and boyfriends receded to the far edges of her mind as she pulled her bowstring taut and felt the thrill of whistling arrows into each small target that she saw in her mind. People gathered to watch, apparently genuinely impressed. Her knee-bends and push-ups, though they had required every scrap of self-discipline she could muster to practice back home, seemed to really be paying off in her trail work. She would run and leap onto a rock, or push off a tree and turn in midair and still shoot with accuracy. She found that, here on the training grounds, people were only too happy to throw little pea-stuffed sacks into the air for her, and she'd pin them with her shafts. An hour and a half flew by, and August found she'd really held her own, boasting the second-best target score for the day. She even seemed to gain a measure of respect from some of the girls who had given her the fake-nice earlier; now they seemed genuinely warm and respectful towards her.

A group of a dozen or more young lasses took their neatly boxed lunches beneath a tree, and August followed. "I can't believe how warm it is for this time of the year, can you Adair?" one of the girls ventured, staring at the boy and waiting for acknowledgment. He grunted in the affirmative while stuffing a rather large sandwich in his face.

"This is pretty fancy dining for hunting camp, or whatever this is," August said to the group as she untied the string on her box.

A girl with long red braids spoke up. "Me mum always makes them with my aunt. She can't hunt anymore, or use weapons at all really—she does it to be useful. That's as she says, anyway."

August pulled out a large sandwich, a big hunk of cheese, an interesting variation on carrot sticks and some shortbread cookies. She had been feeling conspicuously hungry until her mind wandered back to Faolan. She wished she had some way to check in with him. Even just a phone would have been nice. She picked up the sandwich and tore into it, and guzzled down water from a canteen.

"Tell your mom thanks from me," August commended the girl, who smiled broadly and nodded, her braids bouncing with enthusiasm.

They all gave August their first and last names again and invited her to the bonfire that was to happen later at somebody's house, after they got back to the village, even though August demurred and told them that her boyfriend would be picking her up.

Again, seemingly out of nowhere, Merindah walked over, towering above the sitting girls and eating something that looked like beef jerky. She said, "Your man will not be picking you up at the designated time. You should attend this bonfire. These are your people. This is your land. These things, they are all you. She is you. He is you. That rock is you. That tree is you. You must tame this urgency and get to know your people, child. If you do not, you will regret the things that come to pass." She squatted down next to August. The entire hill was silent, even the wind and birds made no sounds.

242

Merindah examined August, as she drank from a decorative woven pouch that hung from her waist. With the woman so close, August was overwhelmed with her scents—dried grasses, wood, some earth smells that were probably from the pigments she was wearing, along with the furs, animal skins, and even the dried meat, which smelled heavily of pepper. Merindah also seemed to be putting some mint in her mouth to chew. Other smells, too—almond or macadamia nuts maybe, and either sage or yarrow root, which August only recognized because of her time working at Leigheas.

August didn't look directly at Merindah, as it seemed like it would be a trespass—like not curtseying before a queen or something—but she felt the woman's presence almost like an embrace.

Merindah put her finger under August's chin and turned her face towards her and their eyes locked. The warrior woman was seeing something deep inside her, and August suddenly felt naked, yet protected. Held. Merindah's words stretched like a bridge between their hearts. "I feel your resistance. Your will is strong. But you must do as I say."

August swallowed, even though her mouth had gone dry. It felt as though a mystical truth had been given to her as a gift, and she was going to honor it. "I will," she said simply. And once again, Merindah was simply no longer there.

The rest of the afternoon was spent wrestling and trading stories about the village. August answered a lot of questions about America, New York City, Maryland and burger joints. She talked about her gran and how she had suffered, losing so many of her children, and August felt their sympathy and understanding like a balm. Some of them were even outraged on August's behalf for the murder of her father, and the pain that made her grandmother turn inwards. It was as though they could feel her losses along with her, and as they told more of their own family stories from the 60s, August realized that some of them had lost loved ones as well. They truly shared her scars.

When supper time rolled around August was exhausted; she wasn't used to training all day, and every muscle she had was reminding her of that fact. She'd also delved into emotional depths she rarely let anyone else see, and that brought its own kind of fatigue. Everyone gathered their equipment and piled it next to the barn, until the only person left with August was Adair, who seemed to be intentionally lagging behind.

"You don't have to wait for me," she asserted, thought half-heartedly. She was glad for his company, and to see he cared about her enough to linger.

"What makes you think I'd be waiting for ye?" he replied with faux innocence. "I am simply picking up my things and settin' 'em down."

August let out a chuckle.

"Supper's over there." He pointed to several rows of tables behind the barn. People were already getting plates full of food and taking seats.

"I'm not feeling especially hungry at the moment, though. Adair, would you mind walking with me to that building over there? I want to get my cloak. The man who took it said it would be ready by supper."

Adair gave her a sweet smile as they each shouldered their equipment. "I'd love to," he said, then took her hand, and it felt natural that August let him. *Like friends*, she told herself.

The only person in the shed was Gavin. He was bent over the machine, the needle chewing away at a length of red velvet. At the end of the stitch he snapped a lever and pulled the velvet away. He nipped close to the fabric with a small pair of scissors, flipped the light off and stood up.

August and Adair set down their gear and waited as he smoothed the garment down and dusted it off.

"Here. If ye don't like it, don't bother comin' t' tell me."

"Thank you," August said with a blink, and shot Adair a look. He let go of her hand, and she missed it immediately. "I'll take it Gavin, thanks." She stood there with it in her hand, feeling awkward and unsure what to say. She couldn't understand why Gavin seemed so bothered by her.

"Well go on, put it on. I have t' see if it fits. Er if yer highness needs any more adjustin'."

August's face went warm with a rising irritation. She turned her back to Adair so he could put the cloak on her.

"You need to put your arm in." Adair said.

"What? Oh … It didn't have sleeves before." She put her arm in the slightly belled sleeve, and then the other, and shrugged it on. It fit perfectly. It was shorter now, about mid-thigh. It was more of a coat, nipped in a bit at the waist and had silver buttons with Celtic knotwork on them, and a wooden bead at the throat that could be fastened into a loop. She could tell the wood was mistletoe. Ever since she'd begun having transformation episodes, she seemed to be more sensitive to mistletoe oil, though still not too bad. Gavin watched intently as she looped the button, possibly waiting to see if she was allergic. He seemed satisfied.

Gavin took her by the shoulders and spun her around to look in the mirror.

It was the same, yet completely different. Instead of her father's mantle, it was her own garb, a herald of her identity and heritage for those that could recognize it. It didn't hurt that it also showed off her figure considerably better.

"It's beautiful. It's just ... perfect. I love it. Thank you, Gavin!" She threw her arms around him and Gavin nearly cracked a smile, but quickly suppressed it.

"Just doin' my job. I'm going to go have supper now if you two don't need me to slave away at anything else."

August gave a small smile. "Enjoy your supper, Gavin."

Adair and August were left alone in the big room. August walked around looking at all of the garments, many of them like the ones she and Adair were wearing, along with scabbards and quivers of various types.

"Wow, they really can make anything."

"It's a special talent. Everybody has one."

"Aren't you supposed to be a cloak-maker McCabe or something? Why are you training?"

"Well, Little Red Riding Hood, I'm half McCabe, on my mother's side. My da is a Hunter, by name, though his mum was Blackwood."

August turned away from the racks and unbuttoned her coat, slipped it off while tossing an over-the-top fashion-model stare at Adair, and sauntered over to lay it on top of her things.

"What do you suppose people are stuffing their faces with out there?" she wondered casually.

"Probably lamb and potatoes. Are you hungry?"

"Are you?" August said, tilting her head a little.

"I'd rather stay in here and talk to you, if it's all the same."

245

That was what she was hoping he would say, though now she felt kind of wrong for hoping it. *Ah, what the hell—you only live once,* she reassured herself. *Carpe diem. Or carpe boy.*

"Everybody here has been so nice to me today. Well, except maybe Merindah. She scares the hell out of me."

"Though she did save yer neck, it looked to me."

"Ah. Right. That."

"I think being around your people is good for you. Not that I know you very well," he added with a wink.

August leaned her bottom against the edge of a table. Adair sidled up beside her and did the same. His pinkie was touching hers.

They talked for what felt like twenty minutes, but when August looked out of the big double doors again she saw the sun had gone all the way down.

"Shit, how long have we been here? We must've been talking for an hour or something." She shifted her weight and the table gave, sliding out from her bottom before she had gotten her balance. Adair reached out and caught her and pulled her up. They were face to face. Belly to belly. She could feel his breath on her mouth, he was so close. He smelled of grass and dirt, sweat and apples.

August breathed out, "Why do you smell like apples?"

"I ate the one you shot right before we stopped shooting." His voice was also low and breathy.

"Oh." She couldn't stop breathing him in. She didn't want to.

They stood there like that for an eternity that was really only a minute, his gravity drawing her closer, her swaying towards him, touching her lips to his. Just barely. They both stood there, inhaling each other, the electric tingle of touch pulsing through both of them.

A clacking came from outside. It sounded like wooden sticks, dozens of them, being banged against each other, and snapped them out of their reverie.

"The fire!" They both remembered they were supposed to be at the ceremonial pyre at sundown. They took off for the hillside together.

A girl there caught them holding hands. "Yer boyfriend in't gunna mind that, I reckon." She turned and said something to her friend and they both giggled. August had a vivid flashback to her old high school in Manhattan and its gaggle of gossiping glamour girls.

About ten hunters where standing near the pyre and banging together large boomerangs, and the primal sound of rhythmic beating became hypnotic for the crowd gathered around them. The heat of the conflagration was intense. The beating became faster and faster.

August felt a sudden awareness of her place in the larger world, the life that she came from, and she let go of Adair's hand. She wondered what all her tangled feelings meant, but before she could blink twice Merindah strode out beside the pyre. She was wearing a short skirt, with pelts and textiles tied at the waist, which exaggerated her hips. Her hair was adorned with a headband of what looked like tiny orange feathers, tightly stacked, and strands of knotted yarn or fibers hanging down to her shoulders. She had a necklace almost like a lei, with feathers ending in a large weaving of a sun, fringed with thin dried grass. Her face had more dots and lines, and they continued onto her arms, chest and legs in bold patterns delicately outlined with more white dots. There were more little feathers tightly strung around her ankles, and her feet were bare. As she passed by them and stood close to the flame, half of her body became dancing shadows, emphasizing and then hiding her features in quick flashes.

The clacking of the boomerangs reached a fever pitch, then stopped.

Everyone was silent, waiting for her to speak.

"The Dreamtime is the dawn of creation. My people have been on this world since this time. Since before all others. We were the first to see what the Rainbow Serpent made of the world. He is known by many names, but my people, like yours, have much respect for what the Rainbow Serpent wrought, and also for our ancestors, who can send us great knowledge from their time."

There was a wave of whispers through the crowd. Merindah seemed to not mind this, as she probably knew the information would be miraculous for those who had not been enlightened. The murmuring quickly settled; they could hardly wait for what was to come next.

"To speak to your ancestors, you must first take colors from the land they walked on and adorn yourself, as I have done with my ochre and grasses, feathers from my Koori, and wool, wood, and stone from Summerblynd. You must contemplate their sacrifices and open your mind to their spirit. I am going to dance to invite one of my ancestors

247

to fill my vessel with their spirit, then you will do the same."

The boomerangs started up again. Merindah picked up a bundle of long thin sticks in one hand and began shaking them, they banged together making their own sort of wooden music of a different, higher pitch than the heavy deep boomerangs. The effect was snakes, teeth chatter, wind, thunder, all of the sounds of nature coming together under a dim sky that watched sparks snap into the air, then turn to ash and float to the ground as Merindah danced, stomped and shook, made trills and hoots, calling out to her ancestors. Then she stopped and stood tall, humming a long, low music that sounded like several voices at once.

August gasped and was instantly covered in gooseflesh. She thought she could see something—she hesitated to call them ghosts—skittering across the hillside. She wondered if Merindah was channeling her Scottish or her Aboriginal ancestors. She wouldn't have believed it, but Merindah made it believable as she changed in front of August's eyes. It was almost imperceptible, but she seemed to take on a slightly different shape—and maybe it was the dancing light of the fire, but her eyes seemed to spark of something otherworldly. She went into a trancelike state, her humming becoming more deep, her feet planted firmly on the ground as her body swayed and rocked. Merindah then threw the sticks down and put both of her arms out, shook them and exhaled a scream that seemed to come from the very center of the earth itself, or maybe from halfway around the world in Australia. She stopped, inhaled deeply several times—closing her eyes and turning her face upwards—then hummed quietly and opened her eyes to the stunned crowd.

"My ancestor has communicated with me. I am not to share it, and I will obey. If your mind is open and you channel your ancestor, you will know what you must do when it is done." She pointed at a large wooden bowl with mud in it. "Here, I have made a paste of Summerblynd earth; put it on your bodies. Make a crown of rowan berries and oak leaves. Tie the wool yarn around your wrists and in your braids. Identify yourself to your ancestors."

The group crowded around and formed something of a line. Some of them seemed less than convinced, and they muttered to each other and hung back, but August was inspired by what she had just seen. When she reached the bowl she scooped a handful of the mud

248

and stepped aside to dot her face and make an armband. She dragged the fingers of each hand across her chest, leaving streaks of mud on her breast. She bent over and wiped her hands on the cool damp grass and grabbed rowanberry clusters and small branches of multi-colored oak leaves from a pile near the mud bowl. One of the younger girls handed her several lengths of undyed wool yarn, and she took them over to sit on the backside of the fire and make her crown.

She was close enough to the pyre that the warmth enveloped her, and glowed on her outstretched feet as she made a V of her legs, putting her craft project on the ground in front of her. She was hoping Adair would come sit with her, but she was also hoping he wouldn't— though she didn't have to fight that internal battle for long because he soon was on the ground next to her with a similar pile of crafting materials.

"How do I look?" August laughed gently and turned her face this way and that, to give him a good view of her mud makeup.

"Bonny. Me?"

"Same." And she meant it. Their eyes stayed locked for a moment. He was truly beautiful in the firelight. His strong jaw had almost no hints of a stubble shadow, something she'd grown so used to on a man she took it as normal. His chin had a slight cleft that shifted when he smiled. She was letting her guard down again. She wanted to let her guard down. She wanted something, anything, to be easy for once. The eye-contact became almost unbearable, compelling her to take some action, so she looked away, nonchalantly, at her supplies. "Craft time at hunter camp. Guess I shouldn't be too surprised."

August and Adair twisted the pliable twigs together, weaving in rowan berries and vibrant oak leaves. August made two braids in the front of her hair, weaving in the wool yarn and wrapping it around the ends. She could see Adair watching her as she worked, and she liked it.

"You're good with your hands," he said.

"So I've been told," she grinned, flirting.

They both let out easy laughs. At one point their elbows grazed and made August long for more grazing and hot breath.

"How many clans are here, anyway?"

"Most of them here have mixed heritage, mostly otherkin. Some are mixed with human. I don't actually know all of them. As far as the original clan lines represented, there's some from all five—six if you count the two Huntar lines as two. Honestly, it's gotten pretty confusing since the 60s. A bunch of kin left, or at least went away for a bit, came back with new husbands and wives. That was a bit of a baby boom—the results of which you see represented at this lovely event." He laughed. It was an easy laugh, maybe a bit cocky, but not in a bad way.

"I haven't been around this many people my age in a while," August confessed. "I don't think I've ever been around this many people my age that I actually get along with."

"Really? Ye seem easy to get along with t' me." He bumped her knee with is.

"There," she said, and put her crown on top of her head. "What do you think?"

"Tis a mickle better'n mine," he said, holding his up. The rowan berries sagged off of the sides and the oak leaves were tucked willy-nilly, leaving awkward gaps.

"Give me that," she said, yanking it from his hand. She accidentally tore a couple of leaves and sent berries to the ground. She sighed. She had been going for impish and charming, not brutish and childish.

"Well, ye don't have to destroy it, lass, it's not all that bad!" Adair scooped up the remaining leaves and the put them nearer to her working hands.

She started working on it quickly, her hands bending and tucking at lightning speed. "Sorry. I was trying to be funny."

"Such the worrier. I think it will work as well ugly."

"Do you really think? Shouldn't ceremonial things be beautiful, so they … I don't know … please the gods or something?"

"Hmm. I honestly don't know, Archer. That is a point, though. You'd better finish fixing it then. Wouldn'a want to displease the gods."

In moments she handed him a fully fledged, well-crafted wreath. She rolled up onto her knees and waddled over in front of him, scooting up between his V'd legs to place it on his head.

"There."

Her bosom was level with his face and he looked up at her, and she looked down at him. The burning wood popped behind her and showered them with sparks, floating down and turning to ash the moment it hit their skin.

"You're very pretty, August."

She kneeled back down on her legs and looked at his face. "Thank you. I feel beautiful right now."

The night was humming with magic. She felt a little drunk, without a drop of alcohol. The fire and sparks made her think of summer fireflies back home and her chest swelled with emotion. The sky was so big, all of the stars winking as they emerged from the fading twilight, and the deep quiet of the forest made life seem timeless and full of possibilities.

She rolled over onto all fours and crawled to the edge of the pyre, where she stuck the end of a stick into the flames and caught the end on fire. Adair watched her bottom sway as she waved the stick gently through the air. He tried to hide his excitement by bending his legs and adjusting his kilt. August turned back around, catching him as he adjusted himself, and averted her eyes back to the flaming stick, pretending not to have noticed his want for her. She extinguished the small flame in the grass and blew on the ember, making it glow, then fade, until it went cool and dark.

She put the tip to her breast and drew a crude arrow down the center of her chest. She knee-walked back to Adair and touched his shirt. He nodded and she opened the laces and drew an ash arrow in the middle of his chest as well.

"Ready?" He asked.

"Ready," she replied, standing and dusting off her bottom. "Do you think we need to be in bare feet?"

"Couldn't hurt. Closer to the earth, and all that." They both took off their boots and set them at the base of a nearby tree. They walked around the flaming stack to see the last few people were tucking leaves into their wreaths and gathering around.

Merindah took her place by the fire again.

"Open your minds. Feel your feet on the land. Spread your arms out to the stars and move your bodies. Call out to your ancestors and invite them into you. Ask for their wisdom with a silent mouth. Listen to their secrets with ears that hear nothing. Listen only with your heart. Connect to all of the things around you and accept the knowledge without fear. Now close your eyes and begin to sway. Begin to hum. Find the vibration of your people and of your land."

251

August felt a little silly at first, but she closed her eyes and began to sway. She started with a low, quiet hum, and soon she forgot that she was with anybody else. Her body began to tingle and pulse. Her lips felt like they were throbbing; she could feel her heartbeat shaking her ribcage. She felt as though she were floating free, closer to the stars, all of them glittering in brilliant colors as though somebody threw diamond dust through sunbeams, the velvet night as a backdrop. This color pulsed too, and the diamond dust arranged itself into a shape. It was the face of her father.

He took on a three-dimensional form and touched down to earth with her. August felt her hand reach out as if he were right in front of her, scattering the sparkling figure, but he quickly reformed.

"August, I'm sorry sweet girl. I'm sorry I let you down. I wanted to tell you all about your history. I wanted to find a way to make peace with the Veritas before we reclaimed our lives here."

She heard herself speak to him, though her mouth was not moving. "Daddy. I can't believe it's you. I didn't even think about trying to call out to you. I'm sorry. I miss you so much." She was crying. Her face was wet, she could feel the tears dripping off of her chin. "Why didn't you tell me? Why did you leave me?"

"Darling girl, we don't have much time, please listen to me."

"Of course, Daddy. I'm listening." Things sounded a bit echoed and slightly distorted. She tried to focus on what he was saying. Her head pulsed harder and her ears and fingers were tingling.

"You must spend this time with the hunters wisely." His voice was going in and out like a bad connection.

"That's what Merindah said. I'm trying. I promise."

"I need you to be careful. We all need you to …" There were a couple of words that didn't come; she could see his mouth moving, but no sound. " … and don't try to be something other than …" More fading and missing words. The glitter began to look windblown—she was losing him. "August, you cannot trust …" What? He was almost nothing now. The stardust of Fletcher's image blew away and it was replaced by a wolf face, also luminous and sparkling, but larger, and it came at her, jaws open, snarling.

She could feel emotion engulfing her like a firestorm. Her body was light and sky. It began to crackle and tingle and twitch. Her gums dripped blood and her ears felt like rubber bands were snapping them.

252

Her clothes strangled her, then went slack. She opened her eyes and everything looked different. She howled up at the night sky, long and loud and wild. The entire group was looking at her, some had taken out their weapons and watched, stunned and muttering to each other.

One of them nocked an arrow and pointed it straight at her, when Adair stepped in front of her. "Put it away mate!"

"She's a sodding lycan!" The young man said. She recognized him as the guard at the gate. His colors were wrong. Everything looked bluish.

"She's also a sodding Archer—your blood! Now put it down!"

"She's not my blood. I'm not kin to any of those animals!"

Merindah stepped into the scene and between the young man, and Adair and August. "She is as much your kin as I am. I am Archer."

The young man took down his arrow and lowered his bow. He glowered sullenly at Merindah. Whispers rippled through the group, and faded within moments.

August's body started changing back as everybody craned their necks to see around Merindah and Adair. Flashes of her flesh started to show through rapidly thinning fur. She panted and heaved until she was a puddle in the grass, naked and weak. The whispers started up again, louder this time, a few giggles from some of the girls, and Adair turned around and saw August vulnerable on the ground. He pulled out his dirk and chopped off the long shoulder plaid from his kilt, laying it over her. He bent lower, scooping her up in his brawny arms, and toted her off toward the flower van, scowling at the crowd as he strode by. He hollered "Nia, home!"

Nia said something to her uncles and to some of the other people. She grabbed August's ruined clothes and belongings and ran to the van. She tossed everything in the side seat and they headed back to the village, Adair on the floor in the back, cradling August the whole way.

Back at the village Adair took August to his family's house, barely a mile from the circle. He helped her stand and make her way into the cottage on her wobbly legs. He walked her though the tiny front hall and into the bedroom in the back, flicking light switches on along the way. He helped August to the bed, where she sat on the edge, looking utterly drained. He pulled a shirt out of the closet, a plain natural muslin with lacing at the collar. He helped pull it over August's head as she stood, putting her arms in the air. Her nakedness flashed, exposing breasts and a thatch of dark hair as the tartan dropped and the muslin settled over her body. It was almost mid-thigh on her tiny frame, and the lacing was open enough that one nipple was peeking through the opening. Adair tugged the ends of the laces and closed it up enough to provide some modesty, then helped her under the covers.

"I'll get ye something to eat. I know you're gunna be hungry."

August made a gravelly grumbly sound and snuggled deeper into the bed, pulling the covers tightly around her.

It seemed like ten minutes later when August was awakened to find that Adair had brought her a tray of food loaded with cheese and bread and smoked fish, as well as some ale and water to drink. He'd also changed into jeans and looked freshly washed. She wiggled into a sitting position and propped some pillows behind her back, taking the tray and demolishing the meal in a flurry of bites and sloshes. A few minutes later she pulled the napkin across her mouth and tossed it onto the tray.

"Impressive," Adair said with a bit of a smile.

"It makes me tired and hungry," she said, looking a bit sheepish, almost ashamed.

"Good to know." He whisked away the tray and sat it on the dresser.

"It happened once before. I didn't even know I could transform until a couple of days ago." She looked up at him and looked away. "I suppose I shouldn't be giving secrets away to the enemy." She half-grinned, though there was no joy behind it.

He walked over and sat beside her on the bed and brushed a dark corkscrew of hair away from her eyes. "The enemy," he said with a gentle smirk and a soft touch of her cheek.

"How'd you get all that food ready so fast?"

"Actually it took the better part of an hour."

"Really? What time is it?"

"About ten. You were asleep most of the time. I kept checkin' ye. Did ye have any dreams?"

"Hmm. I don't remember."

The phone rang and Adair reached across August to the opposite bed table to answer it. She tried not to notice how warm he was, and how good he smelled, and how much she liked him being pressed against her legs when he leaned.

"Oi? Aye. Yeah. It's been a long day. She's had a bit of a nap. Aye, no problem, hang on." He held the receiver out to August, "It's for you."

August swallowed and took the receiver and hugged it to her chest. She noticed she was a bit disheveled and uncovered and tugged at the blankets, but they were stuck under Adair. She tugged more insistently and gave him a stern look. He grinned and hopped up. August gave a shooing motion with her hand and he scooted out of the door.

August took a deep breath. "Hello."

"Lass! So lovely to hear your voice. How are ye?" He sounded weird. Like he'd been drinking, maybe. Just too chipper.

"I guess that depends."

"On what?"

"On why you're calling."

"I'm supposed to be picking you up in an hour or so. I wanted to check with you and see, well ... see how you are."

"It's been one hell of a day, I'll tell you that." Then August remembered she couldn't tell him about most of her day, so she didn't have much else to say.

"Do you want to tell me about it?"

"I will when you come get me," she said it like a challenge. As though she knew what was coming next, and it wasn't going to be him speeding over to the village circle to pick her up.

"Well, that's what I sort of wanted to talk to you about. I'm afraid I'm a bit in my cups here. And it got so late chatting, that I didn't realize what time it was."

"Mmm-hmm."

"Anyroad, I'd like to pick you up tomorrow, if that's alright."

"Wait, where are you?"

"I'm at Issy—Iseabail's manor." He didn't sound quite as chipper with that confession. August got a knot in her stomach and was worried she was about to lose all of the food she just ate.

"So, you plan on sleeping there?"

Several moments pass and she was wondering if the call dropped.

"Faolan, you plan on staying the night at Iseabail's? Is that what you're telling me?"

"Do you trust me, lass?"

August thought about it a bit too long, for both of their comfort.

"Lass?" He sounded hurt. "Love, I'm asking you to let me have this time. I'm askin' ye to trust me."

"Do you think this is a good idea? I mean, what if she wants to … you know, what if she gets physical. Unless she already has—wait, did she already—"

"Red, don't worry. Whatever happens, I'm still yours."

"That wasn't exactly an answer to my question."

"I'm sorry, I'm trying to be honest and I am a bit swept up with emotions."

August gnashed her teeth. "Faolan, you're asking me if you can stay the night at this woman's house who you have loved for longer than I have been alive. You just said you were swept up."

"I don't want to pretend to you that it's easy, but I won't do anything to hurt you. I'm asking you to trust me."

"What if she …"

"She won't. All we've done is talk. She's cried a bit. It's been grief for both of us. I will tell you all about it. She knows I am bonded to you. She said that she doesn't want to interfere with our relationship. She wants me to be happy. She said if our reunion—our reconnecting, I mean—is hurting my relationship with you, she will certainly remove herself from the situation. I don't think she's going to try anything."

August's mind was racing. What am I supposed to say to this? If I say no, then I'm possessive and childish and keeping him from some important connection. Some important purpose. She felt trapped into not being able to have a say at all. "I'm not going to make you drive drunk to come get me, Faolan. I'm not going to rip you from the apparently lovely little reminiscing you're having with your long lost dead lover." She wasn't even trying to hide the resentment.

"It's going to be alright, August. I love you best, always remember. You're the one I belong with, and want to be with. I can care about her, but still want to spend my life with you, can't I?"

August inhaled sharply. It was settled for her, there was nothing to be done. But beyond his being drunk, and as much as it felt like it was begging for trouble for him to stay with the woman he has idolized

256

for decades, August had to be able to trust him, or it was all for naught. She felt a little sick, but there was nothing more to discuss tonight. She shuddered.

"I will be there bright and early. I'll bring you some scones. Alright? You can call me if you need to, here's the number ..."

August jotted down the number onto a little notebook in the side table.

"I hope we aren't making a mistake," she said, and it sat there for a moment.

"We aren't. We can handle this. Our love can handle this."

She nodded and wanted to say she loved him, but she couldn't bring herself to say it first. She wanted him to declare his love first, then she could at least hang up the phone and not throw up.

"I love you, August. Dear girl of my heart. I'm your boy, don't ever doubt it."

"I love you, too." She felt her heart swell and sent the words to him like bullets through the phone, wanting him to feel it, hard.

"Have a good rest of the evening. I'll see you not too many hours from now."

"Ok."

"Goodnight, love."

"Goodnight, Faolan."

She listened, waiting for him to hang up first. She didn't hear a click, and after a while he said, "Are you going to hang up? I can't hang up if you don't hang up."

She let out a small laugh. This little dance comforted her.

"Okay, goodnight." She smiled when she said it, in spite of her concern.

"Goodnight."

She hung up the phone. As soon as she did the disconnection from him enveloped her and made her feel a million miles from him. A star away. Two stars—which is a star too many for sure.

Adair leaned into the doorway. "So?"

"Were you eavesdropping?"

"Not ... on purpose. The place is small. It is a cottage, August, after all! So?"

"He's not coming tonight."

Adair strode over to the bed. "Get up, we're going to the

bonfire."

"I don't feel like—"

"August, if ye stay here, even if I'm here with ye, yer going to feel the minutes creeping by. If yer at all well, let's go do something together. It'll keep your mind occupied. It'll help the night go faster."

She knew he was right. She hopped up from the bed, and Adair couldn't help but take in the sight of her. The thin muslin was lit from the lamp behind and he could see the shadow of her shape. He felt a swell of desire and tried to talk himself away from it. Most of August's things were forgotten in the flower van, so he took some clothing from his dresser for her: a pair of jeans—which were way too big, so she cinched them with a belt and rolled up the cuffs—and a David Bowie tee that was a little loose, but so soft it must have been washed a hundred times. She turned away and took off the blousy shirt, showing her bare back to him. He wanted to reach out and stroke her, enfold her, but instead he turned away and chatted about smoked fish, and Merindah, and who all was coming to the bonfire.

August slipped on the shirt, her bra having been lost somewhere in all of the confusion. She wasn't used to running around braless any more, but right now it seemed like a stupid thing to be worried about. She was just thankful that he'd found a pair of plaid boxers tucked away in the back of his drawer, despite the fact he must have outgrown them by the time he was eleven. She'd felt intimately close to him when she slipped them on, rolling the waistband down a couple of turns for a more girlish fit. Now somewhat put-together, she caught a glimpse of herself in his dresser mirror—the jeans bagged up and the soft tee draped down from her breasts. She gathered her hair up in the back and grabbed a thin strip of leather from a bowl on the dresser to tie it. She looked like she was on her way to a concert, or on her way home from one. She saw Adair had given up his kilt for jeans as well.

"You needn't worry that people won't want you around," Adair volunteered, correctly picking up on one of the things worrying her most at the moment. "Mind you, they might have been a bit surprised, but they know you're more hunter than anything. And your cousin who was so keen on loosing an arrow into you—he was uninvited in no uncertain terms. So don't worry. Everybody that will be there is just curious about you. That's okay, isn't it? To be curious?"

August shrugged. She wasn't used to getting so much attention from such a large group of people. She felt a little like a sideshow freak.

"They may ask you some questions, is all."

"I probably don't have any answers. All of this is new to me."

He nodded and watched her slip her boots on, which had made it back along with her coat. He wanted to go to her and hold her and tell her not to worry.

"Have y' ever had a hot toddy?"

August shook her head. "No."

"Well, we'll be having some 'round the fire."

"I usually have hot cocoa and toast marshmallows."

"Yer gonna like the hot toddy." He said it like a flirt.

"Well, okay then." She flirted back.

She put her newly tailored red coat on, he grabbed a bottle of whisky and a hand full of cinnamon sticks. "Grab those mugs, will ye?" She picked up two earthenware mugs, which must have weighed two pounds each, and they headed out into the clear November night.

A Fire

About half a mile from the cottage Adair pointed out a much larger home. She could hear laughter and see the glow of a fire behind the house as they approached. She got a bit of a knot in her stomach.

"Don't worry, August. You're welcome here." Adair put his arm around her and guided her to the back yard.

There were only five other people there. One of them was a plump, pretty girl with long gold hair, and two young men, both attractive in different ways, sitting on a log close to the fire, one on each side of her.

"August, you might remember Rose from earlier today. These are her boyfriends Charles and Edward."

"Oh … okay. Hi." She shook everybody's hands.

Charles put his arm around Rose's ample waist and squeezed. She smiled and kissed him on the cheek. Then turned and kissed Edward on his.

Charles studied August for a moment and said, "That was some show you put on today."

"Yeah. Sorry about that." August felt her face grow hot.

"Och, I didn't mean it as a judgment. I was truly impressed. I'd heard you were mostly hunter and—"

Adair interrupted, "She's mostly hunter." He gently grasped August's ponytail and gave it a squeeze, and it struck her as oddly intimate.

"I don't care what ye are, so long as y' c'n keep yer mouth shut about our secrets," Rose proclaimed. "Don't want any of those hounds sniffing about."

August felt challenged, almost accused, but she had the sense they didn't mean to be insulting. She wrote it off as defensive speciesist thinking—probably they would feel more comfortable once they got to know her better.

"We've got to be prepared for whatever those dogs throw at us," Edward chimed in. "They'll do anything to take over these lands. They're monsters." He seemed to notice August's pained expression. "I don't mean you, of course, lass. Yer as much us as y' are them. More, the way I hear it," he added, nodding to Adair.

Adair hoisted the bottle of whisky into the air. "Oi, lads! Why don't we all have some bloody hot toddies and talk about something fun?"

"Sounds like a party to me," Rose replied. "Got me cup right here."

"Shite. I forgot the pot."

"I reckon they'll just be toddies then!" piped Charles. Everybody looked at him for a moment as if he'd grown a spare head, but, as he was correct, there were shrugs and mutters of agreement, and Adair commenced pouring whisky. Rose went behind him with dollops of honey, which only sank to the bottom of their cups, since it wasn't warm enough to mix, and no one had remembered spoons, either.

"We're a mess," August laughed, and to her great relief, the rest laughed with her. They tipped their cups back and held them out again. Charles snapped off a twig as an improvised stirring stick, hoping to inspire the sludgey lump of honey at the bottom of his mug to mix in a bit.

"Makes ye warm even without the fire!" Edward said with a smile.

The other two people there—a brown-haired girl and a boy in cargo pants—came over now and shook August's hand, but she forgot their names almost as soon as they said them. Her body was warm and she was getting a little buzzed. The fire was cozy and enticing. She picked up twigs and kept tossing them in, watching them curl into glowing worms and fall apart into ash. A few more people arrived, then a few more, and they all came over and said hi to August, who by then was sitting on a log with Adair near the fire.

More people meant more bottles of whisky, and they were big on sharing. A tree of a boy named Garrison came over. "This is the good stuff," he said to her, and poured a couple of fingers into August's mug. She sniffed it and it smelled smoky like the fire. She took a sip and was surprised how much she liked the smokey flavor.

"Thanks!"

After three rounds, everybody started sipping a bit slower.

The fire was getting quite toasty, and August felt a glow inside. She and Adair talked about the cloak shop, the various lineage mixes in the village, who was dating whom. They talked a little about Merindah, but it felt weird and maybe wrong to discuss her outside of the context

261

of the hunting grounds. There was something sacred about her that made you want to keep it close and to yourself, mostly. Every few minutes somebody would say something funny; August would laugh, then lean against Adair. He would do the same. It went on like that for an hour or so, when the day and the whisky finally started to catch up to August.

"The fire looks like creatures dancing."

"Watch this." He reached over into a pail under Rose's bench and grabbed a handful of something and threw it on the flames, which burst into crazy hues of turquoise and green. He grabbed a handful from a second bucket and threw it on, making the fire purple.

"Amazing. How'd you do that?" She was beaming up at him. Tipsy and happy and, for the moment, not thinking at all about her Faolan troubles.

"It's simple chemicals, is all. Makes it a bit more exciting, though, eh?"

She smiled and nodded. "Yeah."

She tipped back her fourth cup and stood, nearly losing her footing. Adair reached out and she caught onto his arm.

"Oops, you almost fell," she said in all sincerity. "Good thing I was here to catch you."

He grinned big. "Good thing, aye!" He tipped his own cup back, poured one more and downed it as well. "Ye kinda look as though ye want to leave now."

"Aye," she said, winked, and wobbled towards the front of the house.

"Adios, amigos!" Adair bid the crowd goodbye with a wave. "Thanks for a bonny fire!" They raised their mugs to him with cheers, and shouted farewells after August, who was halfway down the drive but came back to blow big kisses to everyone.

She overbalanced and he caught her, a little unsteady himself. When they reached the road she went left instead of right.

"You don't know where you're goin', lass."

"I do too!" She hiccuped and made a funny face and walked off in the direction exactly opposite from home.

He took her by the shoulders and gently spun her 180 degrees, while she just kept walking along, not skipping a step. The two of them sang a bit of "The Safety Dance" while they laughed and zig-zagged their way to the cottage.

He opened the door for her and she reached in to turn on the light, but the switch was already up. "You're lights are broken. Or burnt on. Out. Something." Another hiccup.

He reached around her and flipped the switch down and she blinked in the bright yellow glow. He helped her over to the couch. "Here, you sit here, I am getting us some water."

"And popcorn," she called after him.

August kicked off her boots, one of them flying towards the television, a narrow miss. "Oopsies!" She covered her mouth to stifle a giggle. She unbelted the jeans and they fell off. She threw them over the end of the couch and sprawled there in the giant Bowie tee and Adair's underwear while the room gently spun.

"Popcorn, right," he called back to her, searching the kitchen cabinets for something resembling popcorn, but there was none. "Would you settle for crisps?"

"Crisps? What the fuck is a crisps? Where's my cuppa whisky?"

He appeared with a glass of water and a bowl of potato chips and set them on the table in front of her. He certainly noticed her being half-naked there on the couch, but pretended not to. He grabbed a soft knit blanket from the back of the chair and tossed it to her, and she sat up and spread it across her legs.

"We're having water, remember? I'm out of whisky." While August was having a drink he reached around behind her to the cabinet where two bottles of whisky stood, and tucked them behind the couch.

"Oh, these are potato chips. Chips, not crisps-ps."

Adair took a couple of gulps of water himself and threw some kindling and logs into the fireplace. He was proud of how quickly he got the fire going considering how hard the whisky had hit him. Once he was satisfied it would keep going he plunked down heavily on the couch, close to August. He popped a few chips-not-crisps in his mouth and crunched and looked over at her. She was leaning back looking at the ceiling.

"I think I'm drunk."

He leaned back next to her. "Yeah, me too."

"I like the fire. Thanks."

"Yer welcome." He smiled, triumphant.

"I like you Adair. I'm sorry I was mean before."

"I like you, too, August."

"Some people call me Red."

"Is it fine with you if I prefer August?"

"It's fine with me ... yup." She made the "p" pop at the end, and popped it a few more times, trying to watch her lips with crossed eyes.

Adair echoed her with the same "p" popping, and soon they were laughing.

"I made a mix tape for you," he said abruptly. "You wanna hear it?" He sat up a little, looking hopeful.

"What? How?" She rolled her head to face him, her body apparently rooted to the upholstery.

"I knew ye were comin' here, so I thought I would make a tape for ye. Stuff I imagined you might like."

August was unabashedly flattered. The fact that he thought about her after their meeting made her warm to him even more.

He hopped up, and almost tipped over.

"The getting up is the tricky part," she counseled.

"Aye," he said, and grabbed the cassette from his jacket pocket to pop into the boom box on the bookcase. "Ignore the adverts, I didn't always pause it in time."

She closed her eyes and listened to the unfamiliar music, which sounded a bit like rock. Country rock, maybe? She heard flutes and mandolins in there. A bit of advertisement cut in at the end, then there was a slow song, a kind of sad romantic ballad, with just guitar.

"You know what I like?" she asked.

"I canna imagine—what?" He sat down next to her and leaned back. Their thighs were touching. She pressed hers into his for a moment.

"I like that knowing you is not very complicated."

"Eh?"

"I mean, you're a hunter. I'm a hunter ... mostly. Mostly. Right? We're close to the same age, right?"

"I think so, yeah." He closed his eyes too, and folded his hands on his stomach. It helped the room stay a bit more still.

"It's just, well ..." She sighed.

"Ye can tell me."

"You're my age, we're both hunter, we come from the same village, you like cool music, I like cool music. Plus ... well, you're not

264

hard to look at. There I said it. You're goddam good-looking, ya jerk."

"Jerk?" He opened his eyes and lifted his head a little. She opened hers and turned a little on her side to face him. "Well you're dead cute yerself, so what do ye think o' that?" He said it as though it were an insult.

"Damn you. Where were you two years ago? Before I met Faolan Conall and my life got so ... complicated?"

"So the lycan is why your life is complicated, eh?" He smiled and raised his brows. "I'm thinkin' *you* might be why yer life is complicated."

"Ooh! Damn! Right in the heart!" She feigned being wounded, made ludicrous dying sounds and sat back again, her hands folded across her stomach.

"August," he turned to her and put his hand on her hands.

"Mmm-hmm?" She didn't open her eyes.

"Hey, August ... ?"

She opened her eyes and looked into his. She laced her fingers into his, sending a warm surge of desire though both of them. "What?"

"I wish I'd met you two years ago, too. Before yer life was ... complicated."

She turned to him and leaned a bit closer. Their noses just inches apart and their warm whisky scented breath filling the hollow between them.

"My heart hurts. Adair. My heart has been hurting for years. I want it to just be happy, ya know? I don't want to think about my dead father, or that my boyfriend is sleeping with his old fiancé tonight. I wan—"

"Wait—he's sleeping with her?"

"Well, just at her place. Not *with* her. I just want things ... I just want love to be simple."

"Are you sure that's what ye want, lass?"

She nodded, then moved in closer and touched her lips to his, barely brushing them with her soft warm pout. They stayed that way for a moment, then he pressed his mouth to hers, and they both parted their lips. She met him hungrily, their tongues plunging and swirling together, their heads lifting from the couch. The heat growing between them made her writhe and press in closer.

She tossed the blanket aside, threw her leg over him and

straddled him. He held her with his hands on her hips and then grasped her naked thighs as they kissed again, stroking them up and down. She could feel how hard he was through his jeans and she began kissing his neck. He reached up and cupped her breasts through the soft tee.

His hands felt so good, touching her aching body. She pressed hard against his erection, feeling his heat through the thin cotton of the boxers, and steadied herself with her hands on his shoulders to rock back and forth on him. He pushed up her shirt and put his warm, wet tongue on her nipple, rubbing and squeezing the other one. A little too hard, but it still felt so good to be thinking about nothing but this moment.

She bent forward to run her fingers through his hair, but it wasn't the wavy steel and black hair she had fallen in love with. It was Adair's short locks. And his hands were smaller, and smoother, and she could see them on her breasts, trying to please her, and suddenly it all felt wrong.

She stopped rocking and leaned back, pulling her shirt down. "I'm so sorry. I just can't. It feels wrong."

Adair caught his breath. "What? Are you alright, lass? Did I hurt ye?"

"No, no … You're really sweet. You are. And so, so sexy. I mean, I want to, but I just can't. I'm in love with him and it would be wrong." She leaned forward and touched her forehead to his. "Even though it feels so … so, so good. I'm sorry."

He nodded. And helped her back into her spot on the couch. "If you're alright, could you excuse me for a moment?"

She nodded and pulled the blanket up over herself. She lay there curled up under it, cursing herself for being so selfish while she heard him running the water in the restroom. After a few minutes he returned, seeming more relaxed. She was relieved he didn't seem upset at all.

"I'm sorry. You're so sweet Adair. I'm just such a jerk sometimes."

He waved off her concern as he sat back down on the couch. "Dinna worry yerself about it, please. I'm sure I've done worse m'self. Did you want some more water?"

She shook her head. "Could I snuggle to you though? Just, you

266

know, to be close."

Before he could even answer she had her head in the crook of his arm and within minutes she was asleep. Once she started snoring gently, he slipped out from under her, put a pillow beneath her head, and covered her up with an extra blanket. He watched her for a moment, stroking her hair, and kissed her cheek. Then he went to the bedroom, leaving the door open so he could keep an eye on the couch, and crawled into bed and passed out.

Anarchist's Uniform
Conall Keep

The morning was misty and everything was covered in a glittering edge of hoarfrost. The trees were in top form, all but the firs on fire with color. Engres Laithenskye arrived at the keep in his long black coat, his long black hair streaked with swaths of red and brown. Beneath the open coat he wore black as well, and his fingers were covered with heavy gold rings engraved with arcane symbols; the boldest of them bore an effigy of a wolf's head. Everything about him was calculated to exude darkness and depravity, of the sort normally associated with vampires. His pale gold eyes waited placidly for the door to creak open and behind it he saw Katie, her tiny bony frame tugging at the heavy oaken planks.

She gave a bit of a curtsey. "Come in, sir, they're expectin' ye."

She clopped down the hall ahead of him in her sensible shoes. He followed in long silent strides; even the hard heels of his boots seemed to float above the surface of the stone floor, soundless.

She stopped at the archway leading to the sitting room, extended an arm and directed him in. He perched on the edge of the chair, legs apart, hands resting on them, looking as though he could either accept a cup of tea or pounce on an enemy at any moment.

Ciardha entered the room, his face still a little green, and it did not go unnoticed to Engres, who could have smelled the illness even if it wasn't physically obvious. He feigned ignorance to anything but Ciardha's healthy alpha stature.

Engres stood and put out his hand to shake Ciardha's. He squeezed hard, his rings digging into Ciarha's fingers. Ciardha suppressed a wince, stood firm and squeezed right back. The men's eyes locked.

"Keer," Engres said, not blinking, still squeezing, and stood tall.

"Gres," Ciardha replied, narrowing his eyes slightly and standing a bit taller.

Engres relaxed a little, allowed his head to lower a bit beneath Ciardha's, released his hand and sat down. Ciardha, satisfied his position as alpha was obeyed, then sat across from him.

"I see yer wearin' yer anarchist's uniform today."

Engres's face was still, impassive. He blinked a couple of times, but said nothing.

"What's the news, then?" Ciardha asked, popping open his case of papers on the table next to him.

"I have word that they are gathering forces, Keer. It's been difficult to infiltrate them, but we have one who might do it. It's risky, as he could be a double spy."

"We don't have much to lose. So what if he spies on us? He won't be permitted to meetings. He won't be given any sensitive information."

Engres nodded. "Aye."

"What does he want?"

"He wants some money, not much. He wants a few bits of red tape taken care of that are in his way to getting some business off the ground in Perth. He is, evidently, aware of your connections in Perth. And, he wants information about a girl named August. She's a mixed lycan, and American."

"That's curious. When did he ask this of you?"

"Last night. Why?" Engres slid back into his chair and crossed his legs. He rubbed his chin.

"My brother is in town."

"I heard something of the kind." Engres tilted his head and waited.

"The woman he's with is this woman yer askin' about."

Engres leaned forward again, his focus sharpened. "What about that?"

"They're lovers. Says he loves her."

"Your brother always was a weak cunt. Is he a jobby jabber?"

Ciardha shot him a sharp look.

Engres shrugged it off. "What does that mean for the cause?"

"Nothing. I don't care about what happens to her," he lied. "Go ahead with your mole. Our intel is thin."

"How much lycan blood is she? Can she transform?"

Ciardha screwed up his face and looked to him for explanation.

"I need to tell this young man something. He wants to know more."

"I don't ken the bloodlines beyond her mostly hunter parents." Ciardha spat. "Her mother has the lycan blood, but canna transform.

Her father was pure hunter. Generations back. Ask this lad what he already knows about her."

"So mostly hunter?" Engres seemed disappointed with this news. "I heard she's attractive. Sharp tongued."

"Aye. I'd agree with that last assessment. I've not seen her, but Blair has told me."

"This girl, if she can transform, she could be valuable to our cause. She's inferior, of course, but ... We need to find out if she can transform."

"I'll decide what we need to know." Ciardha, despite a wave of nausea, sat up tall and forced color into his face. "I will look into the matter with my brother."

"Sounds like your brother is even further away from the cause than before. Why'd he bring her here?"

"He dinna say. But I have leverage with him I didn't have before, with this girl. It's too bad she's not full blood."

"So you say, Keer. And how is Blair?"

It was an impudent dig, but Ciardha let it slide—probably not the smartest move, and he knew it. Even a wisp of authority taken from him compromised his alpha position, and his situation with his hunter wife had made him vulnerable as a Veritas leader. He hadn't yet built up enough consensus in his argument for mixing breeds.

Engres seemed to follow his train of thought. "Seems like this hunter girl is just what you want to help promote your idea of mixing-with-intent. Aye?"

"I thought you were against all of that, Gres."

"I don't mind fucking them, Keer. I don't even mind breeding with them, so long as they take care of the little spawn." He shrugged. "Who knows? I might even be able to bond with one myself. But they will always be less than us."

Ciardha looked grim, but nodded. "Aye." He knew Blair was never going to be his equal, no matter how much he loved her. Besides, she so often didn't believe he loved her, it was a constant irritation having to prove himself.

Ciardha didn't want Engres to be the one presenting these ideas to the Veritas. They were too radical, too important to let him take credit. Ciardha needed to find a way to make it clear that he alone came up with it—that he had earned his alpha position. In the old days he would have leapt across the table and ripped out Engres's throat. His position as leader and alpha would be unquestioned for another generation. The wicked thoughts must have flashed in his eyes because Engres was more alert and seemed ready to spring. It was then Ciardha realized that, in his weakened state, it would have been Engres who'd have leaped across the table and tore *his* throat out in the old days, to claim his place as alpha.

"We should present this at the meeting," Ciarhda finally said.

"Would you like me—"

"No, I'll do it. It has to come from me."

Engres nodded. "I do want to meet that girl." He stood.

"I'll see what I can do. See you tomorrow night."

They shook hands and Engres glided out into the hall, through the door Katie held, and disappeared into the forest.

"Blair! Blair!"

Blair, hands folded in front of her, stepped into the room. "Yes, Keer."

"I need to eat some meat. I can't stomach any more of that stew, just have Katie roast up some meat, and bring me some raw, too."

"I'll do it, Keer. We need you feeling better. The Veritas would fall apart without you."

"I don't reckon about all that. Gres probably has some witch doctor poking pins in me, or had a curse put on me."

"Keer, superstitions? Come now, I've never heard you speak of such silliness." She had the tone of a mother ashamed of her child.

"Don't talk down to me woman, I'm sick. There's no explanation for it."

"Well, you are getting older, you know. It happens to everybody. Maybe it's just a weakened immune response, from stress and age."

"Woman, don't try me. Get me some meat."

She kept her hands folded and her demeanor was even, almost ghostlike, in its calm.

"I will make you some lovely meat, Keer. I have at least a dozen huge cuts of beef in the kitchen. I will get you something raw right away. There is a bit of marinade left, I'll season the roasts with it."

Ciardha was looking through papers, still looking peaked, only half paying attention to her, "Fine, that's fine."

"Keer … did you, by any chance, have plans on seeing Liam any time soon?"

He looked up at her and narrowed his eyes. "Why are you asking about Liam?"

"He's my son, I miss him. That cannot be hard for even you to understand."

He set his papers down and cocked his head to the side. "Even me? What's that supposed to mean?"

"It means, you say you love me, but you don't care how much I suffer."

"I know what's best for you. I will let you know when you can see your son."

Blair wanted to say more, but she bit her lip and gave him a glare instead. She turned on her heels and headed to the kitchen.

She grabbed the meat in the back of the icebox that had been marinating for days. She'd skipped all of the fancy herbs and flavorings, this time it was mostly water and the wild white parsnips and some salt. She put on her rubber gloves, pulled all of the meat from the container, toweled it off, added a bit more salt and laid a mound of the meat on a plate and headed back to Ciardha.

She came back to the kitchen, rinsed the marinade down the drain, washed the container, and then threw the remaining scraps of parsnips into the kitchen fire. And waited.

The Morning After
Hunter Cottage, Summerblynd

August blinked away sleep from her eyes. Everything was a little fuzzy, and she was having trouble focusing on anything. She sat up, slowly, her head feeling like there was a large lead marble rolling around inside of it. She didn't recognize anything around her for a moment. *Where the fuck am I?*

Then visions from the night before began to trickle into her mind. A fire. Her father. Another fire. Kisses. Hands. She saw the door to the bedroom was open and leaned to see the bed. She stood up, and felt the room shift a little. When it stopped she saw Adair on the bed, still in his clothes, fast asleep.

She made her way to the kitchen—carefully—to pour herself some water and look for some aspirin. She found a cabinet stocked with some medical supplies and located some headache powders. She had to read the little instruction packet, which she found quite quaint. She dumped the powder into the water, gave it a swirl and a swish, and drank it down. For a moment she thought it might come right back up again, but it stayed put. She tried to discern if she was hungry or nauseated. She figured hungry was something she could fix, so she'd give that a try.

She found some eggs and a rasher of bacon in the icebox. She found bread, the end piece moldy, but the rest looked okay, so she set about making bacon, eggs and toast. It took a little while to find the things she needed, from the pans to the percolator, and even the coffee cups. Fortunately the kitchen was small, and had all of the basics for a full breakfast. She found a can of baked beans like the kind Faolan put with their breakfasts, so she opened that up too, and warmed them in the pan in the bacon fat.

She started setting everything on the small round table in the dining nook by the kitchen. It had a lovely little alcove of windows that looked out onto the mist-covered town. It seemed like it must be about seven or eight in the morning. Everything was quiet and dreamlike. The cottage smelled wonderful now, with bacon and coffee aromas filling it up. Even the toast smelled great. That proved it was hunger gnawing at her stomach.

Just as she was setting the last bit of food and flatware onto the table, Adair emerged from the bedroom rubbing his eyes and yawning.

"I made breakfast."

"I see ye did. Gorgeous."

She paused. She realized she needed to put some firm boundaries into place. What had happened the night before was still coming into her mind in bits and flashes, but she had the distinct impression some things had gone too far.

"I think maybe we should just ... you know ... keep it friendly."

"What?" He seemed puzzled.

"You just called me gorg— Oh ... You meant the food."

He laughed. "Yes, the food."

She felt her face flush, but she was too hungry to linger on her mistake for long. Besides, she was getting quite comfortable with Adair; a little faux pas here or there seemed not nearly so mortifying any more.

"Let's eat then, shall we?" She smiled and pulled out his chair, "Tuck in!"

"Och—not so loud."

"Yeah, it was too loud for me, too."

They smiled at each other as they scooted their chairs in. He raised his water glass and she picked up hers and they clinked it very gently. She felt warm towards him again, but in a different way than before. Brotherly, but not exactly like a brother. More like a lover, but without the sex. Something she didn't have a name for, somewhere between brother and lover. She wondered if he was feeling it, too.

"I'm sorry about last night," she apologized in a low voice. "I shouldn't have got you all worked up like that. I was drunk. I was feeling lonely. Not that that's an excuse. I was mad at Faolan. But scared about him too, y' know? I don't know how I'm going to tell him about it. I don't know how he's going to react." She started in on her eggs and bacon, small bites and gentle chewing. The headache powder was helping.

Adair broke into his yolk with the point of his toast and bit it off. He looked thoughtfully at her. "We were both drunk. We were both feeling alone. And let's face it, we're both exceedingly good-looking." He smiled wide and she caught that it was a joke and gave him a small grin for his trouble. "I'm glad you spoke up. I would have felt terrible if

274

you hadn't, and regretted it later. I wouldn't want to be somebody's regret."

She nodded and nibbled on a buttery edge of toast. She picked up the heavy coffee mug and let it warm her hands as she inhaled the vapor, closing her eyes. "Oh my god this smells so good."

"Thanks for making breakfast. Ye did a cracking job of it."

She gave a little nod, guessing that was a good thing, and began dumping several spoons of sugar and a double shot of cream into her coffee.

"Have a little coffee with your sugar and cream," he teased.

"Yeah, I'm bad about that."

"Black for me. The darker and bitterer, the better."

She made a face. "Yuck."

"Ye didn't touch yer beans."

"I'm still not used to them. You want them?"

He leaned over the table and grabbed her plate and fork and scooped the beans into his mouth.

"Okay, you're being gross." She sipped her coffee and peered at him over the mug, brows raised. He froze, lifted his eyes to her, then set the plate down and took out his napkin and patted his chin.

"Sorry."

"Boys."

"Girls."

"What time is it?"

He finished up the beans in a more dignified manner and began to clear the table. "About half-past. Eight."

"I would have thought it was later than that. It does seem awful quiet out there, though."

"When is Faolan coming to get you?"

"He didn't say."

"What, honestly?"

"He just said he'd be here bright and early. I think we've passed bright and early."

She helped him tidy up the table and wash the dishes. They chatted. Bumped elbows a few times. Smiled a little. The energy between them was still good, and she was relieved. It was good to have somebody she could talk to about ... everything.

"Did you ever meet somebody and get to know them a little and feel like you could just say anything?" She wiped a dish dry and put it in the cabinet.

"Not really. Maybe it's a girl thing."

"Hmph. Maybe. I never thought of it that way. Well, I feel that way with you. Like I can talk to you, and trust you."

He paused and looked at her, searching her face for sincerity, and found it there. He smiled and went back to scrubbing.

"You're not going to make me regret it are you? Adair? You're not a gossip or a blabber mouth? Or maybe you have some dark secret like you have sex with llamas or something, right?"

He handed her the dish he'd washed and said, "I'm not a gossip. You can trust me. And I am deathly allergic to llamas."

"Really?"

"Yeah, never gossiped in m' life."

She bonked his hip with hers, "No silly, the allergic to llamas thing."

"No, I'm not really allergic to llamas. See? I'm a big liar. Can't be trusted."

"Oh, you!" She made a face, wrinkling up her nose like a five-year-old.

She finished putting away the dishes. He drained the sink, dried his hands and turned towards her, accidentally knocking into a low-hanging copper pot and causing a clatter that made them both wince a bit.

"I wish you could come back to the hunting grounds and practice some more. I heard you're leaving in a couple of days."

She crossed her arms and leaned against the counter behind her and frowned thoughtfully. "Yeah. Maybe I can come back for another visit after the winter."

"I'll be in the States next summer m'self. Maybe I can come visit you, too. Well, if nothing goes really wrong anytime soon with all this lycan stuff. I'll need to stick close by home if it does."

"Shit, I hadn't thought of that. I was so pumped up yesterday about all that stuff."

Adair gave her a funny look. She thought maybe it meant, *Really?*

"It's not like I want shit to go down, Adair. I just like being ready for it if it is."

"Are ye sure you don't want any shite to go down? I heard about

Ciardha. What he did to your family, August. It's kind of a thing that went around the village."

"I thought you didn't spread gossip."

"I didn't say I don't *hear* gossip."

She narrowed her eyes.

"What? Yer family is kind of a legend around here, ye ken?"

"They are?"

"Yeah. Killing Ban, for starts. Your family hiding out and helping other hunters—anyone who was done with the lycan uprisings and wanted to just try and live a regular cumanta life."

"My family did that?"

"People got sick of the constant threat of violence. They worried about their kin. Besides, it seemed like the old ways were dying out, with the modern world closing in on every secluded place. It made sense to some folks to just get out."

"I mean, I knew about Ban—that was self-defense."

He looked at her and blinked.

"Wasn't it?"

He shrugged.

"Hmph. Anyway, I didn't know that other stuff, about helping people move to the States and hide. Is that how Ciardha found my family?"

"I don't know. Could be. It wasn't just the States, it was all over the world. Your da being with the university, he helped with a lot of the red tape."

"I'm … stunned. I really just had no clue. In fact, I don't think my dad ever talked to me about work."

"We always tried to keep the lycan from finding out about the hunters that wanted to go live in peace. There were a lot of vengeance seekers on the wolf side. But there were some angry hunters, too. They felt like the ones who left, they were cowards. They weren't protecting traditions or bloodlines. Or the land."

"I think somebody could make the argument that they were definitely protecting bloodlines."

"When people are upset, or feeling cornered—"

"Or abandoned."

He nodded. "Or abandoned—logic goes out the window."

"Every time I learn new things about my dad, I feel a little like

I've lost him again."

"Ah, lass … Let me give ye a hug."

She spread her arms and he came over and hugged her. She put her head in the nook of his neck and tried to let her tension flow away. He gently rubbed her back and she sighed. He gave a little, almost imperceptible, twitch and said, "That's enough for now," and stepped back and put his hands in his pockets.

"Really?"

"I'm a young buck, y' know. Practically rutting. I'm still attracted to you August, and my whole body wants me to bond with you. I reckon it'll pass when I find somebody else to get all hormonal about."

A knock came at the door. "Shit, I should put some pants on," August said. "Why didn't I think of that an hour ago?"

"He's seen you in your underwear."

She rolled her eyes at him.

"He hasn't? What?" Shrug.

"I mean, he'll know *you* saw me in my underwear. Actually, *your* underwear!" She whispered hard through her teeth.

He shrugged again.

"Oh, you're no help!"

August strode over to the door and opened it as though she had nothing to be ashamed of. But it wasn't Faolan. It was the other Archer boy. Henry. The one who'd pointed an arrow at her.

"What the blazes are you doing here?" He demanded.

"Of course it's not my boyfriend. Of course it's some strange boy who wants to murder me."

Before August could even turn around to open the door wider so the Archer boy could see Adair, Faolan's car pulled up and he got out. His clothes were wrinkled, his hair mussed and he had on sunglasses, despite the mist. He strode up to the door, looking like a laird who owned the whole village.

August felt a lump in her throat. It was as though a halo followed Faolan around and there was nothing, not even the idea of him sleeping with another woman, that could shake her feelings for him. The idea of him being with another woman hurt. It hurt like bloody hell. But it didn't change her feelings for him. She supposed that the glow she felt for him, this unshakable affection and longing, was what he'd felt with Iseabail.

But at the very least, August had gotten a taste of the possibility that, if she really wanted to, even at this point, she might be able to get over him if she had to. With somebody like Adair. Would that be fair to Adair, though? Would that be using him? Even if it was, would he mind? So many questions she couldn't resolve.

Henry pushed past her. "Rude!" she shouted as he stalked towards Adair, who was leaning against the counter in the kitchen.

"Mornin', love." Faolan leaned down and gave her a peck on the cheek. He held out a brown paper bag. "Scones. The best."

She took the bag. "Thanks. You look terrible."

"You look nearly naked. Is this how you always hang out with other men?"

She tossed the bag to the couch and crossed her arms. "Maybe you should give me some idea of what you were wearing last night before you go critiquing my clothes."

"Sorry, lass, it was a joke. Sincerely sorry. I should've known you'd be tense."

"Tense? How about nervous, worried, hurt, sad, scared, confused? How about any of those?"

The two in the kitchen stopped their loud whispering argument when her voice reached a certain decibel. The Archer boy seemed to have a good chuckle at her expense. She flipped him the finger and turned back to Faolan.

"I'm not saying you don't have a good reason to be—" he began.

"Damn right I have a good reason!" she said to Faolan, and "Mind your own fucking business!" to Henry. In his agitated whisper he said one last punctuated thing, which August could barely understand since it was all very Scottishy, and turned to leave. As he passed he paused and took in Faolan, then looked at August.

"Yer a bossy little cunt, ain't ye?"

August gave him a hard glare while Faolan, almost a full head taller than the Archer kid, lowered his glasses.

"You'd better learn some sodding respect, mate."

"I'm not yer mate, you animal." He then pushed past Faolan, trying to shove him. But Faolan was a rooted tree and the kid pretty much bounced off of him across the porch, then ran into the edge of the woods and disappeared.

Faolan stepped into the living room area.

"Guess I'll go put some clothes … um …" August faltered.

Faolan handed her the bag he had slung over his shoulder. "Here, love. Your clothes were at the flower shop where I left you yesterday. The lovely Nia had retrieved them, along with your bow and gear. She sends her best wishes and her hopes for your return soon."

"You can do as ye please with my pants," Adair said from the kitchen breezeway. "I'm gunna need my Bowie tee though. I've had it forever."

"Oh, right. Sure, sorry." She walked a few paces to a corner of the living room and pulled on the pants she'd had on yesterday morning, then slipped out of the tee. Adair leaned a little to watch her naked back. Faolan rotated his head toward him and cleared his throat. Adair looked away, as nonchalantly as possible.

"So, how was your night, Faolan?" he ventured.

"Dandy. Yours?"

"Same."

Faolan nodded slowly, his face remaining studious. He sniffed the air and raised a brow towards Adair, then looked back to August.

August turned back to them with the Bowie tee over her arm and handed it to Adair, then pulled on her red coat.

"Is that yer cloak?" Faolan asked, puzzled.

August threw him a stern look that said *Don't ask me questions right now*.

"Adair, thank you so much. For everything." She pecked him on the cheek.

"I mean it, August, about seeing you in the summer. I'd like to see that big house of your grandmother's. Hell, I'd like to meet her."

"Let's make it happen, then. Write me, okay?" August peeked over her shoulder at Faolan, wondering if he would think something of them staying in touch, on top of her sleeping there in Adair's underwear. Which she was still wearing.

They hugged and she whispered one more "Thank you." She let go and dashed out of the door ahead of Faolan, who was a little slow on the uptake.

"Thanks, Adair. Tell your folks I said oi."

Adair nodded and unfolded an arm to wave goodbye, without much enthusiasm. Indeed, he looked very sorry to see August go. He watched as they got into their car and drove off, then closed the door.

A Poisoned Mind
Conall Keep

Ciardha dropped large cubes of raw meat into his maw while he made notes for his speech at the Veritas meeting the next night. At first the meat felt like it might stay down and the smell of the roast in the kitchen was actually appetizing. But an hour into his notes and he felt a little queasy and stopped eating.

"Blair!"

She entered the room and stood in front of the low table he was working on. Her arms crossed, she tilted her head. "Would you like some bicarbonate?"

He leaned back and put his hand on his stomach. "Is that meat bad?"

"Of course not. Katie brought it from the butcher just yesterday. Cubed it up and put it in the icebox."

"I don't have time for this. I can't be seen like this in front of the Veritas. I have an important speech to deliver!" He broke out in a cold sweat and turned yellow-green.

Blair took a slow route to the kitchen at a leisurely pace. She mixed up some baking soda with water and walked it back to him.

Ciardha took the drink and drained the glass. He burped and looked like he might faint.

"Blair, help me upstairs, I need to rest before tomorrow."

She put out her arm and he grabbed on and hoisted himself off of the couch. They made their way up the stairs and he crawled onto the bed. "Bring the basin over here."

She brought over the basin and set it on the bed. He rolled on his side and half curled into a ball and hugged it.

"Pick out my suit and tie for tomorrow," he ordered between moans.

He was always like this, worried he would be late. For somebody who didn't care what anybody thought, or who he hurt, he liked to be punctual. Blair used to see it as a good quality. Now she saw it more as an affect of the negative sides of his personality. It was all about appearances and control.

She selected his favorite dark suit, the one he thought he was hot shit in. He liked the pleats and the full half-break at the ankle. He liked to wear it with his most expensive silk tie, which he bought on their honeymoon. "Fit for a world leader," he'd said as he held it up for her. Painted with swirling colors of red, orange and yellow, it gave the effect of fire. Ciardha didn't generally favor suits. He liked his bad-boy hunting leathers, his suedes and linens, flannels. He fancied himself rough and manly and she felt self-loathing creep up into her throat for having bought into all of his manipulative games. His façade of being a man. He was nothing more than a boy with a grudge, a child with a want, and the power to do something about it.

She hung his suit on the garment rack and set out his socks, shoes and tie. She headed back downstairs and went into the living room and rifled through his papers. Most of it was the sick rantings of a prejudiced mind. She read the speech, and it was full of speciesist hate, but cleverly organized as reasonable arguments. It hit all of the points: tradition, bloodlines, survival, power. He spent a couple of paragraphs on how cumanta are crowding them out and segued neatly into how mixing with the lycan, urwulf and canis clans of other lands might help build their race again, but that there would be complications about land rights—where they would live and what lands they would protect—and internecine war was a possible outcome. But, he countered, mixing with chosen hunter strains would bring forth stronger children with the abilities of both hunter and Scot lycan. She could feel her face getting hot. All these years she's been keeping everything quiet and low. She gave up her family, her identity, her very dignity, and only now that she's at the end, now that she has nothing left for him but contempt, he tries to make something legitimate of their relationship.

She dropped the papers back on the table, and noticed a folder in his case marked "HM Prison, Perth." Her hands started to shake. She held her breath and opened it. There was a photo, a prison photo of Paden, the man she loved, the father of her child. Her heart started to pound and her eyes welled up and dripped tears as she took in the face she hadn't seen in three years. His kind eyes, his strong jaw, the face she knew so well. Even the harsh flash of institutional photography couldn't take away from the regal quality he exuded. She sat on the couch and traced the outline of his face with her finger.

She looked through the contents of the folder, which included a variety of legal papers regarding his conviction and incarceration. His conviction—a total farce, and Blair knew it well. It was Ciardha's doings, his jealousy, that got Paden locked up.

There were some incident reports from the prison—trips to the infirmary, reprimands for being where he shouldn't and things like that. There was a list in the back called "lessons" and dates. She realized that the seven or eight incidents that ended with infirmary visits shared the dates with the "lessons." The most worrisome though was a short note tucked in right behind the photo. It simply read:

> C—
> *It's being taken care of December 17.*
> *Is this to be the final lesson?*
> —*Professor*

Lessons. She shuddered. She imagined him with the injuries listed in the report—black eyes, stabbed in the arm with a sharpened toothbrush, even the idea of people being cruel to him every day broke her heart—but this, this combination of emotional torture and physical violence was unbearable. She blamed herself for his suffering. If they hadn't fallen in love, if Ciardha hadn't been insulted and angered so deeply, he wouldn't be there. He'd be with some sassy round lass cooking him fry-ups every weekend, enjoying life. Taking his place as a leader in the hunter clans.

December 17th was Liam's birthday, just about six weeks away. Her anger began to simmer, then to boil when she realized he meant to have Paden killed on Liam's birthday. She wavered for a moment, wondering if she wasn't making a mountain of a vague note, but kept thinking of how much Ciardha had escalated over the last couple of years. He had been angry at Fletcher for some time, but it boiled over when Ciardha discovered that it was her brother that had introduced her to Paden. It was such a casual mistake, really. Somehow Blair had let it slip. She didn't even really consider it a secret—not exactly. But it was all the reason Ciardha needed to fan the flames of his vengeance.

The back of the folder had a pocket, and it was stuffed with something a little fatter than the rest. Blair reached in and her heart sunk when she pulled out three letters that she had asked Katie to smuggle out. Still Ciardha had caught them. And Katie was never punished, so she must be Ciardha's spy too. He hadn't even bothered to open them. Paden never read her desperate messages. Did he even know how much she still loved him? How sorry she was? Did he suffer every day, locked up and cursing her name?

Blair's veins grew warm—she could feel them pulse through her body with the leaden weight of regret, so deep she almost couldn't breathe. She had sacrificed everything for her passion with Ciardha, a bond built on nothing beyond rebellion and sex. Only after years of propping up her sham marriage out of a misguided sense of dignity did she find real love with Paden. Love based on intelligence and respect, on kindness as well as passion. The difference between these men— and how her mind and heart connected to each of them—almost couldn't be compared.

She couldn't let Ciardha hurt Paden any longer. She couldn't let him take Liam's real father away from him in a fit of jealousy. Blair's regret made her heart beat hard. Her hunter aspect came upon her and she felt as though she could crush Ciardha like a flea at that very moment, and end all of this misery. No more hemlock-soaked meat— she was going to go upstairs and cut his throat like the hunter she was.

The sound of Ciardha retching drifted down the stairs. Blair felt no empathy whatsoever. Not even sympathy—not a blink. She was going to end this now, and save Paden and Liam. It was high time she did something worthwhile with her life.

Upstairs Ciardha filled the basin with vomit. He was breathing hard and his body was churning between surges of healing and feeling like he might collapse. His ears pointed out and his fangs tried to emerge, but he was weak. He let out a pitiful howl that echoed through the loveless halls of the keep. He fell asleep to a vision of himself standing in the front hall with Blair. There were three small children running around and grabbing her skirts, which were swollen with more bairns. They were happy, finally.

The Tell Tale Heart
On the road from Summerblynd

The mist was starting to lift with the late morning sun and August wasn't sure if she should start, or wait for Faolan to talk. *Why is he being so quiet, anyway?* She herself was quiet because she had a confession to make, but when it occurred to her that he might have a similar reason, a wave of nausea washed over her and she started to feel slightly panicked.

"You're not talking because you have something to tell me that you know I don't want to hear."

He kept his eyes on the road, and replied evenly, "What makes you say that, lass?"

"You're only this quiet when I'm running my mouth. We've been driving for ten minutes and you haven't said a damn word."

He inhaled deeply and let it out.

"You're acting weird," she said, a little quiver in her voice.

"I'm sorry, I don't mean to act weird. It was a long night. I drank too much, I'm tired. I'm also emotionally exhausted."

"That's not the shirt you had on when you left. Why, what ..." she looked around the car and spied his shirt from yesterday on the back seat, ripped. His pants, too.

"Did you transform last night?" she demanded.

He bowed his head a little, then re-focused on the road. His jaw flexed, "Can't we talk about this when—"

"Oh my god, you did! You transformed!" August had a memory of his early letters with Iseabail, where she wanted him to transform while they were having sex. She felt her heart start to ache and throb as though somebody had physically reached in and jabbed it with something sharp. An energy began to grow in the center of her. But it was not her wolf aspect; it was her hunter that had started to swell in her. She felt the tingling not in her ears or gums—this time it was electric zaps all through her, like flashes of adrenaline, though more visceral. Her senses all twitched and tingled and August saw images come into her mind like the glittering stardust of her visions the night before. She saw Blair—or maybe felt her. She knew she was about to do something drastic. Something final. August couldn't really understand what this all meant, but it was in the most ancient and instinctual part of her brain. They had to get to the keep. Right now.

"Faolan—something's wrong ..."

"I'm sorry, lass, it's nothing to worry—"

"No! Faolan! We have to get to the keep, right away. Something bad is going to happen to Blair!"

"Are you having hunter visions?"

"I don't know what it is. I can't ... It's kind of like the dream vision I had yesterday around the pyre. It's hard to explain. Just—we have to go right now!"

Faolan stepped on the gas and they headed in the direction of the keep, taking dusty corners and narrowly missing the edges of tree roots, the Rover becoming airborne at moments, two wheels at a time.

They arrived within ten minutes, much closer to the keep this time. They both hopped out and sprinted for the front door, the wooded landscape blurring past. Faolan struck the door hard at the latch, and they both ran past a stunned Katie who was polishing the furniture.

Faolan was breathing hard, pausing to let August sense the direction they should head. They took the stairs three at a time, and rushed the door to find Ciardha on top of Blair, half-wolf with his paw-hands around her throat, his claws pressing in. Spots of blood started to rise where they dug into her flesh.

She had a dagger in her hand. She was trying to hold onto it, but it was slipping. She was trying to talk, but could only make sputters and grunts. Tears rolled down her red cheeks, which were beginning to turn purple.

Ciardha was cursing and thundering, shaking her like a doll with each damnation. "I loved ye! I loved ye! You slut! I loved ye, you sodding whore!"

August yanked out her sgian dubh, which she had tucked in her boot on their way there. She felt all of her hunter ancestry awake and pulsing around this attacking lycan. She also felt her vengeance welling up, her deep outrage, and wondered how much peace it would bring her to kill the man who killed her father. Her only hesitation was in calculating where her best strike might be, but before she could lunge Faolan was past her, already transformed into the werewolf form. His enormous paw met the side of Ciardha's head and almost knocked him

286

off-balance, though he loosened his grip only slightly on Blair. August watched in awe as Faolan seemed to grow even taller. He growled, teeth bared, and opened his claws. He struck his brother with a blow that rang through the room like iron on wood, his claws ripping across Ciardha's face and neck, knocking him onto his tail on the stone floor, gasping and vomiting. He looked up at his younger brother, utterly stunned, and tried to close up the torn flesh from his face and neck. Blood spurted and he pressed his half-paw over the gash.

August rushed over to Blair, who was sitting on the edge of the bed coughing and gagging and trying to catch her breath. She held Blair's head, watching the scene on the other side of the room unfold as she petted her pale hair.

Faolan towered over Ciardha, daring him to move, snarling and growling. Ciardha gave a weak snarl, then whimpered like an injured puppy as the life started to drain from him. He tried to paste the ribbons of flesh and fur into place with sticky blood, but the dark pool spreading around him was too big to mean anything but death. He finally collapsed onto his side, his paw releasing his neck, and what little blood was left in him spilled out.

He was gone. August expected she would feel a sense of triumph, or at least relief. For as long as she had wanted to say, "There, you got what you fucking deserved!" instead she felt sick and sad and didn't want to say anything at all. She looked to Faolan, still in his werewolf form, though smaller, his clothes ripped at the seams. He stood, breathing slowly, immobile, unreadable.

August felt like she was watching it all from a gauzy distance, as her aunt's coughing and gagging subsided. She could relax about her family's safety, now that Ciardha couldn't come after them again. But none of it would bring her father back. Or her aunt and uncles. So much loss, and for what? Old grudges. August shook her head and held her Aunt Blair a bit tighter.

"You're safe," August told her. "He's … he's gone."

Blair looked over her shoulder at the pile of fur and shredded flesh that was once her husband—once a man she had loved, that she had wanted to have children with. Now she felt nothing but relief to see him lying dead.

"He got what he deserved," she said, her voice hoarse and strained.

August saw Faolan was back in his human form, all but naked in the remnants of his ruined slacks. He sat down slowly on the edge of the bed, looking at his brother and holding up his own bloodied hand. August's mind whirled, trying to imagine what would come next and how on earth to handle it.

"Faolan?" August coaxed gently but clearly. "I've got Blair. Why don't you go wash up, sweetheart?"

Her heart ached to see how slowly he rose and went to the sink, and she listened to his vigorous scrubbing. A short while later he emerged from the closet wearing his dead brother's denim and flannel. He seemed to be trying to make sense of something.

"Blair," he finally spoke. "We need to call Dr. Haggerty."

She nodded. "Downstairs, Faolan. His number is by the phone on the desk."

Faolan came over to the bed and stood by August for a moment, then kissed the top of her head. She kneeled up on the bed and gave him a hard hug around the middle. Then he walked with deliberate steps out of the room and down the stairs.

"They're going to do an autopsy and know that something weird is up," August said to Blair. "People don't just get wounded like that. He doesn't even look human …"

"You needn't worry, niece. Dr. Haggerty is very good at making weird things appear normal. Blair then locked eyes with her. "Thank you, August. I gave you a hunter call. I could see myself reaching out to you in my mind. I didn't know I could still do that. You were here so fast."

"You're going to have to explain some of this hunter call stuff to me. Anyway, it was partly coincidence that we were out in the car on the road already." Then August remembered what Merindah said, and her vision, and began to wonder if it was coincidence after all. "Anyway, I'm glad we were here."

August stood and pulled her aunt up on her feet. She didn't think either one of them needed to be sitting there in the room with Ciardha's body. They headed downstairs for the sitting room.

"Are you gonna let Gran know you're alive?"

Blair lowered her eyes and picked imaginary fuzz off of her knee. "I don't know if she wants to know I'm alive."

"Only one way to find out."

Blair nodded.

"Are you going to be okay?"

Blair nodded again. "I think so. But this thing … Keer dying … it's going to cause some new troubles."

August cocked her head to the side, hoping for more explanation. "Blair, what happened, anyway?" she finally asked.

"I think he went crazy. He's been sick, as ye know. I think he might have eaten some hemlock."

"What? Why would he eat hemlock? How do you know?"

"Sometimes after he would hunt, he might cook up some meat for himself if Katie and I were off doing other things. His favorite was a rabbit stew. He killed about a dozen hares a few days ago. At first I thought maybe the hares somehow made him sick. The lycan, they get well so quickly when something happens to them. Well, I noticed my bowls of herbs and roots was missing the hemlock. They look a little like wild parsnips. I think he might have eaten it."

"Did you tell him?"

"No, I thought he'd just get better … And, well, he could be violent when he blamed me for things."

"It wasn't really your fault he ate them."

"He wouldn't have seen it that way."

"We'd better let the coroner know, so they aren't surprised to find hemlock in his system. If they are even looking for it."

Blair nodded.

"Look, I'll tell Faolan. Don't worry about it."

"I'm not sorry he's gone. Is that terrible? Life is going to be so much better. The first thing I want to do is send for my son. I want to have him brought home tonight."

"I didn't know you had a son," August said. "Gran would want to know that, too."

"No one knew," Blair said blankly, then blinked. "Alright."

Faolan joined them in the sitting room and he looked grim. August felt terrible for him. As many times as she'd wished he would do it, she'd never thought about what it would actually mean for him to kill his own brother. She walked over to him and put her arms around him. He wrapped her up and held her tight. He didn't weep, but she felt his grief in his arms, in his chest. She took him into the hall and told him about the hemlock. He asked, without accusation, if she thought Blair had done it on purpose. August shrugged and said it didn't really matter at this point. Things would be better now. The head of the Veritas had been cut off. It could usher in an era of interspecies peace. He hoped she was right.

They went back into the sitting room.

"Haggerty will be a few hours yet. Though I don't know how he'll pick him up from the road," Faolan said to Blair.

"Katie's seeing to that already," she replied.

"Ah. I reckon we have a funeral to plan. Let us help ye. Maybe ye want to rest a day?"

"I've got a lot of phone calls to make today. You two might as well go on with your visit to bonny Scotland, aye?"

"Right, we'll just go have a picnic by the stream then? Blair, ye know we'll not go anywhere until we've done what needs."

"Of course we'll be here helping you make calls. Just give us the lists and tell us what to do," August said.

Blair looked at the two, then slipped them some sheets with tasks already written out, alongside names and phone numbers. "I appreciate yer help. Truly. I'm going to go take a shower."

"This is very organized," August said once Blair disappeared around the corner.

"Aye." They exchanged looks, but divided the work and got to it.

They sat at the table with paper, pens and lists, taking turns making calls and jotting notes. There was even a floral catalog from Perth's biggest florist in the stack. August figured maybe rich people just kept floral catalogs around. Blair returned to the room in sweat clothes, a sweater and big socks, and August couldn't blame her for going with comfort. They all worked quietly together, the sounds of pen scratching on paper and pages flipping being the only sound between phone calls.

Blair broke the silence between them. "This is so odd—the little duties that go with death, they seem like a thousand other things you do, don't they? But this is for death. Such an odd mix of ordinary duty and grim circumstance."

"Loss is another process, I reckon. The lists are the artifacts of going through it; they may have the same shape and feel as 'normal' lists, but they aren't. Maybe it's how the brain helps us make it through?"

290

Blair nodded. "Aye, it could be, that."

Faolan next called the proctor. "Funeral's in three days," he announced after hanging up. "They are going to make sure things push through quickly with the official report. Oh, and the funeral home wants a suit for him to be buried in, and a photo of him."

"I have the photo." She pulled a large yellow envelope from the desk and handed it to Faolan. "Would you mind taking it?"

"Aye." If Faolan thought it odd she had a display photo ready, he didn't let on. "And the suit?"

"Right, there's one already picked out," Blair said.

This time Faolan and August both looked up and studied her.

"That does sound odd, doesn't it? Ye see, I picked him out a fine suit only a few hours ago, for his meeting tomorrow. He asked me to. So that's the one. Only a few hours ago. Life can change so suddenly, can't it?"

Flowers, food, casket, memorial, burial plot. So many things to figure out rather quickly, but Blair didn't seem to be having much trouble with it. In fact, she had all of the information they needed handy.

In a matter of hours, they'd checked down the whole list together. Blair sat back and sipped some tea. She appeared to be relaxed and perhaps relieved. Katie had come in twice and offered food. The first time they all demurred; the second time, nearly at the end of the lists, Blair accepted a tray of bread, grapes and cheese. Faolan and August again exchanged glances as she popped a grape in her mouth and made notes. Both of them were still far too shaken by the experience to be hungry, despite Faolan's having transformed.

August gathered up all of their notes and slid them across the table to Blair, who tucked them into a folder at her elbow.

"Should we stay, then? Await the coroner?" Faolan asked.

"I'd rather have the time alone, actually. If ye don't mind, Faolan?"

"Aye. Anything else we can do ye before we go?"

"Are you staying for the funeral?"

"Of course. Did ye want to come back with us to the States after?"

She shook her head. "I have too much to do. I will write a letter to Mom though, if you could give it to her for me. Maybe it's the best way to test the waters?"

He nodded and gave her hand a squeeze.

August leaned in and gave her a hug. "I'm glad you're okay. Take care, I guess. See you at the funeral. Or sooner if you need us."

"Thank you. I think I'll be alright."

August nodded a last farewell and she and Faolan went out into the afternoon sun.

Blair closed the doors behind them, then went to the table and opened her address book. Most of Ciardha's family was dead, but there were a few cousins. She popped another grape in her mouth, spread some soft cheese on the bread, and washed it down with a glass of wine. Then another. After her third glass she started calling the lycan list—Ciardha's few friends, Veritas members and what remained of his family. She mustered her best upset widow façade and told them that he had simply fallen ill. *The poor foolish man had taken the hemlock for wild parsnips when he was making his rabbit stew. No, nobody else had eaten it. Yes, that's quite a lucky thing indeed.* The Veritas were mixed in their reactions. Some called her an abomination and hung up. Others sent their condolences. She wondered what the funeral was going to be like.

Her final phone call was to Kester. She told him of her husband's death and asked to meet with him the next morning—she had an offer he would want to know about. Katie came in at the end of the call, and informed her that the gate was now open and the road cleared of the worst of the vegetation.

After the coroner had come and gone, Blair went to the safe in the study and opened it to count the contents. She was surprised how much remained, including gold and diamonds, bonds and jewelry. She filled a small satchel with bundles of £100 notes and tucked it under the desk. She shut the safe back up and went to the sitting room to call the boarding school and arrange for Liam to come home due to a death in the family.

She called a car company and gave them exact instructions for finding the obscure keep. She changed her clothes, barely looking at the room where Ciardha had died, and dabbed makeup on her bruises. Widowed only a few hours, Blair Conall strode out the front door a free woman, hopped into a waiting sedan, and headed towards her son.

The Confessions

They remained silent on the ride back to the inn. August kept seeing images in her head of Ciardha, the look on his face, trying to put his skin back together. Not understanding he was dying. Not understanding how his own brother could do that to him. She watched Faolan driving, his attention resolutely on the road. She had never understood how powerful, how terrible, he could be. If she was going to marry this man, she would be married to that power. She would have to be ready to stand by him, even if he had to do something as horrible as that. Before she could give him that loyalty, she knew she had to be able to trust his love, no matter what. But she didn't yet; not when it came to Iseabail. She tried to focus on the big sky and the reflection of her nose in the side window.

"I'm gettin' hungry now," he spoke up. "You?"

August nodded when he looked at her. "Pub food? I like the Scotch eggs. I would love a beer."

"Aye. Or four."

Once back at the inn they took separate showers. August shut the bathroom door tight. She felt like she was mad at Faolan, though she couldn't pin down exactly why. She also didn't want him looking at her; she was feeling protective of herself. She hurried washing everything down, and then dried her hair carefully as not to make her hair a bush of frizz, while he quickly slipped in and out of the shower. She couldn't help noticing he shut the door tight too, and it made her suspicious, and resentful. What did he have to hide, she wondered—what was he showering away?

In fresh sweaters and jeans and clean shoes with no blood on them, they walked over to the pub and ordered food and beer. They grabbed the corner table and ate quietly until they weren't so hungry, and as the eating slowed, the conversation started.

"I'm sorry, about your brother. I'm not sorry about him being ... Well, I'm sorry you had to do it."

"Are ye then?"

"Why would you ask me that? Of course I didn't want you to have to do that to your own flesh and blood."

"I think ye did. I think you'll be much happier now knowing I

293

finally did something to protect your family, won't ye lass?"

August wasn't sure how to respond. She started to say something, but it caught in her throat because it had nowhere to go. She huffed. "You know what Faolan? I think you're going to be happier knowing that, too."

Faolan nodded and popped a whole Scotch egg in his mouth, then drained his pint in three swallows and called for another.

She watched him wipe his mouth, take a swig of beer, brush something off of his leg.

"You are different," she finally said.

"I'm not, though. Beyond killing the last remaining member of m' family, and reacquainting m'self with the ghost of my first love." He looked at her directly. "It's been quite a week, ye must admit. Are you feeling suspicious? A little threatened maybe? Or just jealous?"

"It's not like I *want* to be jealous. It's a terrible feeling. I know I don't own you. I don't want to own you. I just want that sense of belonging together to be there. Do you feel like you belong with me?"

"Aye, I do. Of course I do. That's why I brought you here. That's why we work so hard to figure out how to love each other better." He reached over and took her free hand. She set down her fork and waited for more. He was quiet, looking at her face for a long moment, but finally said, "We belong together. Whatever else is going on."

August looked around at the crowded pub. There was a din of diners swigging and munching, laughing and talking. There was a man sitting at the bar regaling his neighbors with a pub song, rather mellifluously. One of them said, "Oi, Danny, sing us another!"

Faolan scooted his chair around the table so he was next to her. They held hands and watched the other diners for a bit. Nibbled at the food.

She finished her beer and started on the lemonade she'd asked for—which she forgot would be lemon soda, not lemon juice, sugar and water. She wanted to be clear in her discussions, without the fog of alcohol clinging to her.

"This is weird, huh?"

"What's that, love?"

She sipped her soft drink and sloshed the ice around. "Just sitting here eating dinner after what happened today. Just, you know, like nothing happened. We've got to eat, everybody does. When my dad died I was upset that time didn't stop. It felt like everything should freeze for a while. Not a long while or anything, but just for a bit. I wanted to scream at people for doing things, just normal things. I wanted to make them understand what a wonderful man was ripped from the world and I wanted the world to feel the loss the way I did. I know that doesn't make sense. Why would somebody who didn't know my dad feel that loss the way I do? I couldn't think straight. I resented people who weren't suffering the way I was. I was … well, indignant."

"It does seem as though the world ought to stop and take notice when a hole like that is ripped open. There are people who won't ever ken what they're missing, while others will always be keenly aware of it. But, you're right, we've all got to eat. And it wouldn't do any good t' sit in the room and stare at the walls, would it?"

"Do you ever look around and wonder the shit people are going through? Like that guy who's singing. Why is he singing? We all are enjoying his singing, but why does he do it? Do you think there is any pain behind that story? Like a dead wife? Do you think he's a widower? Why is it widower when it's a guy?"

"Lass, do you want to talk about last night?"

"Do you?" She jumped on it immediately.

"Aye, I think it's best."

"You're not going to tell me something that's going to hurt or scare me are you?"

"Scare you?"

"You don't know it's scary when somebody is about to tell you they love somebody else, or don't love you the way they thought, or maybe will be staying behind in Scotland indefinitely when you've already decided you love that person and that you want to spend all of your time with them?"

"Take a breath, Red. It's alright."

August felt her stomach muscles tighten and her hand tensed up in his.

"Love, relax. Be calm. It's going to be alright." He knew what he had to tell her, she thought, but if he knew what she had to tell him, maybe he wouldn't be saying that. If he knew that her naked breasts were in Adair's mouth last night, and she was kissing him—kisses that she meant—maybe he wouldn't be saying it was going to be alright.

She was at least as worried about what she had to tell him as she was worried about what he had to tell her. How would he react? Now her brain was a jumble of worries and she just sipped her soda and tried to relax her muscles and fool her body into thinking everything was fine.

"You're shivering," he said, and took off his sport coat and put it around her shoulders. The warmth he left behind clung to the liner and made her feel a bit safer. Faolan called for coffee.

"Thanks. I'm nervous is all."

"I understand. I think maybe you're worried more than you need to be. Look, lass, I did transform last night, but not for the reason you think."

"What? I didn't think any reason. What kind of reason do you think I thought you would think I—"

"Shhh … Hey, hey. Listen." He squeezed her a little and leaned his cheek in close to her, his arm wrapped around her shoulders, their legs touching.

"I transformed, but I really only did it because I was drunk and she asked me to—"

August looked to him sharply.

"Not, not like that. She just wanted to remember how I looked, to see me once more. We didn't do anything."

"I didn't realize this would be a thing, but I don't like it when you transform for other women. Wow, that sounded really weird."

He made a thoughtful sound. "Alright."

"Alright, it's alright for me to feel that way?"

"Alright, it's alright for you to feel that way, and not so weird, I think. And alright, I won't do it again."

"I didn't ask you not to."

"It bothers you though, so why would I do it when it bothers you?"

Just like that. No arguing. No blaming. She felt like a terrible person, so ready to be territorial and demanding, when he was so ready to accommodate her.

"Well, I have a lot more I wanted to ask, but now I feel like you're being so great I should just shut up." But she knew she couldn't shut up. "I guess … Well, after you not selling the store, and holding on to those letters and things for so long, I just … um, what happened with the trunk?"

"I left it with her. So she could read all of the journals and letters."

"Do you think that's a good idea? It might just fan the flames for her."

"I hadn't really thought of it that way. I guess I wanted her to read them as much as she wanted to read them, so I just handed them over."

"You basically just said why it's a bad idea. I wish you hadn't."

He nodded. "I ken your point. I don't actually think it's going to fan anything, but I'm sorry. Anyroad, it's done—I'm not going to go take them away from her. They are the past for me. Whatever they mean for her, I canna help that. But she deserves to know that she was being thought of."

August had many objections to this, but none of them sounded sane or mature, so she kept her mouth shut. It wasn't really her business what he did with his trunk, even if he did make a promise. Life doesn't follow a script. Plans change.

"Anyroad, how did your day and night go? Once you were able to forgive me for not picking you up and being so un-gallant."

"The day was amazing. We did huntery stuff. I'm not supposed to tell you because it's some big secret." Faolan seemed completely unconcerned about whatever secrets she may have been given, so she plunged on. "But it really was kind of amazing—I had a vision of my dad, Fe."

The words touched her heart as she spoke them, and she swallowed hard. Faolan leaned in and kissed her temple.

"Then I had a bonfire and whisky with a bunch of hunter kids. This one girl, Rose, she had two boyfriends."

"She told you that?"

"She had them with her!"

"Unusual."

"Yeah. Anyway, the bonfire was just down the street from Adair's cottage. So we walked over, talked to the kids. He and I spent all this time just talking about all kinds of things and throwing back whisky."

Faolan continued to listen intently. August's story seemed to get slower and slower. He sipped his beer and waited.

"Anyway, once we were back … Once we were at the cottage

again, we both just sat down on the couch and talked some more. And …"

"Yes, and …" He took another sip of his pint.

"I'm too ashamed to tell you." Her face was flush and she felt stupid for being so jealous of what Faolan might be up to, when she herself had been kissing and putting her hands all over this other man.

"Ashamed? Why?"

She took a deep breath and sipped her soda again. She looked around the pub, but everybody else seemed to be oblivious to the tight little vortex of drama she felt at their table.

"Things went a little too far."

Faolan pushed his drink away and angled his body towards her and looked her in the eyes.

"Eh?"

"We were drunk … And, honestly even if I wasn't drunk, who knows … It's not like you were there to get me like you said you would. If you had, then I wouldn't have been so upset. In fact I wouldn't even have been there. You realize, don't you, that this is mostly your fault? Because I was really was scared and upset. Can you blame me? You're so complicated, Faolan. Things between us, they're so complicated sometimes. So even if I hadn't, if we hadn't been drunk, maybe it would have still gotten a bit out of hand. I'm not using that as an excuse. I think that there is some room to question how reasonable it was to think, whether I was drunk or not, that I might be upset with you, or even think you might not come to pick me up at all … and …"

She sputtered out a bit and didn't know what to say next. Even if she did know what to say next, she wasn't sure it would come out coherently.

He stared at her with what appeared to be a cross between wonder and amusement.

"Are you about to fucking laugh at me?" she hissed.

He stifled a grin. "No." His lips struggled to stay neutral, bowing and flexing in one corner, then the other.

She pursed her lips and crossed her arms. "This isn't funny in the least."

He shook off the amusement, and made a more serious face. "I'm sorry, go ahead. Things got out of hand."

She looked down at the table and felt hot salt tears welling up in her throat. "I'm sorry, I kissed Adair."

"Ah. I see. I forgive you."

She was instantly a bit suspicious of this. Why would he forgive her so easily? Maybe he had bad stuff to feel guilty for too, and he figured this evened things out a bit? But her more rational mind would not let her get away with such an obvious self-deception. *He said he didn't do anything, and you know perfectly well he wasn't lying. All of this is just about you feeling guilty, August! Now tell him the rest.*

"There's more."

He raised his brows, but he seemed calm. Way more calm than August could be with news like that. Why was he so calm?

"More?"

"We … well … I got half naked. Like, it was bad. Wrong. I was straddling him and my shirt was off and I didn't have a bra on. He put his—"

"August—love, stop. You don't have to tell me. I can see you're upset by this, but it's alright. I can see you didn't mean it to go further. You're here with me."

"What?" She looked at him in disbelief, a tear rolling down one cheek. "But I—"

He put a finger to her lips and leaned in and pressed his cheek to hers. "You don't have to tell me. It doesn't matter."

She started to cry a bit harder as he held her. She forgot for the moment they were in a room full of people as she buried her face in his shoulder and let some of her shame out. She emerged a minute or two later feeling pretty safe and cozy in her corner. Nobody even seemed to notice what was going on between them, each table its own little world.

He then took a more serious tone, and her heart sunk a bit. "I will tell you this though …" Faolan paused, waiting for her to focus.

"What?" Heart pounding.

"You don't get to blame me for the things you do, love. Ye ken?"

He was right. She nodded. Heartbeat normalized. "Yeah."

"Finish up the coffee. I'll get some cheesecake to go, how's that sound?"

"Sounds wonderful."

They collected their things and went back to their room, pulled off their clothes down to their underwear and climbed onto the bed and ate cheesecake together.

"I love cheesecake. This cheesecake especially," August said, pushing her fork into the white creamy confection, leaving little ridges along the edges. "Oh my god this is so good."

"It is rather enjoyable, I'd have to agree with you on that one."

"And the blueberries, with the lemon swirl. Just, come on—who thinks this stuff up? Unfair."

"The strawberries are good too," he said, peeling off a slice with his fork that included a big red strawberry. His method was different. He turned his fork sideways and cut the creamy cake, leaving a smooth edge.

"You know I love strawberries." She let him feed her the bite. Her eyes widened, she made yummy sounds and poked her fork into her cake and pulled off a chunk with blueberries and lemon and fed it to him.

"Mmm," he chewed and looked at her like he might like to take a bite out of her as well.

She set her plate on the bed and used her fingers to pinch off a piece of his cheesecake and put it in his mouth. She removed her fingers and he licked them.

He then set his plate down and pinched off some of her cake and fed her. She took his finger in her hands and licked off the cheesecake, sucked the end of his finger while looking into his eyes.

They leaned towards each other and their lips met. First slow and warm. A gentle and sensual *hello, I missed you.* The kisses became more hungry. More insistent. Soon the cheesecake was crashing to the floor and August was on top of him, straddling his lap. The only thing between them was their respective undergarments.

They kissed and rocked together, but Faolan's body was not reacting the way she expected. He was kissing her deeply, his loving energy surrounded and embraced her. But he wasn't getting hard, and she started to think maybe she smelled funny or he was thinking of Iseabail. She tried to just keep kissing and push through the awkward, vulnerable feeling, but she stopped rocking and sat up. He looked surprised, which surprised her.

"What's wrong?" He asked, breathlessly.

She cocked her head slightly. *Come on, really?*

"What?"

He has to know what, she thought. Maybe he was embarrassed? Maybe she was wrong, maybe she just wasn't feeling things right?

"You don't seem … ready." She did a little head bob to say, *You know, down there.*

He scooted up a little, and she rode forward with him. She went to throw her leg over to dismount him, but he caught her thigh, and put his hand on the other, and held them both. Then he squeezed her hips and then cupped her face in his hands.

"I've got a lot of things running through my mind." He spoke in a tender, yet matter-of-fact way that lowered her defenses.

"I thought guys only had problems like that if they weren't—you know—into the person."

The corners of his mouth went down. "Red." He looked away for a moment, collecting his thoughts, she imagined. "August, love, you know I'm more than into you."

"I've never been with a guy who didn't … who had this issue. Are you sure everything's okay?" He gave a small nod and there was a long pause. "Are you … thinking of her?" The words themselves were almost an accusation, but her tone was one of vulnerability and defeat. As if she already knew the answer was yes, but needed him to break her heart with the words before she could even begin to accept it.

"August, sweet girl, it's been a very rough week. I'm not thinking of her, not like that. It really has nothing to do with you. What I did today—my brother … That was not an easy thing. I'm enjoying kissing and petting you, if you'll let me. It's actually giving me a great deal of comfort. I don't have to be inside of you to be close to you."

August felt stupid. And insensitive. Selfish. She then lined up this new information about men with what she knew from her previous young lovers, television, movies, books and music. It seemed like she was lacking a certain education in this regard and was willing to acknowledge as much. When she thought about it, it was kind of shocking that they were even in bed enjoying each other. It seemed like they should be doing something more to mourn Ciardha, even though August had no intention of being sad about his death. There was also something about being close this way that was life-affirming. She supposed they both needed to touch each other to remember what is vital in the world, and appreciate it.

301

She leaned in and kissed his forehead. She cradled the back of his skull and ran her fingers up through his long wavy locks. She put little kisses on his cheeks, on his eyelids. She leaned in and whispered into his ear, "I love you."

He kissed her mouth, tenderly, deeply. Kissed her breasts, caressing, cupping and pressing his cheeks to the firm little bumps. He turned her onto her back, kneeled between her legs onto the bed and bowed to press his mouth to her belly, skimming her skin with warm soft lips, from neck, to breast, to belly, to hips. He pet her thighs, then the thin tender skin behind her knees.

At first she watched him. Now, with his hands caressing as much of her as he could with his smooth palms and curious fingers, her eyes closed and she let out sighs and moans. She heard herself whisper, "Yes," several times, and the rise of pleasure blotted out the rest of the miserable trip, and all that was in focus was Faolan.

It was worshipful the way he touched her, kneeling between her thighs. He grabbed the sides of her panties and tugged them down a bit, bent forward and nuzzled her soft fuzzy mound. He then put his hands under her knees and guided them to bend, parting her thighs wider, making her softest folds vulnerable to him. He stretched his legs back and lay on his stomach, his face just inches from her there.

He started with gentle kisses. As she felt herself swell and her excitement mount, he licked and tickled her with his tongue, up and down, until her hips urgently rose to him. She begged him not to stop, as her hands alternately touched his hair, then grasped at the pillows behind her head, seemingly of their own accord. Her hips wiggled, and he started to hum against her, rocking his head, pressing harder into her, rocking, pressing, creating a quake in her that worked its way outwards until it reached her chest and the spark in her head became an explosion. She reeled out into space, unconscious to everything but a flood of ecstasy, and fell back to earth again, breathless.

He came up from her, almost reluctantly, and lay his head on her mound as he petted her thighs. Then he reached up and petted her all the way down her sides a few times, gently scratching her tingling skin, before climbing up to settle beside to her.

As she came back from the heavens she tucked in under his arm and put her hand on his chest. Bliss.

"I love your sweet songs," he rumbled against her. "The little sighs and moans you sing to me." He then made an adorably dog-like "woof" and kissed her temple.

"You always have such a beautiful way to say things, Fe."

They lay there, softly talking about their earliest days sitting by the stream. All of the pretty little things that brought them together— literature, constellations, dinners and picnics. They listed off her favorite flowers, and his favorite ales. Celebrating their happiness together. There was no reason to fret right now over what was concerning them, what ills had reared up since their arrival, or even why Faolan might not have been ready for her. No reason to ruin this moment, and they both seemed to take to that idea without even discussing it.

Faolan hummed low, some sweet old tune August didn't know, and the vibration enfolded her and sent her off on a loving boat, floating her to sleep.

Paden & Liam
Conall Keep

Blair was up before first light. For the first time in over fifteen years she woke up feeling promise in her day: the light joy you feel in your heart when you know you will be holding your child in your arms; the sense of possibility that lifts up your spirit when your lover is steps closer to your door, and the relief of knowing you are in charge of your own life now, without belittlement or abuse, without unwanted touches, or gifts that you pay for many times over.

She put on a smart suit, with pants instead of a skirt this time. She went to Ciardha's room and pulled out his thin blue tie, to set off her eyes. She didn't even pause to ponder her husband as her heels clicked past the corner where he bled to death. Blair took a small tack-pin out of her pocket—an A with an arrow through it. She hadn't worn it since she was a teenager. Her dad had given it to her for her birthday when she was fourteen. It used to have a place on her purse strap. Simpler times. Innocent times.

She peeked in on Liam, who was still sound asleep, splayed across the bed in his school uniform. She sighed and smiled and closed his door quietly.

Downstairs she pulled an apron on over her suit and hummed as she prepared tattie scones, his favorite. She did this despite the fact that Katie would be arriving before he woke up; it felt good to do something motherly for Liam, to try to make up for the time they'd lost. It was just the beginning of all of the things she would do to make up for that.

She drank some tea, polished her nails with red lacquer, and as it dried she watched birds and a fox out of the window. She thought about the dog she might get now that Ciardha was gone. He had been so jealous of anything drawing her attention that he had killed her dog, not long before he left for America to hunt down Fletcher Evan. She might get two dogs—a puppy for her and one for Liam.

At precisely 8 a.m. a knock came at the door. She strode over to it with the confidence of a runway model and pulled it open. Kester was standing there, in an expensive though not too expensive suit; it would be unseemly for a government man to look too well-compensated. His highly polished shoes were a little dusty from the walk up the drive. Short and no-necked, but clean-shaven and smug, he fiddled with a cufflink and eyed her in the doorway. "What do you want Blair?"

"Come in Kester," she answered in her best business posh manner. "Let's go have a little talk in the study, shall we?"

Kester hesitated, but came in and followed her to the study. She rounded Ciardha's desk and sat in the chair. "Have a seat."

"I don't need—look, what happened to Keer?" He looked around the room as if the answer to his death might be written on the walls or the spines of the books.

"I think you've guessed there won't be any more payments coming to you to keep Paden locked up, so sit the fuck down and we can talk about an arrangement. Ye ken?"

Kester went white. He was used to Ciardha's bluster, but Blair's posh tone never changed. This woman was a viper—he would have to be very, very careful with her. He cleared his throat, narrowed his eyes and sat down.

She pulled a satchel up from under the desk and plopped it on the blotter with a thunk.

"This is fifty thousand pounds. It's what he would have paid you over five years' time. You can have it all in one go if you get Paden out immediately." She pulled five bundles of £100 notes out, tossed them in the desk drawer, and locked it with a flourish. "Half of it's still in the bag. You get the rest when the deal is done. And to make it a little easier, I've left ten thousand more in there in smaller notes, to help you bribe whomever you need to. You keep what you don't have to use."

"So, I walk out with thirty-five thousand in that bag? And I get the other twenty-five when he's out?" Kester studied her and flexed his jaw. He pressed his lips together and finally asked, "What happened to Ciardha?"

"He poisoned himself by accident." She raised her brows and gave a tiny smirk. "Turns out the man didn't know the difference between a wild parsnip and hemlock."

She knew Kester was a fringe Veritas supporter. But she also knew he loved money more than anything, and expected he would take the deal. She was proven right.

He stood, adjusted his waistband over a bulging belly, and

straightened his lapel and tie.

"I've got no loyalty to that grouchy bastard." With an air of deliberateness he grabbed the handles of the satchel and lifted it off of the desk. "I will have your man out by Monday week."

"That's not soon enough. He's already endured—"

"It's the best I can do, or I leave the bag here."

She gnashed her teeth and pressed her mouth into a thin line, then gave a single resolute nod.

"Well then, Lady Conall. Pleasure doing business." Kester turned on his heels and hurried himself down the hall in his short graceless strides, and Blair followed him to the door. She could see his car parked in the drive—still a novel sight. She imagined he was only the first of many who would stop there, now that the old gate was open and visitors could drive right up to the keep, as befitted a proper house. It was remarkable how quickly Katie and the groundskeeper had gotten it cleared; perhaps she wouldn't fire the girl after all, now that her loyalties would not be so divided. Blair thought she might set them to work on the weeds and vines choking the front of the house as well. She was planning on making something of the place. Or selling it with Faolan. Or selling her half to him. Her life was hers once again, and it was going to open up in any number of new directions.

Blair taped up some storage boxes, popped open a new box of trash bags, and started pulling things down from the shelves. She sorted out books she thought might be worth money while the rest went into boxes. She polished the wood and whistled and hummed as she worked. The sun cut beams across the desk and the dusty air, and she felt closer to total joy than she had in a very long time.

Weaving the Silver Cord
Meikleour Inn

When August woke up, Faolan was already awake, still holding
her in the crook of his arm. She snuggled in closer, though she really
couldn't have been any closer.

"You feel so good."

"You too, lass." He kissed her on the corner of her head where
his chin had been resting.

"Can we just have breakfast right here and stay in bed all day. I
don't want to hear from the rest of the world. I want to read books,
and write in my journal and pretend this little room is all that exists in
the world."

"The weather would seem to agree with you today. Looks like
clouds are rolling in."

"Good, then we have a great excuse to just eat pastries, drink
wine and spend time together. Just you and me."

They got out of bed and took a shower together. It was a little
awkward, with the old fashioned surround curtain trying to cling to
them, and August had had to take a giant step to get into the tub,
which made her a little self-conscious. She hated feeling as though she
looked like a little kid. But all of that washed away as they began
soaping each other. The suds were sensuous and fun, making their
bodies slick and clean, it was like play-time with a friend rather than
something sexual. She liked that—the urgency wasn't pressing her to
do or be something, she was just being in the moment, having fun. The
warm water was relaxing. And there was no place to rush out of the
shower and get dressed for. If the hot water lasted, she could stay in
there for an hour.

"Use the cloth, it feels nice and scratchy." August enthused, and
presented her backside to him. Faolan soaped up the flannel and
rubbed her pink.

"When I was a little girl I would take long baths and pretend I
was a mermaid," she remembered as he scrubbed. "I would make up
crazy songs. I still remember some of them. Did you ever do anything
like that?"

"Not really. My mother did sing us songs though. I was

humming one to you last night."

"That's sweet."

They exchanged more childhood stories, but only happy ones, and Faolan avoided mentioning his brother and father. It kept the conversation loving and connecting, each heart-share a balm for their battered spirits.

They spent the next several hours ordering in breakfast and playing chess and Faolan read some poems for her. August picked up one of the books she brought along and ventured to read a bit out loud as well. It wasn't often she did, because she would get a little stage fright and tighten up at the throat, even with Faolan, but she elected to forge ahead anyway.

"I found this at the book store just a week before we were supposed to leave. I can't vouch for its quality. I've never heard of this guy, have you?" She held the book up, *The House of Wolf*, by Basil Copper, with the cover image of a snowy locale and some people and a big wolf.

"Never heard of him."

"Yeah, me either. I thought it would be fun to find all of the werewolf books I could. What do you think?"

"Lass, so long as you aren't touchy about people writing nonsense about you or your kin, I'm game. Some of the canine lore is kind of far-fetched." He waited a beat, then winked.

"Punny." She rolled her eyes in mock chagrin and opened the book. The fire was cozy, she had a mug of hot tea and the rain beat down on the window. There couldn't have been a more perfect moment to read a scary story.

The day went on like that, the sun hidden behind heavy gray clouds, the steady pelt of raindrops creating a comfortable background music. Faolan ran out to the pub at some point and brought back boxes of sandwiches and some ale. He reported that the rain had caused a bit of flooding in the parking lot, and the little streamlet they crossed to get to the cabin was now touching the underside of the footbridge. After lunch he took a turn reading the next few chapters of *The House of Wolf*.

They both were visibly lightened, feeling close and connected again. Almost normal. It might be temporary, August thought, but she'd take it.

The Veritas
Conall Hall, Perthshire

The Veritas Council, the senior members of the order, met an hour earlier than they had originally planned to in order to discuss Ciardha's death. Even though Engres Laithenskye was not on the council—largely because he owned no property and was too young and outspoken—he was asked to attend the special meeting as well.

They had been gathering in Conall Hall for ages, long before Banning's death some twenty years ago. Not far from the western edge of Summerblynd, it was a handy distance from Ciardha's keep, and the main hall was large enough for full membership meetings, which in times past had been as many as eighty lycan. After he inherited it, Ciardha had kept it staffed and leased it to the Council, and had much enjoyed the extra prestige of hosting Veritas events.

Four men and one woman sat on one side of the long table at the end of the hall; Engres sat on the other side, facing them. Toren, with his tight gray ponytail and his pinched face—the oldest of the Council, and maybe the oldest living lycan—spoke first.

"Gres, these are precarious times, not just for our order but for our race. We've got only two full-blooded breeding females left among the Veritas, and not many more in the greater community o' the midlands. Among the other females, those who are half or less typically leave the clans when they reach their moon cycles. None hae been able to transform. Ciardha believed he had a plan that would help strengthen our bloodlines and bring our numbers back. We needed his leadership to make the Veritas strong again."

Engres listened attentively, ramrod straight, eyes intense. He crossed a leg gracefully and folded his hands to rest them on a knee. He looked to each of the council members as the old man spoke, but only Toren merited his concern. He looked back to him again.

"You met with him Gres, more than once, and we, the Council, want to ask if ye kenned t' what Ciardha was to present tonight?"

The council members all nodded in agreement.

Engres rubbed his chin with ring-clad fingers. "I do not wish to speak ill of the dead."

The council members all exchanged glances and mutters and

fixed their eyes on him again. Toren said, "We suggest ye do so anyway."

Engres nodded and stood. He moved with the grace of a hawk as he paced, seemingly in thought, then stopped and turned toward them with gravitas. "Ciardha wanted us to accept his hunter wife, so he had hoped to convince the Council that mixing with any otherkin, regardless of how inferior their genetics might be, was the way to increase our numbers and bloodlines." He said it with disdain, but in a way that felt like a deep truth was just laid bare.

"You do not believe this is the way?"

"I do not," Engres declared. "I believe that we must use modern travel and technology to help us make alliances with other lycan cultures around the world. Marry canine to canine whenever possible. Bring new blood. This part is the long route. Many will not want to move here and protect these lands unless we give them funds to resettle. With Ciardha gone our financial strength is weakened. His hunter widow won't give us anything for our coffers; we may not even be able to meet in this fine hall again. But for those we can convince to come to us, we will raise the young ones to be Summerblynd lycan. And for those of us that go elsewhere, we make a blood pact that they have as many babes as possible, quickly, and bring them here, to be raised as Summerblynd. And as we grow we will attract others."

"Won't that sow resentment among the other wolfish communities?"

"Perhaps. But if we time it well, and only approach communities weaker than our own, it won't matter. They won't be able to do anything about it. Will they?"

The Council pondered this and they whispered among themselves, then nodded.

"There is more."

"Go on," Toren said.

"There is an American here now with Ciardha's brother. Her name is August Archer. She is only a small part lycan, the rest is purebred hunter. But I have been told she is capable of full transformation. I believe that she could be the key to building our strength up again quickly. If I were to have her for a mate we could easily gain five bairns in six years. There must be others like her, in her bloodline. Her mother is the lycan carrier. German blood. Obviously superior genetics."

"I know who August Archer is. Ye seem unaware that it was her family that killed Banning Conall. Ye really should do more research, Gres."

Engres felt ire rising in him, but he remained visibly unaffected and simply gave him a single nod in reply.

"Ye do make an interesting point, however," Toren went on. "I had nae realized the Archer girl could transform. But you are speaking as though she will come willingly to you. It hardly seems likely."

"I can be very persuasive."

"And if not, what do you intend? If she be young Conall's mate she is of no use to yer plan, Gres. Unless o' course he rejoins us, and takes his brother's place as alpha." Toren smiled, indulgently. "Better, wouldn't you say, that ye invested yer efforts there?"

Engres let the jibe pass unacknowledged. Toren seemed determined to needle him, but he would not give him the satisfaction of seeing it irk.

"Perhaps the mother then," Engres resumed his argument. "I'm sure you could charm your way into breeding her, Toren. She's a Jaeger, as it turns out, but has already proven herself capable."

Toren was silent, but his eyes glowed with more than mischief. If young Laithenskye had intended merely to barb him for his advanced years, he had in fact set him to thinking in a new direction.

"And how are we to convince the mother to come to us and breed more bairns, Engres?"

"We will have her daughter."

Toren peered at the upstart, trying to see in his eyes if he really meant what he seemed to be implying. Laithenskye reeked of ambition, but Toren had to admire his grasp of the old ways. He nodded. "Aye."

One of the other council members started to speak up and Toren turned to growl at him. He backed down and bit his tongue.

"If indeed ye have five bairns with this girl, that could be the seeds of a new, vigorous lycan society by 1990," Toren speculated. "Archers have been known to twin, and if a good number be girls, we breed them with the oldest full-blood lycan males from different lines once they hit their moon cycles. We could be starting a second generation before the millennium, and have well over a hundred in thirty years or so."

"You're going to make them all brood mares?" The woman, Teagam, spoke out of turn, too appalled to keep still.

"Are you unclear about the hazard of our position, councilwoman? Should we stand by and watch our kind expire on the altar of law and decency?" Toren seemed more patient with her than Engres would have expected. He wondered idly if they were sleeping together. Toren went on. "If even half o' them can transform, we will be poised to take over the whole of the village and infiltrate Perth. By the time the cumanta kenned t' what was happening it would be too late."

"How would they even realize it, Toren?"

"Ye dinna think we'd be hiding in the shadows forever, did ye, woman?"

"But it's for our own protection."

Toren snarled, and all murmuring stopped. Engres smiled placidly as he turned back to him.

"Gres, find out what you can with the Archer girl. Report to us the moment you have any information."

Engres was pleased; he already had intel on August in the works. It was going to make him look very good to the Council when he came back quickly with answers.

"I will see to it today." He stood, gave a little bow, and in three strides he was out of the room.

It was only ten minutes later that the first meeting attendees started to trickle in, most of them sagging and gray. A few of the younger ones were twitching with adrenaline to do something, anything, to the cumanta. They went to each meeting hoping for a directive to kill and eat humans. Some of them found their way into the cities or went on far away vacations and did their damage there, then would return home. The idea of thinning or blending bloodlines was too abstract for their attention—all they heard was their own bloodlust in their ears.

Soon the room was packed with more members than they'd had in months, maybe years. The news of Ciardha's death brought them out for answers. Toren intended to spoon-feed them outrage instead.

Preparing Goodbyes
Meikleour Inn

Faolan and August spent the rest of the evening snacking and talking about the science and history of otherkin. Finally they felt sleepy enough to climb into bed, and Faolan read only a few pages of the wolf book before August was snoozing gently, lulled by his low voice and the patter of the rain, finally tapering off.

Faolan watched her sleep and petted her naked shoulder. He tried to brush away thoughts of Iseabail that intruded. Her pale ginger hair. Her blue eyes, still startling, though now much greyer and wiser than he remembered them. He had tried several times to talk about their lost child, but she'd change the subject and he guessed it must have been too painful for her to remember.

He tried not to think about her now reading those letters she had never seen, the conversations he had imagined with her and recorded in his journals. But he couldn't help wondering what she would see in it, how all of it would make her feel. Loved? Missed? Honored? Cherished? Obsessed over? Perhaps August was right, and he shouldn't have handed over the trunk. He kept coming back to the central question that had plagued him these last few days: why had Iseabail let him believe she was dead all these years? She'd told him she feared for him should he interfere in her life, told him how closely her husband and then her brothers kept watch over her, all but a prisoner in her own home. Perhaps it was as simple as that. But over the better part of a century, did nothing present itself? Maybe some of what he sought would be in the bundle of letters she'd given him at the church. He had reckoned that this trip with August was not the time to read them, and had already had them shipped home—a moment of wisdom in all this, he smiled ruefully to himself. Perhaps he wouldn't ever read them— how could it serve any purpose other than to further complicate a situation that should be simple?

He kissed August's warm, sleepy head. He had been ready to let Iseabail go, ready to release the past and embrace the future. What did it change, really, for Iseabail to be alive? Indeed, couldn't he now let her go with a lighter heart, knowing he no longer had to live her supposedly too-short life for her? She had been doing that for herself all along. Without a word to him. He closed his eyes and imagined the silver cord between them, unmooring it from his center and setting her adrift, free to float on in another direction.

He spent his final moments of consciousness playing with a springy curl of August's hair and remembering how he felt when she first spoke to him, that full moon two years ago, in the wee hours of All Hallows' Day. How his heart sped up in spite himself. How he had wanted to breathe in the scent that had led him to her, so powerful once she had lowered her hood, and how he wanted to kiss her neck. He had also wanted to keep his promise to protect her from harm, so he kept his distance. He wondered sometimes if she had sensed the chemistry of his attraction, and that was what drew her to him. Perhaps it was the other way around, but it didn't really matter—he and August could never have ignored each other for very long.

When they woke the next morning the sky was still grey, but the clouds were high and thin and the air was crisp and dry. Mindful of the mud, they pulled on boots, ate breakfast at the pub and headed out to the keep to check on Blair.

Car rides were always a good time to talk because there wasn't much else you could do but look at the scenery. August thought how some of her best conversations with Mom were in the car, and she suddenly felt how much she missed her; even though it had only been little over a week since she'd seen her, it felt more like a month.

"Faolan, thank you. For yesterday. I really needed it—just a day of nothing but peace. A chance to reset. All the sweet things you said, and reading to me." She snuggled to his shoulder. "I don't think I could have gone another day."

"Me as well, lass. I thought I was a tough customer, after all these years of life and its frequent insanity. But there's been nothing like the last few days. It could rend a man's soul. So thank ye love, for yesterday and all."

"I don't think we'll have time to finish the wolf book before we head home."

"We can catch up with it when we get back. Ye like a spooky story, aye?"

"I guess I do. Didn't used to. Now, it feels like I almost have to." August had a sudden image of Ciardha on the stone floor, his neck covered in blood. She had a flash of Tanner, and blood on her own neck. She shuddered.

"Y' alright, love?" He reached over and put his large hand on her thigh. His touch was warm and it comforted her. He made her feel safe. Mostly, anyway—and even if she'd felt a little uncertain at times lately, she still trusted him.

She tried to clear her head, and let out a long sigh. "This has been a wild vacation. I think we're going to need a few weeks of lazing around, eating junk food, and reading trash books to recuperate."

"Sounds perfect to me."

Where the drive had once dead-ended in a wall of vines and grown-over gates, now the greenery was trimmed back neatly and the gate was open. The road continued on toward the keep.

"Boy, that didn't take long."

"Aye."

"Faolan?"

He pulled up in front of the keep and parked.

"Do you think Blair poisoned him?"

He blinked a few times, rolled his eyes up a bit in thought. "I think that we need t' say goodbye to all o' the things that tore the family apart. I think asking questions like that could just make a new wound while the old one is finally closing."

"Do you think that's what's happening? Old wounds are closing?"

"I do, aye."

"What do you think Sorcha's going to do when she finds out Blair is still alive?"

"I actually think Sorcha has always known. She just couldn't bring herself t' face it."

"But, she blamed you all that time—if she knew, then she knew you didn't kill her."

"Ye remember what she was like when you met her? She needed something t' help make sense of Blair taking up with Ciardha after all that he and my father had done. I think she needed Blair to be gone, and she needed it to be a Conall that did it. When somebody ye love that much turns their back on you, all that's left is finding a way to

315

cope."

"She was so awful to you."

"I can take it."

August gave a sympathetic grin, wrinkled up her chin and gave him a peck on the nose.

"I like what they did to your cloak." He reached out and petted down the sleeve.

"I know, isn't it rad?"

"Rad, indeed. Alright, here we go. If she doesn't need us we'll just head out and try to have a nice last day in Summerblynd."

"If she doesn't need us, I'd like to stop by Iseabail's and say goodbye to her."

His face registered surprise. "Would ye now?"

"She is my great-grandmother after all. Is there some reason I shouldn't? Are you going to find it hard to be around her or—"

"No, no, I'm fine. Just surprised you want to see her."

"I can be a grown up about this."

He nodded.

They knocked on the door and Katie pulled it open and invited them in. Blair's heels were clicking around in the study and they walked over to her.

"Hello," she said, rather chipper. She looked very put-together. Her hair was up in a twist, her pantsuit was wide-legged slacks in cream with a short dark red blazer and a silk cream blouse peeking out from underneath. She looked like a business woman. A CEO, in fact.

"Hi," August said and they went in for an awkward hug. August wanted to try to be closer to her Aunt Blair, but it was going to take time, and she still didn't quite trust her. She noticed a little gold pin on Blair's lapel: the letter A with an arrow across it. She realized that Blair was re-claiming her Archer heritage, which August considered a good sign.

"Blair," Faolan said, giving his head a little bow and kissing her hand.

"I don't need any help, really, except for taking the suit upstairs to the funeral director. And the photo, don't forget. I do appreciate ye coming by to check on me."

"You're alright then?" August asked.

"Shouldn't I be?" She shifted her focus to August's coat. "Was

316

this your cloak?" She reached up and fingered the fine velvet trim of the sleeve hem. "Who did this? This looks like McCabe work."

August grinned wide; she was more excited to talk about her new coat than she realized. "Yeah, this grouchy old guy named Gavin ran it up in a few hours. And check this out." She pulled open the front to show the grey and green interior. "It's reversible. If I ever need it to be." They both glanced briefly at Faolan who was pretending not to have any idea of the implications of that comment.

"I'll just grab the clothes," he supplied, excusing himself to head upstairs. He found Ciardha's suit and tie hanging on the hook, with his shoes and socks on the floor beneath, and gathered them all up. As he walked past the spot where Ciardha had died he stopped and gazed at the scrubbed flagstones.

"Brother, I hope you find peace now, fer auld lang syne."

Back downstairs he hung the suit on the coat hooks by the entry and grabbed a bag from under the bench to toss in the rest. He headed into the dining room where the envelope with the photo was still sitting, with a pile of neatly organized papers.

The door to the kitchen was propped open and he could see a boy eating at the island counter. He realized this must be the son Blair mentioned, though he didn't smell any wolf on him. Perhaps he was too much hunter, Faolan thought—he certainly favored his mother— though he did wonder why he'd never heard tell of him before. Faolan stepped in closer and the boy looked up and wiped his mouth.

"Hullo, I'm Faolan. I'm yer uncle."

"I'm Liam."

"Pleasure to meet you, mate. You takin' good care of yer mum?"

"Aye."

"Good."

Faolan went back to the study and chatted a bit longer, then he and August collected the suit and the rest and pointed the Rover towards Summerblynd. Their business at the funeral home hardly took a minute, and then they were back in the car and headed toward Raven's Loch and Iseabail.

"Do you think it's okay to just drop by?" August asked.

"I suppose I should have called her before we left the keep. I didn't really think of it. We're very close now. We'll just drive up and see if it looks like she's home and give 'er a knock. Try not to be too worried about it."

"I'm not worried."

He looked skeptical.

"Not much. I'm just nervous." *And boy am I*, she thought. Her stomach was a twisted knot. Part of her did want to say hello and goodbye to her great-grandmother, but she also felt like she needed to test the temperature between Iseabail and Faolan for herself. The house was on a hill up a winding drive. It wasn't a cottage or a keep. It was instead a big old stone house of turrets and gables that looked like two Blue Rooks could fit in it. There was some bustle on the property. They were setting a canopy up out back, and there was a catering van and people toting crates of wine.

"I wonder what's—"

"I forgot. She's preparing for a whisky and wine social. You dress up in fancy clothes and sip wine and talk to people who own businesses. Her brothers both died this year, within just a few months of each other. They were a bit stifling, as she put it. She plans on having a big party on Friday night and I guess they're getting a head start."

"I wonder how many people are coming. This looks like it's going to be huge."

"About a hundred she said."

"I don't think I even know a hundred people."

"I don't think she actually knows most of these people. She seems to be gearing up some kind of business ideas. Her brothers had a lot of contacts, so she went through their Rolodex and started calling people, setting out to build her own network. She said something about wanting to start a clothing line."

"Really?" August scrunched up her face in disbelief. "A clothing line?"

"Aye, like knit clothing. The best Scottish wool. Maybe even tartans. This is her first foray into all of it, she said, so she wasn't sure where it would lead her."

They made their way up to the door, August positioned herself a little behind Faolan and let him knock. She could feel herself tightening. Would she see any heat between him and Iseabail? Any unresolved passion?

Iseabail herself pulled open the door, and she seemed a bit

harried. "Thank you for—oh Faolan, it's you." She furrowed her brow. "Did you come to talk about the trunk?" Her demeanor softened, and so did her voice, into a lower register and almost a whisper, "It's been so lovely reading your letters, your musings." She reached out to take his hand, "I can't tell you how much—"

He shook her hand, formally if warmly, and let it go, stepping aside to reveal August. "Iseabail, actually August came to say goodbye to ye. She felt she should have a moment with her kin."

Iseabail took a step backwards and her face became more serious again. "Oh, I see. Of course." She stepped back and waved them into the house.

The hall was warm and full of rich pale fabrics and a mix of heavy and dainty furniture along the walls. It was dominated by whites, off-whites and pastels of yellow and peach. Considering the place had belonged to her brothers only a short while ago, it struck August as a rather feminine tone.

"It's lovely in here," she said, taking in the large oil paintings of flower bouquets set in fancy wooden frames of pale gold.

"Thank you, granddaughter."

August tilted her head a little, and made a face.

"Not yet? Fair enough. August, then?"

August nodded, and smiled. "I wouldn't have thought your brothers—my great-uncles I guess—would have decorated quite like this."

"I set about redoing the place some months ago, after James died. Bruce didn't mind either way. Some of the furniture and family treasures, I kept. But most of what passed for décor consisted of plaid, dog paintings and various weaponry on the wall." Iseabail smiled. "It actually struck me more of a boy's-own room, but the whole house was that way, other than my wing. Like living in a hunting lodge."

"I'm sorry about losing your brothers. But I'm glad you're making the best of inheriting the place."

"Actually, it was always my place, August." Iseabail had a thoughtful look in her eye. "My brothers simply had … a lot of influence, shall we say?"

August knit her brow slightly and nodded, even though she wasn't totally sure what the woman meant. She supposed it didn't matter—she was just glad that her stomach was not so knotted up anymore. Something, though, was still making her nervous.

"I'm sorry I don't have a lot of time to visit, with the people setting up and bringing supplies for the party. I understand you'll be gone before Friday night, otherwise you'd be welcome to come."

August watched Faolan out of the corner of her eye. She wanted to lean hard into him, make sure he wasn't going to bolt, or melt, or just embrace Iseabail right in front of her and announce he wasn't coming back to America. August thought he was maybe caressing Iseabail with his eyes, but she knew enough to imagine she was just being suspicious, in her distressed state.

"We don't want to keep you," Faolan finally said, cueing August that they were about to leave. She wondered if he too was feeling something. She didn't know what—but it did seem odd for him to do that. Then a worker opened the doors at the back end of the long central hallway. The air rushed in, carrying a faint scent that both Faolan and August recognized immediately. It smelled of lycan. They looked at each other, and August's ears were tingling. A moment later the sound came—squeals and laughter, as two children, a boy and a girl that looked to be about four years old, came tearing through the door, nearly knocking into a man carrying a crate of wine glasses.

"Granny, Granny! I got dirt on my new jumper!" They both shouted at Iseabail about it, as the little girl held out the smudged tail of her sweater. The two wore matching grey sweaters. Iseabail looked at Faolan and August and her face drained of color. She swallowed.

The children stopped at their feet and looked up at Faolan and August. Though they had grey eyes, both looked strikingly like Faolan. Their chins and lips in particular could have been Faolan's as a child. It seemed to August that Iseabail's face told her something was being seen that wasn't meant to be.

Faolan looked absolutely stunned. August opened her mouth to say something, but nothing came out. She was almost out of air before she realized she was holding her breath.

"Who's this, Granny?" The little boy asked.

"They're guests, love. You can have some biscuits from the jar on Granny's special shelf, if you take just two each and then go back outside to play, alright?"

"Alright," he said in his tiny voice, his dark wavy hair pasted to the edges of his sweaty little face. He dashed toward the kitchen. The girl waved at them, her perfect cherub face smiling up, then she grabbed a fistful of her skirt and walked on her perfect miniature legs after her brother.

Faolan followed her with his eyes as she went. He was turned away from August, but something about his breathing seemed odd to her. He turned back and fixed his unbelieving eyes on Iseabail's. There was a tear rolling down his cheek.

"Issy?" He asked it so softly, and it cracked in the middle like he might start sobbing.

She folded her hands in front of her and averted his gaze.

"Why?" he croaked out. His brow furrowed, his eyes screwed up. Tears began streaming down his cheeks.

"I think you'd both better leave now," she said low and soft. "It's time to say goodbye."

August was frozen in disbelief at what she thought she just witnessed. She felt a warm wave of tears start to roll up inside of her and she swallowed them with a tight throat. Faolan was immobilized.

"Come on, Fe," she said gently. She took his hand. She thought if she pulled it too hard, it might come off. She gave him a tug. He was still looking behind him as he took his first stumbling steps, before turning for the door.

Back in the car Faolan sat behind the wheel for a moment, trying to compose himself.

"Did what I think just happened, happen?" she asked, in her smallest voice.

Faolan nodded his head, looking a bit hypnotized and shattered all at once.

"We'd should go back to the inn now, sweetheart. Do you want me to drive?"

He shook his head, straightened in his seat, and started the car up. The ride was quiet and lonely as the landscape blurred by in the afternoon sun.

Back at the inn their feet sucked their way through the parking lot mud. They kicked off their mucked-up boots and went inside. Faolan sat in one of the reading chairs, laced his hands behind his neck and bent forward, and began to sob.

August hesitated, then walked over to touch his shoulder. He took her hand and she stood in front of him, he put his arms around her and squeezed, his body wracked with sorrow. She petted his hair while he cried for all of the things he felt he missed, or lost, or couldn't have. Her heart tried to wrap around and protect his, but it couldn't. This pain was too private. All she could do was stand there and catch his tears.

Once he had quieted August made them some tea, and she sat in the chair next to his. She put the tea on the table and nodded at it. He inhaled deeply, held it, and then let it out slowly. He picked up the cup and sipped.

"Those are your grandchildren aren't they? Or, I guess your great-grandchildren?"

"I don't know."

"Faolan."

"Why would she do that? Leave me to suffer that way? All those years ago. All those years." His voice was strained and pitiful.

"I don't know, Fe. I'm sure she had her reasons." August couldn't believe she was trying to make a case for her rival. What's more, she couldn't believe she was trying to encourage him to not be enraged by this flagrant violation of his trust.

They talked like that for next few hours, or tried to talk, coming up with no new insight—going around and around about why somebody would do something like that, with Faolan occasionally stopping to sob. He looked older than she'd ever seen him. All of the lines on his face were creased and dark, showing his years, his grizzled stubble only adding to the effect. She didn't know how to help him, except give him empathy and tea. Squeeze his hand. Pet his hair. Say soft things. Offer him food, which he kept refusing.

August knew this week had been harder on him. Maybe as hard as the one she was having last year at about this time, thinking her mother was dead, seeing her family attacked and her home wrecked and bloody, expecting a monster to appear at any second. She couldn't imagine what all the bond between Faolan and Iseabail was made of, but it was wrecking him.

The Funeral

Faolan woke in rumpled clothes with half-empty tea cups and biscuit crumbs scattered all over the place. His face was puffy and for the first time in his life the vital glow of otherkin strength had dulled. He looked like an old man.

They had both fallen asleep on the bed in their clothes. He reached over and brushed a cloud of frizzed curls aside to find half a chocolate biscuit stuck to August's cheek. He kissed her temple and heaved himself out of bed. He caught sight of himself in the mirror looking sallow and bedraggled, and grunted at that miserable Faolan in solidarity. He went to get a shower.

Standing there naked under the hot water, he refused to think about anything, allowing the uncertainty and stress to drain from him, if only for a moment. He pushed his ears and fingers to transform just a little, to feel his lycan blood, to revitalize his body a bit and hopefully his spirit.

He opened his eyes as the curtain parted and August's naked body stepped in. They didn't talk. They washed and held each other in silence, the water making rivers and waterfalls over their bodies. He wrapped his energy around her. He visualized the cord between him and Iseabail fraying, pulling taut, threads snapping. He was not the same man he'd been a week ago.

They got out and toweled each other with tenderness and got dressed. August had fortunately brought one black dress on the trip, though she'd imagined wearing it to a nice dinner, not a funeral.

It turned out no church near Summerblynd wanted anything to do with Ciardha's funeral, so the service was held in the funeral home's largest room instead.

August and Faolan arrived quite early, but even so Blair was already there, wearing an elegant black dress and hat with netting that half-covered her eyes. She had on white gloves and red lipstick. She looked like something out of a movie. The whole scene struck august as cinematic.

They walked toward the front where the casket lay closed. The photo of Ciardha had somehow been blown up overnight into a large framed piece, now set on an easel at the head of the casket. The picture was obviously from a few decades back, and August shivered as she looked into his brutally handsome features, but she could see something of the man he must have been when her aunt fell in love with him. Faolan made no outward display, but she could tell from the way he gazed at the image that his feelings ran deep.

When they turned back August saw a teenager in a suit, sitting in the front row by Blair folding one of the programs into a paper airplane.

"Blair," Faolan said with a nod. He then turned to the boy, "Liam, hello there, lad."

Liam looked up. "Hello, Uncle Faolan."

"Liam, this is August, I don't think you've met."

Liam's eyes got a little larger and he straightened up and checked his tie as he smiled at her.

"Your cousin August," he amended.

The young man slumped a bit, but his smile didn't fade as he extended his hand. "Aye, cousin August, nice to meet ye."

August blushed a little. "Nice to meet you. Although …" She glanced around the room. "I'm sorry it's under such circumstances." August had that one handy because somebody had said it to her at her own father's funeral. "I'm sorry about your dad."

"Yer probably the only one," he said and stood up, tossed the paper plane. It made a loop and a long glide towards the back of the room. He put his hands in his pockets and looked back at her. August was stunned and didn't know what to say. *Yeah, your dad was kind of a murdering asshole* seemed inappropriate about now.

"We're cousins, I can say that to ye," he said. "I ken who he was."

August nodded and felt her heart pulse hard in empathy for him.

"That's a pretty awesome glide on that airplane. Where'd you learn to make them like that?"

"My Uncle Paden."

August tilted her head, "Uncle Paden? I haven't heard of him."

"He's in jail. He taught me how when I was little."

"In jail?"

"Yeah, I don't know what he did. We don't talk about it. I don't care, he was good to me."

"Oh. I get that." August nodded and didn't know what else to say. "So … well,"

"Yeah, I don't ken what to say either. Nice to meet ye, I reckon."

"Yeah."

He jogged to the back of the room and picked up the paper plane. She watched as he examined it, pinched the nose of it and smoothed it flat as he left the room.

Faolan had been having a quiet discussion with Blair.

"It doesn't matter if they didn't like his policies, Faolan, they'll be here. It's a matter of fierce loyalty to the alpha for them. No actual thinking is part of the equation," Blair was saying as August sidled up alongside Faolan.

Faolan and August helped her lay out programs on the seats.

"Where are the flowers?" August asked Faolan.

"They don't give flowers for a man. They'll mayhap send food, tartans, quilts, silver pieces, or money. It's tradition when the husband dies not to waste your resources on items such as flowers, but things that the family can use for sustenance. Blair doesn't need that kind of help, of course, but it's tradition, and if they are nothing else, the lycan are strict traditionalists."

"Oh."

A small band of musicians arrived. One with a flute, one with a fiddle, and bagpipes of course. They set up and started to play from the front corner of the room.

A slow trickle of people started to come in. For all the world they looked to August like a gang of Scottish bikers or something, many of them a good bit older than Faolan, though some also a good bit younger. She watched as a parade of men eyed the room with suspicion, some nodding to Blair, bowing, or shaking her hand, others giving her a cold stare as they took their seats. It was an odd sight, these beleaguered-looking men in their tartans, weapons and leathers trying to contain themselves, each perching his enormous presence on a small beige folding chair.

Liam came in from outside, folding his plane and tucking it in his pocket.

"How old is he?" August leaned over to Faolan and asked.

"Thirteen." He whispered back.

"Just a kid."

Faolan nodded, then said, "No more or less than any hunter at that age."

"You look really rough today."

"I'm feeling rough. My brother. And … the other thing."

"I know." She put her arm around his waist and leaned in for a moment, then took one of the empty seats near Liam.

August realized she was only a few years older than Liam when her own father died. Though it was a very different experience for her. She missed her father terribly. He was a wonderful man and full of good. *Shit, his dad killed my dad. This is so fucked up. Why do these hateful men have to drag innocent people into their vengeance?*

She felt sorry for Liam, that he couldn't know what a great father was like. But she was glad that he didn't lose a great father, too.

The room was almost to capacity when the bagpipes stopped and one last visitor glided in the door. He looked otherworldly, like a vampire. He exuded something seductive and confident. He rounded the last row of chairs in the back, all the way diagonally opposite from August, and she watched him over her shoulder. As he went to take the last seat in the last row in the corner he looked directly at her and held her eyes for a moment. She wasn't sure what was happening, but she felt something pass between them. She broke eye contact and turned forward in her chair, but she could feel his gaze still on her.

We are totally surrounded by lycan, she thought. She stayed alert, allowing her ears to tingle a bit, just in case a change was called for. But what good could she do among all of these lycan? Then she remembered Faolan's concern about keeping her ability to transform a secret, and made herself calm down. She took comfort in knowing Faolan was there if any shit were about to go down.

It was Blair who stood up, taking a place at the podium in front of the crowd, and the hall went silent. Even the water cooler had ceased to hum. August was a little concerned as Blair cleared her throat. She was not a lycan, and despised by many in the room. *This can't be an easy moment for her*, August thought, even if she wasn't too sorry her husband was dead. Blair sat a paper down in front of her and removed her white gloves, draping them over the edge of the podium.

"Very few of you have ever met me. I am Ciardha's dirty little secret."

A wave of discomfort rolled through the room. People inhaling and clearing their throats. She stared at them and waited for silence.

"I am the hunter wife he has loved these long years and kept hidden away in his pitiless castle, and I now claim my right of redress, as your own tradition demands. You people and your vendettas made our love impossible. You people and your agenda of purity and tradition have torn apart lives that could have otherwise been happy. I refuse to stand and pretend that the lot of you abide by high ideals of order and prosperity, as once I believed. That you are high-minded advocates of purity, or members of a master race that will make the world a better one. I ask, for whom are you making the world better? For any lycan who dares love somebody other than another pure lycan? Or even for yourselves, as you stew in your hate and speciesism? You lot don't give one rat's ass about making lives better. Even your own. I don't think a single one of you even kens what that means. You wouldn't recognize happiness if it walked by and lifted your kilt. The only thing you love is power, and forcing others to bend to your will. That's it. So ask yourselves, do you carry these stones of indigence and resentment every day because you are oppressed? Do you imagine that you cannot find comfort, or love, or prosperity, in a lover's hand? A warm breakfast? A good glass of whisky? What are the things you imagine are being stolen from you, because somebody in your world chooses a love you do not approve of? It is your own self-fulfilling prophecy of alienation that robs you of happiness, brought on by your own ugliness, and exclusion from those who are 'other.' My hand was by Ciardha's every day, but he cursed it because it was not the right kind of hand. He tried to lead all of you in the direction he felt lycan culture could go, should go, to fulfill the promise of your strength and intelligence, but his effort was misguided. You are all misguided. The people you are trying to dominate, to control, to breed out of existence—they are not the enemy. If you want to see your enemy, look in a mirror."

She stood there, firm jaw, steely eyes, daring any one of them to say a word. The place seemed to be holding its breath. She picked the paper up and looked at all of them as she crumpled it into a ball and threw it onto the floor. She snatched her gloves off of the podium, stepped around it, and looked to her son.

"Come Liam, I don't want you near any of these speciesist fuckers." They strode down the center aisle. The entire room watched as she exited, her head held high and Liam following behind red-cheeked and frowning, glaring back at any who stared at him, until they were out the door. The heads all turned forward again, but the room remained silent long enough to hear her car start up and kick stones as she tore off down the road.

Faolan stood up and walked towards the podium. That was when heads started turning towards each other and whispering, throats were clearing and a few of the older men got up and walked out. The younger lycans were mostly crossing their arms and flexing their jaws at this point. The collected exhalation was making the room stuffy. The vampire man in the back corner was not giving away his feelings either through facial expression or body language, August noted. In the brief moment she had assessed him, he looked again her way and she diverted her eyes immediately this time, turning them to Faolan.

He stood behind the podium and cleared his throat.

"I'm Faolan Conall. I'm pretty sure most of you know who I am, but in case some of you younger bucks don't, I am Ciardha's brother."

Another wave rippled through the room, sounds of surprise and possibly of condemnation, August couldn't really tell.

"My brother had some very specific ideas about how to preserve lycan culture and community. He and I didn't agree on a great many things, but we did agree on one thing: we both loved hunter women. Neither of us saw this as a betrayal of our heritage ..."—he paused only briefly as grumblings and sounds of denial rose up from the group—"even if Ciardha did feel it was a betrayal of his politics. He was a complicated man and a firm-handed alpha. He was a brother who loved fiercely. Throughout his life, Ciardha Chaill Conall put family before all else, even if his ideas of family were conflicted. We have no reason to ignore the lessons his life has to teach us. Thank you for coming to pay your respects. I understand there are four of you who have agreed to be pallbearers. We will now take the casket to the hearse, then those of you who wish can follow us to the gravesite by Conall Hall."

Four burly men made their way to the casket and lumbered out to the hearse with it. They all followed to the small cemetery at the outer edges of the property, where about fifteen of them remained for the burial. Blair and Liam did not show.

They all gathered tightly around the hole in the ground. The dramatic-looking man August had noticed earlier was standing across from her, his arms elegantly crossed. His suit was narrow, giving away his lankiness, with a long grey wool scarf draped over his shoulders. His dark purple dress shirt was unbuttoned at the top, and a gold necklace with some kind of pendant glinted at her. With his smooth black hair pulled back into a long ponytail and his fingers covered with rings, he looked like a rock star. His confidence was palpable, but his intensity made August distinctly uneasy. Every time she looked his way, he was staring right at her. It was beginning to make her uncomfortable. She edged in closer to Faolan, and as one of the other lycan, some kind of holy man, said words about Ciardha being a strong alpha and a good guide for the future, August whispered to Faolan, "That guy won't stop staring at me, he's making me really uncomfortable."

Faolan looked in the direction that August had nodded and took in the man, whom he didn't recognize. Faolan looked right at him, and the man returned his glare. They remained like that through the words from the speaker, as August felt the tensions rise. She knew instinctively that Faolan was going to have to maintain eye contact until this man broke away, and she could feel the electricity coming off of him, the rage of the last few days surging inside him. By about the four-minute mark Faolan had shifted his body and distanced himself slightly from her, only staring harder. The stranger finally smirked with half his mouth and looked away, and pretended to talk to somebody next to him.

Faolan tried to shake it off, but remained distracted through the burial. At the end, they both watched as the man smoothly stepped over to his little black sports car, slipped in and tore away, spitting dust and pebbles when he hit the gas.

"I don't know who that was, but I don't like him," Faolan said. "Come on, let's go."

There's No Place Like Home

They got in the car and waited for all of the other vehicles to pull out ahead of them, then drove straight for the inn.

August began gathering toiletries and checking drawers. "Well this vacation bites. This was not what I thought it was going to be." She threw her clothes into her suitcase, each toss a grumpy exclamation point. "Should I laugh? Should I cry? Who knows?" She just kept on grumbling as she rounded up scattered shoes and checked under the bed and in the nightstands.

"I ken. I'm sorry. I truly am."

She turned to look at him, slumped and defeated. "I'm sorry, Fe. I shouldn't complain. I know it's been harder on you. I just feel like we're cursed or something. Doesn't it feel like we're cursed or something?"

He nodded.

"I sound like a kid, don't I? I should write you a letter. It may take more time to say what I want, but I'm able to edit it until I at least sound like an adult."

"You do write a grand letter. I miss them." He folded a shirt and placed it neatly into his bag. His whole suitcase was tidy and everything fit well. Her bag was a monster pile of clean and dirty laundry heaped in the middle.

"I'm looking forward to getting home, aren't you?"

"This is my home. Or was." He bundled a pair of socks together and tucked them in a row that ran alongside the clothes.

She sat down on the edge of the bed next to his case and looked at him. "I'm sorry, I know you wanted this to be a good birthday present. I know that. I can't stand it if you start to get all gloomy again."

He patted her on her hand and continued to look grim as he neatly folded his clothes.

Once they'd loaded up the car they said their goodbyes to the inn staff and the few other pub patrons they recognized and started for Kilmarnock.

"It's a little town that's closer to the airport. I'm sorry we aren't doing the route I had intended. I had more surprises in store, but all of it is colored with loss and uncertainty at the moment anyway."

"More surprises huh? Not sure I'm into surprises anymore."

"Aye, I canna blame ye for that!" They both laughed slightly. It was the first moment that felt normal for days.

"Shit—did you remember to ship my archery stuff back to the Rook?"

"Aye."

"I wish I'd had a chance to talk more to the folks who I spent time with in Summerblynd. I know it was just a day and one night, but it felt like I'd known some of them a long time. It was weird. And I met this woman—"

Then August remembered she wasn't supposed to share anything about the training with Faolan. They didn't know Faolan like she did, but she had promised. She looked out of the window and watched the countryside float past.

"This woman?"

"I'm not supposed to tell you." She ran her hand across the dashboard and left a clear path where dust had been collecting. She wiped it onto her black jeans, leaving a streak of dust on them.

"Not supposed to tell me?"

"Yeah, we did this training day thing. I was sworn to secrecy. Hunter stuff."

"I see, well that's very mysterious."

"It did have an air of mystery, if I do say so myself."

He reached over and put his hand on her thigh and gave it a squeeze. She took his hand and laced her fingers into his. She stared at the grey dashboard and poked at the vents, flipping them up and then down with her finger. She cranked the window down just a crack to let in some fresh air.

"Anyway, I met a really cool woman there. She's from Australia. I would have liked to have spent more time with her."

"I thought maybe you were not talking about it because you might like to spend more time with Adair."

August's face got hot and she shrunk in her seat, loosening her grip on his hand. "No," she said in a very small voice.

He gripped her hand tighter. "Let's talk about something else."

"Like what?" She was fighting under the weight of embarrassment to let the issue float away.

"How about Christmas and Hogmanay."

"Wait, you forgot Thanksgiving. Thanksgiving comes before those things."

"I ken that, but I am aware how fond of Christmas you are."

She pondered this in a deliberately silly manner, twisting her lips and studying Faolan's face. "Well, that's true. It's like you know me or something."

"I think if you look back, it's been over two years."

"Well, technically we met two years ago, but it was months and months before you would even tell me your name."

"Aye, that's true. You've got me there."

"I like the fat trees with the long needles. Want to pick one out after Thanksgiving?"

"Lass, I would love to do that with you. I'll even wear the red cap your gran made me."

The trip went like that for almost two hours. They drove right through Glasgow, with memories both happy and uncomfortable for August, before reaching Kilmarnock, where they checked into a tiny inn by the river. The day turned gloomier the closer they got to the coast, but their mood was brighter, so August didn't mind the grey and chill. They didn't bother to unpack, just dropped off their main suitcases at the room and headed into the local pub for a bite.

"On a better year I could hop all over Scotland checking out pubs. And frankly, hot guys in kilts," she added, as two strapping young men exited the room.

"Is that so?" Faolan replied with mock outrage, peeking over top of his pint at her, then taking a swallow.

They took turns picking at the pile of fried pub food they'd ordered. She gazed at him, and he looked older. If he were human, she'd say he aged ten years in the past week. Her heart was full up, but also hectored with doubts about things working out for them. It seemed almost as though the world didn't want them to be together, for some reason. *But what does the world know?* she thought with a spark of defiance.

Her mind flitted as they sat in the warm pub, the sounds of people chatting and dishes clanking. She wondered how Faolan forgave her so easily for her fling with Adair. She also wondered why his mind wasn't riddled with questions of what they did or her feelings for the young hunter. She knew that if it had been her on the other end, she would have tormented herself with wanting to know every painful detail. She thought about her parents in some pub somewhere when they were younger, drinking a pint. She thought about her gran Sorcha and Abel visiting family in the Deep South. She wondered how she could do some of the meditations that Merindah taught her. She wondered if she could connect with Merindah through the mediations. She remembered two things Nia had included in the bag she sent with Faolan: a new set of hunter clothes, and a plastic zip bag full of Summerblynd soil.

"You have many thoughts in your eyes." Faolan's voice was deep and gentle.

"My brain is buzzy with stuff. We need somebody to sing a good pub song for our last night in Scotland."

Faolan grinned wide, stood up and called out, "Mates! Mates! Oi!"

The room settled a bit and August slid down in her chair. She pulled her sweater sleeves up over hands and put them up to her face.

"This is our last night in bonny Scotland for a while. My beautiful lass would like a song," Faolan gestured towards August and she covered her face even more as everybody looked at her. "Would ye join me in a song, then?"

Some men stood up and held out their pints and a man with a very deep voice boomed out the words *"Hill yo ho boys, let her go boys ..."* then the rest joined in for a boisterous though somewhat sad little song about farewells and arrivals and the people you left behind. It was a fine and fitting song and August uncovered her face to hoist her pint to them in thanks.

After the song several men came over and slapped Faolan's shoulder and tipped their hats to August and wished them well, then just as casually returned to their food and drinks and conversations.

"Friendly lot," August said, smiling.

"Aye. Could have easily gone another way with a different pub."

"Well, we were bound to have some bit of good luck eventually."

"I'll drink to that!" Faolan drained his mug and they paid and went back to the inn.

They both took off their clothes and August pulled on a comfy tee and cuddled up to Faolan in the bed, which was cozy, if not exactly

333

the most comfortable mattress.

"Let's just talk about Christmas stuff until we pass out," she said, snuggling herself tightly into his side and throwing an arm across his chest.

"Let's do that."

So she started with her favorite cookies to bake, her favorite pajamas when she was seven, and the places in New York she used to visit during the holidays, some with animated mannequins, small trains you could ride through fake winter scenery, and very realistic Santas.

He told her about his favorite Christmas and Hogmanay when his dad had been away for a month and his mum had gone crazy with baking traditional sweets and decorating and wrapping a pile of presents. He got a little choked up when he spoke of his brother, but pushed through it. Then he started talking about the things he wanted to do with August, and this farm that he could take her to a couple towns over from Mahigan Falls that has animatronic elves, and a "Christmas shoppe" with ornaments and fancy, gigantic candy canes.

August listened to the deep timbre of his voice, felt the warm cotton of his shirt on her cheek, his smells and breath like a lullaby for her, and she drifted off with visions of sugar plums dancing in her head.

In the morning, following one more round of fry-ups for their last meal in Scotland, they drove to Prestwick and dropped off the car. The airport was a misery of fog and chill, with flight delays and stressed-out travelers lining the halls, but August's mood was good because she was heading home to the comfort of her mother, her books, her whole closet. All the talk of the holidays had kept her looking ahead to something good and loving, rather than fretting about things that were sad, or hard, or complicated. The holidays were simple. Pine and cinnamon. Cookies and velvet dresses. Big dinners, new pajamas and presents. She loved giving gifts even more than she liked getting them.

She rubbed the pearl of her necklace, the family heirloom that Faolan had given her when they were new to each other. She thought about how much faith that took, to trust her with this. She pretended she didn't remember that Iseabail once wore this same necklace.

They finally boarded for their long flight, settling into first-class seats on the port side of the plane. Faolan insisted August have the window, and she watched as the earth dropped out from beneath them and the cars and ships and then the coastline got small. Then all there was for miles was grey and water.

They played mini-checkers and Faolan did some magic card tricks. He read in a low voice and recounted a few pleasant stories, for which he received a few kisses. It reminded her of the kinds of things her dad would do with her when she was bored. It was cozy and lovely and another silver thread wound around and wove into the others that connected the two of them, making the cord stronger still.

The day was fading as the sparkling lights of the American coast came into view. August's excitement was buoyant as she watched the rosy skies in the west, knowing she was so close to home. "You give an old dog new life, love," Faolan told her with a kiss on her forehead. He pointed out the window, to where the full moon was rising in the east behind them.

"Ooh! Should we howl?"

"Well, it'll be a bit fuller tomorrow. Perhaps a little one, then."

They howled quietly to themselves so as not to disturb their fellow travelers, and August figured as long as they were already puckered up, they might as well kiss.

Sylvia and Two Feathers were at the airport to give them a ride home. Her mother looked radiant and August ran towards her. Sylvia braced for impact as August threw her arms around her.

"I misst ye sae muckle!" she said into her mother's hair.

Two Feathers laughed and patted August on the back. She let go of her mother and gave him a hug as well. Even though Two Feathers would never replace her father, she had grown quite fond of him and his way of quiet contemplation.

Faolan and Two Feathers shook hands, "Good to see you made it home in one piece," he said to Faolan.

"Yes," Sylvia added. "No tragedies."

"Aye! It's good to be back."

When they got to the house Smoke and Snow were waiting at the door, sitting like good dogs but with tails wagging butts, and whimpering to leap and lick. When August put her arms out they tackled her and she rolled on the hall floor in a tangle of dog fur and tongues and puppy growls and yips.

August had held back so many tears in the moments she couldn't cry, but now that she was back at the Blue Rook they all came flooding out. Sitting in the glow of the living room fireplace she and Faolan detailed the tragedies of their visit as Sylvia and Two Feathers looked on speechless. Snow and Smoke each lay on one of August's feet, staring up at her with deep concern in their wolfdog way.

They left out some of the things that occurred between August and Faolan in regards to Iseabail. It was too personal to share, and too embarrassing—particularly some of August's jealous behavior.

After a good cry and a good dose of comforting from her mother, August was ready to head uphill to the Den and get cozy for the night. She was all cried out and emotionally exhausted. She knew the next few days would be about laying around and writing in her journal and trying to figure out her feelings.

"Oh—when are Gran and Abel coming home?"

"The week after Thanksgiving," Sylvia said.

"After?" August whined in disappointment.

"We'll still make dinner. Abel hasn't had Thanksgiving with his family in years. It's their turn by a long shot."

"Okay," August sighed, resigned to it. "We've got to come up with some new traditions. Shit is all scrambled up. I need something to look forward to each year, ya know?" August scratched both of the dogs behind the ears and got up. "Let's go home, Faolan."

Faolan nodded and got up. August hugged her mom.

"Come on Snow, home." The dog snapped to her feet and wagged. Smoke didn't bother to even lift his head, and let a sad whistle out of his nose.

"Don't worry Smoke, Mom is staying here with you." Smoke groaned. August gave the large canine's head one last pet before she left with Faolan and Snow.

HM Prison Perth
November 8, 1984

"Huntar, get your arse over here."

The prisoner padded over to the bars, close to the guard who summoned him, and the man grabbed the cage and leaned in toward the prisoner's ear.

"Word is that Ciardha is dead."

Paden Huntar leaned back, examining the guard's face for the hint of a lie.

"When?"

"Dinna ken. A day or so. Maybe a bit longer."

"How'd he go?"

"No word."

Paden nodded.

"The clishmaclaver is, yer gunna be released."

Paden stared again, peering intently at the guard, letting disbelief wrinkle his brow.

"Aye, y' heard. The Professor scheduled a meeting, we're to fetch you to his office in the morning."

Paden nodded again. "His majesty comin' in on a Friday. That's different. Thank ye Clyde."

The guard nodded and walked back to his rounds.

Third Day's the Charm
Mahigan Falls

Saturday, November 10, 1984

We've been home three days. Three days. It feels like both an hour and a month. I missed Snow so much. I didn't realize it until I saw her, and since then she hasn't left my side. I think things were so crazy in Scotland that I didn't have time to worry about her. Guess that makes me a bad dog mom. I'm glad she was hanging out at Mom's with Smoke, tho. Those two just adore each other. The best of buds. One of my favorite things to do is lay between those two beasts and feel their bodies rise and fall with breathing. They put out these sleep-waves that knock me out every time. Mom calls us the Three Dog Night when it happens. It feels good to be back home, around those kinds of things.

I'm pretty bummed that Thanksgiving is going to be so small with Abel and Gran gone, but at least Brigid and Mom and Two Feathers will be with us at the table. Now I can't remember if TF even has a first name. He is supposed to tell us the real story of Thanksgiving. I don't think it's going to be a cheery one.

I've spent most of the past two days sleeping, eating starchy foods, reading and cuddling with Snow. I really ought to get outside a bit, but I suppose I'm allowed a few days to get over the crazy ass trip we had. The weather has been gloomy, anyway. It's like I brought the grey Scotland skies with me.

I'm still adjusting to the reality. I can't stop thinking about Iseabail having grandkids that look like Faolan. Doesn't that mean she has—fuck, they have—a kid around somewhere? It has to. Though that kid is not really a kid, I guess. He'd be almost 90. My head is spinning. Do I worry about it? Or do I do my best to just bond tighter and tighter to Faolan? I mean, what's the next step here?

At least I'm feeling somewhat human again. That counts for something doesn't it? Haha, I just said I feel "human again." This is never going to be right.

I had a dream last night. It was like one of those glittery images from my dreamy meditation that Merindah invoked. My dad came to me, he sang me a song in Scottish Gaelic. I'd never heard him do that before. I wonder, did he do that as a boy? Why didn't he ever do that when I was a kid? I feel like I missed out on so many things with him.

My dream eventually shifted to a bit of nightmare where Adair and Ciardha were chasing each other. Adair with his bow and Ciardha with his teeth. I was lucky enough that I woke up before anything scary happened. It was just ... so tense. Is it a nightmare if nothing seriously scary or gruesome happens? Is it a

338

nightmare if you're just supremely uncomfortable the whole time?

As soon as I put down this pen I'm going to go into the kitchen and make a healthy dinner that has some vegetables involved. I'm going to make Faolan get off of the phone, which he's been on nearly non-stop the past two days. Most of it sounds like business, but some of it sounds like research or detective work or something. Honestly, part of me doesn't want to know. Honestly? Do I need to convince myself that I am speaking honestly? Anyway—or anyroad—I think some of it is Iseabail related and I feel a little sick when it looks like he might talk to me about it all. I can see he is suffering, but I can't handle it right now. I cannot take on the weight of his lost love. I have to focus on my own heart and if his comes along with mine, that's what's meant to happen. Why is it so scary just to <u>talk</u> about it? My dad always said that fear was often motivated by the idea that we are going to lose something. Am I afraid of losing something? Of course I am. What do I do with that, though?

Where Love Comes From and Where it Goes

They ate at the kitchen table, the sun catching in the stained glass strip that ran along the top of the sink window, throwing shards of color onto the side of Faolan's face. It gave him a magical quality.

"I'm nervous," August said, pinching a bit of pickle left on her plate.

"Nervous?" Faolan downed the last bite of sandwich and swallowed the last gulp of ale.

"I kind of want to know what all of the phone calls are about, but I'm afraid what you will tell me will hurt, so I kind of don't want to know, too."

"Ah. I ken your dilemma." He wiped his mouth and leaned in, taking her hand. "You've nothing to worry about, love."

"So … you aren't hung up on her?" August felt that now-familiar knot in her stomach.

"Lass, there is much I am still digesting. Much that I never imagined I would be trying to work out. My feelings about Iseabail are evolving, shall we say. I think perhaps I kept her so close to let her have a life, when I thought hers cut short. But as we know now, she had a life, and I wasn't part of it. She is not the woman I have long held her to be, of course. How could she be? But remember this, August: I love you. I choose you, and a life with you, over any other. No matter what any of my feelings for her ever were, this is where I want to be."

August nodded. He had looked into her eyes. He meant every word he said. She tried to believe this meant he loved her more than he loved Iseabail, but some little voice in the back of her mind tried to tell her, that isn't what he actually said. She didn't want to listen to that voice, even if it was right, so she shut it down and allowed herself to feel the warmth of his hand, and swim in his troubled eyes.

They went for a short walk in the crisp November evening and came back to warm mugs of mulled wine. He professed his love to her again, and again declared she was the woman he wanted to spend his life with. Then Faolan went back to his study to make some calls while August took a shower and dug one of his cozy white cotton tees out of a drawer and threw it on over her panties. She padded downstairs and fed Snow, then they curled up together in the game room and August put on a mindless Saturday night line-up of *T.J. Hooker* and *The Love Boat*. She fell asleep cuddled up in Snow's thick winter coat.

Howl at Your Beauty

"Lass ... Lass? Wake up, love. Little Red ... August, time to go to bed." August woke up and rubbed her eyes. Faolan's beautiful face hovered in front of hers, almost as if in a dream, and she reached out and pulled him to her, kissing him. He was leaning across the couch arm and nearly lost his balance, and they both laughed. A bit more awake, she stood. Her hair had dried a little crazy. She had lines on her left arm and the left side of her face, and possibly a bit of dried drool. She inhaled deeply and stretched and took a sip of water from the side table.

"I shouldn't have laid on my hair wet. It feels like a giant shrub."

"It's beautiful. You're beautiful." He said while holding her fingertips. He smiled gently, and she did the same. He looked vibrant and alive, more like himself than he had in days. She shuffled towards him, and put her head onto his chest.

"You know, we can get you some more pj's," he told her while petting her head. Then he petted her back and she looked up at him.

"I like wearing your shirts. They smell like you."

He nodded. "You're a hopeless romantic."

She nuzzled her head back into the warm cotton on his chest. "So are you," came her muffled reply.

"Fair enough. My love, my true love, I need to ask you something. Something important. About us."

She came awake quickly, her heart beating faster. "What about us, Faolan?"

"I know I've been rather impossible lately, leaving you to doubt my feelings, but I think I can tell you some things."

"Good things, right? Not scary things?"

"Good things, aye. True things. A bit scary for me, actually, but here goes. For the love of you, August, I was ready to let go of a ghost, and again for the love of you, I was ready to let go of a love back from the dead—or at least, to let go the love I had carried for her. But this week past I've been mourning. Mourning the loss of a family and a life that never was, but also mourning a betrayal. For Iseabail not to have told me in some way that I was a father, and then a grandfather—well, I'm still trying to forgive her for keepin' that away from me."

August looked up at him and touched his cheek. His eyes were shining.

"So my darling girl, I come to you with even more baggage than before. Iseabail is not my love, and I let her go with a full heart, but now it seems she is family, mine as well as yours. And more than that, those bairns are my kin, my own, and I canna leave them behind, and this is what I must ask: Can ye love a grandfather, Red? Because that's what I am and what I intend to be. And out there in the world, I have a son, and I mean to find him."

Somewhere in there, in a confession that might have spelled the end for a happily-ever-after life with the man of her dreams, August heard something else—the chance for a happily cluttered, ridiculously complicated, truly loving life with a man who was so much more than a dream. Whether it was hope, or hormones, or just trying to love the best way she could, she convinced herself she could accept this new complication, together, with the man she loves.

She held his face between her hands and stood up on her toes to kiss him.

"I believe you were about to take me to bed?"

Faolan wrapped his arms around her and hugged her tight, laughing. "Och, Red you're the best! The best!"

They walked up to the bedroom and August felt her heart speed up again. Faolan had lit candles all around the room—a couple dozen or so, with several of them around the head of the bed.

"What's this?" she said coyly, leaning into him and squeezing his hand tighter.

"This, love, is for us. Unrushed. No ghosts. Just us." He let go of her hand and walked over to the stereo and put on a record. "I've been listening to this song quite a bit since we came home, and I'd like to sing it to you, while we dance."

August tilted her head and some organ music queued up. *Organ music?* she thought, but she just went with it as Faolan reached out his hand to hers and she took it.

"May I have this dance?"

"I'm not really dressed for such romantic overtures—"

"You're perfect. Absolutely. Perfect." He held his hand in place as she took a step forward, then he pulled her in close. The organ music made way for a deep crooning voice that warmed August.

343

Faolan began to whisper the song in her ear, about the moon and beasts, about longing and forgiveness—"*Please, please ... I'm your man.*"

As they slowly turned together, August watched them in the few mirrors around the room. She saw their bodies, kissed by candlelight. His arm snugged around her waist. She studied them as they swayed—his head bowed against her hair, her bottom curved out beneath his arm. Him in his button-down dress shirt and slacks, still wearing his belt and tie, her wearing nothing but that plain tee-shirt and string-bikini panties. And she felt sexy.

The sultry song and his whispers and words made her flesh bump up, her nipples bump out. She could feel his excited parts against her too, rigid and warm and wanting.

Then he leaned back a little and sang louder with the low rumbling voice on the stereo. She could feel his passion coming off of him in waves and when the singer paused he said, "I love you, August. I'm sorry that I hurt you." He let go of her hand and took a few steps back. Then the voice crooned about falling to his knees and crawling to his lover, and Faolan sang along, dropping to his knees and crawling to August.

She laughed, but because it was fun, not funny. In fact it was powerful, primal, and unbelievably sexy. He was making himself so vulnerable to her and she admired him for his courage. The heady mix of adoration, tenderness, and helpless desire made parts of her catch fire.

He looked up at her, holding her close, and she looked down into his face, the image of love and sincerity, and got down onto her knees, too. She kissed his singing mouth, twice, softly. Faolan let Leonard Cohen finish the song alone as they kissed deeply, tongues dancing and plunging. Gasping, pressing, clutching. They stood together, their mouths not leaving each other. She started to tug at his tie, slipping the knot down, pulling the long end until the knot burst apart in her hand and the slippery silk was laying on the floor in a pale blue jumble.

He started saying, "I love you ... I love you ... I love you ..." each time punctuated with a kiss. He watched as she unbuttoned his shirt, then he tugged it free. He threw it off with a snap and yanked his undershirt over his head, throwing it in the other direction. They were both breathless and swimming in each other's eyes. August pushed one

344

more hard kiss against his mouth, letting the rough of his chin sting hers. She stepped back a pace and slowly pulled the shirt she was wearing up over her head and dropped it on the floor in front of her, then kicked it aside.

Her hair was wild, and her green eyes shone over her freckled nose. She could feel her ears and gums begin to tingle and prickle a little, but Brigid's tea was helping her keep her transformations controlled now. She stood there, feeling like a goddess with moonbeams shooting from her pores, casting her silver light of love onto Faolan. He gazed at her, taking her beauty in, savoring each curve and valley. The halo of hair over her soft, blushed cheeks. Her delicate neck, the bump of her clavicle sliding down in a wide v, leaving a dainty hollow perfect for kissing. Her breasts, tender mounds, so soft to the touch, so firm in his hands, with rosebud nipples bumped out, eager to be tasted. His chest rose and fell as he panted, his desire unbearable. He yearned to kiss her belly, to kneel and worship at her altar.

She smiled and inhaled deeply, feeling her breath run the length of her body, and gave him a sleepy-eyed blink, like a cat, and a small come-hither nod. He scooped her up off the carpet and into his arms, cradling her and gazing down at her face. Her eyes were solemn, but warm and open to him—what was about to happen was important, a moment to be entered into with full intention, and they both knew it. And neither of them wanted anything to ruin it. He kissed her forehead, butterfly soft, and lay her on the bed. She sunk into the silk and down bedding, a porcelain beauty in a sea of garnet. She felt the silk on her back, sliding her arms over it, as if she were making snow angel wings in the bed. She turned on her side, her face propped in her hand, and watched Faolan as he pulled at his buckle, loosening his belt and sliding it from the loops, slowly and deliberately. It made her tingly. It made her want to bite or lick something. Watching him unbuckle his belt, then unbutton and unzip his trousers, stirred something primal. She felt an animal lust flow through her veins, her heart pounding hard and her body—lips, breasts, and between her thighs—growing hot and swollen.

Faolan stepped out of his clothes, and he was there for her, naked, his cock sticking straight out. She was mesmerized with the power of it—the power of Faolan and his hard cock to hold her under this spell, pin her to the bed, and she liked it. She wanted more of it. All of it. All of him. She rolled onto her back and beckoned him and he climbed in, sinking into the bedding with her.

"Take off my panties," she gave a breathy command, and relished the feel of him putting his powerful hands onto the small strings of powder-blue lace at each hip, edging them down, revealing her downy thatch.

He swept away the fabric and threw it onto the floor with the rest of their clothes.

He made a canopy of himself over top of her. He bowed his head down and gently kissed her forehead, and each shoulder. He slid his warm lips across her collarbone and peppered her belly with kisses. He lay a cheek on the flat surface of her hip and petted the other hip, tracing the plane, then the mound with a long finger. He kneeled back up and she watched the flesh of her thighs give way to the gentle squeezing of his hands.

"Are you ready, my beautiful lass?" he rumbled. She answered with parting legs. He wrapped his hands around under her bottom and lifted her into his lap, then put his arms under her back and raised her body up towards him. She instinctively wrapped her legs around his middle and he turned with her, so that he was now laying back and she was on top. She was spread, the center of her pressed against his belly, and she rocked against him there for a moment, the pressure, the friction from his hair, so sensual, as the tip of him pushed urgently against her bottom. She wanted to rub herself over every inch of him, but nothing could hold back her desire to have him inside of her right now.

Their eyes were open to each other, speaking in a language older than words. She lifted up onto her knees and grasped his cock, lowering herself slowly to it. All of the world, all of her thought melted away as the firm blunt tip pressed into her swollen cleft. She took him in, her body surrounding him, consuming him, holding him inside of her, and she felt like ripening fruit, so full, so ready to burst, the thin skin wanting to split and give way to juice and essence.

He moaned, "Yes, love … August … love …" as his cock filled her up, and she put a hand to her belly and could almost feel him press against it, so deep inside her. She grabbed hold of the headboard as Faolan cupped and rubbed and kissed her breasts, teased her nipples with his tongue, and took the mounds almost whole into his mouth.

Her eyes closed and her mind reeled with an explosion of images—the moon, the panting of wolves, a forest of trees. Then flowers, buds swelling and then cracking open, tender petals unfolding, blossoms becoming fruit, fruit swelling fat and juicy and then splitting. She pressed and rubbed, overwhelmed with the sensation of being filled with him, the irresistible pressure on her swollen bud, and she wanted to swallow him up whole. She wanted to take all of him into her, to keep pushing and rocking until the top of his head disappeared inside of her.

She began to chant his name, and he echoed her rhythm with "Love" and "August" until she leaned forward onto him, pushing, sliding, and riding to an ancient rhythm. They were both pressing as much flesh to the other as possible, moving together. August felt the ocean tide in her rising, and the waves cresting, pushing her up towards the stars and the moon in her soul until she was howling, and she felt below her a pulse, a surge, and then Faolan was howling too. They howled together, arching and shaking as they both lost themselves to their love and ecstasy, both beginning to transform, with pointed ears and fangs and fingers.

August collapsed on top of Faolan, panting hard, and he put his arms around her and rolled her onto her back, releasing her tenderly and kneeling between her legs, laying his head on her belly almost as though he could hear the shift in her.

She let the euphoria wash over her. There were the glitter stars of her dream visions swirling at the edges of her eyes as she tangled her fingers into his wavy hair and traced his temple with her finger.

They laid there unmoving for a while, as the world started to spin again, as their hearts slowed, and their breathing shallowed, and their spirits weaved together in silver and gold threads, bound together. They opened a new chapter of their story. With no ceremony other than their own, they became husband and wife.

August wasn't sure, but she thought she could feel the difference. Or the change. Something inside was different. But she could almost see it, too. They were connected now, in a way she'd never been connected with anyone before. She wondered for a moment if she should be frightened at the finality of it all, but if anything it made her feel more brave. Like anything could happen, and it would still be okay.

They would still be okay.

Faolan crawled up beside August. He pulled a soft cotton cloth from the side table and gently, sweetly, patted her clean. They got under the covers, August turning on her side and pressing as much of her back as she could into his embrace. He wrapped an arm around her, his face buried in her hair and her fingers laced into his.

"I love you, August. I'll have no other." He said, low.

"I love you too, Faolan. And I'll have no other."

A promise. An ancient wedding.

"Are you sleepy, lass?" He spoke into her cloud of curls. He treasured the way they tickled his lips.

"I'm a little awake, actually. Adrenaline, I guess. My brain is contemplating a thousand things. 'Big questions of life'–type stuff."

"Aye. I'm sleepy. How do ye feel?"

"I feel … At peace. In love." She let out a little laugh, he made a sleepy laugh, too. "I feel good right now. In this moment."

"That's really all life is—the things we do from moment to moment, and how we feel about them."

She took in a deep breath, and with it exhaled the frenetic energy of her mind. She accepted what he said as an answer to the life-type stuff. "This then, is a good moment."

"Aye, 'tis." He again kissed her cloud of hair and was soon adrift in an indigo velvet sky somewhere. He dreamed of a star. And moons. And spoke to old loves, apologizing for his slights, wishing them all the best.

August was not far behind him. She dreamed of flying through space, or maybe time, seeing nebulae and Saturn's rings and sparkling, glimmering images of her father. They walked through a shining emerald version of Central Park, her small hand in his as he talked to her about love and honesty and integrity. Then she was bigger, and he introduced her to Faolan. *You can trust him*, he said, and when they turned back her father was gone. She started to cry, but Faolan mumbled into her hair, *Don't worry, he'll be back.*

The candles had sputtered out in their jars. Snow padded into the room and curled up by August's side of the bed. Moonbeams glowed through the high window and shone gently on them as they slept.